SF

D0435747

MAR - 2006

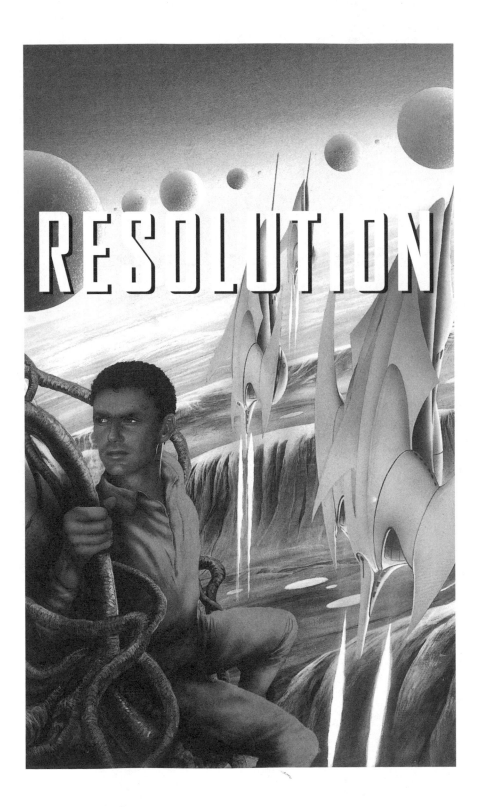

Other Pyr® titles by John Meaney

Paradox: Book One of the Nulapeiron Sequence

Context: Book Two of the Nulapeiron Sequence

RESOLUTION

BOOK THREE
OF THE NULAPEIRON SEQUENCE

JOHN MEANEY

an imprint of **Prometheus Books**
Amherst, NY

Published 2006 by Pyr®, an imprint of Prometheus Books

Inquiries should be addressed to
Pyr
59 John Glenn Drive
Amherst, New York 14228–2197
VOICE: 716–691–0133, ext. 207
FAX: 716–564–2711
WWW.PYRSF.COM

10 09 08 07 06   5 4 3 2 1

Library of Congress Cataloging-in-Publication Data

Meaney, John.
    Resolution / John Meaney.
        p. cm. — (The Nulapeiron sequence ; bk. 3)
    Originally published: London : Bantam Press, a division of Transworld Publishers, 2005.
    ISBN 1–59102–437–4 (hardcover : alk. paper)
    I. Title.

PR6113.E17R43 2006
813'.6—dc22

2005035119

Printed in the United States of America on acid-free paper

Remembering Pip,
now bounding with his sisters among the stars

1

NULAPEIRON AD 3423

A lean figure, wrapped in a long cape, stood atop a slender footbridge spanning Gelshania Boulevard. It was an hour before dawnshift. High above the boulevard, attached to the baroque, ornate panels of the concave ceiling, bronze-and-platinum glowclusters shone dimly, as if sleeping. Down below, the boulevard's floor was of polished butter-yellow metal. At this hour, only a few servitors walked there, carrying out their errands.

I was once like you.

Tom Corcorigan was a Lord, and there were people in power who knew the part he had played in the War Against The Blight; but nothing could eradicate the memory of his lowly childhood and the deprivations of his years in servitude.

Beneath the cape, his missing left arm ached.

There was movement, far along the shrinking perspective of the boulevard tunnel. Tom recognized the vanguard immediately for what it was: a cohort of greystone warriors, neither human nor living statues but somehow both, their slit-eyes covered with nictitating membrane and impervious to sporemist or smartwraith, their bodies formed of granite and morphstone, tensing to unbelievable hardness in the heat of battle.

Expensive, Tom thought. *Who is it that can afford their services?*

This was the Primum Stratum of Demesne Kalshuna, an old rich realm that had suffered during the war. What reason could the Liege Lord's clan-members have for sneaking around before dawnshift? As far as Tom knew, he and Elva—she was fast asleep in their guest apartment—were the only visiting nobility.

The procession drew closer.

Oh, Fate . . .

Behind the greystone phalanx, a levanquin floated, moving ponderously above the metallic yellow floor. Eerie blue reflections slid across its bubble-covered carapace; inside, a bulky, shaven-headed figure was barely visible. Behind the levanquin, more greystone warriors walked, and among them shuffled twin rows of manacled servitors, dressed alike in shabby blue livery.

Haven't I tried enough to eradicate this?

The vehicle's occupant was an Oracle, and these servitors could surely bear witness to the intense, perverse stimulation that most Oracles required to bring their strange, fragmented mentalities into a semblance of coherence, to match their thoughts to normal timeflow.

Like every Oracle, this one would be a product of the Collegium Perpetuum Delphinorum. The nearest Collegium (for there were three sites in the world) had survived enemy occupation during the War Against The Blight . . . and it was Tom's and Elva's destination. This was the eighth night (or early morning) of their honeymoon; their peregrination would end at a place which took innocent children, with their families' consent, and turned them into monsters.

And one of those abominations occupied the levanquin sliding at this moment beneath the footbridge.

I could kill you now.

A drop onto the bubble-canopy, a swift cut from the graser-bracelet he wore—a wedding present from Elva—and Tom would be inside. Then his bare hand would be enough to dispense justice on behalf of those who suffered so that Oracles might thrive.

Whether Tom could escape from an enraged cohort of greystone warriors was another matter . . . but he knew already that he was not going to try. He had no intention of making a widow of Elva so soon.

Elva . . .

A soft smile alighted on Tom's face, and he turned away from the sights below, pulling up his cape's hood, and strode on across the foot-bridge, heading back towards his and Elva's temporary home.

Tom walked the length of the apartment's hallway. Its floor was square-patterned, milky violet quartz and hard transparent glass, beneath which lambent orange lava flowed. Just for a moment, he caught a glimpse of hexagonal flukes as a thermidor wriggled and swam through blazing hot magma.

A doorshimmer evaporated, and he stepped through into the darkened lounge. An oval window overlooked the Benbow Cavern, containing a scene of joyful debris. Down below, torn banners floated in ornate pools; discarded flagons decorated quiescent fountains which last night had flung polarized streamers of thousand-hued water in high, triumphant arcs. There were a few sleeping bodies; on one tilted lev-bench, a Lord-Meilleur-sans-Demesne lay sprawled against a commoner.

Mesodrones were scooping up the litter.

Sooner or later the victory celebrations would have to cease, and everyone would turn to rebuilding their lives. For now, why not? The Blight had been a vast malignant lifeform, enslaving millions of minds as it reached throughout the realms of Nulapeiron, and they had been lucky to beat it back and destroy it. They had caused it to confront an entity which lived in mu-space, a possibly god-like being that had once been human, whose name was Dart. It was the Dart-entity which had defeated the Blight.

So why aren't I happy?

But Tom knew that the Blight had been a spawned seedling, and that during the final battle it had been trying to contact its parent organism: the vast worlds-spanning hiveform known as the Anomaly. That Anomaly had already subsumed entire planets. Even in Nulapeiron, where the teaching of history was tightly controlled, the Anomaly was a dark legend synonymous with fear.

And the closer Tom and Elva drew to the Collegium Perpetuum Delphinorum, the less Tom was able to sleep. During nightshift, he kept snapping awake, convinced that the Anomaly was already aware of Nulapeiron's existence. If it had any curiosity concerning a world capable of killing its offspring, it might turn its attention here . . . and Tom was under no illusion that the trick they had pulled off against the Blight could be made to work again.

The Blight had nearly destroyed Nulapeiron. How humanity might fight the vast malignant entity which had spawned the Blight, Tom had no idea.

A crystal sideboard stood against one wall of the elegant chamber. On the sideboard, atop a platinum tray, was an oval outline in shadow. Tom assumed that Eemur's severed head was asleep, or in some state that might pass for sleep; but then her words sounded directly in his mind:

Can't sleep, my Lord? Did something come up?

Tom stared into the gloom.

Or fail to? Shame, on your honeymoon.

Thank you, Eemur, for your kind empathy.

Tom could not have said exactly when he became aware of the link between them. It had occurred during the past few days, growing continuously stronger, and he was already taking it for granted. He had not mentioned it to anybody else . . . not even Elva.

You're worried about the Anomaly.

Of course I am. Aren't you?

Tom made a control gesture, and a glowglobe detached itself from the ceiling, flickering brightly as it floated lower.

Naturally. But no-one else will be in the mood to listen, and you know that.

But the danger—

Is based on what? Your intuition? My Sight? You know what they're worth.

Fate damn it.

Now the light glistened on Eemur's flensed and disembodied head: her blood-wet striated muscles, including the odd three-way strips beneath grey-white cheekbones; her long exposed teeth; the bulging spheres of her eyes. There was something new: a black moirée cap covering the remnants of scalp and sparse, sticky strands of lank, blood-soaked hair.

You know I'm right.

Her head balanced on its tangle of sinews and severed arteries, testament to the clumsy beheading five centuries before.

You know I don't have to like it. But, yes . . . You're right.

So what are you going to do?

Down in the Benbow Cavern, the glowclusters were beginning to shine a rosy hue, marking the commencement of dawnshift.

I'm going to work out. Is that all right with you?

Whatever you say. Don't mind me.

Then the contact between them became muted, a kind of mental hush falling in the chamber. Tom nodded, and gestured to the glow-globe to return to the ceiling. As it rose, he shucked off his cape and tunic. Bare-chested, wearing only dark training tights, he stood relaxed, taking in deep breaths.

No comment came from Eemur's Head.

Tom worked through his warm-up routine, then his squats and one-arm press-ups (the only kind, as he sometimes remarked to Elva, that he would ever be able to do). Then he ordered the morph-capable ceiling to extrude a loop, for a series of one-finger pull-ups (each finger in turn): a traditional exercise used only by élite-class climbers.

The first part of his workout was over. Tom gestured a section of flooring into laminar-flow mode, stepped onto it and began to run. After a few minutes, he pushed up the speed, and the flow accelerated to match.

His bare torso was slick with sweat.

Anomaly.
Running.
I will not let you do it.
Running harder.
I will not let you take my world.

Tom ran on his hurtling journey to nowhere, faster and faster on the spot, concentration narrowing until he was pure movement, all fears and thoughts forgotten.

When his training was finished and his breathing had slowed, Tom stood in the bedchamber doorway, still soaked with sweat, scratching the stump which depended from his left shoulder.

"*Remove an arm.*" Lady Darinia's words echoed across the years. "*Either arm will do.*"

On the bed, his beautiful wife Elva lay sprawled and contented. The chamber's glowglobe painted her skin dawnshift-pink, full of promise.

Then she stirred and opened one eye.

"Well, my good Lord. I hope you haven't exhausted yourself."

"I am pretty tired."

"*How* tired, sir?"

The smartsatin sheet furled back.

"Not very," Tom said.

"Then come here."

2

NULAPEIRON AD 3423

While Tom and Elva were eating breakfast, he noticed a change come over Eemur's Head, where she stood atop the crystal sideboard. Her flensed flesh had been growing scaly and purple over the past few days; now she was glistening like fresh blood.

Tom put down his tine-spoon and stared at her.

Lady Lavnaxar just died.

For a moment, Tom could make no sense of her silent words inside his head.

I'll talk to you when I've finished feeding.

Tom looked away.

"What is it?" asked Elva, but Tom merely shook his head. He had speculated before on how the dead Seer maintained nutrients within herself. Now he knew: her spacetime-warping abilities allowed her to suck fluids and other substances from a just-dead Lady.

Would you rather I hadn't waited for her death?

Tom closed his eyes.

"If you're too tired," murmured Elva, "we could postpone our shopping trip."

"No." He opened his eyes and smiled. "Let's go. I'm looking forward to it."

But he had little appetite for finishing his breakfast, and ate only a mouthful before pushing his plate away. Then he got up and headed back to the bedchamber to change his clothes.

To maintain their schedule and arrive at the Collegium on the appointed day, they would have to leave Demesne Kalshuna this evening. In the meantime, since Elva had heard the shops were well-appointed in this realm's Primum Stratum, they took the opportunity to look around.

For a while it was magical, simply walking around the marble halls with Elva at his side. Every now and then a noble or freeborn person or couple would recognize them and perform an ornate bow: to the precise leftward angle required for congratulating newlyweds (with the freeborns correctly inclining themselves some fifteen degrees further forwards than the Corcorigans' noble peers). None of them tried to make conversation; that would have been impolite, for this was the couple's own time together.

"I could get used to this, Tom."

"Well, my Lady Elva, you may have to."

But for all their happiness, they had little money left, and no realm to return to: the demesne briefly ruled by Tom (which he had then abandoned) had long been subsumed into Realm Shinkenar, and he had no prospects of other employment before a Convocation could be held.

In the meantime, they had a debt of honour to fulfil. Tom hoped that the Collegium Perpetuum Delphinorum would be accommodating, but he had few grounds for optimism. Though he had worked alongside Collegiate personnel during the war, now that the conflict was over they would have little sympathy for someone of his background.

In some circles, Tom was known as The Oracle Killer.

"The Jack may be dead," said Elva, guessing that Tom was thinking of the Collegium.

"No, I don't think so."

The blasted, ruined cyborg, its remains welded into a wall by the force of the explosion which had burned its body apart, should have died long before. Tenacity had been programmed into it at the deepest cellular levels.

When Tom was lost, searching for Elva in the Collegium corridors after Blight-subsumed soldiers had captured her, it was the near-dead Jack which had sniffed the air—his preternatural senses still functioning—and struggled to produce a whisper, telling Tom which direction to follow. Without the Jack, Tom would not have found Elva.

"It's almost as if he can't die," added Tom. "And we owe him everything."

Elva touched his arm. "I owe him much, from what you say. But you're the one who rescued me."

"That's because I love you, Lady Elva Corcorigan."

"Ah, my Lord. I love you." She stopped before a fabric store, looked Tom in the eyes, then turned him to face a daistral shop where a flock of singing glassbirds was hovering. "And because I want you to *keep* loving me, I suggest you go and drink some daistral while I look around in here. All right?"

"I don't mind—"

"You lie beautifully, as a trained logosopher should. Now go and drink some daistral."

"Yes, ma'am."

"And whatever I buy, tell me later that you love it."

"Yes, ma'am."

"Good. Now go."

Tom sat at a hexagonal quartz table, sipping whiganberry daistral with cream on top. Nearby, two Ladies drank from floating lev-cups and watched their children playing together. Towards the rear, an ancient noble couple—the Lord so feeble that he moved within an exoskeleton's support—shuffled towards a table which had been readied for them by a vassal who greeted them by name as well as rank.

It was over half an hour before Elva turned up smiling, followed by a long-haired servitor carrying a handful of black velvet bags.

"The mall-master wouldn't let me carry my own goods."

"Well, of course not," said Tom. As Elva sat, Tom dug inside his waistband for cred-slivers, but the servitor shook his head.

"Sorry, sir," he muttered. "Master Zagrix says as how we shouldn't accept tips, see . . ." A miserable expression caused his spotted face to droop.

"Thanks for your help, young Wiklan." Elva took the bags from him; for a moment, he stared at her in awe. "That'll be all, thank you."

"Er, yes, ma'am. Thank you, ma'am."

Wiklan bobbed a bow, then turned and moved away at a kind of fast shuffle, as though he had grown too fast into his body to be coordinated.

"Those aren't bolts of fabric," Tom pointed out, as Elva opened the first of the velvet bags.

"No, I found a much more interesting place." Mischief danced in her grey eyes. "Wait till you see." She drew out a set of shining brass knucks. They clacked as she placed them on the quartz table. "See, they've got retractable spikes. Aren't they cute?"

"You found a weapons shop."

"Could be. Look here . . . This is a crystal gun, and the needles are almost invisible. Got a range of loads: that one's incendiary, then neurotoxin, and a nasty little smartvirus that—"

"You're an obsessive hoplophile, dearest Elva."

"Tom, you say the sweetest things. And look . . ."

She drew out a whitemetal poignard and placed it carefully on the quartz. Then she spun the weapon around, so that Tom could see the pommel and the insignia inscribed upon it: two archaic characters, kappa and alpha, intertwined.

"Where did you—?"

"Kilware Associates"—her smile was cute enough to break Tom's heart—"are back."

One of the things that had made Elva such a good security chief—of Corcorigan Demesne—had been her eidetic memory. She remembered Tom once giving an order to find a weapons store called Kilware Associates. That search had been unsuccessful; but when she saw the golden insignia on the store today, she had remembered everything.

Now, as they walked along creamy cathedral-high halls towards the store, Tom told her for the first time of his dealings with Kilware Associates.

"I think they may be observers," he said, "under Pilots' orders."

"Pilots!"

Tom had been fourteen Standard Years old when he had met his first Pilot: the woman who had given him her log-crystal shortly before the militia caught up with her and their graser beams tore her apart. Tom still forgot that, for most people, Pilots existed only as figures out of legend, dangerous folk who traversed the fractal wilds of mu-space, carrying ordinary humans in their ships as unconscious cargo. Yet how else could Terran emigrants have colonized Nulapeiron, some twelve hundred Standard Years before?

"I suspect," said Tom, "that Pilots maintain an intelligence service, and that Kilware Associates are part of it. At any rate, when I entered one of their shops, a man called Brino caused some kind of tacware to be embedded in my nervous system."

"Without your approval, you mean?"

"Or knowledge, at first. It was quite useful for hand-to-hand conflict: it highlighted vital targets in red, made me see attackers as a mass of points to strike. But the 'ware is long gone . . ."

Tom's two lost years as an alcoholic derelict, after he had fled a revolution which seemed no better than the corrupt regimes it sought to replace, had destroyed all traces of the implanted mindware. Perhaps some psychological carry-over had occurred: when Tom now practised his fighting skills, he still focused on places to hit, not on his opponents' actions.

"The day of our wedding," Tom added, "a stranger called to see me. A Pilot. He said his name was Janis deVries, and that the Pilot I met all those years ago was his mother. And he gave me a dagger"—he pointed at the whitemetal poignard—"just like that. It's in our luggage."

Elva had known none of this. "What else did he say?"

"Only that we'd be meeting up again. Nothing more."

Tom and Elva halted before a wide storefront draped with black velvet curtains and banners, behind which jet-black opaque windows stood. A discreet golden kappa-and-alpha logo glinted by the doorway.

"I guess," said Elva, "we should say hello."

The store's interior was hushed. It was a place of grey shadows and black drapes, with crystal-clear points of light illuminating display cases where polished weapons shone. From the rear, a lean, shaven-headed man walked towards them. He wore a goatee; last time Tom had seen him, he had been clean-shaven.

"It was a woman called Yeira," murmured Elva, "who served me earlier."

"Right," said Tom. "And this is Brino, that I told you about."

Brino stopped and bowed, with a gymnast's—or a master-fighter's—litheness.

"My Lord and Lady Corcorigan. So good to see you."

A short woman stepped out from behind a sword rack. "My Lord." She bobbed a curtsy, then said to Elva: "Nice to see you again so soon, my Lady."

"Hello, Yeira."

Yeira turned to Brino and said: "You were right. They *were* followed. Seven watchers are stationed outside. Deepscan shows they're armed."

Tom looked at Elva.

"We noticed nothing."

"And they're not yours?" Brino gestured, and a string of cubic holo images hung in the air before him. Inside each, an impassive man was shown. "My guess would be an Action League. They're not local, anyway."

Elva's hand went to the graser pistol tagged to her hip. "Who are they?"

Tom said: "What's an Action League?"

With a two-handed control gesture, Brino caused a black membrane to slide down across the doorway and vitrify into hardness. "We're protected now." He made a further series of gestures, then stopped. "My Lord, you've heard of the Circulus Fidus."

"Reactionary think-tank," Tom said, thinking: *And that bastard A'Dekal tried to recruit me to their cause.* "Are you saying the Circulus has become militant?"

"Not exactly. Action Leagues are affiliated to the Circulus, and they're springing up in every sector. Strategically, their thinking is sound. With the war over, they have to re-establish the old regimes quickly, before realms start experimenting with new forms of government. It's a chance for change, or to knuckle down beneath the same old iron fist."

"Your words could be interpreted as treason."

"Perhaps . . . Would you drag me before Duke Kalshuna, my Lord?"

Tom had to smile at that. "Maybe not."

Inside each of the seven holo images, the men suddenly stiffened, and their eyes rolled up. They slumped to the floor.

"Don't worry." Yeira checked a scan display. "They're unharmed. A bit of a migraine when they wake up, is all. They'll be out for an hour.

Oh, and . . . they're wearing eyebranes with high-zoom capability: it's no wonder you didn't spot them. They'd have hung well back."

"Thanks for that," said Elva. "Perhaps I'll have a little chat with one of them."

"You'll learn very little," Brino told her. "My recommendation would be to make sure you're on board your arachnargos tonight. Realm Vilshan is well guarded, and you should be safe there."

That realm was Tom's and Elva's last stop before the Collegium itself. "You seem remarkably well informed, Master Brino."

"I try to be, my Lord."

Elva had edged towards a display case. Now, before Tom could react—he remembered the toxin-laden membranes that had protected the weapons store's displays—Elva reached inside and picked up a small dartbow. "Very nice." She held it down and to the side. "Isn't it dangerous, selling weapons for a living?"

Brino held her gaze.

"No, my Lady. Safest place in the world."

Elva looked at him for a moment longer, then replaced the dartbow on its velvet cushion. At that moment, Brino reached inside his tunic pocket, took out something small, and tossed it towards Tom.

"A present, my Lord."

Tom snatched it from the air; Elva frowned at the lack of protocol. She was a commoner by birth, but a peacekeeping officer by training, and therefore disciplined.

"A crystal." Tom clenched it in his hand. "May I ask what's on it?"

"I think you know," said Brino. "It's a copy of the one that was destroyed."

"From the *Pilot*?"

"Janis deVries sends his regards."

"What? No, wait—"

Then something strange happened. Brino made a control gesture such as Tom had never seen before, and the air began to move. Blocks of transparency slid around them. Display cases shifted, weapons glinting as they rotated and folded out of existence.

Invisible bands constrained Tom like a fist.

"Are you caught?" he asked.

"Yes," said Elva.

Brino seemed wrapped in shadows: nearby, yet somehow distant. "Farewell, my Lord and Lady. I hope you're successful."

"Wait, I want to—"

Brino was gone. So was Yeira.

Shadows, shadows all around . . .

An eldritch twisting of the air itself.

Then the invisible force released Tom and bright light sprang into being on all sides. He toppled backwards onto the floor, flagstones banging hard against his buttocks. Elva was sprawled on one side.

They were sitting on the floor in the bright-lit hall, and passers-by were stopping, shocked at the sight of nobility sprawled on the ground. Where the weapons store had been was a blank, wide alcove.

"That's a neat trick," said Elva.

"Isn't it?" said Tom.

Then Elva giggled, and in a moment they were laughing hard enough to cry as they sat there on the floor, while all around them strangers stared at the insane aristocratic couple who had dropped into their ordinary lives.

3
NULAPEIRON AD 3423

The original crystal had been some kind of diary or log, but in the young Tom's possession it became much more. Adapting itself to the environment, the crystal posed teaching questions, and allowed Tom to study logosophical disciplines long before he enrolled in the Sorites School which made him a Lord.

It was also a history of the Pilots, though how much was true and how much was drama for its own sake, Tom could not tell.

Yet the crystal could also function as a mu-space relay, and Tom made use of it several times. Accessing communications processors of the mu-space universe enabled him to subvert an Oracle's future memories, by immersing the Oracle in a perfectly simulated but false future. Only in a fractal universe (where mathematics was not constrained by Gödel's Theorem) could such a detailed lie be constructed.

The crystal's last feat had not been at Tom's hand. Instead, a squadron of volunteers flew with it above a giant Blight-constructed crystal building up on the world's surface (and this was exceptional: most of Nulapeiron's ten billion inhabitants would collapse in agoraphobic fear if they saw the surface or the sky). Those volunteers opened the gateway through which the Dart-entity warred against the Blight, and defeated it.

Back in the apartment, Tom held the crystal in his hand for a long time, simply staring at it. This one, he was sure, had no mu-space comms capability; Brino would not hand over such technology. But even if the crystal held only the old teaching tales, the ones that Tom had already experienced over and over, that would be enough.

It was a link to his past, in a dislocated, fluid world.

Elva kissed him, then made ready to leave. She had booked an hour in the training chambers of the local security forces, so she could practise with her new weapons against fighting mannequins.

"See you later, Tom."

"Be careful, darling. Or at least—"

"—be vicious, right. Later."

Then she was gone.

Tom did not fully immerse himself in the old story. Instead, tapping his holopad, he opened an introductory static image: a holo depicting a slender woman and her two teenage sons. The sons were twins, a little older than when Tom had last seen them in the original crystal's tales, but still recognizable.

They looked normal, because they wore contact lenses to disguise the true appearance of their eyes: obsidian orbs without surrounding whites, jet-black eyes which could stare upon a fractal space no ordinary human being could comprehend.

Tom looked at the image for a long time.

What's wrong?

It was that feeling of *threat*, the feeling that had been growing stronger as he drew nearer to the Collegium. Surely it could only be nerves, knowing that he might be placing himself and Elva in the hands of his enemies. And yet, and yet . . .

It was something real, he knew: something more than fear.

Then a familiar silent voice sounded in his mind:

Tom? Is that you in there?

He chuckled and headed towards the lounge, holopad in hand. As he stepped inside, he made to shut down the image, but Eemur's next words stopped him.

No, don't . . . There's a link here, my Lord. A very strange but important link.

What kind of link?

A form of entanglement? I'm not sure. But something . . .

Tom shivered.

The nervous systems of Elva and her twin sister Litha had been quantum-entangled since an early age. When Elva's body had perished (or, as she said with no trace of humour, the *first* time she died), her consciousness had instantaneously displaced Litha's mind in Litha's body. But this could not be what Eemur was talking about: setting up such a link was a long, tricky process, and fallible; Elva sometimes woke up amid fading tag-ends of dreams that were not hers.

"Eemur?" Tom spoke aloud. "How can there be a link? These people must have perished centuries ago."

There was no reply.

"Eemur?"

Then her words came with an odd, eerie overlay: **I haven't given you your wedding present yet.**

"That's all right."

Let's do it now.

"Don't worry about—"

But you have to kiss me first.

Confusion whirled inside Tom. Once before, he had picked up Eemur's Head and kissed her like an automaton, not knowing why he was doing it. While Blight-subsumed soldiers had threatened them, Tom had kissed two sapphire tears from her eyes and gained strange abilities, just for a few moments. For long enough.

But now—

In some fashion, Eemur's Head had saved his and Elva's lives. Now, Tom knew he should refuse her request; yet he could not. Deep inside, he did not *want* to refuse.

Eemur.

Tom leaned forward, and then Eemur's black-and-purple tongue was slithering, slick and icy, inside his mouth. Sucking the warmth from him.

Sapphires sparkled.

What . . . ?

Cold lightning seared his lips.

Congratulations, my sweet Lord.

Tore his universe apart.

Tom fell *into* that explosion, whorls of brightness flashing past, arced around atoms grown the size of galaxies; fell through the humming strangeness of quarks, the scream of incandescent spacetime whose warp and weave stretched to encompass him.

He dropped through.

Twisting along the Calabi-Yau dimensions, sliding through hyper-geometric crawlspaces beneath the subset revealed to human senses . . . he could almost comprehend the mosaic, the eleven-dimensioned tessellae slotting together to form the universe. The human universe, realspace, was just a brane's width away from . . .

Tom slammed into normal size.

He lay on black, gleaming glass, panting hard.

Where the Chaos am I?

It was a cold great metal hall, formed of abstract sculptures: jagged flanges and polygonal sheets of alloy struck odd angles everywhere. Razor-edged obsidian formed angular archways too high and narrow for humans.

Cold . . .

Overhead, a vertical hanging sheet of bronze crawled with dark-red crystals which spread in fractal trees, blackened into death, then glimmered red once more. Criss-crossed black hawsers webbed the hall; spinning copper disks moved along them.

Interesting place you've chosen.

The air felt thick, cold and oily.

"*I've* chosen?" Tom's words sounded flat. "What is this?"

More flanges materialized, sliding into place. A jumble of metallic sheets moved. An angular carapace shifted, and steel eyes opened.

Tom, I think you'd better . . .

But Tom was already moving.

Where in Nulapeiron is this?

Stupid question. He ducked behind a sharp-cornered buttress. Had it seen him? He had caught a glimpse of questing pincers which could snip him in half without noticing.

Quickly.

There. A jagged entrance to . . . something. Tom pushed away from the buttress, ducked beneath a protrusion which could have taken out his eye, and was into the tunnel.

Things clacked behind him.

Not in Nulapeiron. This was not his world.

There was a jutting sheet of dull metal which formed a natural hiding place, and he sank down, breathing hard.

"Where?" he whispered.

As a boy, Tom had dreamed of leaving the marketplace, perhaps to visit the merchants' homes in the stratum above . . . and now this: another world.

This may be Siganth. Tom, I'm sorry. I followed the link . . .

Siganth?

"Don't be insane."

I've made a mistake, but you have to—

"Chaos, Eemur. I believe you."

Siganth was a distant hellworld out of legend and he could *not* be here, not in any rational universe. Yet Eemur's silent words rang with truth as well as fear.

"Eemur? Can you bring me b—?"

The metallic ceiling hinged open, extended black and copper claws, and reached down.

Run, Tom.

He lunged to his feet.

Run fast.

Blades snicked behind him.

4
SIGANTH AD 3423

Scrapes followed him. Clattering filled the air as Tom squeezed between thin flanges which sliced his tunic, drew a dozen scarlet creases along his torso—*Chaos!*—as a series of serrated blades skimmed past his ear. Tom slid through a sharp-edged slot, hauling himself into open air—

No. It can't be.

—where he hung, blood dripping, fingers hooked onto a corroded flange, and stared down at the streaked metallic cliff-face plunging below. It spread many kilometres to either side, and reared high above. The sky shone purple, streaked with starless black.

A different world.

Or nightmare. But his cuts ached, and they were real.

It was a vast canyon, and the distant opposite wall was chalky and bone-grey, slashed with dull bronze slanted sheets and vanes, each too big to contemplate. In the intervening air, strange, pulsing vortices whirled and broke apart. The breeze which slid across his skin was slick and cold, like frostsnail slime.

Snick-snack sounded from the shaft behind him.

Time to move.

Changing his grip, crimping hard, Tom swung out onto the exposed metallic cliff-face, squatted into a climber's frog-position, and boosted himself up.

Movement was odd. Lighter gravity but viscous air . . . perhaps. Everything was off-kilter, but there was no time to stop and analyse the differences; he had to keep going.

Tom worked for the climbing moves, used bolt-like protuberances on the metallic cliff to spider his way up. The surface felt rough-smooth, as though covered in fine rust, and when he came to a jutting ledge he stopped, unable to climb further along the blank, sheer face.

Below, a black stalk extended from the shaft he had used, and Tom pulled himself onto the ledge, out of sight.

Did it see me?

There was a steel eye at the stalk's end. He was almost sure of it.

Eemur. Get me out of this place.

Primeval wails of fear sounded in his mind.

Tom lay shivering on the hard ledge, trying to control his breathing. Inside his lungs, the air felt different from the cold gelatinous atmosphere pressing against his skin. Could he somehow be breathing Nulapeiron's air, though his body was on a distant world? Was Eemur maintaining some kind of connection across the light-years?

It gave Tom the tiniest hope that she was working to drag him back.

Then he twitched as down below, inside the abyss, something dark and massive began to ascend. It was metallic, formed in overlapping armoured sections, bristling with antennae.

A vessel? A creature?

Tom suddenly felt that in this place there was little difference between construct and organism, between machinery and life. Either one could kill him.

It was rising towards his hiding place.

He pulled back close against the metal face, but that was dangerous: too much pressure would bounce him off the ledge and into the void. The vessel-thing continued to rise.

Oh, Chaos.

Tom pulled his legs beneath him, formed a squatting position, and got ready for the only manoeuvre he could think of. If it had eyes upon its back, he was dead.

Still rising.

He shut his eyes, rehearsed the jump. The muscles of his thighs began to quiver with stress and cold.

Now.

Tom launched himself from the ledge.

He seemed to fall slowly.

Slowly . . .

And then it was very fast, metal surface rising towards him and he struck feet first against the hull, rolled and lashed out, grabbed for an antenna—*missed*—and rolled again, unable to stop with the edge of the carapace in sight, the fatal drop waiting for him and then another antenna—*grab*—and this time he got it.

The vessel/creature was still rising.

Splotched oval patches decorated the dorsal surface. Membranes, amid the metal?

Hurry.

Carefully, knowing it would be easy to slip and slide right off the hull, Tom crawled to the nearest patch, pressed down with his finger-tips. They sank into soft, membranous material.

Get inside.

Tom rolled forward, and dropped through.

He crouched on a cold metal deck, scanning the empty corridor, then chose a direction at random and took it.

I'm still breathing.

It was a reminder. If he was breathing his homeworld's air then Eemur was maintaining a link and there was still some sort of chance.

You don't know that for sure.

Siganth was an Anomalous world. Just as a human body is formed of trillions of cells whose individual identities are irrelevant to the whole (indeed, to avoid cancer, the body must command many of its cells to commit suicide), so did the Anomaly consist of trillions of once-human and alien beings it had subsumed. To be Absorbed was to become an unthinking component of an unimaginably greater whole: individuality no more relevant than a single cell's or bacterium's chemical drives.

Tom's skin went cold, scraped by electric tension as he crouched in the corridor. It was dread, and there were only two choices: to slink away or face it. *Something* lay ahead. Fate, not chance, had led him to this vessel; he could feel himself being drawn forward.

Nerves wailing, Tom advanced.

There was a diamond arch. Beyond it lay a great chamber in which jagged metal buttresses grew from the walls, stippled with viral crystals. Shards of black glass floated in the air, some spinning, some hanging still.

Tom crept closer.

Oh, sweet Fate.

The air shone like ice, and at the chamber's centre a figure hung suspended, writhing.

A human figure.

He was unclothed and screaming, though no sound reached Tom's ears. The man's face was half-coated with silver scar tissue and his right hand was a claw, but those were old injuries. What happened next was different.

Invisible fingers hooked beneath the captive's skin and peeled it back, stripping his flesh bare. The skin seemed to twist through an impossible angle, and disappeared from sight. What was left was a writhing, agonized, flensed victim. Even as he struggled, something dragged greyish fat from his body; the globules rotated, then winked out of existence. Arteries broke loose, whipped like cables cut in a storm, pulled themselves into nothingness, were gone.

Still the man lived, and suffered.

The vivisection continued, taking his eyeballs, then plucking out the bones one by one until only this remained: a fine tracery of thread-like nerves in the air, connecting to his floating brain. Everything was gone, save the ability to sense massive, agonizing pain.

No . . .

Something worse occurred.

As Tom watched, the field reversed the process, pushed bones into place and layered strips of striated muscle over them and popped the eyeballs in, then draped skin across the ensemble until the captive human being was whole, entire again.

Writhing in the energy field.

Until invisible hooks tugged at his skin and the process began all over.

There was an energy field, and an unaided man could not hope to break through, but as Tom watched the captive suffer he knew he had to try. He looked around the chamber for something which he could thrust inside the field, saw nothing. Perhaps if he climbed up to the ceiling—a series of angled flanges would provide holds—he could drop inside the field from above and haul the poor man free.

But even as he thought this, a torture cycle completed and the man's body was whole once more, for a few seconds. This time he saw Tom approaching . . . and then the strangest, bravest thing occurred.

The man raised his hand and shook his head, yelling silent words that could mean only one thing: warning Tom to stay back, not to risk himself. If Tom had been the captive, he would have been screaming for help, unable to comprehend danger to others when his own nerves were racked with agony.

How long have you been here? Days?

Tom crept closer, as the man's skin began to twist, as invisible hooks inserted themselves. Tom would have to time it right, enter the field when the captive was whole.

Or years?

Then Tom stopped dead. In the overwhelming horror of the sight, there was something he had not noticed. The eyes, the eyeballs which the invisible field was tearing at again . . . were totally black, a shining obsidian. This was no ordinary man.

A Pilot!

This was why Tom had been drawn to this chamber. Eemur had talked of a link, and now he felt it. Some part of Tom tasted a distant echo of the tortured pain the Pilot was undergoing; he could not understand how the man survived.

"Hang on. I'm going to get you out of there."

Even as his flesh peeled back, the Pilot tried to wave Tom away. Tom reached up to the nearest flange, took hold—

Then the walls seemed to come alive as white light flared—an alarm—and great encrusted metal limbs reached for Tom with talons and blades—*snick*—as doors slid down, shutting off the corridors—*snack*—and there was nowhere to go.

Blue sparks rose in the air—sapphire blue: the hue associated with Oracles and Seers.

Eemur?

A low hum.

Get me out of here!

Something slammed him downwards.

Then he was plunging into a slick electric-blue tunnel that blazed and shone as he fell through nebulae that were atoms with electron clouds greater than worlds, and he yelled as unstoppable forces squeezed and spat him through the gaps of reality, through the holes in a network of vibrating strings of spacetime, flung him down and down—

I've got you, Tom.

—until the path curved and he spun upwards, grew, flew in all directions and tumbled out and fell, back to normality once more.

Tom was on his knees and retching on a soft carpet. There was a faint woody scent of boxed fluorofungus upon the air. Lambent orange of a floating glowglobe cast diffuse shadows on the floor.

You're all right.

Tom looked up.

"Easy for you to—"

But her disembodied head was dry and scaly, and Tom knew he could never appreciate the effort behind her abilities.

"Interesting present, Eemur . . . Are you all right? Do you need anything?"

I'll be fine.

Nodding, Tom dragged himself to his feet. "We need to talk . . . in a while." He staggered from the lounge, through to the bath chamber. There, he gestured for the aerogel bath to activate itself in full medical mode—his cuts would need cleansing—and pulled his clothes off, dropping them into a reclamation bin.

Tom winced as he climbed down into the bath. He held his breath, slid under, until he was completely submerged. His skin tingled; the burning in his wounds began to fade. Inside the gel, he started taking shallow breaths.

Then incredibly—in reaction to the trauma and the knowledge that he was safe—Tom drifted into sleep.

5

NULAPEIRON AD 3423

The arachnargos which took them to Realm Vilshan was long and streamlined, its upper carapace coloured a deep metallic violet, melding into chocolate-brown and grey at the sides, becoming shell-white across its underbelly. The violet-and-grey tendrils were long and strong; they whipped outwards with a speed and manoeuvrability Tom had never seen with a vehicle of this size.

As they travelled, Elva sat up front in the control cabin, while Tom went back into the thoracic hold. There, he sat on the deck near an upended case, atop which Eemur's Head stood on a tray. He took out his crystal, pressed it into his holopad, and flicked on the image of Ro McNamara and her sons.

"A link," he said, "between me and Pilots."

That's right.

"Perhaps the captive was a descendant of this family."

It could be. When the link was forged, or *will* be forged, I can't tell.

Tom stared at her flensed head.

"*Will* be forged? What do you mean?"

What I said. The linking event may not have occurred yet.

For all that he had grown up with the notion of Oracles, the idea of backward causality made Tom shudder. The future should not affect the past; that was not the way things ought to work. Even the Oracles saw only their own future memories, their own perceptions untied from the arrow of time. Yet when ruling Lords acted now on information perceived from the future, wasn't that a form of reverse cause-and-effect?

Tom let out a long breath.

"I haven't told Elva . . . We need to equip a rescue party for Siganth." It was another debt of honour, though harder to explain. "How we'll afford it, I don't know. Perhaps I can persuade Corduven to mount a commando operation."

I don't think so.

"Why not? What's the maximum number of people you can send through to a hellworld in one go?"

It's not exactly "sending." In one sense, you remained in Nulapeiron the entire time.

Tell that to my cuts, Tom thought. *Elva hasn't seen them yet.*

Still, Tom knew that existing logosophical theories could not adequately describe a Seer's abilities. Pilots travelled by inserting their vessels into another universe: the fractal mu-space which underlay all continua. Seers had no access to mu-space, but they could perceive and use the hidden dimensions of realspace, unknown to most human beings (who have evolved to act within three spatial dimensions, not the full complement of ten: time is the *eleventh* dimension).

The Blight had been able to manifest its once-human components, teleporting them into place using powers which were surely similar to Eemur's.

The way is blocked. I cannot reach Siganth again.

"Fate." Tom stared into Eemur's bulbous eyeballs. *Blocked by the Anomaly? Because it knows I was there?*

It knows *somebody* traversed the Calabi-Yau geodesics.

Fear accelerated Tom's pulse. He had worried about the Blight, that it might have contacted the Anomaly, albeit briefly. What if he himself had compounded the disaster, by making the entity aware of Nulapeiron's existence?

Does it know which world I come from?

A pause.

I don't know.

Tom turned away. Ignorance could bring no comfort.

Two days later, with a border checkpoint in sight up ahead, their hired arachnargos entered a great cavern, passing beneath a huge holobanner which read:

*** COLLEGIUM PERPETUUM DELPHINORUM ***
*** where Oracles are created ***
*** not born ***

For a motto (or a sales slogan) it seemed obscurely threatening. From the forward cabin, Tom stared at the ornate triconic symbols as they slid past overhead. Then the arachnargos was at the checkpoint, and the pilots were bringing it to rest on a vast polished platform of blue stone. Down below, guards in matched black-and-yellow capes stood to attention.

An exit hatch puckered and opened, then fine tendrils lowered Tom and Elva to ground level. A mesodrone drifted down alongside them, containing Eemur's Head along with all their luggage.

Just how the authorities would react if their scanfields detected a severed Seer's head inside the drone's shielded carapace, none of them knew. Eemur had insisted that they not leave her behind someplace; and neither Tom nor Elva had been able to think of an adequate reason to overrule her wishes.

Tom's skin tingled. They *were* being scanned.

Above them, the arachnargos, its commission completed, was already turning away. As Tom watched, a lead tendril whipped out with a *thwap*, its gekkomere pads fastening onto a broad stone pillar. Then the arachnargos was in motion, tendrils flicking out faster and faster, accelerating along the broad natural caverns until it reached the arching exit, accelerated even more . . . and was gone.

Tom turned to look at the Collegiate guards.

"Nice to be back," he murmured.

The last time he and Elva had been here, the entire realm was under the control of Blight forces, and they were fighting for their lives. Now, less than a hectoday later, they had little idea what to expect.

It's a debt of honour, he reminded himself.

What if he was risking Elva's life in trying to repay the near-dead cyborg, the Jack which had helped him to rescue her? But Tom had talked it over with Elva, and she had been firm: "*At the least, I had extra days of life, and the chance to marry you, my Lord.*"

There had been nothing Tom could say to argue against that.

Now an officer in a black-and-yellow cape was marching forward. As he drew close, the troopers behind him raised their weapons to port-arms. The officer halted, and stamped to attention, then bowed deeply.

"My Lord and Lady Corcorigan. I bid you welcome here."

The troopers quick-marched to fall in all around them, forming an escort.

"The guest quarters," the officer added, "have been made ready. I hope you'll find them adequate."

Then they moved off along the broad stone platform on foot, followed by the floating drone.

Farsight Broadway was long and richly furnished with velvet hangings, and with morphglass sculptures dancing in its marble alcoves. The central carpeted strip slid into laminar flow, carrying Tom and Elva and their armed escort. Collegiate scholars and other noble visitors were walking among the cloisters and colonnades which stretched off to either side. Everything, it seemed, had been restored to its accustomed glory . . . except that, looking carefully down side-corridors, Tom glimpsed the occasional burn-mark, or channels carved in stone by wild graser fire. Collegiate forces had fought hard before falling to the Blight.

Elva looked up at a decorative bronze ceiling-sculpture.

"Milligrasers," she murmured. "In gatling arrays."

Tom raised an eyebrow. He had not noticed.

"I wonder how legal the targeting system is."

"Not very, if they're sensible."

For centuries, the anti-Turing provisions of the Comitia Freni Fem'telorum had kept weapons relatively dumb. Handheld grasers were the energy weapons of choice; and blades were used for formal duelling among the nobility . . . but none of this was state of the art, for it was over a millennium since smartmists and other killing fem-totech had been developed. The problem was that, when you utilized such weaponry, all tactical choices (and ultimately strategic and even political decisions) were made by the weapons themselves: they acted and reacted too fast for human intervention.

Yet the recent War Against The Blight was making people reconsider. Perhaps humankind needed the deadliest armaments it could muster, not having the luxury to consider the drawbacks of entrusting their Fate to devices of their creation.

The flowing carpet was decelerating.

"I guess we're here."

Before a peaked archway, a holo bird formed of orange flames manifested itself.

"This way," it sang.

The soldiers bowed and remained on the spot as the bird floated slowly along the corridor and Tom and Elva followed, with their meso-drone moving alongside.

What happens next? Tom wondered.

Steam rose gently from three red-brown bowls of indigoberry daistral, which stood on the purple glass conference table. The aroma made Tom smile. While the Collegiate Magister was dismissing the servitor who had brought the drinks, Tom reached over for the nearest bowl, then sat back in his chair, holding the daistral but not yet drinking: that would be rude.

"Don't wait for me," said Magister Strostiv. "After that long journey, you must be dying for a decent daistral."

"Pretty much," said Tom, and took a sip. "Ah, thank you. That's excellent."

Elva waited until Strostiv was sitting down before she picked up her own bowl and drank. "Mm. Not bad."

Strostiv ignored his drink, and sat with his elbows on the tabletop, fingers steepled together. His white hair, unkempt as always, stuck out at odd angles. He was an Altus Magister of the Collegium Perpetuum Delphinorum, and no-one would dream of telling him to smarten up his appearance.

"Congratulations on your wedding, both of you."

"Thank you, Strostiv."

When Tom had last talked to him, Strostiv had been acting as a tactical adviser to Corduven's military Academy, and had revealed as much as was understood about the Blight's true nature to Tom and the other executive officers. He and Tom had not exactly been friends; Tom wondered if they were enemies now.

"Your message said that you wanted to reclaim a damaged Jack-class cyborg, designated Axolon."

"Is that his name?" said Tom. "I didn't know."

Strostiv frowned at the word *his*, rather than *its*. Perhaps a man who helped create Oracles had difficulty in assigning personal qualities to those who were no longer truly human.

"At any rate, the Collegium is happy to renounce all title to the Jack. As far as we're concerned, it—*he*, if you like—is a written-off asset. We have checked with the Klivinax Toldrinov, and they have no particular wish for you to return Axolon to them. They consider it irreparably damaged."

Tom looked at Elva. If the Klivinax Toldrinov, the Guild which created cyborgs, had written off the Jack, then what hope was there?

But we have to try.

Elva nodded, as though she had read his thoughts.

"We're going ahead," she said. "No matter what it costs."

Tom tried not to wince at the thought of their dwindling wealth.

"That," said Magister Strostiv, "is very noble of you."

Elva placed her daistral bowl down on the tabletop, very quietly. Strostiv might do well not to provoke her, Tom reckoned.

"The thing is," Strostiv continued, oblivious to the threat, "we're all very grateful to you. Corduven's forces have received all the credit, but those of us in the know are aware that you, sir, provided the crystal and the strategy which brought us victory."

The replacement crystal suddenly seemed large and hard, tucked inside Tom's waistband.

"Avernon," Tom said, "was the one who implemented the strategy. A team of world-class logosophers *might* have produced the same results, given several tendays. No-one else could have pulled it together in a few hours, singlehandedly."

"You might be right. Do you know where Lord Avernon is now?"

"No . . ." Tom thought that Strostiv's tone had become falsely casual, and he wondered why Strostiv would need to contact Avernon. "The wedding celebrations were still in full flow when Elva and I left. Avernon was there, but we didn't really get to make proper farewells."

It had been a whirl of happy impressions, accompanying their sudden departure in a tiny yellow arachnasprite built for one person (inside which they had both squeezed, laughing) while a similar hired 'sprite followed with their small amount of luggage—and Eemur—stowed aboard.

"And . . . Lord d'Ovraison? What of him, my Lord?"

"There was talk of rebuilding the Academy," said Tom. "And of promoting Corduven again, though to what rank, I'm not sure."

Corduven was already Brigadier-General Lord Corduven d'Ovraison; there was not much else for him to achieve within a strictly military hierarchy. Any higher appointment would be overtly political.

"I'm . . . not sure, either." Strostiv's gaze shifted, betraying some concealment. "He is your friend, isn't he?"

When Tom had been a servitor, Corduven had been the first Lord to treat him as a human being.

And how did I repay him? By murdering his brother.

Tom had killed the Oracle who had foreseen—and in doing so, caused—the death of Tom's father, and who had stolen away Tom's mother. The Oracle had foreseen his own eventual death of old age, but Tom had given him the first surprise of his life . . . and death: a violent, bloody death; a paradox unexpectedly resolved.

Redmetal poignard, sinking in to the hilt . . .

The Oracle was Gérard d'Ovraison, brother to Corduven whom Tom had called friend, and still did.

"What are you getting at, Strostiv?"

For a moment, Strostiv stared at him. "The Jack called Axolon was part of the manhunt, after Oracle d'Ovraison was killed in the terraformer sphere. You can't appreciate the scope and depth of that search. We knew that truecasts had foreseen the Oracle's long, uneventful life . . . It shook the foundations of *everything*."

It was supposed to, thought Tom.

Beside him, Elva grew very still.

"You were the first commoner in Gelmethri Syektor," added Strostiv, "to be upraised to Lordship during the past hundred Standard Years. Your logosophical potential might not have been at Avernon's level—his kind appears once every three or four centuries—but you were still outstanding. And yet you failed to contribute anything to official research . . . until you came on the scene with astounding techniques of war *and access to mu-space*."

"Not many people are aware of the details."

"But some of us are in a position to put the picture together. You weren't a prime suspect at the time of the Oracle's death, but in retrospect your guilt is obvious. Even though the killer directed the terraformer's drones to clean up the interior, there must be *some* forensic evidence we can retrieve, even after all these years."

Tom kept his composure.

"I don't know what you're talking about."

"Well, my Lord, I think you do. But the point is, it doesn't matter"—Strostiv formed a control gesture, and a holo image winked into being above the purple glass tabletop—"because of this. You're specifically exonerated, by the one man I should have thought would want to see you dead."

The image held a legal declaration, Tom saw, witnessed by officials at a Convocation, and at the heart of it was one simple statement:

I do hereby forgo all vengeance-claim upon Lord Thomas Corcorigan, in my absolute faith in his innocence.

Below it, a simple signature-knot tricon hung:

Brigadier-General Lord Corduven d'Ovraison

Tom closed his eyes.

"In the light of this"—Strostiv's words sounded from far away—"no-one could bring you to task. No-one, my Lord."

Corduven.

Tom could not understand why Corduven would support him. With such a document, even if a tribunal were to find Tom guilty, they would have to absolve him from punishment.

You did this for me?

Tom opened his eyes and looked at Strostiv.

"What do you want?" he said.

"To help." Strostiv spread his hands. "Only to help, my Lord."

6
NULAPEIRON AD 3423

Two hours later, Tom and Strostiv stood on a rough stone balcony overlooking a quadrangle which was decorated with purple and scarlet moss. Below them, on the hexagonal flagstones, stood a dozen-strong team of techs and engineers. A pair of utilitarian mesodrones hovered a metre above the ground.

Elva was briefing the technicians as though they were commandos going on a raid.

"You . . . Harin, is it? Good. Your team consists of Alen, Xindor and Frayne." She pointed to them in turn. "You'll take that drone."

"Ma'am."

"The preliminary analysis is your job. I'll want a rundown of whatever additional gear we need. Debriefing at Snapdragon Hour, on the dot."

"Yes, ma'am." And, to his team: "OK. We're moving."

As they left, Elva addressed the others. She had met them minutes ago; already, she knew their names. "You're with me. First stop is the scanner workshop, and I'll need your recommendations, Sharlyn," she said to a heavy, strong-looking woman who bowed. "No need to go for the most expensive gear, people, but no skimping either. All right?"

"No problem."

"Right. Let's get on it."

As they left, Elva made a small nod towards the balcony, not looking up at Tom. Then they trailed out, and were gone.

"Good luck," Tom murmured.

Strostiv frowned. "Is everything all right, my Lord?"

"What do you mean?"

"Lady Corcorigan didn't wave goodbye, so I . . . I beg your pardon, sir. Not my business."

"No offence taken," said Tom. "Military officers don't make emotional farewells; not in front of the troops."

"But they're not—"

"—soldiers, right. With Elva in charge, they might as well be."

Strostiv said nothing for a moment, then: "You're proud of her, aren't you?"

"Oh, yes. Are you married, Strostiv?"

"No. A long time ago, nearly . . . But it doesn't matter."

As he turned to go, Tom reached out and touched Strostiv's sleeve. "It's not the done thing to talk in these terms," Tom told him, "but you know, love is the *only* thing that matters. What else makes life worthwhile?"

Old sorrow darkened Strostiv's eyes.

"Yes," he said. "You're right."

Tom left it at that. He followed, as Strostiv walked back to the inner chamber and sat down at the purple table.

Strostiv had asked that Tom remain behind, while Elva began the task of evaluating the ruined Jack's situation. As their talk proceeded along the minutiae of restoring the Collegium to its pre-war condition, Tom began to grow impatient. Just what was it the man wanted?

Then Strostiv said: "I've a technical expert called Zilwen who would love to talk to you, my Lord. We'll meet back here in an hour, if that's all right."

"Um . . . OK. If I've an hour to kill, I might as well follow Elva and offer my—"

"If you like, of course. But I thought that you might want"— Strostiv gestured; antique bronze doors swung open at the chamber's far end—"to meet up with an old friend."

The antechamber beyond was in shadow. A narrow, cloaked figure stood in the gloom.

Corduven?

Then the man moved forward into the light, his oriental Zhongguo Ren features lighting up in a broad smile. "Tom, old man. Fancy seeing you here."

"Zhao-ji!" Tom had seen him at the wedding, but there had been so little time to talk.

They embraced, pounding each other's backs, then stepped away.

"I guess," said Tom slowly, "I've always known you must have dealings here."

More than once, he had come across glowing sapphire fluid which was somehow linked to Oracular (and possibly Seers') abilities; and there were hints that it was Zhongguo Ren secret societies who transported the stuff in clandestine fashion. And no society was better at technical matters than the Strontium Dragons, to whom Zhao-ji belonged.

Strostiv said: "I'll leave you two to reminisce."

"No, please." Perhaps Tom had judged Strostiv too harshly. "You're welcome to stay with us."

"I think Zhao-ji wants to give you the full tour—"

"Definitely. I'm ready to go now."

"—and I'm afraid I can't follow."

"Why not?" said Tom.

Zhao-ji wouldn't lead me into danger . . .

Yet things had changed since their days in the Ragged School; Zhao-ji's allegiance was to the Strontium Dragons now.

"Come on." Zhao-ji took hold of Tom's arm. "You're going to be impressed, I tell you." And, to Strostiv: "See you later, old chum."

It was not the most respectful way to address an Altus Magister.

A few minutes later, Tom learned why Strostiv had left them. Zhao-ji led the way through a glistening membrane into a vertical shaft. As magnetic gel surrounded them and whisked them upwards, Tom shouted: "*Are we going where I think we're going?*"

His words echoed faintly through the thick gel. The shaft wall appeared to slide downwards, but it was relative motion: they were ascending, and fast.

"To the surface, yes!"

So Zhao-ji had undergone agoraphobia-desensitization. It was in character: Tom remembered his first days at the Ragged School, seeing the slight figure of Zhao-ji launch himself at three much bigger praefecti, hands and feet swinging in hopeless bravery. Tom had never known him to back down from a challenge.

Just for a moment, as they ascended, he caught a glimpse of glowing sapphire at Zhao-ji's wrist. Then Zhao-ji tugged his sleeve down and looked upwards, towards their destination.

Their ascent began to slow.

The gel-flow twisted, spilling them onto a white ceramic floor, then curled back inside the shaft proper. Tom and Zhao-ji were crouched in a low chamber; before them, a metal door was opening. Grass and dirt spilled outside: they were in a hollow hillock, hidden in the landscape.

"'Madmen lead, fools follow.'" Zhao-ji went first through the opening, then looked back at Tom and grinned. "So which one are you?"

"Grow up, why don't you?"

But Tom was smiling as he passed through the doorway, and stepped out onto the open ground. He took in a deep breath of cool, sweet air.

"Fantastic," he said. "I love this place."

Now even Zhao-ji was looking doubtful. "Fate, Tom. I can put up with the surface. That doesn't mean I love it. What's wrong with you?"

"Madmen lead . . ."

"Right."

They walked out onto grassy heathland.

The sky was warm yellow, blotted with chocolate-brown clouds. The long grasses held a silvery sheen. It would have been perfect, but Tom had not figured their exact position: as they crossed a ridgetop and looked down at a glittering expanse, he suddenly realized that the Lake of Glass lay below.

Why did you bring me here?

The glass had once formed a vast ornate structure reaching up above the surface. Within it, a quarter of a million subsumed men, women and children had melded into the greater Blight, attempting to beam its cry for help across the light-years to the parent Anomaly. Tom had played his part in destroying the Blight and saving the world, but the price . . .

Encapsulated in the glass, mouths open and eyes bulging, swirling hair forever frozen, were the two hundred and fifty thousand people who had perished in a single moment, when the Blight vanished from existence.

Zhao-ji placed his hand on Tom's shoulder.

"Look," he said. "No. Look *up*."

Something was descending from the sky.

A white shuttle moved between a gap in the clouds, disappeared for a moment, then slid back into visibility, drawing closer to the ground by the second. As Tom watched, it decelerated hard, adopted a level attitude and hovered.

"Whose is it?"

"You haven't guessed? It's the Collegium, Tom. That's a Collegiate shuttle."

"And what do they want with orbital vehicles?"

"That, my friend, is what I'm here to show you. For the moment . . . just watch."

The Strontium Dragons, like their peer societies, were capable of formulating game plans that lasted centuries. Tom wondered what part he was playing in their advancement right now.

An area of heathland glimmered beneath the sun, and Tom realized it was a wide patch of membrane, big enough for the shuttle to drop through. As the membrane liquefied it shone more brightly; and Tom could almost hear a wet sucking sound as the shuttle lowered itself through and disappeared from sight, with the membrane re-forming in place above it.

"Who's aboard?" said Tom.

"No-one. D'you expect *people* to go up in those things?" Zhao-ji's grin twisted. "We're not all as mad as you are."

"So it's AI-controlled. Then what's the cargo?"

Zhao-ji shook his head.

"Why don't we just go and take a look?"

Then he turned around and headed back towards the hillock, and the concealed drop-shaft which would take them back into the buried safety of the civilized world.

Perhaps it's not the Strontium Dragons who have something to gain, Tom decided, as he followed Zhao-ji. *Perhaps it's Strostiv who has a goal here.*

The grassy doorway opened.

Tom and Zhao-ji entered, then stepped side by side into the viscous metallic gel, and sank down inside the shaft together.

They walked into a large bay. The bay adjoined a huge hall shaped like a horizontal cylinder, stretching the best part of a kilometre. A thick transparent view-window separated Tom and Zhao-ji from the interior.

"That's hard vacuum inside," said Zhao-ji. "We can see everything from out here. Look."

He pointed. A long balcony, offset from the hall, ran alongside. Like this bay, it was partitioned off by thick windows.

"Look at what, exactly?"

"Well, this . . ."

The shuttle, held in place by great metallic clamps in the body of the hall, was cracking its dorsal doors open.

"They're collecting the harvest," added Zhao-ji.

"*Harvest?* What the Fate do you harvest in orbit?"

"Something very important. We've been doing it for centuries."

Tom noted the *we*. Perhaps the collaboration between Collegium and Zhongguo Ren societies went deeper than he had thought. Perhaps the Strontium Dragons' involvement in the abortive revolution had been more equivocal and manipulative than anyone realized.

"All right, Zhao-ji. Show me."

Shepherded by drones, a misty cloud rose out of the shuttle and hung billowing in the vacuum. Inside it, tiny points of hard white light were shining.

Tom opened his mouth, closed it. Zhao-ji would explain in his own time.

"This way, Tom."

They stepped onto a dark strip that ran along the floor. Zhao-ji gestured, and the strip began to flow. It carried them to the bay's edge, flowed around a corner, and then followed alongside the vast cylindrical hall.

Inside the hall, the misty cloud was moving along the hall's central axis, at approximately the same pace.

They tracked the cloud's progress to the far end, where a huge cone formed of magnets collimated the cloud into a narrow beam, pushing it along a solid horizontal shaft that was hidden from sight.

"Now what?" said Tom.

"Now you see what this is all about." Zhao-ji looked more glum than Tom had ever seen him. "And I hope that you don't hate me for it."

The moving strip bore them onwards through a dark windowless tunnel, then brought them out into a bright-lit observation chamber where medics in orange gowns stared through view-windows, manipulating med-drones with intricate hand gestures.

What the Fate?

In the chamber below, on the other side of the glass, drones were working on a shaven-headed child who lay on a couch. Tom could not tell whether it was a boy or a girl. Whichever, the child lay quiescent, eyes open, oblivious to the robotic arms peeling back his/her scalp and lasing tiny holes into the skull.

All around, drones used magnetic fields to marshal the misty cloud and its load of shining white geometric points, funnelling the stuff downwards, into the child's freshly exposed brain.

Oh, sweet Destiny.

Tom had forgotten where he was: the place where "Oracles are created, not born." The thing was, no-one outside knew about the process itself; it was the most heavily guarded secret the Collegium possessed. There was *no* reason to reveal it to a sworn enemy.

"Zhao-ji. What are they doing?"

"What they've always done, my friend. Exactly what they've always done."

7

NULAPEIRON AD 3423

Strostiv was waiting for Tom in his antechamber. Zhao-ji took his leave, departing amid an escort of hard-faced 49s, footsoldiers of the Strontium Dragons, trained in wu shu and weaponry and utterly ruthless in protecting their senior officers. They caught the vibrations from Tom's repressed anger, and kept watchful gazes on him until they were out of sight.

Tom had not spoken a word since they left the medical chamber.

"My apologies," said Strostiv, "if I have offended you."

There was no reply that Tom could make, short of striking out with a half-fist to the larynx and ending Strostiv's life here and now. And what good would that do? The Collegium and its work would still go on.

Finally, Tom exerted all of his self-control and said in a tight but civilized voice: "There was a technical meeting you wanted me to attend?"

"That's right." Strostiv looked relieved. "That's exactly right, old chap."

"So where—?"

"Do follow me, my Lord. Right in here. We're all set up and waiting."

Strostiv's technical expert was a man called Zilwen. An obsidian skull-cap clasped his head. Whether it fitted over his scalp or replaced it, Tom could not tell.

They convened in the same chamber as before, with the purple conference table over which a large abstract holodisplay was now billowing. Zilwen gestured an intricate network diagram into being as Tom took his seat.

The core equation modelled the expansion of the entire universe from the viewpoint of notional metaspace. Its relevance was obvious: the future lies (always) in the direction in which the universe is bigger. *All* the basic equations of physics are time-reversible: swap the sign of the time variable in any particle's trajectory, and you merely get a particle moving in the opposite direction.

There is *no* preferred past or future at the tiniest scales. It is the great temporal mystery.

If the universe begins to collapse . . . the ancients' notion was of a Big Bang, expansion, then collapse to a Big Crunch. But by symmetry, Tom knew, you actually get *two* Big Bangs, both growing towards the future time when they meet and join.

These are the equations, Tom thought, *that led to my blade in d'Ovraison's heart.*

Would the cross-over time actually occur? Irrelevant. Provided you replicated conditions *as if* the universe were shrinking, you obtained regions of spacetime where time flowed in the opposite direction. Some of the neural groups in Oracles' minds experienced just such negative time: it was the basis of their abilities and their damaged, fragmented personalities.

No-one knew how such a feat of spacetime engineering was possible, only that it had been done. Living Oracles were the proof.

"Perhaps you've wondered," said Zilwen, "how Oracular minds can be constructed."

"I'm willing to learn," Tom muttered.

All the better to destroy you.

Zilwen gestured, and the display rotated and transformed. It showed a white spherical cloud—a hollow sphere—surrounding the world.

"From space, it doesn't shine so obviously"—Zilwen brightened the display further—"but it is there, in exactly this configuration."

"*What* is there?"

"The spinpoint field, of course." Zilwen glanced at Strostiv, who did not react. "What did you think you just observed? The spinpoints we've harvested from orbit."

"And what," asked Tom slowly, "is a spinpoint?"

Zilwen was one of those brilliant fools, technically hypercompetent but unable to explain his thoughts, and his mouth worked as he tried to find the words.

Then Tom held up his hand, forestalling him.

"Fate! You've got singularities—"

Strostiv was smiling now.

"—of negative time. That's what a spinpoint is: an infinitesimal knot where time is reversed."

Zilwen nodded. To Strostiv, he said: "He got it, fast enough. I'd say he's able to do the job."

Strostiv shrugged, smiling at Tom in apology for Zilwen's manner. But at least Zilwen was not concealing his goals.

"You want *me* to work for the Collegium?" Tom stared at them. "Are you serious?"

"It's the perfect place for your research interests, don't you think? You have no demesne to rule, and the money must be running out, particularly with the cyborg affair: I know how much those technicians cost."

"It'll be fun." Zilwen gazed at him with round, almost childlike eyes. "We have top of the range equipment. Absolutely the best."

Tom remembered another child, with cut-open scalp and the drones removing humanity from the wet, exposed brain.

"I don't see . . ." Tom would milk them of information before refusing outright. "I still don't see how you create the spinpoints in the first place. It seems impossible."

Zilwen frowned.

"Um . . . I thought you realized . . ."

"We're working on it," Strostiv interrupted with a politician's smoothness. "Whether it's the next year or the next century, we'll get there. We're guaranteed success, don't you see? What could be better than allying yourself to a project that *you already know* will be a winner?"

Even with the logosophical model hanging over the table and the hints contained in Strostiv's words, it took several long moments for Tom to put the pieces together and blurt out his reaction. "My Fate," he said. "You don't know how to create spinpoints. You don't know—"

He was out of his chair and standing now.

"—because *they haven't been created yet.*"

Waves of silence seemed to crash in the room, and then Strostiv sighed, reclaiming a sense of normality. "That's the nature, I'm afraid, of negative time."

"The spinpoints' origins lie in our future. Our descendants will create them."

"Or we will, tomorrow." Strostiv raised his hands, palms up. "Who can tell?"

"And you want me to work on this?"

"Well, of course we can discuss your—"

"You know so much about the nature of time. Do you understand the word *never*?"

Tom kicked his chair aside. It spun across the floor and fell clattering. Then he strode from the chamber breathing hard, not looking back, knowing he might kill someone if he did.

An hour later he was on a lev-platform accompanied by four greystone warriors, skimming through raw, broken tunnels only fitfully lit by glowfungus. In some, the fungus was sparse or diseased, and therefore the air was bad; they moved through those tunnels at high speed, mainly for Tom's benefit: it was said that greystone warriors could function for many minutes on end without breathing.

The escort, he assumed, was not for Tom's protection so much as the Collegium's: they might wonder what he was capable of doing.

(The warriors might, just might, have been assigned to get rid of him, now that he knew the Collegium's secret. Tom half-hoped they would try; he had an awful lot of anger to purge.)

But then the lev-platform was descending without incident, and the officer was saying in an incongruously soft voice: "The Lady Elva is through there, sir."

A dark opening in the rockface emitted clinks of sound. The technicians must be already working on the Jack.

"Thank you," said Tom, stepping off the platform.

It rose and spun away, then flew back the way it had come.

Tom stepped through the opening.

Elva was there. Tom took in a deep breath and let it out in a sigh, releasing his rage, letting it dissipate. One of the technicians, kneeling, glanced up at him, then continued with her work.

On the rough stone wall, the Jack's ruined half-head turned slightly. Its—*his*—one intact microfaceted eye focused on Tom.

"You . . . came . . . back."

"I said I would."

"Promised . . . death."

Tom had sworn to end the Jack's agony. "I'd rather bring you life."

Charcoal sprayed across the rock. Remnants of the cyborg's destroyed torso melded with charred stone, fused into the damaged wall. Any other lifeform would have been obliterated; but tenacity was at the core of a Jack's programmed being.

"Axolon?" said Elva. "We need to take you offline now, for a while. All right?"

". . . ess."

The cyborg's head drooped as if tired. Tom could not imagine the pain and exhaustion he had undergone.

"Now." The kneeling tech gestured, and the Jack froze still.

"Whew." Elva rubbed her face, then smiled at Tom. "It's going to be a lot of effort just to prise and chip him from the rock, even with micro-cutters. After that . . . I really don't know how we're going to fix him."

"But we have to try."

"Yes." Elva stared at the near-destroyed form. "Yes, we do."

It was hard to imagine Axolon at the height of his power, with hyperfine senses and weaponry to match a regiment. (Tom had once killed what he thought was a Jack, but in Klivinax Toldrinov terminology that had been a nymph; as a full Jack, Axolon would have been invulnerable in hand-to-hand combat.) It was even harder to imagine a power capable of doing this to Axolon, but that was what the Blight had been: unimaginable.

And its parent Anomaly was greater and darker by far.

Then Elva was handing Tom a crystal—the ordinary kind—saying: "A courier left this, an hour ago. It's DNA-sealed, for your eyes only."

"Well"—Tom thumbed it on—"I've no secrets from you, dear."

But the lightness dropped from his tone as he read the message. All its meaning was wrapped up in two, concise triconic ideograms:

Please come immediately. It concerns Corduven. The sharp-edged configuration conveyed this: **Fully urgent.**

And it was signed:

Lady V'Delikona.

Elva placed her hand atop Tom's.

"You can go in the morning. I'll keep the work going here. Your absence won't slow things down."

"I can always postpone—"

"It says *most urgent*, Tom, and she's never asked anything of you before."

"Perhaps . . ." He blew out a breath. "Perhaps I should go right now."

"In the morning, when you've rested. Our tent's down that way. You can go freshen up, while I make your travel arrangements."

"We can't afford—"

"Do what I say."

"Yes, ma'am."

"And I'll be with you in a minute."

"I . . . Thank you, darling."

"Any time, my love."

Next morning, Tom left at dawnshift, in an arachnargos less impressive than the one which had brought them here, but functional. The pilots offered to let him ride up front, but Tom preferred to sit in the thoracic hold, alone.

There, he reached inside his tunic, and drew out the metal stallion talisman which his father had made, a lifetime before. His fingers formed the same old control gesture, and the solid metal clove apart, revealing the crystal hidden in its hollow core.

It was the crystal which Brino had given him, replacement to the one which had been Tom's companion over the years, with its teaching puzzles and tales of the first Pilots. For a long time, Tom held it in his palm, smiling with anticipation, before inserting it into his holopad.

Then he activated it in full sensory mode, and sank inside the tale.

8
TERRA AD 2160

<<Ro's Children>>

[1]

It was a December night, black and cold over Zürich. White snow slid softly from the sky. From the false Christmas tree, formed of wide floating disks decorated with greenery, with boughs of pine and sprigs of holly, the choir's voices rose sweetly into the chill air.

Bystanders, their shopping temporarily forgotten, stopped to listen.

Ro, in her heavy jumpsuit and muffler, stood between Dirk and Kian and hugged her twin boys towards her. They stiffened before giving in: they were fifteen years old, identical, alternately awkward and mature.

Golden holoflames flickered among the children in the six-metre-tall artificial tree, while very real white snow was caked atop the green pine branches, and on the shoulders and red caps of the children. They sang:

"Stille Nacht, heilige Nacht . . ."

It was a small square off the luxurious Bahnhofstrasse. The miniature park was surrounded by cobblestone pathways where vendors hawked intricate craft items from tent-like stalls, and sold hot chestnuts and fat-spitting sausages from crackling braziers.

Beyond, over the Bahnhofstrasse thoroughfare, long rows of white/gold holo stars glimmered in the air, overlooking some of the most exclusive and expensive stores in Europe. They were still open, this late on a December night: the Swiss take their Christmas shopping seriously.

A lifetime ago, Mother had taken Ro to this very square.

I miss you.

But she was gone. Last year, as summer slid into autumn, Karyn McNamara had slipped quietly from the world.

Dirk's infostrand beeped. He wore it wrapped helically around the bronze torc encircling his neck: all the fashion this year.

Sorry, he mouthed to his mother, as bystanders looked round.

He walked away, muttering to the holo image lased into his grey contact lenses.

After the call was finished, Dirk remained where he was. Frowning, Ro gave Kian's sleeve a tug, and they went to join Dirk.

"It was Josette," he said to Kian. "She's in the café."

"The Royale?"

"*Ouais, d'accord.*"

"Well, what kind of *espèce de crétin* does she think you are?"

Ro, who was as quintilingual as her sons, said: "Not the kind to stand her up, I hope. *On m'a posé un lapin* when I was her age, and I was pissed."

"Mother . . ." Dirk looked pained. Kian checked that no-one nearby had overheard Ro's coarse language; in her youth, it would have been considered mild.

"The thing is," he said, "Dirk's too soft to give her the heave-ho."

Ro looked at Dirk.

"Josette and Lorraine had a little meeting," he said. "They *decided* that Josette was the one who was going to have me."

"And which of them," asked Ro, "do you prefer?"

Dirk shrugged. Kian answered for him:

"Neither one of them."

In the artificial tree, now lit by bright white light as the snowfall grew heavier, the school choir began to sing in Latin, calling the faithful to the cause.

"Adeste fideles . . ."

"You have to tell her, Dirk." Ro chucked him under the chin.

Dirk refused to be annoyed by the gesture. He was growing up.

"I know I should, but—"

It was Kian who finished the sentence:

"—I'll do it instead."

"Now look, boys . . ."

Ro let her voice trail off. Kian was already striding away through the snow.

"What?" Dirk shrugged. "I'd do the same for him."

"You would?" said Ro. "Or you already have?"

"I—"

"No." Ro held up her gloved hands. "I don't want to know."

They're growing up.

Dirk chuckled.

Way too fast.

Part of the problem, Ro concluded, as she walked arm in arm with Dirk towards the main station, the magnificent old Hauptbahnhof, was the length of time she spent away.

A red thermoacoustic tram, with a man dressed as Santa in nominal control (the onboard AI was in charge, freeing Santa to dispense jolly bonhomie), hissed past above the snow-covered cobblestones. The lighting was a cheerful golden glow. Passengers smiled at each other or peered out, delighted at the sights.

If I were thirty-seven, she wondered, *would they take me more seriously?*

That was the age Ro would be, had she remained earthbound. In fact, she bent the ultra-relativistic mu-space geodesics to far greater limits than UNSA planners suspected. No wonder she looked more like the twins' sister than their mother.

They crossed the street, passed the seated statue which frowned down upon the waiting travellers, seated in their bubble-lounges waiting for trams. Inside the station proper, transparent laminate covered the stone, preserved its baroque splendour. Holo adverts gleamed in shop windows. New-fangled morphslides had replaced the ancient escalators; Ro hoped that bioarchitecture would not replace the old buildings.

"Dirk? You want to go down?"

The boys, when they were younger, had loved to descend to the platforms and watch the big yellow double-decker mag-trains whisk away, or deliver crowds of passengers, many with snow-shoes or skis, into the city's heart.

"No thanks, Mom."

Growing up.

Josette, with slightly pouting lips, her honey-coloured hair drawn back with a papillon mag-clasp, was hunched over an espresso, reading the tabletop display. Fashion news, Kian guessed.

Josette looked up, and wiped the display to neutral navy-blue.

"*Grüezi,*" called Alberto from behind the zinc-topped counter. "*Wie geht's?*"

"*Guten Abend.*" Kian used the local pronunciation: *oh-bent.* He spoke Schweizerdeutsch by default, could switch to formal Hochdeutsch when required. "*Also gut. Alles ist hier OK?*"

"*Ja, natürlich.*"

When Kian sat down opposite Josette, he automatically switched mental gears.

"*Tu vas bien, Josette?*"

"What do you think, Dirk?"

"I . . ." Kian stopped. Exactly what had happened between her and Dirk?

"André's not too happy, either. You'd better stay away from him for a while, *hein?*"

Kian thought that Josette's elder brother was a clumsy fool, but that was irrelevant.

"All right. Um, how did things go today?"

He knew Josette was trying out for the gym team. Like himself and Dirk, she came into the city three days a week for school; the rest of their studying was in EveryWare.

"Vernadski hates me. I score 75 in biochem, or he drops me from the alpha group."

Josette leaned back in her chair, took a tiny vial from her pocket, squirted a pleasant, understated fragrance beneath her ears.

Why does Dirk want to break it off?

It seemed a shame. Josette was very nice.

He'd do the same for me.

"What about gym?" he asked.

Josette gave him a strange look.

Merde. Something you forgot to tell me, bro?

She opened her mouth as if to deliver a scathing reply, but just then Alberto came round from behind the bar, and deposited two tall glasses of warm dark *Glühwein*.

"To keep out the chill."

"Thanks."

"*Merci.*"

Alberto nodded, and set about delivering similar free drinks to the other customers.

A touch on the back of his hand whipped Kian's attention downwards. With a sultry smile—or as near as Josette could get to one—she wrapped her fingers in his.

"You know it doesn't matter," she said, "about my knee. Getting injured. It was worth it, darling."

"I don't—"

"You can try again. You know what I'd like?"

Kian's tongue was dry. He swallowed, tried not to flinch as Josette leaned across the small table and whispered in his ear.

"Jesus Christ."

"Huh?"

Kian could feel his face burning. "You've been doing what?"

Josette, suddenly pale, sat back in her chair with a thump.

"*Kian* . . . ?" Then, raising her voice to stop all conversation in the café. "You're not Dirk. You pervert!"

"Oh, *merde*." But Kian could not help smirking. "No wonder you strained your ligaments. Don't you think that was a little, er, ambitious?"

Josette's hand arced through the air. Kian shifted slightly, and her palm smacked into the wall.

"*Ow!* Now look what you've done."

"Me? All I . . ."

But he let his voice trail off then as she placed her injured hand in her lap, covered her face with the other, and began to sob.

Accusing faces, all around, stared at Kian.

"I'm sorry." It sounded inadequate. "Look, see . . . Dirk couldn't face having this conversation. You mean so much to him. It's just not working—"

"*Bâtard!*" She hissed, an indrawn breath between her teeth, then: "*Espèce de con! Je te déteste!*"

"I don't—"

"I hate your brother, and I hate you. Both of you!"

Kian pushed his chair back. It was time to leave. He signalled to Alberto: the universal handwriting-on-palm gesture which had survived into an age when no-one used pens.

There was a hiss. His left eye stung.

The fragrance bottle was in Josette's hand and he knocked it aside. It arced through the air, bounced off a pillar onto the floor and lay there.

"You bitch." Kian rubbed at his eye.

"I didn't—"

He used his thumbnail to lever off the contact lens, blinked rapidly. He ought to rinse—

But then he saw the expressions on the other diners' faces, shock mingled with something else, and he slowly rose. There was a mirror on the far wall, inscribed with an advert for Toblerone chocolates. In the reflection, his exposed eye glittered darkly.

Obsidian. Jet. Shining black with no surrounding white.

A Pilot's eye.

Something Dirk didn't *share with you?*

Josette was frozen, the tears down her cheeks beginning to congeal. She *knew* that Dirk and Kian lived at the convent which doubled as the Pilots' School. Had she never put the picture together?

"Alberto?" He fingered his infostrand-torc. "How much do I owe you?"

Ponderously, Alberto came around from behind the counter, scanned the patrons of his beloved café.

"Nothing," he said. *"Nichts, nul. Rien."*

Kian took a breath, trying to ignore the pain in his eye.

"But you'd prefer I didn't come back, am I right?"

Alberto said nothing more, but his meaning was clear.

My kind is not welcome here.

Kian looked at Josette.

"See you around."

He left quickly, hiding the trembling in his shoulders, feeling sickened.

Outside, the night was icy black and unforgiving, but Kian kept his hood down as he walked, his eye burning, preferring December chill to the stony hardness of his supposed friends' hearts.

<<MODULE ENDS>>

9

NULAPEIRON AD 3423

Sitting there, in the half-lit cargo hold of a speeding arachnargos, Tom wondered about the nature of obligation and duty. When Axolon was cut free and later restored, what then? Tom had the future to think of, yet no plans beyond attending a Convocation and trying out for any vacant positions. He did not even know when the next Convocation would be held.

None of this distracted Tom from his unease, from his fear of the Anomaly's turning its attention towards Nulapeiron, and from the memory of Siganth. Eemur had said there was a link between him and the imprisoned Pilot; she implied that her "gift" could have been a shared trip to almost anywhere, yet Tom had ended up in a hellworld.

The Pilot did look familiar. Now that Tom had spent time immersed in the old tale, he was struck by the man's similarity to Ro and her sons. Though burn-scars distorted his face and his right hand was a claw, Tom decided he must be a descendant of the McNamaras.

I wish I could help you, Pilot.

The arachnargos slewed to a halt. A voice sounded in the hold: "We're stopping to take on board another passenger, my Lord, if that's all right."

"Not a problem," said Tom. "You carry on."

"Thank you, sir."

The man who shortly climbed inside was a lean, taciturn courier called Markilon, who nodded towards Tom as he sat back against a bulkhead, placed an aerolute across his lap, closed his eyes and promptly fell asleep.

A quiet companion, anyhow.

Soon the arachnargos was under way again.

They stopped overnight in a raw cavern in interstitial territory, away from any civilized demesne. The two pilots, Feltima—a short woman with cropped hair and shoulders as broad and muscular as Elva's—and the older, leaner Velsevius, joined Tom and Markilon in the hold.

"We could sleep outside," said Velsevius, "but I always feel safer onboard."

"Suits me." Tom glanced at Markilon. "What do you think?"

In answer, the courier picked up his aerolute, strummed a chord, and began to softly sing:

> *"A fighting Lord who lacked a limb*
> *Asked suff'ring proles to follow him*
> *And glad they were, against the Blight*
> *To focus their enragèd might*
> *When hope of victory seemed dim . . ."*

Then he plucked a final chord, and allowed the harmony to die away.

"You're a man with hidden depths, Markilon," said Tom after a moment.

"Many people are, my Lord."

"So *you're*—" began Feltima, staring at Tom, but a gesture from Velsevius cut her off.

"We don't enquire," Velsevius said, "about our passengers' private lives."

"But we have friends, *a* friend, in common, my Lord and I." Feltima looked boldly at Tom. "Some people say I manoeuvre vehicles exactly like her."

Tom had deduced that Velsevius and Feltima had swapped roles during the day; for part of the time, the vehicle had been flung through some wild, exciting turns that seemed familiar. It was an old memory that surfaced now.

"Limava?" he asked. "Were you trained by Limava?"

"Yes." Feltima was beaming. "Before she moved on to better things. You know she became a squadron leader during the war?"

"No. Did she—?"

"As far as I'm aware, she made it OK. We haven't been in touch."

"Good." Tom nodded. "That's good."

He and Limava had been short-term lovers. When she broke it off, Tom had felt relief as well as disappointment. Tom had been a delta-class servitor then: not a great prospect for the future.

Not that I've any wealth now.

Markilon was sitting up and looking watchful, but Velsevius had already tucked himself into his sleeping bag, pulled down the opaque face-visor, and rolled over onto his side. Tom followed Velsevius's example, sliding down inside his bag and giving an exaggerated yawn.

He allowed himself to slide into a relaxed trance, superficially asleep but in fact alert. His sleeping bag was military issue, designed to shred itself apart in action, freeing up his limbs should he need to fight. Still, while Markilon's presence was unexpected, Tom sensed no danger from him.

Feltima and Markilon chatted softly for about an hour. Finally, they turned in, and the hold's lights dimmed. Tom's trance drifted towards sleep.

Yet he wondered, before he let go of consciousness, just why it was that Lady V'Delikona should summon him on Corduven's behalf, when Corduven was more than capable himself. Why was the summoning urgent?

Blackness carried him to dreams which would fade before he woke.

They travelled through the day, and arrived in what would have been nightshift in almost any other demesne. (Once, Tom had remarked that Terran timezones had depended on where you were, instead of being standard across the globe. His friend Lady Sylvana had shuddered as she deduced the geometry, and said: "How deliciously *quaint*. That's what you get for grubbing about on the surface.") But Realm V'Delikona was different: it was known as The Realm Which Never Sleeps. Each of its inhabitants chose which of three diurnal rhythms to adopt; workplaces were continuously open; all public corridors and halls and caverns were permanently and brightly lit.

The arachnargos slowed before a platform which overlooked a sheer drop: three hundred metres to the cavern floor. This was the largest cavern in the demesne, and one of the most impressive. Glowing morphbuildings slowly altered shape below, and on the cavern walls. The air was strung with crimson tubes hanging in catenary curves, carrying ovoid passenger-cars like corpuscles through arteries.

Down on the platform, despite the late hour, a regal white-haired figure stood, dressed in a long violet-and-white robe with a raised silver collar. Around her, the Palace Halberdiers were at ramrod attention.

Tom, squeezed into the rear of the control cabin alongside Markilon, heard Feltima's gasp. "Is that Lady V'Delikona down there? The Lady herself?"

With a sense of mischief, Tom could not help saying: "Well, she *is* an old friend."

Feltima glanced at him with an awe which had not been present before.

"Taking up position." Velsevius spoke in a crisp, professional tone.

"Ready to lower you now, my Lord, if you'll make your way aft."

"I will. Thanks for your hospitality and . . . entertainment." Tom winked at Markilon, who grinned. "Take care, everybody."

"It's been our honour, sir," said Velsevius.

Then Tom clambered back into the thoracic hold, where a slender tendril wrapped itself around his waist only a second before the floor puckered then gaped open. A cold wind was blowing below.

The tendril lowered him.

It *was* windy, and as his feet touched the ground Tom was almost bowled over, but the tendril lingered long enough to steady him, before whipping up into the arachnargos hold. The vehicle sealed shut, and was already moving away when Lady V'Delikona grasped Tom's hand and said: "Thank Fate you made it, Tom. You need to be here."

The Halberdiers closed in all around, providing a shelter from the buffeting wind. High overhead, Tom could see glassbirds being flung against the stalactites. For someone who loved the surface, he was still discomfited to be in a cavern large enough to manifest *weather*.

"Why's that, my Lady?" He let her lean on him as they walked towards the rearing entrance. "Why the urgency?"

"It's Corduven." Lady V'Delikona stopped, wisps of white hair escaping from her platinum clasps. "He's here, and . . . He's dying, Tom."

"*No . . .*"

"I'm afraid he doesn't have much time. Prepare yourself for a change in his appearance."

"It can't be."

"Tom. You learned to face harsh realities a long time ago."

He blinked at the gusts which assaulted his eyes.

Corduven, my friend.

But Lady V'Delikona was right. He had long given up expecting fairness from Destiny.

10

NULAPEIRON AD 3423

Polished floors were tuned to deep, vibrating purple. Morphsculptures in alcoves stood frozen, their pseudometabolisms halted as a mark of respect. Servitors clad in grey tunics or surcoats dropped to one knee as Tom passed.

In a hushed pentahedral antechamber filled with ice-like furnishings of frosted glass, a shaven-headed priestess—a senior Antistita—bowed to Tom, sweeping her thurible to one side, dispensing heady violet smoke. At the chamber's far end, tall doorshimmers evaporated, sensing Tom's approach.

"Prepare yourself for a change in his appearance," Lady V'Delikona had said, but the figure propped up in the bed was still a shock. Corduven's cheeks were sunken and his eyes were glazed; yet only a tenday ago he had been bright and cheerful, acting as best man at Tom's wedding.

Too cheerful. Doped up with 'tropes. In retrospect, Tom could see it. *You've always driven yourself too hard.*

The narrow, skeletal man in the bed was the greatest strategist of the current age, according to some military observers. Always highly strung, he took immense doses of logotropes, especially at the height of the war, sometimes going a tenday without sleep.

Fragile eyelids fluttered open.

"Knew . . . you'd . . . come. Tom."

Fingers raised weakly, let fall.

"Corduven. Fate, Corduven."

Tom knelt by the bed, took that frail hand and held it, head bowed.

After a time, a low cough roused Tom from his thoughts. It could not be Corduven: he was sleeping, hanging onto the last shreds of life. Tom looked up, blinking. A man was standing at the foot of the bed; and his eyes were reddened from crying. It took Tom several moments to recognize Jay A'Khelikov, his one-time colleague in the intelligence corps of Corduven's Academy.

"Jay . . ."

Tom swallowed, released Corduven's hand, stood up. Suddenly, he realized what Jay was doing here, and the nature of his relationship to Corduven.

I didn't know.

Corduven had confessed, once, why his marriage to Sylvana had failed and been annulled. It was a vulnerability that Tom could have exploited: in noble society, men who were close to other men could not hold responsible positions or inherit the privileges of their parents. In that respect, commonfolk in some lower strata had more freedom than their aristocratic rulers.

Corduven and Jay.

Tom had not even known they were acquainted. He also knew that Jay had had an affair with a female operative, called Lihru . . . but there had been something odd about it, an internal struggle which Tom had thought due to the charged situation in their clandestine, betrayal-filled world, at the height of the war when defeat seemed inevitable.

Jay shook his head, unable to speak.

"I'll leave you alone," said Tom.

As Tom walked from the bedchamber, holo images from Corduven's past sprang into being in the air, circling the bed: happy memories, helping to ease the transition from life. Children playing in a stone piazza, one a girl with blonde ringlets and bright blue eyes whom Corduven would some day marry; another, from a later date, showed a muscular, bearded man dressed in a silken gown, and quaffing wine: Corduven's brother Gérard, whose ability to function in normal timeflow was greater than normal Oracles' . . . and formed one of the reasons why he was able to steal Tom's mother from her family, and condemn Tom's father simply by foretelling his death.

Corduven.

Tom stopped in the antechamber, remembering the shock in Gérard's eyes as Tom's redmetal poignard rammed into his heart.

Cord, my friend.

Doorshimmers froze into place behind him.

Tom was at the outer doors when a soft female voice behind him called his name.

"What—? Sylvana."

She was his age, pale-skinned and blonde-haired. Sylvana blinked her tear-damp eyes. On a couch in an alcove, she was sitting with her hands clasped in her lap.

"I didn't see you there," Tom added. "My apologies."

"No need . . . Jay's with him, is that right?"

"Um, yes."

Tom crossed the chamber, knelt on one knee before her.

"We're closer than . . ." Sylvana looked at the closed doorshimmers. "I *was* closer to Cord than anyone. We could talk about our hates and loves. Including . . ."

She stopped, but her meaning was obvious.

Including me.

Tom took her hand, as he had taken Corduven's. Hers was so much warmer, and his skin tingled in a way he did not want to remember.

"We did make love once, Cord and I." Sylvana answered a question which Tom could never have asked. "Not too successfully. Not like you and me, Tom. I never knew my skin could burn like that."

Tom let go of her hand. Slowly, he stood.

You're very beautiful.

He had thought so even on the day Sylvana had bought him as a servitor, thereby saving his life, while casually mentioning that his arm should be removed as punishment for theft. Her mother's order confirmed the suggestion.

"Tom. I'm sorry for . . . I treated you like a chattel. Something to be bought and sold."

"Yet you rescued me. Let me attend the Sorites School, have Mistress eh'Nalephi as my tutor."

Sylvana swallowed. Her throat was slender, soft-looking.

"Tom . . . Stay with me a while? My chamber is nearby."

"I'm sorry."

"I don't mean . . ."

"Yes, you do. Take care of yourself, Sylvana."

Tom walked away with silent footsteps and did not look back.

Tom descended.

There were depths to Realm V'Delikona he had not experienced. Twelve strata down, he accidentally blundered through a security barrier—it would have stopped most people, but his thumb ring of rank had allowed him to pass—and was caught up in a bladed feud. It was Vendettenday, when laws were abrogated for a time in a tightly defined section of one stratum, and three men mistook him for a contestant.

He left them broken and bleeding in an alleyway behind a tavern. They would live.

Corduven. My friend.

Another six strata down, the tunnels grew clean once more. Tom walked, feeling a sense of dislocation, aware that he should sleep but not wanting to: this realm had no sense of the night. Instead, he found a place to sit and rest. From a cosy daistral house, he watched a small marketplace in operation; it reminded him of his childhood days in Salis Core. *Before the Oracle destroyed everything.* But that was not Corduven's fault.

Tom and Corduven. At least they could forgive each other. Perhaps there was more on Corduven's side, a feeling that Tom could never reciprocate; he hoped it did not cause his friend pain.

Once before, in a different realm, Tom had descended to the lowest stratum of all. Then, his head had been injured, and he had been fleeing the revolutionaries he had thought were his friends, but turned out to be more violent and vicious than the rulers they sought to displace. It was alcohol, the burning dragon that still tempted him, which had become his new false friend.

Today, Tom would climb back up. Never again would he give in. He could face everything; even his friend's death.

Earlier, walking through the peaceful corridors, Tom had noticed a cultural meme, in that things seemed arranged in fives, and pentagonal chambers were popular here. Several small boutiques had five proprietors' names on their banners; in the taverns, groupings of five people seemed casual, unplanned, but were more frequent than other numbers.

It reminded Tom that the proto-logosophers who founded this world had based their society on memetic engineering, seeking to depart from the Terran cultures which gave them birth. Nowadays, such a blatant cultural symbol as a preference for one number was a primitive throwback, a relic of earlier times when manipulation had been cruder and experimental.

Perhaps Tom, too, was an incidental tool in the great plans hatched by manipulative minds and developed over centuries, handed down among the ruling nobility . . . or perhaps he was a man, capable of fighting for what he believed in.

Corduven . . .

Tom could have faced being there at the end, but it was not his place. Jay deserved that privilege; and it *was* a privilege, though a painful one.

In the daistral shop, Tom rose to his feet, left payment and a too-large tip upon the table, and walked out into the market-chamber.

Familiar scents of hemp and fabric filled his nostrils as he threaded his way among the stalls. Sweet nuts and boljicream patties on a vendor's warm tray produced mouth-watering aromas, but Tom fought down the temptation. He stopped briefly before a table filled with second-hand drama crystals, then made himself walk on. Some other time.

In the centre of the chamber, Tom halted. Then he did something which the child-Tom, in his humble home, could only have dreamed of doing. He pushed back his cape, reached up his hand, and the noble-house ring sparked brightly on his thumb. Overhead, brass ceiling flanges arranged in a circle began to rotate.

As the flanges descended, Tom stepped aside. The metal slatted into place, forming spiral steps to the level above. All around, shocked marketgoers stared at Tom, mouths open as they realized what kind of man had been walking unrecognized among them.

I'm just like you, he wanted to cry.

But perhaps that was no longer true. Tom looked around, gave a solemn bow, then looked up, and began to ascend the steps.

11

TERRA AD 2160

<<Ro's Children>>

[2]

The triple towers, with their slow-moving glassine spiral skyways and linking bridges, stood proud above the city, white and gold in the evening sun, framed against bruised purple storm clouds gathering in the north.

On Ellis Island, the comparatively small statue stood with its once-upraised arm broken off at the elbow and deliberately unrestored. Not long before, Ro had seen the original in Paris, now silver in its flowmetal sleeve, designed to withstand any attack short of an X-ray laser burst. There, it was an open secret that anyone thought to own xaser technology was liable to be gunned down by combat squads of the Police Judiciaire, no questions asked.

Ro stood on the Manhattan shoreline, by a small jetty reaching out across the choppy waves, wondering where her contact was.

There.

Senses she could not have named registered the presence seconds before the white conning-tower broke through grey waves with a rush of foam. Water poured from the submarine's upper hull, as a protuberance grew from the smartceramic shell.

Within two minutes, the slender extrusion reached to form a gangplank from sub to jetty. Then a hatch sighed open on the hull, and a slender grey-haired man climbed into sight.

He noticed Ro and nodded, then turned his attention to crossing the narrow walkway without falling into the cold waters. When he reached the jetty's worn planks—they were almost silver with age—a relieved smile twisted his narrow face.

They watched as the sub retracted its walkway and sank beneath the waves.

Then they shook hands.

"How do you do, Monsignor Grayling."

"You can call me Father"—still holding her hand—"if you really must. But I'd rather you called me Ed."

"All right." Ro released her grip. "But I thought your name was Edwin."

"Only Ma called me that. And Mike, when he wanted to wind me up."

"Yeah. Gramps had a wicked sense of humour."

"And the best *ikkyo* I've ever seen, besides your mother's. Have you followed the tradition?"

"Kind of." Ro shrugged. "There's more to fighting than twisting wrists."

The monsignor looked as though he was going to protest, then reconsidered.

Just as well.

Jesuits were not known as God's Soldiers because of fighting ability, though some were warriors. This one, if he had trained in aikido, no longer had the look of one who practised daily.

Still, he was a friend of the family.

"Come on." Ro tapped her infostrand to summon a taxi. "I'll buy you dinner."

Soft rain began to slide downwards.

"There's a storm coming."

"Yes, there is." Ro gave a tiny smile.

A real one.

She knew the double meaning was intentional.

And I intend my young Pilots to survive it.

The aircab never came. Shrugging, they decided to walk instead of hunting through EveryWare for another service.

"This used to be a go-ahead place," said Grayling. "Full of impatience and energy."

"Really? It reminds me a lot of Rome. Kind of friendly and sleepy, you know? Incompetent, but not malicious."

"Cities change. So do nations."

By now they were in a long dark street where steam rose from gratings as it had for four centuries: more from tradition than necessity.

"Very atmospheric," said Ro.

"Special effects." Grayling winked at her. "For the tourists."

They passed a row of brownstone houses, then came to a restaurant set below ground level whose entranceway shone with inviting holos. A giant disembodied hand pointed a commanding finger down the steps.

Enticing aromas of pizza reminded Ro more than ever of the Italian Confederation.

"What do you think, Ed?"

"Suits me. I'm vegetarian, but this place should be fine."

As they descended, Ro caught sight of a tiny smartbat high overhead, recalled to its eyrie in the face of the gathering storm.

Scanning us?

Farther down the street, slow-morphing bioarchitecture buildings were smoothing out their curves and reinforcing their buttresses, ready for the gales and heavier rain to hit.

"*Buonasera.*" An obsequious waiter smiled as they passed through the door. "A table for-a two, is it, lady and gentleman?"

"*Ciao.*" Ro raised an eyebrow at the waiter's laboured accent. "*Mio amico è vegetariano.*" And, pointing at the holo menu nearby: "*Scusi, cosa ci sarebbe per lui?*"

The man froze, his smile becoming a rictus of embarrassment.

"I'm-a sorry," he said. "It is my wife who eez Italian. I just pick up-a the accent, see?"

Grayling sighed.

"The food smells wonderful. I'd love to eat here."

The waiter almost fell over in a relieved bow.

"Yes, sir. This way, please."

Ro followed along, murmuring, "Very smooth, padre."

She hoped his compassion extended to some two thousand children with obsidian eyes who, according to some fundamentalists whose EveryWare forums were such a colourful delight, held Satan's hot fire where human beings kept their souls.

Three hours later, Ro was alone in her small hotel room, remembering the final sentences of her conversation with Monsignor Edwin Grayling, SJ, Ph.D.

"There are superiors I must consult within the order. I will do anything I can."

"And the matter compilers?"

"Livermore security is tight, but I have my privileges."

"But no promises."

"Exactly right. You do have my blessing."

Ro closed her eyes. She was putting her trust and hope in an ordained member of a faith in which she did not believe, all for the children's sake.

"So you think mu-space-born have souls, at least."

"Everyone's a child of God, or we're all in trouble."

Rousing herself, Ro tapped the infostrand wrapped bracelet-wise around her wrist, placed a realtime call to Sister Francis Xavier. It was 5 a.m. in Switzerland, but if the nun was not already up and about, Ro would be surprised.

Nothing.

There was no reply, not even a netAgent proxy to take a message.

"Shit."

She tapped the strand again, told it to access the convent house AI. A pale orange holo of two hands spread, palms up, appeared above her strand. No go. The AI was blocked: offline from EveryWare, or crashed.

Dirk and Kian would be asleep. No point in calling them.

Shaking her head, she rose to her feet, took a turn around the small hotel room, then grabbed her coat and left.

The holosign was a green-white-gold extravaganza denoting an ironic lack of originality: *Paddy's Bar*. At least Ro hoped it was irony.

Inside, the regulars were on stools at the counter, staring at the mag-hockey game in the HV above them. Ro took a table in a rear booth and used her infostrand to order coffee.

"Be right with ya," called the barman.

Ro raised a hand and nodded.

Most of the booths were empty. The one Ro could see from her seat contained a middle-aged couple with expensive clothes and coiffed hair and bodies that looked slender but soft: style over substance.

"Here y'are, doll."

"Thank you."

"Shall I leave ya a menu?" He had a hardcopy folder in his hand.

"I'm not hungry, but I'll take a look."

There was a half-hearted cheer from the barstools. In the HV display, the arena's crowd barriers were lowering and spectators were streaming onto the polished metal court.

With a shiver, the image changed to a newsNet channel. There was a menu, with directional choice so that anyone who wanted could request a separate image with holo audio beamed at them.

Ro took the International News section, then Central Europe, wondering how often those choices were made in Paddy's Bar.

"Hey!" One of the beer drinkers waved a glass.

"What's that?" said another.

"Awright, boys. Just a glitch." The barman called to Ro: "Miss? The HV's on the blink. There's no private view-vectors. If you change channels, everybody sees the same . . ."

His voice trailed off as Ro launched to her feet.

"Miss? Is everything—?"

In the image, crowds were demonstrating on the Bahnhofstrasse, in peaceful Zürich where Christmas choirs had sung. Then the viewpoint shifted to a hospital ward, and the battered face of a bandaged boy maybe twelve years old lying half-conscious on a pillow.

One of his eyes was partly open. Beneath the bruised lid, the eye glittered black.

Jean-Pierre!

His name was Jean-Pierre Delahante and he was one of the two hundred or so children at Dirk's and Kian's school. Ro blinked slowly, momentarily aware of the contact lenses she wore so casually.

In the image, the boy's skin held a greenish cast, and the eerie lighting lent his obsidian eye a reptilian look which bore no relation to the way he looked in life . . . not in his normal healthy condition.

Ignoring the barroom crowd, Ro used her infostrand to call the boys.

"What the hell happened?"

"Mom . . . We weren't sure you'd be—"

"—still up. He's going to be OK."

It was her-ears-only audio, and the drawn but alert faces of both boys were lased directly into her eyes.

"Willya lookit that?" came the barman's voice.

Ro shook her head.

"It's young Annette," said Kian. *"A friend of Jean-Pierre's."*

"From town." Dirk swallowed. *"She's got some skeletal deformity, a twisted spine they can't cure. The other kids—"*

"—don't leave her alone. And Jean-Pierre saw them bullying her."

Ro let out a breath.

"How many of them?"

"*A dozen, or more. Bigger boys.*"

Kian's voice deepened in half-controlled rage. "*Made sure there was no-one else around to see.*"

"I'll talk to you again in a few minutes."

Ro shut down the comms.

"Devil spawn," the big-haired woman was saying in the other booth. "Don't belong with human kids, I'll tell ya that."

"I hear ya." Her husband scowled at the HV. "Should round 'em up, and investigate whether they got mortal souls. And if they don't—"

"They don't."

"Well, Mary-Ellen, you just could be right."

At the bar counter, the native NYers talked differently but the sentiment was the same.

"—Riker's Island, and lose the key."

"Dowse da doity little bastards wit' gas, and light 'em up."

Ro used her strand to transfer payment for the untouched coffee. Slipping from the booth, she passed the midwestern couple without a word and headed for the door.

"Hey now, miss. Is there a problem at all?"

Her aikido-trained mother had striven for the way of peace. But for Ro, blending with an enemy's attack was just a way of getting close enough to reach their eyeballs.

"If the coffee's not warm enough, I can—"

Golden sparks glimmered, half-visible through her grey contacts.

"Devil spawn? Is that what you think?"

Potential building.

Now.

There was a flat bang, and a cloud of dense, yellow-tinged grey smoke billowed from above the bar.

"The HV set just—"

Then Ro was on the street and the bar's door was shut behind her.

Stars were visible in the sky, even with Manhattan's bright lights, and the air felt fresh after the storm. Sidewalks, washed clean, glistened with clear puddles.

I'll show you a storm, if that's what you want.

Her boots splashed through puddles as she walked.

<<MODULE ENDS>>

12

NULAPEIRON AD 3423

In the antechamber, servitors stood in ranks on the polished floor at solemn attention, in stone-cold silence. The doorshimmer leading to Corduven's chamber sparkled at Tom's approach but did not evaporate. He stood there, story crystal clenched in fist, hard enough to hurt.

Corduven—

Inside, his friend lay dying, not yet dead.

Tom stared at nothing, seeing Corduven as he had been last night, sunken and emaciated. It was like Father: wasting away, becoming a wizened skeletal figure that wheezed and breathed fitfully, with those long quiet gaps that made you ask *Was that the final one?* and then the painful surprise of another indrawn, ragged breath . . . until the last, and silence.

For a long time Tom stood there, until frosty brilliance slid down the doorshimmer and Sylvana stepped through. She looked regal, incredibly beautiful, and for a moment Tom felt unworthy even to be in her presence. Her shining blue gaze fastened on him; then she gathered up her ivory robe and walked past him without a word.

The priestess, in her purple death-cape, strode into the chamber. Tom followed her as far as the archway, then stopped, regarding the grey-white corpse-thing in the bed. The dead body was no longer Corduven, but a composite of minerals whose structure was already breaking down, a decaying organic sculpture that bore little relation to the man who had been Tom's friend.

Jay, too stunned to weep, knelt at the bedside, clasping Corduven's dead hand. Behind Jay, Lady V'Delikona stood, straight and unbowed even in the presence of death.

Tom remembered, as a new Palace servitor, walking into Corduven's suite to pick up a faulty smartsatin garment, and the astounded joy on Corduven's face when he revealed a tricon cast in white metal, a joke intended for Sylvana, and found that a common-born servitor like Tom understood the pun: an antinomy cast in antimony. They had laughed together, friends from the first.

Why didn't I stay until the end?

Was it because Jay deserved his private grief, or because Tom had been afraid to stay? There would never be another opportunity to talk to Corduven.

"Tom?" It was Lady V'Delikona. "Walk with me."

She leaned more heavily on his arm than he expected; a show of frailty and therefore of trust: she would never publicly reveal a weakness. They walked through ebon corridors in grieving silence, then came to a halt at the edge of the Great Courts.

A low moaning passed through the Courts, and the hairs rose on Tom's neck.

"What . . . ?"

"The Palace knows," said Lady V'Delikona.

The moan grew stronger, began to ululate, as morphmarble walls vibrated to sing their wordless grief, to mourn the passing of Corduven d'Ovraison from the world.

There was a guest apartment waiting for Tom, and a retinue of servitors ready to perform his bidding; but he waved them away, back to their dorms. Alone in luxury, he felt more poverty-stricken than he ever had as a child.

I wasn't poor. I had the future, though I didn't know it.

There was a couch, a kind of chaise longue, and Tom eased himself back on it, lay down and stared at the ceiling, wondering what Elva was doing now. She had not known Corduven well, but she would be saddened by his death.

Tom remembered a phrase his mother used, *too tired to sleep*, which had never made sense. Now, exhausted and enervated, he thought he might never sleep again . . .

Thinking that, Tom slipped into a dream. Yet it was a fitful thing, featuring a flensed figure writhing in a vivisection field on a distant hellworld. Soon, he snapped awake, breathing hard, his skin drenched with sweat that was already beginning to cool, greasy and unhealthy.

Tom rose from the couch, stripped down to his trews, and in the darkened lounge began to practise his phi2dao fighting forms, striving against unseen opponents, faster and faster as he whirled through kicks, stabbed fingertips into imaginary eyeballs, thrust and snapped and wrenched and threw and locked and strangled, fighting over and over against the deadliest enemy of all, the one that could never be defeated, only held back for a time: the relentless demons lurking in his mind.

Then he stopped, exhausted and panting, and queried the house system for the time. He had been practising for two solid hours.

Tom tugged off his trews, found a glob of cleangel in the bath chamber and slapped it against his bare chest. Then he walked back into the lounge while the cleansing gel spread across his body, exfoliating and disinfecting. He waved open a wardrobe, found a sleeping-robe. By the time he had taken hold of the robe, the gel had already finished its work and was sliding down his body to the floor. He stepped out of the puddle, and pulled on the light robe.

The gel crawled back towards the bath chamber, while Tom found a refreshments cabinet and drank indigoberry-flavoured electrolyte replacement fluid straight from a flagon. Then he headed for the nearest bed—there were at least four bedchambers in the suite—and lay down.

Perhaps he could do more than just sleep. Perhaps he could analyse the captured Pilot's dilemma.

Corduven . . .

Or he might just dream of his dead friend. Either way, as Tom slipped from consciousness, he tried to keep a rational part of his mind in control, directing his dream state. It was a dangerous thing to do, for a trained logosopher. *"Consciousness,"* Tom remembered Lord Velond saying at the Sorites School, *"emerges from neural groups observing neural groups. When I talk to myself, when I control my thoughts, who is controlling whom? For I am my thoughts, nothing more."*

But even as the dream of death took hold of Tom, it slipped beyond his control, and neither the Pilot nor Corduven featured in the images that came next.

He is on his bed, in the open air. A small amber neko-kitten lies curled on his lap, atop the rich orange blanket in which chocolate-brown patterns weave visual paradoxes. Tom's hand, wrinkled and brown-spotted and frail, lies upon the blanket.

He cannot lift it.

Winds blow beneath brown clouds becoming silver as peach-and-yellow dawn brightens the sky. The blanket's patterns almost vibrate in the clear light.

Elva . . . All she meant to him . . . Now it is his time to go. His breathing is shallow, and growing shallower, but there is no pain.

It has been a fine life.

Tom's bed, at his own request, is upon the flat top of a tall glass tower, revealing the final dawn. Remember, he tells himself, how miraculous life is. Our molecules are born in the heart of stars. We are emergent properties of a vast cellular collective . . . These are his dying thoughts.

"Grandfather." On his left, an athletic-looking youth stands straight-backed and true, and his clear grey gaze is Elva's reborn. "Do we have things right?"

Tom cannot speak. With a great effort, he raises his finger, lets it fall.

"He means yes. It is as it should be." The young woman to Tom's right is slender. Her hair is blonde and her eyes are obsidian without surrounding whites. "This is his moment."

She takes up his fragile hand in her youthful, warm grasp.

"I love you, grandfather."

The young man's hand is upon Tom's left shoulder.

"I love you, grandfather."

Beyond them, the sky is vast.

Tom's breath comes intermittently now.

And then the sun is full above the horizon and three huge delta shapes of gleaming bronze and silver spring into being in the sky overhead. They make a slow circle and turn to face the east and hover, waiting.

You came. Thank you. It is time to . . . to . . .

Feel the clear soft air and drink in the scent of rustling grass and heath-land paragorse. A small bird flies overhead as sunlight drapes liquid fire on the great vessels and one more breath as the grandchildren call out their love once more, I know that and thank you for it, everything and always thanks to Elva oh I miss you and I love you with all the darkness and blood on my hand and here is the sunrise, look at it Elva, feel the breeze and who would have believed the miracle of our time together, my sweet.

The need for breath but none to be had.

Fading and the shadows edging in . . . Elva oh Elva I miss you and I join you now at last . . . *In darkness, as the world narrows to a point.*

Hanging on . . .

It beckons.

Let go . . .

Beckoning, the shining gold.

Falling.

Ending.

Black.

As he came awake, just for a moment, Tom thought he saw a tracery of sapphire fire across his skin. Immediately, it faded, and in a second he was no longer sure it had been real.

Part of the dream . . .

He rolled to the edge of the bed, stood up, and ordered the house system to make some daistral. He wanted no more sleep tonight.

Alone, Tom walked through a maze whose corridors must have recently morphed into this configuration. As he neared the centre of the puzzle, he realized that they suggested the tricon for Sorrow, one of the few tricons that was always rendered as static rather than a moving ideogram. The beige corridors contained alcoves of artwork, crystal statues and mag-dust paintings and other works that Tom could not focus on. He stopped. Before him stood a stellate diamond structure that might have represented a star in mu-space, as closely as it could be rendered in the real world.

The quick route out of the maze took him to a broad, deserted lounge overlooking a grand cavern he had not seen before. A scarlet transport tube bore a solitary capsule along its length. Below, a wide expanse of mossgardens, decorated in black and indigo, surrounded an oval quicksilver lake. In the distance, he could hear the Palace's funereal moan, still mourning Corduven's death.

Then a whisper of sound caused him to turn just as three men entered the chamber and fanned out. Each wore a thumb-ring proclaiming noble rank.

"My Lord Corcorigan." It was the shortest of the trio who spoke: shaven-headed, with three burgundy glassine strips embedded beneath each cheekbone. "My name is Surtalvan. Forgive the discourtesy, sir, but I prefer not to introduce my companions."

One of those companions was big and wide-shouldered, looking more like a pitfighter than a scion of some noble house. The third Lord was lean and scarred.

"We've all got something to hide," Tom said.

With a shift in stance, he allowed his cape to fall open, revealing the whitemetal poignard tagged at his hip. (Its twin was out of sight, at the small of his back.)

"Openness can be a virtue." Surtalvan glanced at the dagger, then appeared to focus on Tom's throat. "So here I am, being open. We've all noticed the sorry state of Nulapeiron right now, and I mean every sector. I do *not* hide my concern for our home."

"Our home?" Tom noticed a tiny curved holopin, projecting white revolving rings, half-concealed by Surtalvan's cape. It might have been the symbol of the Circulus Fidus, save that it was pierced by a tiny scimitar. "But you don't live in this realm, do you?"

"It's not just one realm that's threatened with Chaos now."

"But I'm surprised"—Tom allowed his face to display a smile—"to find Action League representatives in this place, and at this time."

Surtalvan's eyes widened. He had not expected Tom to recognize (or deduce the meaning of) the holopin. But Brino, in the weapons shop, had told of Tom of the militant organizations which supported Circulus Fidus reactionary ideas; obviously Brino had not lied.

"We're paying our respects. The Brigadier-General will be sorely missed."

Tom felt anger rise, but held it tight inside him.

"You're early. The funeral will follow the lying-in-state."

"Well, we'd also hoped to talk to you, Lord Corcorigan. We don't seem like natural allies"—he paused as if waiting for Tom to laugh, then continued—"but the world needs consolidation and recovery, you'll surely agree."

"You forgot the need to restore order and discipline. Obedience in the commoners."

"Just so." Surtalvan was not fazed. "That's how they achieve prosperity."

Tom drew his cloak around himself.

"I don't think so, gentlemen."

Surtalvan's eyes narrowed. His lean companion took a half-step forward, and the big man clenched his fists.

Tom moved to one side. Their positions covered the corridor's width, blocking him from the only exit.

"There'll be a Convocation soon," said Surtalvan. "Sponsors and allies might come in handy, when you're looking for a new position."

Tom stared at him.

Allies. People like you . . .

But Surtalvan was operating under several false premises, and one of them was that Nulapeiron was no longer in danger.

"There *is* a thing," said Tom, "that you and I have in common. A desire to keep the world human."

Surtalvan exchanged a glance with the lean man, who stepped back. "What do you mean?"

"I believe that the Blight contacted its parent Anomaly, in the final moments before it perished. You know what I'm talking about."

"Legends . . ." Surtalvan attempted a sneer, but there was doubt in his tone. "I don't think so."

Tom stared at him for a long moment.

Then, "I've told you what I know. Deal with it, or ignore it," he said, and walked forward, brushing past the three men—none tried to hold him back—and strode away.

13

TERRA AD 2162

<<Ro's Children>>

[3]

Hot dry air; the babble of vendors—*¿Le gustan? Los màs baratos . . .*—and holo ads; spicy scents of onions and seared meat cooked on kerbside stoves; the confusion of bright colours. Headmasks and ponchos. Polished guitars. Cheap statuettes of the Blessed Virgin reciting the Hail Mary in overlapping Anglic, Español and Russki.

The dense slam of Mexican poverty.

A coffee-skinned couple, faces webbed with sun-blasted lines, smiled up from their squatting position, revealing stumps of teeth. They offered tortillas from a tiny solar pan, while a metre away thermoacoustic-drive vehicles slid past.

Ro looked back through the border shimmerfield. On the other side, the wavering image of the ground-cab which had brought her here moved farther away, into visual chaos.

Jesus Christ, Ed. Why are we meeting here?

Someone clutched at her sleeve but she twisted and walked away.

Further into Nogales proper, there were few gringos from the Arizona side. A clean-skinned Mexican girl looked up from the corner of a whitewashed building, saw Ro approaching, and turned away with a sassiness already tinged with disillusion.

Behind a church called Santa Teresa stood an open courtyard, and Ro walked inside. A half-door swung inwards at her touch, and then she was in a bare, clean storage room.

Nothing alerted her senses. No detectable surveillance.

"Shit. I don't like this."

Ro let out a slow breath. Then, without using her hands, she sank to the ground in a corkscrew motion, finished sitting cross-legged on dark-grey stone.

And closed her eyes.

Calm now.

Time to wait.

Yesterday morning she had been in the Zürich Pilots' School, sitting in an easy chair in the anteroom to the Mother Superior's office, one leg thrown over the chair-arm, reading a two-century-old novel in hi-res flatscript projected from her infostrand.

Every time Ro chuckled, Sister Olivia, sitting at the anteroom's desk, looked up and frowned. But the story was funny, with surprisingly modern touches. It began with a Latin aphorism and an extended Goethe quotation, though most of the original readership would have been monolingual, in Anglic.

Even the strange-looking *Ich sah* reflected a topical concern, as the current movement to remove the literary Past Historic tense from Français, following the Deutsch tradition, had resulted in controversy and even one death as two academics pummelled each other with leather-bound books in a Sorbonne courtyard.

"The Reverend Mother won't be long."

"Good. Excellent."

Ro read a bit more. For all the absurdism, the short tale had relevant points to make about the nature of time and of human conflict, encapsulating a tragedy which the inhabitants of Dresden recalled to this day.

The pinched-faced nun let out a sigh.

"She'll see you now."

"Thank God for that."

The Reverend Mother Mary Sebastian, aka Jill, sat with her feet up on the glass-covered desk. Opposite her, Ro did the same.

"You didn't get on with my predecessor, did you, Ro?"

"Before she attained Motherhood, she was in charge of facilities management, and I was living here and in my teens." Back when Pilots-to-be came here to be trained by Mother, learning aikido and Feldenkrais body awareness—skills which would stand them in good stead when their eyes were removed during surgery: in those days Pilots traded their realspace senses for those which were virally induced. Back then, only Ro possessed the natural ability to perceive another universe. "I used to take the piss."

Jill smiled at the antique idiom. "I hope you gave Sister Olivia more respect—"

"Not much."

"—though she *is* a prissy little bitch, I'll grant you that. And I will be confessing that lapse."

"Tsk, tsk, Jill."

"I'll tell you this. Old Misery out there won't hear anything said about the kids. Even the ones who are pains in the ass."

"Like me."

"Just as you no doubt were. But listen"—Jill dropped her feet from the desk, growing serious—"there are people in the Order who want the kids out of here. And since that means losing income from UNSA, we're talking serious dislike."

"Is that anything new?"

"You know they're talking about you as the link between two species? You personally."

"The kids aren't actually my offspring. Besides Dirk and Kian."

"But there's something of you in all of them. The general public doesn't know much more than this: that the difference between *Homo sapiens* and *Pan panicus* is one per cent of DNA. So it doesn't take much to form a new species."

"For Christ's sake, Jill. It's one-point-six per cent, and the differences are spread throughout the whole goddamn genome, including control loci, not just one or two isolated genes. Chimps are close relatives, but not *that* close." Ro shook her head. "And the general fuckin' public doesn't know the difference between algorithm and data, because DNA is both and what matters is exactly which—"

"Whoa." Jill held up both hands. "Peace. I'm just telling you that the bishop is wavering, all right? If the Pope made an announcement either way, the uncertainty would be over . . . but she's keeping quiet on the issue."

Ro shook her head.

"I don't believe the kids have souls. But I don't think you or anyone else has one, either. Shit. Can the Vatican even *spell* 'emergent properties'?"

"Only the Jesuits. But, 'falling revenue from church collections'? Or 'rising dissatisfaction among congregations'? They can spell those just fine."

That was yesterday, in the cool, rational surroundings of her Alpine home, far removed from the hard air and stifling heat of Mexican noon. Even meditating in the shadow-painted storage room, eyes shut against the hammering white light reflected from the courtyard outside, Ro was aware of a harsh edge to reality, the faintest hum as a beetle flew to the nearest wall.

Then she was standing, though her eyes remained shut.

Three aircars. Drawing close.

Ed was supposed to come alone.

"Shit, shit, shit."

Ro opened her eyes and popped out her contacts, then flicked the lenses aside. If there was to be any kind of action, she wanted no mistakes.

Two flyers circled low, out of sight behind the rooftops, their sound muffled by the quotidian cacophony of the town. They settled down. Ro imagined armed men spilling forth, running to surround this courtyard.

Wait.

Finally, the smallest of the flyers was overhead, a white speck in a baking azure sky. It hung for a moment, then descended in a puff of hot dust. A pale unhealthy figure stumbled out.

"Ed. God damn it."

Monsignor Edwin Grayling winced at every step, and Ro wondered at the state of his feet. Beating the soles was unsophisticated but effective. They had been careful to leave no cuts or bruises on his face.

Why? You think I wouldn't notice something was up?

Ed walked towards the storage room.

Ro could slide out and get away, sneak through the tiny window at the rear . . . maybe. Abandoning Ed.

She could not do that.

Instead, Ro stepped into the sunlight with a cheery wave, skin prickling as she sensed targeting beams reflecting from her face and body, and called out: "Ed! You made it!"

He moved his mouth, but only a croak came out.

Anaesthetic spray to the vocal cords. Bastards got that right, at least.

Ro gestured back at the building.

"I brought the others. We're all here."

She hoped that would give them pause. The flyer could not hold more than four or five men, but if they were trained that was enough. More of them were outside the courtyard, crouched in the street: close enough that she could sense the trickle-currents of their xaser weapons.

It took more nerve than expected to walk completely into the open, all her senses screaming danger, smiling at Ed as though nothing were wrong. Anguish clawed at his face.

Invisible targeting beams from six different weapons moved across her skin, centred on the same target.

Now.

This was the moment.

Both hands grabbed hold of Ed's shirt as she spun, threw herself in a sacrifice move which hurled Ed to the dusty ground close to the flyer. Then she was continuing the roll, onto her feet—"Stay there!"—and thrusting forward, into a sprint towards the nearest building.

Coherent X-ray beams tore the ground apart behind her.

But she was faster, diving through an open window, registering a glimpse of startled old-woman features, and then Ro was bursting through a wooden doorway and in a narrow stinking alleyway filled with broken crates and remains of rotting vegetables.

Ro hurdled obstacles, brain on fire as she sensed but could not decipher the bursts of microwave communication among the armoured soldiers in the surrounding streets.

Go right.

The decision was instantaneous and a rusty brazier exploded— xaser beam—as she swerved, ran down a short alley towards an open half-door and launched herself headfirst over it. Ceiling–wall–floor whipped past her vision as she used an aikido roll then bounced off a doorway post and spun into a bigger room—fat man asleep on a couch with a hardcopy newspaper draped over his face—then a thrusting wu shu kick to smash open the next door and she was into the street.

Startled faces looking in her direction—*ignore*—and a skeletal out-line beyond the rooftops—there: a half-completed mag-lev station— and she had a place to aim for. There would be cover and few crowds— "¡*Madre de Dios!*" as another beam cracked through the air—and Ro ran faster, in the open again, spotting soldiers ahead but then there was a turning to the right which she took knowing two men were standing here, but taking them by surprise at close quarters.

Thai-style whipping elbow-strikes pummelled them, then she

dropped and kicked from the ground, rupturing their knees with pen-tjak silat manoeuvres they could not see coming. Helmets muffled their screams as the soldiers fell and she jumped up and ran on.

Sparks like fireflies glimmered in the air.

Moving with her, keeping pace.

Come and get me, motherfuckers.

Stink of disinfectant, dirty window—in holodramas people leap through glass all the time but in real life shards would slice arteries and she had to find another route—there, a drainpipe, and she clambered up like a spider monkey while her growing cloud of sparkling lights followed her.

Roar in the distance. One of the flyers, ascending.

Shit.

Red-clay tiles scattered beneath her feet as she ran and scrabbled across the roof, leaped across an alleyway—helmet's mirror-visor looking up from below—and then she was on the next roof, slipping— "Shit!"—on her left buttock as she slid down a slope then kicked off, a moment of freefall, and dropped to solid ground once more, rolling to break the fall then up on her feet and running.

The big flyer would have xaser-gatling arrays and more. The situation was closing in fast and reaching the mag-lev station was no longer an option.

Sparks like fireflies.

Run.

Dodging passers-by, rebounding from a group of shoppers, she saw a squad of soldiers spilling into the street ahead of her and she ran left, into a small shop filled with trinkets and a woman gasped and then Ro was through the storeroom at the rear and out into the alley where she collided with a big soldier twice her size.

The man grabbed at her but Ro used a wing chun trap and triple punch to stagger him, slammed the edge of her hand into his collarbone, feeling the crack as she spun him into a judo knee-wheel and took him down. She would have escaped then but he was armed and could shoot a running figure so she followed him to the ground, took hold of his helmet and twisted into a neck-crank that was pure catch-as-catch-can grappling and he was out of it for good.

All fighting styles become one *in extremis*, and Ro had studied every discipline.

Lights in the air. A growing swarm of sparks.

Soon, I'll stop running.

Moving fast now.

When Ro judged the moment was right she broke into the open, to a wide square where people scattered as the big flyer slid overhead. Its roar pulsed down, pounding the air, drowning the panicked yells of fleeing citizens.

Ro stood in a cruciform stance, arms outstretched, while all around her ten thousand sparks of light swirled and danced. Swarming. Ready to strike.

Gatling arrays swung to target her.

Now.

She lowered her head as the sparks shot upwards.

Sixty seconds later, Ro was walking down a deserted street while in the square behind her wreckage burned, belching black smoke over a gout of orange flames, and no-one was left alive to scream.

The courtyard where she had abandoned Ed was just minutes away, and she knew the small flyer would still be there because she had already seen to that. Only Ro could remove the flight-control block she had induced as she threw Ed to what she hoped was a safe position. So they had a means of getting out of here.

If the other big flyer, currently circling Nogales while firing out bursts of urgent communication, decided to pursue her and Ed . . . well, it might find itself entering an electrical storm that was unexpected and more ferocious than anything its flight crew had ever seen.

You will not kill me.

Ro wiped her sweat-slick forehead, and her hand came away red.

Not before the children are all safe.

<<MODULE ENDS>>

14

NULAPEIRON AD 3423

Tom sent a courier to Elva, so that she would come to the funeral. He wondered if Axolon was still melded to the wall, or if they had finished removing him.

After a time, he asked a Palace servitrix to enquire about Lady V'Delikona. The young servitrix returned within minutes, curtsied, and told Tom that the Lady was in conference with High Lords of several sectors. Invitations were going out, throughout Nulapeiron; Corduven's funeral was to be a major affair of state, a farewell to the most publicly heroic figure of the war.

"Thank you," said Tom, and dismissed the servitrix.

I did that too easily, he thought a moment later, and considered calling her back to apologize. But it was too late.

Have I removed any injustice at all from the world?

Tom had played his part against the Blight. Perhaps that was enough . . . unless the Anomaly truly was coming. Then it was all for nothing.

A chime sounded, and a Palace Halberdier, weaponless, entered on Tom's command. He bowed to Tom, and said: "I have a verbal invitation for you, sir, to visit the Palace barracks. It's from an officer on secondment here, Lieutenant Gervicort. He presents his compliments."

This was the heart of Palace V'Delikona where he ought to be safe, but Tom did not trust such a message. "Is that all he said?"

"If you asked, I was to say, remember when A'Khelikov apologized?"

Tom thought for a moment, then smiled. "That's Adam Gervicort, all right. Which way do we go? I'm ready now."

"If you'll follow me, sir."

Adam had been a servitor in the Academy—formally, the Akademía dell'Guerro—and had startled Tom and Jay, Lord A'Khelikov, as they observed the training grounds. Jay's glance had flickered over Adam as if he were an inanimate object, dismissing him not just as a threat but as a person. Afterwards, though, he had *apologized*, and clasped forearms with Adam as though Adam were an equal, not a servitor. It was the moment when Tom realized the Academy was not run like a normal realm.

Since then, Adam Gervicort had obtained manumission, fought as a freedman and been decorated in the field, promoted to Brevet-Lieutenant in the midst of action.

We should spend time with our friends, while we can.

Tom followed the Halberdier through the main portal of the barracks. Tom's intestines seemed to vibrate just for a moment before he was in the plain corridor: some kind of deepscan with a vengeance.

"Sorry, sir. Should've warned you."

"That's all right. Carry on."

They took a ramp downwards to the next level, where an echo of subdued yells and scuffling feet mixed with the scents of fear and striving upon the air. Tom smiled, breathing deeply. They were nearing a fight-gym of some kind; he felt at home.

At the gym's entrance, they slipped to the left where a hard bench was placed for the benefit of observers. Tom sat, turned his attention to the fight in progress . . .

Fate!

. . . and gave an astounded smile as he recognized the huge, blackskinned warrior in a carl's plain tunic, crouched at the mat's centre, tracking the seven Halberdiers with padded weapons who were circling him. One of them charged forward with a yell, but the warrior spun and lashed out a kick which dropped a different man: the more immediate danger, a Halberdier who had crept closer from the rear.

Then the dark warrior ducked low, grabbed the legs of the charging, yelling Halberdier and straightened up, sending the Halberdier flying.

"Kraiv," said Tom delightedly. "Kraiv, my friend."

The housecarl was all muscle and no fat, yet it was still a surprise to see a fighter of such bulk move so fast. The remaining Halberdiers were canny, using teamwork to attack simultaneously, but Kraiv was having none of it. He chopped down the biggest of their number with a scything kick to the thigh—*He'll be limping for a tenday*, thought Tom—and banged a second Halberdier into a third, heads clashing. Immediately, Kraiv charged the remaining two attackers, taking the offensive, and hit them precisely at the same time. He stepped back as the bodies landed.

A row of watching Halberdiers looked stunned. Then, to a man, they thumped their fists against their chests and yelled their appreciation for Kraiv's skills. His fallen opponents, scattered around the mat, were trained fighters in their own right, not amateurs.

You should see him with a morphblade in his hands.

A narrow, hard-looking man was lowering himself onto the bench beside Tom.

"Have I missed anything good?"

"Adam! Adam, you old bastard."

"Good to see you, too, sir."

They clasped forearms, hard.

"Sorry to hear about General d'Ovraison," Adam added. "We all admired him, but he was also your friend."

"Thank you." It was Jay who deserved Adam's sympathy, but Tom wondered whether he should mention it. Diplomatically he said, "Funny that your message referred to Jay A'Khelikov. He's been here, too."

"Um . . . I think he knew the general quite well, Tom."

Tom smiled, to show that he understood what Adam meant, and that he, too, was aware of it.

Then two massive ebony fists twisted Tom's tunic and hauled him up to his feet, and he was hugged in an embrace he could not have escaped from.

"Tom, my friend."

"Kraiv . . . You can . . . put me down . . . now."

"Thank you, Lieutenant Gervicort." Kraiv's voice rumbled, basso profundo, as he addressed Adam. "Old comrades are well met."

"Who are you calling old?" said Adam, and grinned.

They relaxed in the officers' mess, swapping news. Adam and Kraiv had both attended the wedding, but there had been little time for Tom to catch up with either of them. Now, over indigoberry cordial (Kraiv and Tom) and Golden Angels (Adam), they talked about their friends and families. Kraiv's wife, Draquelle, was happy at the Manse Hetreece, having returned there with their young son Homric after Tom's and Elva's wedding. Adam was less happy with his current posting, as an administrator on Lord Akezawa's staff, which was perhaps why he tossed down the Golden Angels fast enough to make his eyes water. At some point he gestured to the cordial in Kraiv's goblet and said: "Sure you won't try a real drink?"

"He follows the Way of Rikleth," Tom answered for him. "That means he'll abstain."

"Suit yourself," said Adam, but on the next round he switched to daistral, and drank it while it was still too hot for comfort.

Kraiv smiled in approval.

"You know how the Book of the Tri-Fold Path begins? *Distrust every system, including this one.*"

"Ah," said Tom. "I like that."

"I thought you would."

It was an hour later when a Halberdier came up to their table, bowed, and handed over a message crystal to Tom. "By civilian courier, sir. Sorry, we couldn't allow him on the premises. No authorization."

"He's been paid?"

"In advance, sir, by Lady Corcorigan."

"Thank you, soldier."

Tom opened up the brief message, scanned it, shut the holo down. Then he picked up his drink, frowned, and replaced it on the table.

"What is it, Tom?" Kraiv's voice deepened even further than usual. "Trouble?"

"I don't . . . think so. It's from Elva. She's arriving in the morning."

"That's good, isn't it?" said Adam.

"Yes, but . . . She's picked up a travelling companion on the way, she says. And that's *all* she says."

Adam looked at Kraiv, then grinned.

"The Lady's keeping you on your toes, is she, my Lord?"

"I . . . Go heisenberg yourself, Gervicort."

"What kind of bifurcatin' language is that for an officer and a gentleman?"

Kraiv shook his head sadly, and took a surprisingly delicate sip of his cordial. Tom and Adam burst into laughter, which only slowly faded.

Corduven. If only you could be here, too.

Then Tom raised his goblet. "To missing friends."

Kraiv and Adam clinked their goblets against his, and all three drank the toast in unison.

Next morning, Tom was there to meet Elva's blue arachnargos as it danced on slender tendrils to a docking platform, lowered its thorax all the way to the ground, and opened an exit. Elva stepped straight down onto the flagstones. The luggage drone floated past her and alighted, as the arachnargos reared up once more.

"I've missed you," said Tom, then shook his head. "That sounds soppy, doesn't it?"

"It'll do." Elva reached out her arms. "Hug me, for Fate's sake."

Tom did, and kissed her, too.

Then he finally had to ask: "So this . . . companion . . . that you mentioned. Where are they?"

"*She* should be coming"—Elva turned and pointed—"round about now. See?"

A stub-winged grey lev-car came hurtling at a dangerous angle past a tall natural pillar in the cavern system, straightened up, then flew directly towards the platform.

"Um . . . Perhaps we should get out of the—"

Before Tom could finish speaking, the lev-car had twisted to one side, hovered, and dropped down to a silent landing beside them. The bubble-membrane liquefied, and a short, lean figure wearing a soft blue beret strode down onto the wing, and jumped lightly to the ground.

"Hello, there," she said brightly. "You must be Tom."

"This"—Elva was smiling—"is the Lady Renata of Realm Shinkenar. You know."

"I'm sorry, er . . ." Tom looked from Elva to the stranger. "Should I?"

"Well, I *am* Avernon's sister," said Lady Renata. "I presume the little blighter at least mentioned my existence."

"Oh . . . Well met, my Lady."

Tom had been about to bow, but Renata strode forward and clasped his forearm with a surprisingly strong grip, as peers and comrades would.

"You're a climber, I hear." Her voice sounded approving. "I clamber about a bit myself."

"I can believe that."

Renata grinned. "Avernon said you weren't much of a one for noble manners."

In her family, that was obviously a compliment.

When you've your own realm, you can afford to mock pretension—

"There's an interesting route I was looking at yesterday, while I was walking around." Tom looked at Elva and shrugged. "If you're interested . . ."

"Excellent."

"After lunch we can—"

"Why wait for lunch?"

Elva said: "I'll see to that. This evening, we'll probably have formal dinners to attend."

"Wonderful." Renata made a face, then brightened up. "All right, let's get organized."

Then a look passed between the two women which Tom pretended not to notice.

A conspiracy, to cheer me up.

"This way," he said. "I'll get the Palace to put you in the guest suite next to ours."

"Sounds good."

Servitors bustled out of the nearest entranceway, formed neat ranks, then bowed as the three nobles walked past. The servitors, without a word, followed.

15

NULAPEIRON AD 3423

Two hours later, the Lady Renata was dangling one-handed off a narrow rib of stone, and calling down: "You all right, Tom? There's a handhold to your left—Chaos. Sorry."

"Got it." Tom's voice was grim: the position was awkward. "Don't worry."

Renata had not fully adapted to Tom's three-limbed climbing style; but Tom had not excelled either, when it had been his turn to lead. He was too used to solo work.

Below them, the smooth pinkish rock descended two hundred metres to the broken cavern floor. Tom cast a glance down, then up, and continued his climb.

As soon as Tom touched the ledge Renata was on, she was already ascending the next pitch, small and strong and agile, with a direct, level-headed approach to solving problems. Her climbing revealed a lot about her personality.

Then she had reached the top of the pitch and was calling down: "On belay, Tom."

"Coming right up."

On the final pitch, Renata let Tom lead since it was "his" route. Chest heaving, he dragged himself over the top onto a wide, flat table of rock. It led back towards a tunnel entrance where Elva was already sitting on a cushion, beside a neat picnic spread.

"Just a . . . moment," he gasped.

Then he turned and steadied the line until Renata had clambered up beside him.

"Good." Renata pulled herself to a kneeling position and clapped her hands together. "I'm absolutely famished. What about you, Tom?"

"Right," Tom said. "Famished. Of course."

He coiled up the line, while Renata and Elva scooped things onto plates and poured drinks into ceramic beakers, and compared notes on makes of lev-car which Tom had never heard of.

But he remembered the first lev-car he had ever owned, presented to him as a gift when he was upraised to Lordship. Avernon had given it to him.

"You know who gave me my first—?" he began, sitting down.

"Yes, we do," said Elva. "Renata told me."

For a while, they busied themselves with minrasta cakes and the inevitable daistral. Then Tom asked: "How is Lord Shinkenar? I don't really know him, but he was . . . kind to me."

When Tom was a young servitor, he had seen the equally young Avernon collapse in a deserted Palace corridor. Tom's quick reaction had saved Avernon's life, and when Tom became a Lord, it was Avernon's father, Lord Shinkenar, who had split off a portion of his large realm in order to provide Tom with a demesne of his own.

"Father travels around," said Renata, "and spends time talking with old friends, or immersed in old crystal-tales. He's quite content. Officially, he's still the ruler."

"But unofficially . . . ?" asked Elva.

"I didn't want the responsibility." Renata shrugged. "But we can't all be as outstanding as my brother. I still have my own research interests." Then she frowned at Tom. "You weren't going to ask for your old demesne back, were you?"

Tom shook his head. "I hadn't intended to raise the subject, but—"

"That's good." Renata looked down at the ground. "We're a large realm, but what with the war's disruption . . . There's a lot of folk to feed, you see. Always the priority."

In some realms, at least.

Elva busied herself with refilling daistral, not meeting Tom's gaze.

She had no desire to rule a demesne, but she was eminently practical: they had to find *some* position in life.

Then Elva cleared her throat and said to Tom: "I asked Renata to check into Jak's history, to see if she could find out what happened to him."

"The Jack? Oh . . ." Tom realized who she meant. "Jak. Someone else I owe a debt to."

When Tom fled his realm (and his fellow revolutionaries) he had left his senior officials in an awkward position. Elva was a shrewd tactician and had known how to convince investigators of her innocence. She had no idea how Tom's majordomo, Jak, had fared. Elva herself had left the realm quickly, under orders from the secret organization known as the Grey Shadows, to which her whole family had belonged for generations.

Another servitor from Darinia Demesne—Tat, who had served alongside Tom—had said that Jak was in prison somewhere. But that was five Standard Years ago.

"I tried," Renata said now. "And I've had word back. There is no record in Realm Shinkenar that such a person ever existed."

"Impossible."

"For a record to be lost by accident, yes." Renata took a bite of mimmasta. "But to investigators of the Enquisio Scelesto, 'disappear' is a transitive verb."

"You mean," said Elva, "that they *disappeared* Jak."

"Exactly."

"Fate damn it."

Later the talk turned to less painful matters, and Renata told how Avernon, while still young, had taken her to a deserted magma pool and shown her thermidors rising to mate.

"The world's original lifeforms," Renata said, "became my life's study. Both native prokaryotes and Terran bacteria are threaded all the way through Nulapeiron, even deep inside the rock. Did you know that there are *symbioses* between the two lineages?"

"Is that possible?" asked Tom. "They're not even based on the same replicators."

"The bacterial components carry DNA, the native components carry speculuzene chains, and they divide at the same time. Isn't that wonderful?"

Both Tom and Elva smiled at the delight on Renata's face.

"Yes," said Tom. "It is."

And he thought, *You're Avernon's sister, for sure.*

Renata was here for the same reason as all the other nobility descending on Palace V'Delikona: to attend the funeral of Brigadier-General Lord Corduven d'Ovraison. As the arachnargoi and lev-cars continued to arrive, they hung in long queues in the caverns, while servitors rushed to get Lords and Ladies installed as quickly as possible without breaking the rules of decorum.

So many were expected to attend that, according to a message placed in every guest apartment, a full Convocation would be held here. It meant that Tom could apply for some kind of posting, as soon as he found out what was available.

In the meantime, he spent the afternoon relaxing by reading poetry from Zelakrin's two classic collections, *Twisted Cat* and *Gone Up in Smoke*, while Elva serviced her graser pistols, tuning and re-tuning the resonance cavities until they performed to her satisfaction.

"Renata invited us to dinner next door," said Elva, just as Tom shut down his holodisplay. "Want to go?"

Though he liked Renata, Tom would rather see Lady V'Delikona; but he would not dream of disturbing her at this time. The droves of noble guests must be a logistical catastrophe. Down in the kitchens and the maintenance tunnels, senior servitors would be feeling the stress, and snapping at their juniors who were doubtless working long, sleepless shifts to provide the appearance of luxurious serenity to the arriving Lords and Ladies. The one good thing about the controlled pandemonium was that all formal dinners were postponed until the following evening; tonight, visitors were welcome to dine in their quarters or make arrangements with friends.

"All right," said Tom. "I'm ready."

Elva fluffed up her hair, tagged a shining graser pistol to the small of her back, and covered it by pulling on a short half-cape.

"Me, too."

The main door-membrane liquefied at their approach. As soon as they stepped through, they saw servitors coming to attention.

"Relax," said Elva. "We're just going into the next suite."

A gangling beta-class servitor opened his mouth as if to say something, then shut it, gave a deep bow, and backed away.

"I'm hungry now," said Tom.

But the person who rose from a deep chair in the suite's outer lounge bore little resemblance to the Lady Renata. He was old, straight-backed with long white hair pulled back by a platinum clasp. His cane, too, was of platinum, and he looked exactly the part for his rank: Primus Maximus, first choice in this or neighbouring sectors to oversee a noble Convocation, and the leading spirit behind the reactionary and influential think-tank known as the Circulus Fidus.

His name was Lord A'Dekal, and his presence here caused Tom's every nerve to tighten.

"My good Lord Corcorigan. How very nice to see you."

"It's a surprise to see you, A'Dekal."

"But not a pleasant one? Oh, dear. We'd hoped you had matured beyond old resentments. We were all so young once, weren't we?"

I don't think you *ever were*, thought Tom.

"What do you mean," he asked, "by *we*? Have you brought the whole Circulus with you?"

The answer came from a lean man standing beneath an inner archway, clothed in dark velvet, with a long silver poignard on each sleeve, sheathed along the forearm. They looked like decorations, but Tom knew Viscount Trevalkin: the weapons would be real, and he was deadly with blades.

"Not exactly, Corcorigan."

"Trevalkin. You're looking better than the last time I saw you."

Then, Trevalkin had been in an autodoc, bloodied and battered at Tom's hand. It had been a formal duel, with Trevalkin and his cronies expecting a very different outcome, for Trevalkin was a master swordsman and there were some weapons that the common-born, like Tom, had no chance to learn.

"And you're a trifle more civilized." Trevalkin's cold gaze tracked Elva as she stepped to one side, hand hovering near the small of her back. "But that's saying little, isn't it?"

"Viscount . . ." A'Dekal raised a warning hand, but it shook slightly: some kind of palsy.

"Corcorigan and I are old friends, don't worry. Brothers under the skin, eh, my Lord?"

It was the second time he had used that phrase with Tom. This sentiment came from a man who had skinned his enemy's vassals alive, using femtotech to keep them suffering for days before allowing death to claim them. *"They screamed so beautifully,"* he had told Tom, that day in the med-centre.

"Are you seriously," Tom said, "trying to recruit me to your cause?"

A'Dekal's face hardened. Trevalkin merely crossed his arms, tucking in his hands very lightly. From that position, he could cross-draw the twin poignards in an instant.

It was no coincidence that Renata met up with Elva. Tom looked at Elva, and she nodded: she read the situation as he did.

"My friend Surtalvan," murmured Trevalkin, "came back with some preposterous tale about your paranoid beliefs. I can't credit—"

Then the main doorshimmers sparkled and evaporated, and Renata stepped through, followed by a platoon of Palace Halberdiers.

"I set up this meeting, as you asked," she said to Lord A'Dekal. "It doesn't seem quite as amicable as you implied."

"My dear, antagonism can be negotiated away, if one is only *reasonable*."

"Then perhaps"—Tom gestured in Trevalkin's direction—"you should have chosen more *reasonable* company. He hardly makes your case, does he?"

"I don't think—"

Renata's voice cut in: "Please leave my quarters, Lord A'Dekal. Viscount Trevalkin. If you would."

Behind her, the Halberdiers stood ready. Everyone in the chamber knew that their loyalty was to Lady V'Delikona, and she had never favoured the Circulus Fidus. If they had been told to obey Lady Renata's orders, then that was what they would do, even in the face of opposing high nobility.

A'Dekal looked about to protest, but Trevalkin seemed merely amused as he pushed himself away from the inner doorway and sauntered over to Tom. "Nice to see you again, my nearly-brother." And then he performed a deep bow towards Elva, ironic in its exactitude. "My Lady."

Tom and Elva drew to either side as Trevalkin and then A'Dekal left. After the doorshimmer had solidified, Renata stationed the Halberdiers just inside it, then beckoned Tom and Elva to an inner chamber.

But before she could speak, Tom said: "I apologize, my Lady. I've brought trouble upon you."

"No, Tom." Renata bit her lip, then stared back towards the door. "I'd been trying to decide on my own allegiance. They *do* favour rebuilding demesnes' economies . . . But I've just made my decision, haven't I?"

"You can always go back to them and—"

Renata held up a hand to stop him.

"Everyone thinks my brother Avernon is a dreamer, which he *is*, but he's also the best judge of character I've ever met, and you're his friend. It isn't a complicated problem."

"You can't risk—"

But this time it was Elva who interrupted. "Shut up, Tom." And, to Renata: "Thank you."

"You're welcome. Do you think we should have dinner now? I'm starving."

16

TERRA AD 2162

<<Ro's Children>>

[4]

The twins' shared study-bedroom was alight with holodisplays, images and FourSpeak writing suspended over black glass desktops.

"Did the person who invented the word *neologism*"—Dirk pushed back his chair—"realize he was creating one?"

"Definitely. Nice one, bro. Put it in the essay."

A soft chime sounded.

"Later. That'll be the girls."

Kian, nearer to the window, peered out into darkness. An aircar floated above the forecourt, Frau Volk at the controls.

"Time—"

"—to party."

Frau Volk chatted non-stop with Frau Schönherr as they flew through the Alpine night, while the onboard AI did all the work. Behind them, their respective daughters, Hilde and Anna, sat with Dirk and Kian in near silence.

Hilde reached out and touched Dirk's hand.

"*Allons-y*," said Frau Schönherr as they touched down and the gull-door rose. "*So, gehen wir. La noce es bellissima.*"

Her linguistic mix was kaleidoscopic even for this country, to Anna's mortification and the twins' amusement. Frau Schönherr herself seemed unaware of the effect on others.

The four teenagers carried skate-blades as they walked up a winding holo-lit alleyway, its cobbles slick with frost—"Slowly, dears," called Frau Volk—and passed beneath a Gothic arch from which elongated icicles hung like spun sugar.

Fireworks cracked overhead.

Sounds of the Blue Danube waltz grew louder as they neared the fair. The two mothers headed for an enclosed café, passing through the crowd, trusting that their daughters were safe beneath bright lights which rendered the black sky featureless.

Dirk and Hilde, followed by Kian and Anna, stopped at the barrier which surrounded the outdoor rink, and snapped on their skate-blades.

"I'm ready," said Dirk. "Hilde?"

"Ready to show you how it's done."

"Let's do it."

Holding hands, they launched themselves onto the ice and skated backwards through the swirling crowd until they reached a clear space near the centre of the rink.

"Show-offs," muttered Anna.

"Yeah," said Kian. "You want to hold onto me?"

"Yes, please."

Anna held on tight, and stumbled against him often. Kian wondered whether she was unusually inept at skating, or unusually fond of making physical contact with him.

I know which one I'm hoping for.

"Kian, you're pretty good at this, aren't you?"

"I do my best."

At one point a neophyte skater—not Anna—slipped, tangled another person's feet, and in seconds there was a pile of a dozen or more fallen people. Dirk's blade caught in a gouge in the ice and he rolled—*look out!*—and whipped his arm up in a forearm block, stopped hurtling steel by reflex, and a skater fell over him.

"Shit." Dirk disentangled himself, pushed over to Hilde. "You all right?"

"I am. How's your arm?"

"Just the muscle. It'll be bruised." Dirk rubbed it with his other hand. "Better that, than stopping a skate-blade with my skull."

"Right. Amateurs." Hilde looked at the fallen people getting to their knees and brushing off snow and ice-dust, laughing. Then she stared up into the bright-lit café. "Neither of them's noticed."

"Your mothers?"

"Right. Hey!" Hilde whistled to Kian and Anna, who were slowly making their way across the ice, avoiding the skaters who had tripped. "You guys want to go for a walk?"

"Where?" Kian drew close, keeping hold of Anna.

"I know a scary graveyard we can visit."

"*Merde*."

"What, you scared or something?"

"Only of what your mother will do if she finds out."

"Yeah? Then we'll make sure she doesn't, right?"

"I . . ." Kian looked at Dirk. "All right."

They grinned in unison.

Shadowed wings spread against black sky: the tomb's statue might have been devil or angel; in the night, it was impossible to tell. From further inside the graveyard, Hilde's clear laugh came echoing back. All Anna could do was shiver.

"It *is* creepy here," said Kian.

"I know." Anna placed her palm against his chest. "But I'm glad—"

Then they heard Hilde again, but this time she was screaming. *Dirk*—

Golden sparks glimmered in Kian's eyes as he ran at unnatural speed through the darkness, avoiding obstacles, Anna forgotten as he raced to find his brother. He vaulted a headstone, skidded on a path, showering gravel . . .

Blue, it shone: a tracery in the air touched here and there with blazing scarlet.

What the hell is it?

"Kian."

"You're all right?"

"Yeah."

The brothers watched as the twisted maze of light hung roiling in the night air. They moved with unspoken consent to their right, and something in the apparition's shape altered to match.

Watching us.

Then a circle of white light slid across a mausoleum, and the low drone of a police aircar sounded overhead. The glowing apparition winked out of existence as though it had never been.

"Merde alors."

"Got that right, bro."

Above them, the police aircar moved on.

They helped up Hilde from where she had fallen, and led her back to the cemetery's boundary where Anna still waited, too petrified to flee.

"Scarier than we thought," said Kian.

"Some moron with a holo projector," said Dirk.

"Yeah. Probably thought—"

"—that was funny, right."

They headed back in silence to the fair.

Frau Volk and Frau Schönherr had abandoned their demi-tasses of espresso and were scanning the crowd of skaters, their faces pinched in cold disapproval.

"Sorry." Hilde came up behind her mother and squeezed her arm. "There was an accident, a pile-up on the rink, so we got off."

"I couldn't see you."

"I'm sorry, Mother." There was enough genuine feeling in that to surprise Frau Volk, jolting her out of interrogation mode. "I really am."

She would not look at Dirk.

Anna, with an abandoned-puppy look in her brown eyes, moved to her own mother's side, away from Kian.

I did run off pretty fast. *Damn it.*

"Can we go home now, Mutti?" Anna asked her mother.

They walked in a loose group back to the aircar, not in silence but making awkward smalltalk which bounced with odd intonations and pauses; and it was obvious by the time they climbed inside the cold vehicle, breath steaming, that this was the last outing they would make together.

From the forecourt, Kian and Dirk watched the aircar whisk straight up, hang over the convent, turn towards Zürich, and begin its acceleration. The twins stared up at the stars a moment longer, then headed for the entrance.

"No-one's seen a Zajinet since they—"

"—kidnapped Mother and took her—"

"—to Beta Draconis III. Right."

They sensed the scanfields probing them before the doors clicked open. Perhaps they would be safe inside.

"But they can teleport."

"Or something like it."

"*Scheiss.*"

"And *merde.*"

They climbed the granite steps and headed for their room.

Aliens who can teleport? The stories had never seemed real.

Tonight, neither of them expected to sleep.

<<MODULE ENDS>>

17

NULAPEIRON AD 3423

Gleaming black morphglass dragons towed the floating coffin. Chains formed of blinding white diamond emerged from the dragons' shoulder blades and led back to the golden bier, draped with the dark-blue d'Ovraison livery. Behind, legions of the Seventh Army in full dress uniform, polished graser rifles held high, marched to the funeral cadence beaten out by military drums.

For two hours the procession moved along the Via Imperata, while the silent populace watched from ground level and nobles in their floating platforms bowed their heads. As the obsidian dragons drew close to the great bronze doors of the Aedes Sanctuaria, a two-hundred-strong choir of priestesses sang the plaintive lament of *Requiem to A Hero*, and in the crowd below Tom's platform a woman broke down and sobbed.

Glassbirds swooped through the air, making no sound.

Elva stood beside Tom, and her presence was immensely comforting, though they exchanged no words and did not even touch hands. This was a formal occasion, and they would honour Corduven's memory by obeying the protocols of his class.

For you, my friend.

Tom shivered as the coffin slid past their position. The sharp scent of incense drifted into his nostrils, but it could not mask the acidic stench as the tall bronze doors swung open at the broadway's terminus, revealing the swirling green luminescence of the Altissimus Vortex Mortis which would consign Corduven, coffin and all, into chemical oblivion.

For the rest of the ceremony Tom could only watch numbly,

scarcely hearing the eulogies as the coffin unhooked itself from the black dragons and floated above the Vortex, awaiting the temple's command.

Finally, as the long ceremony drew to a close, the descent began.

Corduven!

Downwards the coffin slid, into the swirling acid whose piercing green glow was meant to be an affirmation of life, a memory of the home-world, while all the time filling Tom's heart with a sick dread in devastating reinforcement of the basic fact of life: that everything must end.

So it went; and Corduven was gone.

Tom lowered his head and closed his eyes.

Lady V'Delikona sat on a wide platinum lev-platform with some thirty High Lords and Ladies, some of the most influential nobles of this sector or any other. Tom stared at them for a moment, then made a small control gesture which caused his and Elva's platform to drift back, over the crowd's heads and past a ten-metre-thick stone pillar until they were above a clear area. They settled down upon the flagstones.

"We don't belong here," Tom said in a low voice.

"What do you mean?" Elva asked, but immediately added: "You're right."

"Let's go back to—"

Tom's voice trailed off.

"What is it?" said Elva.

At the back of the gathered commoners, standing beside a stocky artisan whose attention was upon the nobles overhead, a small bare-footed girl was working on a handheld holopad. Tom raised a hand, signalling Elva to wait, then crept closer until he could read the glowing yellow-dominated stanzas.

Shadow forms a caravan
With darkness leading one dead man

Through sombre crowds beyond belief
Whose souls bear witness to their grief.

Tom shook his head. The second stanza, in progress, was more ambitious in its overlaid hues, attempting a counterpoint between grief and irony which was not entirely successful.

Fear the dragons, bravest heart,
Scorn the banners at the start
For he has met his end, you see
The same that waits for you and me.

The girl looked perhaps eleven Standard Years old. Lacking nourishment for growth, she might have been as old as thirteen, but no more.

And who exactly does she remind me of?

Tom touched the artisan upon his shoulder.

"Excuse me, sir." Tom roughened his tones, softening the edges of the patrician accent which he adopted in formal surroundings. "Is this your daughter?"

"Um—" Wide-eyed, not fooled by the accent, the man gulped. "Yes, sir. But what . . . ? She *is* my daughter, my Lord, and we intend to be getting home right now."

Tom wondered what tales of noble high-handedness had popped into the man's mind, and just why he thought a strange Lord would enquire about his daughter.

"That's how it should be." Tom looked down at the girl. "And what's your name?"

She looked up at her father, who nodded his permission.

"Sadia, an it please you, sir."

"And you write poetry. Well . . . So did I, and at your age, too."

"You did?"

"Yes. Is that all you do?"

"Well . . ."

She opened up a logosophical model describing a children's game called Hunt The Narl, with fully coded strategy advisers and conflict/cooperation equilibria for multiple players, drawn in bright primary colours. Tom smiled wide with pleasure.

Fifteen minutes later, he rejoined Elva, who was patiently waiting at their grounded lev-platform. She was staring at the artisan, from whose eyes tears streamed without shame, while his blocky hand clutched the young girl's shoulder.

"Chaos, Tom. I don't even want to ask."

"I just spent the last of our credit."

"You bloody fool."

"I know, but . . . It was the right thing to do."

It would make a small difference to Tom and Elva—it was a tenday's rent for a guest apartment up to noble-house standards—but the change it would make in Sadia's life was radical. For formality's sake, Tom had put safeguards in the account he had set up, to legally ensure the funds were used only for the girl's education . . . but in fact he trusted Glekin, her father, straight away.

In three days' time, when the official mourning was over, Sadia would be presenting herself at the local Akademia Antinomios as a day-pupil. What happened after that would be up to her. If she performed well, she could earn cred-points in much the same way that Tom had earned merits as a Palace servitor; those points could fund more education. It was an opportunity, no more than that.

Elva kissed his cheek.

"Bloody fool," she said again.

"You knew that all along."

"I suppose I did."

They slipped out along a quiet colonnade, and left the crowds behind.

There had been mourners they recognized, among the lesser nobility: Falvonn and Kirindahl, old friends of Avernon's (Tom had never seen them looking solemn before); Colonel Milran, formerly of Darinia Demesne, standing beside Sylvana's cousin, the dark-haired Lady Brekana.

Neither Tom nor Elva was in the mood to talk.

They passed along the floor of a vast cavern, where massed lines of arachnargoi shone with carapaces of every hue. Blue-grey and polished brown speckled with black were most common; but there were resplendent royal-blue arachnargoi and iridescent scarlet vehicles among them. Here and there, a blinding white arachnargos, larger than the rest, stood motionless on tendrils like marble.

High above on the ceiling, smaller arachnabugs hung upside down: shining yellow one-person sports bugs, alongside hard obsidian military models with side-mounted graser cannons.

There were thousands of them in this one cavern alone.

No more than you deserve, Corduven.

Not a thousandth of the recognition that Corduven deserved.

That night, Tom and Elva looked through the list of positions posted for the coming Convocation. It would be held quickly, on Shyed'mday, before the gathered nobles and their retinues dispersed to their own realms.

Flensed Pilot, screaming silently . . .

The thing was, there was more than their domestic life to worry about. If Tom was right, the world was at risk; but judging by Surtalvan's and Trevalkin's reactions, no-one was ready to hear his story.

Hopelessly, Tom checked through the procedure for proposing a motion before the Convocation. There were so many preliminary stages to pass through, Tom did not even think his evidence (such as it was) would go to a general vote.

He started making notes.

It was on the evening of the fifth day after Corduven's funeral that the full depth of Tom's failure became clear. Sadia would have just finished her second day at school.

Without bitterness, Tom thought: *I hope she succeeds better than I have.*

From where Tom sat on a silver seat at the very highest level of a cup-shaped auditorium designed to seat thousands, it seemed that all his efforts had come to nothing. He was at the Convocation, but the advertised positions in the public list had gone to other nobles. Tom had also put up a general posting indicating his willingness to work in any demesne: perhaps someone would grant him a private position.

I'm no politician. Never was.

None of Tom's proposals even passed initial screening. He had tried to put forward several motions, from fully arming a strike force against a renewed threat of Anomalous incursion, to merely slowing down the demobilization process—sending soldiers back to their families in phases over the next two years. None of his proposals made it as far as the holodisplays of most attendees.

Meanwhile, every resolution regarding increased taxation of freemen and strengthening astymonia arsenals had been passed with minimal opposition. Those who agreed with the thinking of the Circulus Fidus were getting their way.

Why am I here?

Nearly three thousand Lords and Ladies, from minor Lords-sans-Demesne to the Archduke Xildran whose realm was greater than most sectors, sat in the tiered concentric circles and voted on the final issues.

Then they reviewed the private noble appointments which were being granted: some deputized to subsidiary committees, others discussed and decided upon here in full session. Two hundred and thirty-seven names were upon the list of candidates—

Elva. What am I going to tell her?

—but Tom's was not one of them.

I've failed.

As far as the Convocation was concerned, Tom Corcorigan did not exist.

Tom left early, while the tall curved corridors surrounding the congress hall were still empty, or nearly so. Up ahead, by an arced sweeping buttress, Jay A'Khelikov and Renata were engaged in a conversation which was just finishing. Renata was withdrawing; seeing Tom, she gave a small smile and a nod, then touched Jay's sleeve once more, nodded, and walked away.

"Jay, my friend. How are you?"

It was inane; but there was nothing else to say. They clasped forearms.

"Numb. Stumbling through the motions." Jay looked away, seeing his own thoughts. "Cord and I . . . We were just beginning to hope for some more permanent arrangement, you know. Sort out our lives so we could live close to each—"

His voice caught.

"Corduven was the best," said Tom.

"Yes."

"How have your family been?"

"They're all right. My mother . . ." Jay produced a wan smile. ". . . is very . . . understanding. I'm still the heir."

Tom thought how precarious noble lives could be, despite the enormous privilege. They had luxury and the power of life and death over servitors, but they could not rest easy.

I can survive without wealth.

"You're going back to your mother's realm?"

"Yes, after the . . . After everything's done. Mother's talking about stepping down, relinquishing the reins of power as Shinkenar has done."

"Renata seems to be coping well."

"I think so," said Jay. "And . . . don't worry about Avernon. Cord had him working on something. That's why he couldn't come."

But Tom's thoughts were sour.

Avernon still should have been here.

Jay was trying to converse as normal but just then a shudder passed through his body. It was obvious to Tom that if Jay did not rest soon he would simply collapse.

Tom gestured to the Palace control system, assuming there were sensors here—they were at the very edge of the Palace proper—and ordered a levanquin. Immediately, an apparently solid marble wall puckered and opened. A gleaming one-person vehicle slid out.

"Fate, Tom."

"I think you should get on it."

"No, I . . . All right." Jay reached out to where Tom's left arm would have been, hesitated, then patted Tom's side instead. "Thank you."

Tom helped him climb into the seat. Jay leaned back and sighed as it morphed to fit. Silent tears began to run.

Tom's command had caused servitors to be notified, and some eight men in V'Delikona livery were rushing from a doorway. They took up positions around the levanquin.

"My Lord A'Khelikov needs to rest a while," Tom told them. "His apartment would be best, I think. Or if there's room in his mother's—"

"We'll see to it, my Lord." The chief servitor bowed.

"Wait." Jay held up his hand. "Tom . . . Back here, on Ahdimday. We're meeting for . . . *Be here.* Please. Snapdragon Hour. I'll send a servitor to . . . remind you."

"I'll be here, of course."

"Good, I . . ."

But Jay's voice trailed off then, and Tom watched as the levanquin rose. It moved off amid its escort of servitors.

Sounds of conversation rose up behind Tom—other Lords leaving the Convocation—and he whirled away, snapping his cape, and strode off into a long corridor which stood empty, with none to see Tom Corcorigan's bitterness or shameful failure.

Three strata down, Tom found himself outside a blue-shadowed establishment called Taverna na'Lethe, where the air was heavy with sweet ganja scents escaping from the masks. Along the tavern's shelves stood row upon row of crystal bottles and decanters that glistened and called to Tom.

The dragon, the one that was always there, coiled and hissed inside his mind.

Tom walked in.

Aquafire was well named. When the drink came it was bright orange with tiny flames licking the meniscus of its surface. Tom held the glass up. His hand did not shake.

Elva, I'm—

Fire rose inside him. A glow. Joy, singing along his nerves.

Everything that happened after that was inevitable.

Shards of perception, fragments of memory. Hand resting in a cold puddle. Shivering as he slept on stone.

Vomiting, and the later stink of it.

And the swaying, as ribbons of the world swam round his head, when strong hands picked him up and carried him, and the cosmos darkened and dwindled in all directions without ever quite disappearing.

Lying on a couch, Tom groaned his way into consciousness, and the sight of a hard-eyed man leaning over him.

"Huh!"

Tom snaked his hand up, going for the throat—too slow—but the man was already moving back, and then Elva's voice said: "This is Dr. Varin, Tom. You're well enough, don't worry."

"Chaos."

Tom sank back, and closed his eyes.

Oh, Fate.

Then, squinting, Tom levered himself up, swung to a sitting position with feet on the floor. "Bath chamber," he croaked.

"Come on." Dr. Varin helped him stand. "This way."

There was a glint at the doctor's hip, a graser weapon, and again Tom tried to react but too slowly. Then he realized: medical treatment cost credit and they had none. The weapon was Elva's, or had been.

Reduced to bartering.

The doctor helped Tom to undress, tossing aside the rank, puke-smelling tunic. Then he lowered Tom into an aerogel bath, submerged him.

"*Rest.*" The voice sounded odd through the gel.

Tom closed his eyes.

Two hours later, Tom climbed from the bath, sober but with every nerve shaking, every cell of his body feeling washed out and sick. At least he smelled clean.

Fresh clothes awaited him.

Dressed, Tom went back into the chamber where Elva now sat alone, and asked her: "What day is it?"

$$\diamond\diamond\diamond$$

Elva pawned a set of diamond-chased stunwhips for sufficient credit to buy a passage back to the Collegium, where the techs should have finished removing Axolon from the wall and encased him in the floating sarcophagus. Where they were going to take the wrecked cyborg, and how they were going to make the final payment for the techs' work in extracting him, neither Elva nor Tom had any idea.

There were two days left until the meeting with Jay which Tom had promised to attend. And it had been *three* days—three entire days—since Jay had told him of the meeting: seventy-five hours of alcohol-induced fragmentation which would never be clear in Tom's mind; nor would he want them to be.

All of his cred-spindles were gone.

Elva sold her second-best graser pistol and Tom's holodrama crystals in a small shop on the Seventh Stratum where no-one asked questions. For the time being, they would be able to eat.

Life reduces to basics very quickly.

On Ahdimday morning, Tom and Elva packed their few belongings, and made ready to leave the guest apartment. Elva had booked the arachnargos for the evening, and there was nothing left for them here save the meeting with Jay A'Khelikov, fulfilling Tom's small obligation to the man who had mattered so much to Corduven.

"I'm sorry," Tom said to the empty chamber.

Then they left.

It was the same amphitheatre that the Convocation authorities had used as a congress hall. Today, the tiers of seats were mostly unoccupied: the few nobles attending the meeting sat down at the front, in scattered twos and threes, totalling twenty-four people. Approximately three thousand remaining seats were empty.

Among the attendees were people Tom and Elva knew: Sylvana and her cousin Brekana; Lady V'Delikona with Jay on one side of her, a red-bearded Duke on the other side; Renata; Falvonn and Kirindahl. The rest, all noble-born, were strangers.

A black-robed Lord entered from the nearest passageway, climbed onto a quartz dais and cleared his throat. "My Ladies, my Lords." A hololattice grew slowly brighter beside him. "We are here to read the last will and testament of Brigadier-General Lord Corduven d'Ov—"

Blood-rush sounded in Tom's ears. He lowered his head, blinking quickly.

I shouldn't be here.

Elva's grasp tightened on Tom's forearm, as she read his intention to leave.

"—collection, including my favourite épée, to Lady Elva Corcorigan, in the hope you will make fine use of it . . ."

With a sniff, Elva nodded.

The disposal of Corduven's possessions was fast, as befitted a soldier. His artworks went to Sylvana and Brekana, save for some shadily specified holoprints which went to several of his old comrades—three of whom were here—along with those items of his weapons collection which he had not left to Elva.

Since Corduven had been military, not a Liege Lord, he had no demesne to dispose of, and that simplified what might otherwise have been a long and involved legal process. Jay sat stiff and pale throughout the proceedings, making an immense effort not to break down when some small favourite sculpture was left to him. Obviously, Corduven had already given Jay whatever major belongings he had wanted to pass on.

Then there were crystals, bequeathed to Falvonn, to Kirindahl—

Tom shook his head, withdrawing inside himself.

Dragon, uncoiling—

He wanted to drink.

—and so seductive.

Then Elva's fingers were digging painfully into Tom's skin.

"—freeborn but then a servitor, from Salis Core to Palace Darinia, and then by dint of endless self-discipline and inborn talent, becoming the first commoner for a century in Gelmethri Syektor to be upraised to—"

Tidal wash of blood-rush in Tom's ears once more.

No.

But the presiding Lord's words continued.

"—and since my parents' death during the war—"

Tom was wrong. Corduven *had* become a Liege Lord, without Tom's knowing it: inheriting his parents' realm.

"—to the man whose efforts were decisive in our victory against the Blight, I hereby bequeath my remaining possessions, including my realm, Demesne d'Ovraison, and the terraformer sphere known as Guillaume Globe, in which my late brother Gérard lived—"

Corduven. Don't do this.

"—to Lord Thomas Corcorigan, my friend and ally. Rule well, Tom, and be happy."

Tom lowered his head.

No.

He closed his eyes.

My friend, no . . .

And wept for Corduven at last.

18

TERRA AD 2163

<<Ro's Children>>

[5]

Spring brought a glistening sheen to Oxford's spires, their mono-molecular protective films shining with promise. Young birds flew over the quiet streets or perched amid bright-green swelling leaves, warbling songs of challenge and invitation. Smartpaths flowed like turgid streams along the old roads—St. Giles, Broad Street, past Keble College and the meadow beyond—while the narrower, cobbled streets remained as they had always been, recognizable to a visitor from a millennium before.

The proud dome of the Bodleian Library's Radcliffe Camera; the quadrangles of St. Hilda's et al.; the Ashmolean's forbidding columns: all retained their stately grandeur. The hidden tunnels beneath the streets still used cables and pulleys to draw books and crystals from college to college, in the hidden arteries of intellectual cooperation.

"What a sodding dump," said Kian.

Leaning against his bicycle's handlebars, he surveyed the twelfth-century architecture and shook his head. Gowns billowing, a group of scholars hurried towards some ceremony—perhaps the Latin swearing-in required of anyone joining the Bodleian Library—and Kian shook his head.

"It's not that bad." Dirk eyed the flapping gowns. "Though I hadn't envisaged the fancy dress, I must admit."

"Trapped in amber. Probably think this is the centre of the universe, when it's really a tiny provincial town."

"Which makes it different from Caltech"—Dirk leaned back on his saddle—"exactly how?"

Kian shrugged.

"Beats me, bro. Where to now?"

Kian had already won his place at Caltech's Feynman Institute. Neither of them doubted that Dirk would pass the post-exam interview to gain admittance to St. Hilda's.

It had not escaped their attention that, nearly a hundred and fifty years before, Gus Calzonni had attended St. Hilda's before going on to teach and perform research at Caltech, where she discovered the existence of mu-space.

Earlier, a young woman showing Dirk around the college had pointed out rust-coloured stains on a crenellated wall, and related the story of the thirteen female students who had publicly and messily committed suicide when St. Hilda's had been opened to males in the previous century.

Dirk had grinned, believing the story but not the discoloration's provenance. Then the woman laughed, as if he had just passed another test.

"Little Trendy Street," Dirk said now, pointing, "is just down there. There's a good place to hang out."

"What? Little *where?*"

"Only townies and bloody outsiders use the names that are on the map. Little Clarendon Street. There's ice cream, in about thirty flavours."

"Well, Jesus Christ, bro. What are we waiting for?"

Four months later, Dirk and Kian were plunged into studies far tougher than they had expected. Life became a maelstrom of social activity and hard work, as they adjusted to their respective surroundings without neglecting to send each other daily h-mails when the time difference made realtime comms awkward.

At Halloween, both of them heard contemporary ghost stories of strange sightings nearby. Neither Kian nor Dirk remembered to mention the tales, which had been relayed to them as jokes by rational-minded fellow students aware that eerie phenomena normally owe more to known hysteria than unknown physics.

Neither Mother nor any other working Pilot (of the old school, their eye sockets plugged into their ships' systems via ultra-high-bandwidth coherent-resonance i/o buses) had glimpsed a Zajinet since that strange sighting in a Zürich courtyard. Perhaps it *had* been a holo, after all.

In December, one night close to the end of term, Dirk was climbing the narrow staircase which led up to his cold room when he heard—not for the first time—stentorian breathing from the other bedroom on his floor. It belonged to Rajesh Mistry, whose main complaint about Oxford was that it was so much colder than Bangalore but who otherwise loved the place, and often delivered blistering insights during maths tutorials that left Dirk wondering just what kind of mind the fellow had.

"More of those strange sexual practices, huh?" muttered Dirk, as he unlocked his own door.

Rajesh's door swung open. Dressed in singlet and shorts, he was drenched with sweat and breathing heavily. Behind him, the room looked unoccupied.

"Dirk . . . I thought I heard you . . . old chap."

"You're out of breath."

"*Baithaks* and *dands*. Great exercise. Listen . . . I have a favour to ask you."

"Um, sure."

"Kaufmannian transitions. Know anything about them?"

"Of course. We studied 'em at school. Didn't you?"

"Not part of our curriculum." Rajesh stood with hands on hips, his breathing coming under control. "Can we meet up in the Common Room, go through the basics?"

"Yeah, if you'll tell me one thing. What the hell are *baithaks* and *dands*? Did I say that right?"

"Perfectly . . . They're what wrestlers in my country have been doing for centuries, and called combat conditioning in the west. Squats and cat-lick push-ups, with some other stuff, is all."

Dirk looked at Rajesh's muscles—Rajesh was bulky, radiating functional strength without any of the polished and injury-prone tightness of a bodybuilder—and Dirk made an instant decision. Anyone who knew the history of fighting arts was aware that Indian wrestlers had ungodly stamina, and could grapple forever without tiring.

"Teach me the exercises," Dirk said, "and I'll teach you everything I know on bio-emergenics. Deal?"

"Absolutely."

They shook hands on it.

That first night of studying together was intellectually uneventful, though Dirk learned a form of exercise which he would practise daily for the rest of his life. It would be springtime before Dirk heard Rajesh being called "a dirty wog" in a snug pub (the "Bird and Baby" in the students' private nomenclature) located on St. Giles and once frequented by Tolkien and C. S. Lewis. (The racial epithet was unfamiliar; Dirk looked it up later.) The verbal insult was swiftly followed by a vicious right hook directed at Rajesh's temple from behind.

The attacker was a drunken rugby player accompanied by three of his mates, and before Dirk could get close enough to help, Rajesh had already demonstrated that he knew more about fighting than just conditioning methods. When Dirk and Rajesh left, four bodies lay sprawled around the small dark pub where a gentle scholar once dreamed of hobbits and dragons.

"Not bad, old chap," said Dirk. "Not bad at all."

Meanwhile, in sun-drenched California, Kian's study-buddy of choice was a copper-haired young woman with copper-coloured eyes, whose name was Deirdre (pronounced Dee-drè in the Irish fashion), with a ferocious intellect and an uncanny ability to stay upright on a surf-board in the wildest of conditions, who made Kian laugh and would have been a perfect soul-mate were she not, in her own words, "a god-damned dyke with attitude."

They often worked together in Deirdre's room, drinking endless cups of lemon tea while Rimsky-Korsakoff's *Capriccio Espagnol* or Zimmer's *M-I:2* played in the background. Or they would take their workpads down to the Conundrum Café and sip cappuccinos (or *cappuccini* as Deirdre insisted on calling them in the plural) while making up fictional biographies of passers-by.

So it went, until Deirdre chose to do a project on ball lightning and interviewed some people who had seen a strange shining shape over the Caltech campus one dry summer night. It reminded Kian of the students who had been frightened the previous Halloween with their tale of glowing lights.

"Could've been the same phenomenon," said Deirdre. "Unusual time of year for it to happen, though."

"What, seeing ghosts and ghouls?"

"Ha. You'll be seein' stars, pal, if you don't—Hey, Kian. What's up?"

"Nothing. Just some weird coincidence."

When Kian h-mailed his musings to Dirk that night, he knew that Dirk would take the sighting seriously.

You and me both, bro.

On second thoughts, Kian directed a copy of the message to

Mother, which she would pick up as soon as she returned from her current voyage through mu-space.

At least we're keeping the insanity in the family.

Rain hissed on cobblestones in the quadrangle below Dirk's window. He stared downwards, seeing nothing, then finally turned and shut down the holodisplay.

I do take you seriously, bro.

Because there had been another sighting, here in Oxford, that Kian didn't know of, and that made three in all. Four, if you counted Zürich.

So there's someone I can't put off seeing any longer.

A lone drop sailed down from a ceiling crack and plopped onto the desktop beside his elbow. Dirk ran his fingertip through the water.

"Right then," he said to no-one. "Let's get to it."

"—and his poncey French, pardon me, Français accent—"

Two male students, clattering down the staircase, passed Dirk on his way up. He recognized the speaker, last seen bloody-nosed and sprawled across a bench formed of wood so old it was black, by a fireplace in a pub on St. Giles.

They were followed by two women, one of whom murmured: "Old Doc Chalou's still got it, in a way that moron never had."

"You fancy Claude Chalou?" The second woman sounded Canadian. She giggled. Then, staring at the two young men who had reached ground level: "I'll bet Chalou could whip their asses, however old he—"

Then Dirk climbed past them, and stood swallowing on the small landing, hand raised to knock, hesitating.

"*Don't just stand there.*" The voice called through the heavy wooden door. "Come in."

Dirk swung the door open.

Grizzled beard, short white-grey hair, sitting in a chair by a blazing thermoglow with a rug thrown across his lap: that was Chalou.

In the silver sockets where his eyes should have been, reflected orange highlights danced.

At his feet lay a barrel-bodied black retriever whose muzzle was flecked with grey.

"Mr. McNamara. I'm pleased to meet you. Sam"—he addressed the dog—"this is Dirk. *C'est un ami, hein?*"

Sam got to his feet and waddled over to Dirk on stiff legs.

"Hey, Sam." Dirk bent down, let the dog sniff the back of his hand, then rubbed the flat top of Sam's head, staring into those brown intelligent eyes. He patted the side of Sam's convex torso. "Good to meet you."

Then Dirk straightened up and shook hands with Dr. Chalou. Strong grip. Chalou looked to be in his fifties, but must have been over seventy, even allowing for the ultra-relativistic effects of mu-space voyages when time slowed down.

"*Ah, bien.* Sit, young Dirk. Over there."

"I'm sorry." Dirk took his seat opposite the ageing tutor. "I should have been to see you before now."

"*Pourquoi?* Why would you want to talk to an old guy like me?"

Dirk shook his head.

Because you're like my grandmother. Because you made a sacrifice I'll never have to.

Chalou tapped his left eye socket with a fingernail, in a gesture which made Dirk's skin shrink, with the clutched-scrotum sensation only a male can know.

"Don't let this *ever* make you feel guilty, my friend. Even if you are the Admiral's son, consider this an order."

Dirk looked quickly around the room, the mullioned window and the dark ceiling rafters, though surveillance bugs would be invisible. He sensed nothing, but that did not mean—

"The room is clean, don't worry. And I think UNSA knows how we refer to your mother, *hein?* So, I take advantage of my age and give you my wisdom, even though you are Karyn McNamara's grandson."

Dirk cleared his throat. "Thank you, sir."

"Ha. Fine. I understand why you were reluctant to come here. I'm not your tutor, after all."

There was an implied question in that, and Dirk chose to answer softly: *"J'ai peur, professeur."*

"Mais qu'avez vous? What's wrong?"

"I think the Zajinets are back. I think Pilots should be warned."

<<MODULE ENDS>>

19

NULAPEIRON AD 3423

Black guilt crushed Tom. He came awake before dawnshift, while Elva still slept, and worked out in the lounge. Some of what Tom had seen in the Pilots' story matched his phi2dao conditioning exercises; under other circumstances, as he bounced like a metronome through five hundred squats, Tom would have grinned as he considered how far back phi2dao's lineage extended.

But the thought of Corduven's bequest beat down upon him.

They were still in Realm V'Delikona. Tom and Elva had re-booked passage back to the Collegium Perpetuum Delphinorum, and reserved the same apartments there. This time, there was no uncertainty about whether Tom could pay the technicians who were working to free the ruined cyborg.

For I am ruler of Demesne d'Ovraison.

Not to mention the terraformer sphere whose exterior Tom had once climbed in order to kill the Oracle . . . he now owned the sphere inside which he had found his mostly-dead mother entombed in a sarcophagus, capable of brief moments of consciousness. She died for real just minutes after the Oracle gave a last, blood-choked breath, with Tom's poignard buried in his side.

Perhaps I can sell the terraformer.

Yet who would want to live among the clouds? Only a few thousand specially trained military could even function on the surface; the rest of Nulapeiron's inhabitants would succumb to agoraphobic catatonia if someone were to drag them from the tunnels and corridors they called home. As a dwelling-place, the sphere was worthless.

Although it was rare to see more than a single terraformer at a time (assuming that an observer was on the surface in the first place), that was because the world was vast. Something like seventeen thousand such spheres floated above the world. If someone wanted to claim a sphere, there was little to stop them: fewer than a dozen were said to be inhabited. The only reason to purchase such a dwelling from Tom Corcorigan would be that it could be moved into straight away, without expensive recommissioning. (And still the buyer might object, if they learned something of the terraformer's bloody history.)

Tom put that aside, and began to work through his new list of obligations.

He would have to register the realm, Demesne d'Ovraison, under its new name of Corcorigan Demesne. Then perhaps, not needing their financial support, he could try again with Trevalkin and A'Dekal, and persuade them to do . . . what, exactly?

What everyone needed—Tom realized, staring into the grey half-light which blanketed the chamber—was a global Fire Watch, like the coastal beacons of ninth-century watchers who surveilled the sea for Viking sails: *not* a standing military force, but a warning system formed of observers trained to recognize the signs of Anomalous incursion.

The Blight had taken over a dozen realms before people began to recognize the danger. This time, with the more powerful true Anomaly, such a delay would leave things far too late to mount any opposition.

If opposition is possible.

Even if it were a paranoid delusion on Tom's part . . . still, the reactionary elements might support him, if it gave them footholds in realms throughout the world. Keeping an eye on each realm's subjects? They would love the idea.

I could help plunge Nulapeiron into harsh regimes which will endure for centuries.

Yet if the Anomaly were truly coming . . .

Then it's our only chance.

In a nearby eatery, Tom and Elva joined Kraiv and Adam for breakfast. Off to one side, a translucent green gel-block, some three metres high, contained the shadowy, etiolated, once-human forms of Wraith Singers. Their nerves and sinews generated the eerie music transmitted by the vibrating medium which nourished them.

Most diners paid them little attention, though Tom found his appetite diminishing. Then he had a sudden thought, and put down his tine-spoon.

"Kraiv?" he said. "Would Lirna . . . ? D'you think she'd be willing to relocate the clan?"

The former ruler, Edric, had not returned from battle. Lirna's *pro tem* position had become permanent.

"The whole clan? Well, actually . . ." When Kraiv shrugged, the big muscles of his shoulders bunched and flexed. "The Bifrost Bridge field generators *can* be moved. 'The Manse Hetreece consists of people, not a place.' Her words, not mine."

In the three years since Kraiv had switched clan allegiance (in recompense for the death of Lirna's son, Horush), he had become a trusted adviser.

"So she might consider a move." Tom was planning rapidly. "With some forces possibly based elsewhere for short rotations, guarding, say, a habitable terraformer sphere?"

"In the sky? Perhaps." Kraiv's chuckle was deep and resonant. "There still aren't enough who've done the agoraphobia deconditioning. It'll provide a motive."

"OK. Good."

It was Lirna as clan ruler who would make the decision; but to have an entire clan of carls based in their realm . . .

"Yes." Elva was grinning. "Yes. We will make your people very welcome, Kraiv."

Not every Liege Lord or Lady liked the idea of berserker warriors living full-time in their own demesne, however useful they found the existence of housecarls when force or the threat of it became desirable. (Even now, Kraiv ate with his heavy jade-coloured morphblade leaning against the back of his chair. Nervous servitors were trying to ignore it.) Elva's obvious enthusiasm might sway Lirna's decision.

Then Tom let out a long, slow breath, and made a decision which was hard for someone who had been private so long, nursing his grievances and focusing on his goals. Without that hidden intensity, he would have achieved nothing.

"There are things I've . . . not mentioned." Tom glanced at Adam. "Not even during Academy debriefings. Perhaps I should have shared them."

Then he related events from New Year's Day of the previous year, when as an Academy-trained operative Tom was running a cell in the Blight-occupied realm known as the Aurineate Grand'aume.

The restaurant is on a wide balcony, overlooking the greater hall below. The diners realize now that something is wrong, for every exit-membrane is blocked by troops in ceremonial scarlet-and-silver, bearing grasers in addition to their sabres.

At Tom's table, Tyentro and Velsivith whip to their feet in one smooth motion.

"Tom, get away!"

Velsivith's beam arcs through the air and Tom drops to the floor, begins crawling. It is his duty to escape.

Something round and palm-sized rolls from Tyentro's hand along the floor: a sphere containing glowing sapphire fluid, captured from the chamber in which the Grand'aume's Seer died.

Graser beams impale Tyentro, lance through Velsivith, and tear them into steaming meat. Tom rises slowly.

"That one." An officer points.

Tom hurls the glowing sphere in a high arc off the balcony, into the hall, then uses his situational gymnastics training for real: chair, tabletop, two quick paces and a vault over the balustrade as emerald beams split the air and then he falls.

Impact, as he hits the flagstones far below the restaurant, and rolls.

Tom tries to catch the sphere.

"I know all this," said Adam. "It was in your report. They were briefing me for a possible follow-up mission, overtly military."

"I didn't catch the sphere. I nearly did, but I fell and it shattered."

"Yes . . ." Adam noticed Elva frowning.

"And the sapphire fluid was gone."

Elva shook her head. "Chaos."

"Yeah. It was *inside* me. Just like that."

Adam looked around at the Collegium eatery.

"Relax, Adam. If we're under surveillance, I don't care. I want them to know this."

"And if we're not being watched, they don't deserve to know?"

"Something like that."

The soldiers are closing in on them, and that was the strangest thing: that he would never afterwards be able to see when the split occurred, when he became them, one Tom Corcorigan turning into two individuals. Then they pass through a door and stop, staring at each other.

"You should go."

Then the disagreement. "I'm nearer to the door. You go on ahead."

"We can both—"

"No, we can't."

Tom Corcorigan runs, surviving the manhunt which is looking for only one person.

Meanwhile, Tom Corcorigan stays, fighting until the inevitable death.

Tom wiped the sweat from his face, shaking at the memory.

"Two of me. And it happened on two other occasions."

Elva blinked. "It seemed like a blur, an illusion . . ."

She had seen a thousand Toms fighting a thousand identical Absorbed opponents, as the Blight multiplied its human component and Tom somehow rode the wave of energies involved and harnessed the same effect upon himself. It was an effect catalysed, somehow, by Eemur's Head.

That time, the ephemeral Toms had conjoined afterwards, become singleton once more, when the action was over. On the other two occasions, a corpse had remained, identical in all respects to the Tom Corcorigan who still lived.

"And I can't explain it," he said to his breakfast companions, "any more than you can."

"But—"

"It relates to the reason"—Tom looked at Elva, then Kraiv, then Adam—"that I'm so sure the Anomaly is coming. It's not just that I think the Blight made contact. With Eemur's help, I made a traumatic trip, or *something*, to the hellworld known as—"

Then there was a commotion at the eatery's entrance, and chairs were being pushed back as a phalanx of greystone warriors marched inside, with Altus Magister Strostiv of the Collegium Perpetuum Delphinorum at their head.

He scanned the tables, stopped when he saw Tom.

"There he is." Strostiv pointed. "Warriors . . . Surround him. *Now!*"

Two dozen figures of living stone rushed forward at his command.

20

NULAPEIRON AD 3423

Before the greystone warriors reached their table, all four were on their feet: Kraiv, gripping his huge jade morphblade; Elva and Adam with graser pistols drawn; Tom with his hand upon his poignard's hilt.

"*No!*" cried Strostiv. "We're not attacking you!"

Then the greystone warriors each went down on one knee and faced away from the table, training graser staves towards every entrance, including the one they had used.

"What the Fate's going on, Strostiv?"

"My Lord, someone's coming after you with false—"

Then militiamen were spilling through the doorway, with a nine-strong group of blue-skinned clone-fighters in their midst. The clones' hides were like lapis lazuli; their eyes were the colour of blood.

Behind them, a nervous-looking Lord entered the eatery.

"My L-Lord C-Corcorigan?"

"That's me."

The Lord lifted a crystal in his shaking hand, glanced up at the greystone warriors in their protective formation around Tom and his companions, and tried to speak, but failed. Beside him, the militiamen's officer cleared his throat.

"Lord Frindolivaunt? D'you want me to announce the charges?"

"I . . . Y-Yes." Frindolivaunt handed him the crystal. "Please."

"These are capital charges, my Lord Corcorigan." The officer cleared his throat again. "In the matter of murder, of one Gérard d'Ovraison, Oracle—"

An excited buzz rose among the frightened diners. The name d'Ovraison was on everybody's lips at the moment.

"—and we offer new forensic—"

"Stop!" Strostiv was causing a holo image to appear. "Read this. You may not bring this charge to bear."

Frindolivaunt paled.

"But I-I've b-been assured th—"

It's a distraction.

The thought must have occurred to Elva in the same instant, because she, too, spun into motion. Frindolivaunt was a dupe. If whoever was manipulating him knew about Corduven's vengeance-waiver, then they knew also that these charges could not be made to stick.

"There!" shouted Elva.

"No!" The militia officer yelled the order. "Clone-warriors, *stand down!*"

A blue-skinned female warrior broke from her group, snarling as she cocked her wrists and graser implants glistened—*move it*—as Tom ducked and rolled, poignard out now and ready—*now*—then lunging to the attack but Elva was in front, blocking the attack as three graser beams spat simultaneously, and then Elva was down.

"NO!" howled Tom.

Elva's shot had burned a notch on the female warrior's shoulder; before the woman could do anything more, her own clone-siblings lunged forward as one, their fists arcing down. Sixteen beams lanced into her. She died.

Then the clone-warriors pointed their hands towards the ground, bowed their heads and froze. It was some kind of capitulation but Tom could not care because *this was Elva* lying on the polished floor, charcoal burns on her clothes, her skin whitened. Elva was not moving, but he could not lose her now, not—

"Tom."

Kraiv's huge hands were holding him.

"She's alive." Adam snapped orders to the greystone warriors. "You, you, and you, let's lift her. There's no time for anything else."

As they picked Elva off the ground, Tom started forward, but Kraiv held him back.

"Tom," he said urgently. "*You're* the target. If you accompany her . . ."

For a moment, Tom fought, but then the words made sense and he stopped, almost fainting with the sudden impossibility of what he faced.

Why now?

Kraiv was right. Anyone associated with Tom Corcorigan was at risk. Now that he had some small power, his enemies were afraid; but the whole world was in danger . . .

In that moment, it seemed there was only one thing he could do. Tom grabbed Kraiv's wrist, squeezed that immense bony joint as hard as he could—actually hurting Kraiv like that was out of the question—and gave him a serious look.

Then, in a sour, strange tone, Tom said aloud: "I was leaving her anyway. Why'd she have to be so damn foolish?"

Adam looked astounded as Tom brushed past him, past Strostiv, past the crouched warriors—*oh, Elva, my love*—and headed for the door, ignoring his accuser and the militiamen who simply stared. None of this was covered in their orders of the day.

Outside in the cavern, Tom ducked off to one side, alert for more enemies, seeing none. Too scared for Elva's life to cry, he stalked dry-eyed along a roundabout route back to their quarters. There, he let himself in and sealed the doorshimmers, then sat down in a chair with Elva's favourite dartbow in his lap, and waited for the news.

The ancient wisdom goes: *The warrior, when attacked, steps forward.*

Elva was a warrior. She had reacted superbly, acting to save Tom. By any means, using any subterfuge, Tom would achieve the same for her. Elva should not be a target because of him.

Always . . .

Yet if she pulled through this, what he had to do might break both their hearts.

. . . and forever, my love.

"Frindolivaunt," said Adam later, "is still apologizing. Lady V'Delikona's investigators are trying to trace the people who passed him the information, but no-one's holding out much hope . . . And he tried to visit Elva in the med-centre, but took the point when I told him he was the last person we could trust inside."

Adam had not left Elva's side until Lady V'Delikona's personal Halberdiers were guarding her, stationed in chambers above and below and to every side. Two squadrons of armed arachnasprites were roaming the approaches.

"What about the clone-warriors?" said Tom.

"Still denying that the group-conditioning can be broken, while simultaneously saying that she acted on her own and contrary to their thoughts. They *do* act shocked, I'll admit."

"But they killed the only one of their number"—Kraiv's voice rumbled deeply—"who could have testified for sure."

"Right. And Strostiv isn't helping. He only says, he knew what he had to do, because he knew he had already done it. First time he's been important enough to feature personally in an Oracular truecast . . . He's proud of it." Adam looked at Tom. "I wanted to kill the bastard."

Tom did not rise to that.

Instead, he said: "I'm going to make some hard decisions, Adam. Can I trust you to guard Elva with your life?"

"Tom? I . . . Yes, of course."

"And tell her that I love her. Because I *cannot* tell her that myself." Kraiv was frowning.

"No . . ."

"Yes. It's the only way she'll be safe."

Even Strostiv had thought Tom and Elva were cold towards each other in public, not understanding the bond that truly joined them. If that were the case, then maybe others would see it as a marriage that had not worked out, an impulse taken too far during the heady victory celebrations, when the air was pulsing with energy and the world seemed fresh because people were astounded to be still alive.

The worst thing was, for the separation to be convincing, it must be real. That was where the danger lay: in fiction becoming fact, despite his wishes.

It's for the best, my love.

Tom waited until the news arrived from the med-centre: she was on the mend, and would pull through. In the middle of the luxurious apartment, alone, Tom dropped to his knees and sobbed.

Two hours later, in the middle of the night, his belongings were packed in a small bag by the doorshimmer, waiting to go.

A green teardrop-shaped arachnabug dropped him at the realm's edge, in a raw cavern where fluorofungus was quiescent, observing night-shift. Then the arachnabug sped through the darkness, heading back towards the bright caverns of The Realm Which Never Sleeps.

This should have been a time of triumph.

Tom stood on a lonely crag, watching faintly fluorescent orange worms slide slowly down the stone below, heading for the cavern floor. Overhead, sleeping edelaces rustled among the stalactites.

Am I doing the right thing?

Something moved at the limits of his vision.

Danger?

Then he could see it: a blob of scarlet moving fast and growing bigger as it approached, bright beams shining for his benefit. It was an arachnasprite, speeding upside down across the cavern ceiling towards him.

Tom picked up his small bag.

In moments the 'sprite was hurtling down the nearest cavern wall, its whipping black tendrils a blur of motion. Then it was straightening out, and coming to rest beside Tom. The black-clad TauRider leaned back in her saddle, and pulled off her scarlet helmet, to reveal blazing violet hair.

"Thylara," said Tom. "You came."

"For you? Any time, warrior."

Tom hefted his bag. "Right."

"Get aboard."

Clutching the bag against his chest, Tom swung into place behind her. The scarlet carapace morphed, encasing his legs and wrapping diagonal bands across his shoulders.

Elva . . .

Then Thylara whooped and Tom's stomach lurched as the arachnasprite wheeled about and leaped for the vertical surface, sped up the rockface, before flipping over and racing across the cracked and broken ceiling, oblivious to the void and the waiting cavern floor below. They careened upside down past obstacles, flipped through a vertiginous arc, then sped vertically upwards once more, almost flying up the thousand-metre shaft at whose distant apex a tiny circle of lemon-yellow sunlight shone.

21

TERRA AD 2164

<<Ro's Children>>

[6]

Rain spattered against the windows, wind shook the bushes outside, pink petals dropping to the grass. The hummingbirds were gone. Shoulder to shoulder, Kian and Deirdre watched the storm.

"This *is* California, right?"

"Unless we slipped into another reality during the night."

They were off-campus this year, sharing a house with three other students. Deirdre's on-off lover Yvette had stayed the night, but left early to get to her job as a rising young architect in the city. Deirdre, at 8 a.m., had come into Kian's room and sat cross-legged on his bed until he woke.

Now, drinking lemon tea, and neither of them with a lecture to attend until the afternoon, they sat and watched the falling rain.

"Come on," she said finally. "Back to my room."

"At last, my luck's changed."

"Ha." Deirdre's reply was automatic, but sad. "Just work, boy."

Kian, carrying his tea, followed her across the corridor and into her room: white-painted walls, everything stacked away, mussed bed which he tried not to stare at. Deirdre caught him looking, and turned away.

"What's up, sweetheart?"

"Yvette, she . . ." Rapid eye-blinks. "She's been offered a job in Toronto."

"Shit." Kian put his cup down, sat down on the floor beside Deirdre, took hold of her hand.

"I knew something was . . . God damn it, Kian. What am I gonna do? I can't drop out of my course."

Kian stared into her copper eyes. After a moment, he said straight-faced: "If only you weren't a lesbian, I'd marry you in an instant."

Deirdre's fingertips brushed his lips.

"If only you weren't a guy, I might take you up on that."

They remained sitting that way, holding hands, as the storm-sounds died and the sun brightened to cast abstract patterns of light glittering like diamonds on the rain-soaked glass.

The holodiagram was yellow and glowing. Every time Deirdre high-lighted a particular feature, a node lit up in blue and a subsidiary image opened up at the periphery, internal details scrolling past.

Kian had work of his own to do, but today it was Deirdre who deserved his attention. An emotional analgesic: that was how he thought of her memetic engineering project . . . except that, as Deirdre talked through the details of research she had shown no-one besides Professor Guillermi, Kian began to be fascinated by the intricate model for its own sake, and for what it revealed about Deirdre's quicksilver mind.

"You know we're in a connected world: six-handshakes-from-the-Pope kind of connected."

"Not the Pope again, dear."

"She's sweet, unlike some of her—Anyway, connectivity. Might've been seven by now, if it weren't for the Changeling Plagues."

"Seven . . . ?"

"Steps removed from virtually any person in the world, chosen at random. Pay attention."

"Yes, Deirdre."

"See, if your closest friends and acquaintances were picked at random from the globe—like, you're as likely to know a rice farmer in

Indonesia as your own mother—then interconnectivity to this degree
would be trivial. But reality ain't like that. You know people you work
with or live near."

"Yes, Deirdre."

"Another way is for *most* acquaintances to be local, but just occasionally to have a long-distance link to someone far away. Village societies are like this." In her holomodel, a virtual landscape showed
groups of settlements: round huts with thatched roofs. "Highly
clumped, very few travellers between them."

"Boring lives."

"Yeah, but . . . Watch what happens when I introduce a plague
vector."

Kian, interested now, tracked through the mortality rates over
time in the simulation, as her little virtual people fell one by one,
coughing up their little virtual blood as their skin erupted with virtual
sores and bubuncles.

"You're enjoying this. Kian, you're a disturbed man."

"Mm."

Diseases which were both highly infectious and deadly killed
entire settlements . . . but did not spread to others. The plague wiped
out its hosts, and died.

"But . . . shit." Kian saw the unsettling implications for the real
world. "Introduce a few globetrotting explorers from the outside . . ."

"And you get AIDS, Ebola, MelterBug and the Changeling
Plagues, spread across the globe. That's what actually happened."

"You're a scary person, you know that?"

After making more lemon tea, Deirdre handed a cup to Kian, then
expanded the diagram. "In large populations, you get a power law network. A tiny number of people have a *very* high number of connections."

"Deirdre, Deirdre . . ."

"*Including* sexual partners, boyo. They're the ones who spread endemic plagues. Same with airborne diseases. Sometimes one super-infecter will contaminate a whole country."

"Which would be good, from the disease's point of view," said Kian, getting it.

"It's almost invulnerable to random attacks, this kind of network. The old World Wide Web was like that, with a small number of highly connected nodes . . ."

Kian frowned. "But the anarchists—"

"Destroyed the Web, yes. That's why we have EveryWare. The old kind of network could cope with *random* attacks, but intelligently directed offensives . . . It's surprising the Net took an entire twenty minutes to die."

It was impressive work, but Kian was confused.

"I thought you were working on *memetics*, how ideas spread like viruses."

The display collapsed in falling sheaves of light, was gone. Deirdre turned to look at Kian, odd shadows in her cupric eyes.

"Recently, Pelkovich in Warsaw and Snyder in Beijing have worked on ways to identify highly infectious memetic nodes: the human individuals and the EveryWare loci who affect the way people *think*."

"They're identifying trendsetters?" Kian wondered why, if this was so good, strain was lining Deirdre's face.

"I examined the body language and oratory of the great manipulators; the use of scapegoats in driving entire populations to illogical and destructive acts; the hypnotic commands embedded in televisual adverts which linked polluting machines to sexual gratification . . . It's been going on for centuries."

Deirdre tapped the desktop. "The thing is, I found ways to do something new: to sugar-coat memetic presentations in ways that make them attractive to the most infectious nodes, the trendsetters, which *guarantees the ideas will spread* through the target population."

"Oh, shit."

"I'm talking propaganda raised to levels no-one's seen before."

Super-propaganda. Deirdre's work wasn't just brilliant, it was dangerous.

"Professor Guillermi's muttering about seconding me to Rand-Miti or UNSA without even finishing my degree. This work would become a dissertation which security-cleared Caltech supervisors would examine. I'd be going straight to Ph.D.!"

"With a thesis that won't be made public."

"Right. *That* practice has been going for centuries, too. Didn't you know?"

"I . . . Deirdre? Why UNSA? What's memetic engineering got to do with them?"

"So far the offworld settlements are just that . . . Small settlements. But terraformers are already spreading Terran bacteria. Eventually, some worlds will have habitable regions."

"With large populations."

"Which UNSA would like to control."

"But . . . They're going to end up designing entire *societies*."

"Yeah, well . . ." Deirdre clasped her hands on top of her head, leaned back in her chair. "They're gonna try."

Outside, gentle rain began to patter once more.

"I've an idea," said Kian. "Let's go to the boardwalk."

"In this—?" She stopped, nodded. "I'll get my slicker."

"Meet you outside in ten."

Grey waves chopped and swirled beneath the timbers. Kian and Deirdre leaned against a rail with a solitary yellow-billed gull for company, while overhead a camera-drone bearing the SMPD logo struggled to maintain position in the gusty wind.

"I wonder how long it can stay up." Kian was eyeing the drone.

"Men worry about that, I hear."

"Ha. You know," Kian said, "there are genes that have identical effects in humans and tomatoes, yet the first time they cloned a black cat, the clone turned out tortoiseshell. And the so-called educated public didn't even pick up on it, much less digest the implications."

"Tortoiseshell?"

"What you call over here, um . . . calico, right? It's not always obvious what's a fundamental concept. Sex is common—"

"Yes, darling Kian."

"—but if that gull's a boy, he's got ZZ chromosomes, not XY. Different mechanism."

"You still worried about your mechanism?"

"Yes. No. Jesus . . ."

Deirdre laid her hand on his arm. "I wrote a paper about gender differentiation when I was twelve. I've *always* been different. I just thought . . . eventually that would be OK, you know?"

"You're worried they can bring pressure to bear? The authorities, I mean."

"I don't know, Kian. I don't know."

In the air, the camera-drone remained aloft. Perhaps it was surveilling them right now.

"You think *you're* different?" Kian hesitated, then reached up and prised away his contact lenses. "Really?"

Deirdre stared at his obsidian eyes and shivered, just as the gull launched itself from the rail and swooped down towards the rushing sea.

"I'll show you from different." Kian pointed with his chin. "See there?"

There was a split second during which the tiniest of golden glimmers inside his eyes caught Deirdre's attention. Then she looked up at the drone.

Feel it.

Kian focused.

Synchronize.

Subverted.

Now.

Aloft, the drone jerked, then coughed dark smoke. For a few seconds it struggled, then it tilted to one side, hung in place for a moment, then slid sideways and down, towards the waves.

Kian turned away, hearing the splash, cursing himself.

Shit. What have I done?

He began to walk.

Rain and seaspray plastered Deirdre's hair against her forehead, and she blinked to keep water from her eyes as she followed, caught hold, and tugged Kian's sleeve, pulling him to a halt.

"You don't get rid of me that easily, pal."

"I'm sorry, Deirdre. I shouldn't have done that."

Gently, she tapped him on the forehead.

"Bad boy. Now let's go home."

"I don't . . . All right."

Wind whipped around Kian and Deirdre as they left the boardwalk, and they leaned into it, heading towards the battened-down Santa Monica strip, combining their weights against the random buffeting of elements which neither knew nor cared about the existence of two tiny individuals caught inside turbulent patterns they could barely perceive.

<<MODULE ENDS>>

22

NULAPEIRON AD 3423-3426

It was a time of despair; it was a time of tightening resolve.

Two Standard Years passed quickly, though not easily: in planning, drawing together alliances, outmanoeuvring political enemies among the Action Leagues and elsewhere; and in research, as Tom brought the best technicians to his floating home, the kilometre-wide stone sphere once known as Guillaume Globe. From its apex, creamy gases spewed, as it continued its centuries-old terraforming task, one sphere among thousands in Nulapeiron's skies.

Then there was Fire Watch.

In realm after realm, internal surveillance organizations sprang up, often with remits which hid their true machinations from the Liege Lords and Ladies who approved their creation. Some of those Fire Watch bodies kept to the purpose Tom envisaged: watching for signs of the Anomaly. Others were more inclined to function as instruments of repression, quashing commoners' movements for emancipation, tightening the punishments for minor infractions of the law.

Tom's missing left arm hurt as never before.

In all of this, Viscount Trevalkin's motives were unclear to Tom: Trevalkin was a reactionary, but one who hated the original Blight with a vengeance (the one thing that Tom would accept they had in common). Tom's head ached when he tried to track the global state of allegiances and betrayals at any time.

And he missed Elva more than he could say.

From the balcony which ringed the sphere close to the apex, Tom would stare down at the slow-passing landscape: quilted patchworks of heaths and meadows; sere blue-grey desert wastes; the blinding Quick-silver Sea.

On occasion, Eemur's Head ventured out with Tom, lowering her lev-tray to the stone balustrade. **Nice world.** Sometimes Tom could not tell whether a thought was hers or his. **Too bad we don't know how to save it.**

The lev-tray had been Elva's idea, and she had sent it along with Eemur herself.

Meanwhile, in the core levels of the sphere, techs worked on hyper-dimensional research—a prime goal being to decide whether there were detectable resonances that would reveal the Anomaly's presence in the world. Other teams attempted to reassemble the near-destroyed cyborg, the Jack known as Axolon.

Strange visions swam through Tom's nightmares. Increasingly often when he woke, there was blazing sapphire tracery that faded quickly, and was gone.

The Aurineate Grand'aume had been a rich realm; now it was suffering because of its status as Blight-occupied territory during the war. It formed a prime recruiting ground.

One of the people that Tom hired personally was Dr. Xyenquil, the red-haired medic who might or might not have saved Tom's life once, from femtocytic infection.

"I don't know why Axolon rejects the regrow-factors," he told Tom more than once. "It's as if his cells—and they're femto constructs as much as biological—have evolved antibody reactions to Jack technology."

"Or he doesn't *want* to be reconstituted as a killing machine."

Xyenquil would shrug. "I can't argue with that, my Lord."

Couriers sent to the Klivinax Toldrinov were met with blank silence. The guild which manufactured cyborgs had disowned Axolon, or were unwilling to reveal their secrets.

"He's not suicidal," Xyenquil said once. "Axolon has no self-destruct facility . . . Not consciously."

Every tenday or so, instead of running on his laminar flow pad, Tom would clamber over the terraformer's balcony and freeclimb around the outer surface of the sphere, buffeted by winds and always conscious that the slightest mistake would spring him into the void.

These were the times when Tom forgot about political subterfuge, about inferring motives and machinations in realms he would never see, based on a haze of doubtful intelligence.

After one such climb, Tom sat in lotus and slid into deepest logosophical trance, attempting to clarify the global situation in his mind. When his eyes snapped open an hour later, his strategic understanding remained shadowy, but he knew exactly what to do about Axolon, and put the matter to him.

The cyborg agreed.

And was reborn.

The terraformer sphere legally became Axolon Array. It continued to drift among the clouds; but now, on the outer surface, mounted just below the equatorial ring, a cyborg's head looked down upon the landscape, his fibres and metal sinews splayed across the stone surface and rooted in it, linked organically with ancient control systems so that he became a composite being: no longer a Jack, but something new and powerful.

Sometimes, Tom would climb down, perch on the narrowest of windswept ledges close to the cyborg's face, and hold logosophical discussions on the nature of life and death and humankind's purpose in the universe.

On other occasions, they would remain silent, watching the landscape slide slowly past beneath, until it was time for Tom to go back inside.

Spies and counterspies; double and triple agents; measures and coun-termeasures; plans within plans. And in that confusion, Elva came to visit: twice in the first year, once the next, always accompanied by Adam who made sure to bury himself in technical discussions for as much of the time as possible.

It was not supposed to happen this way.

How could Tom ask that Elva love him, when they were never together?

Four times, Thylara arrived by shuttle: ostensibly to discuss alliances with the TauRiders and other clans. Two visits ended with a wild ride in bed when she rode Tom like a bucking arachnasprite and he cried aloud with anguished pleasure when he came.

Then Tom returned to work, feeling dirty and driven, surrounded by holodisplays which mapped cause and effect, allegiance and betrayal, making use of every possible resource save Oracular truecasts to determine the state of Nulapeiron.

Pushing himself ever harder . . .

You will not have my world.

. . . until the day a small flyer marked with the charcoal signs of graser fire, its control surfaces so badly damaged that its survival was a near miracle, docked in a transfer bay near the bottom of the sphere, and the wounded occupant came aboard.

Tom received the man in the polished chamber with the chequered blue-and-white floor where, nearly twelve Standard Years before, the Oracle had died.

"My Lord." Despite his injuries, the man went down on one knee and bowed his head. "I have bad news."

The rest was detail, for in that moment Tom deduced exactly what had occurred, and clearly saw the depths of his own failure, and the helplessness with which he and everyone else faced the future.

Fate help us.

The Anomaly was here.

23

NULAPEIRON AD 3426

It was night and white lightning forked through purple clouds. Tom stood on the balcony, dark cloak whipping in the wind as he stared at the sky and saw only failure.

You're achieving nothing out there, my Lord.

In his fist he clenched a crystal delineating the Anomalous incursions. The worst aspects were all-clear reports from Fire Watch bodies in realms which clearly had been subverted. Whom could he trust?

There were sightings of scarlet-clad human figures appearing from black flames; of metallic beings with flanges and wings and talons; mysterious decrees and repressive military occupation by forces whose officers had eyes like stone and the emotional warmth of reptiles.

Sheets of rain, silver and hard, began to fade, intensity lessening until drizzle remained, then nothing: just flat, preternaturally still air, while in the distance lightning blasted through the cloudbase.

Eye of the storm.

They were in the midst of it.

Soon the violence will rage.

Tom turned and went inside. Around a conference table in the chamber where he had murdered the Oracle, his friends and advisers waited. Xyenquil's frown of concern might be for Tom's health, and Eemur on her floating tray merely glistened with fresh blood, but the others looked fearful, knowing the entire world could fall in days.

And what am I supposed to do?

They were looking up at him, expecting leadership. Tom let out a breath.

Then: "Axolon?" he said.

<Yes, my Lord.>

The voice reverberated all around them.

"Ready a drop-capsule. I'm going down to the surface."

While Tom's security teams were checking the drop-bugs and walking through the logistics, Axolon made a strange announcement: <I think you'll want to see this, my Lord.>

Alone in the conference chamber, Tom looked up from the holodisplay. A breeze drifted in from outside, through the tall opening which led to the view balcony. The sky beyond looked clear. Everything was peaceful.

"See what?"

As Tom spoke, a small shape glided into the chamber—*intruder!*—and Tom was going for his graser pistol when he realized that this what Axolon meant. In a combat crouch, though he could not recall having pushed the chair back, Tom stopped and waited.

It was a glassbird, and it circled the chamber once while producing a high, piercing cry. Then it swooped down towards the table—Tom gestured quickly, and the holo image winked out—and came to a scraping halt.

<I've scanned it. There is no danger.>

Tom nodded without speaking.

Then the glassbird opened its polished beak and recited in a singsong voice: "*We should meet my Lord: one psychopath to another.*"

"Trevalkin," growled Tom.

"*I suggest a rendezvous in Realm Buchanan. You'll find the coordinates in this bird's heart.*"

It was a recording, no more. As the words ended, the bird tilted its head, and regarded Tom with an eyeless stare for several moments. Then its body began to shiver.

What the Chaos could you want?

The glassbird melted and slopped apart into a pool of thick, viscous sludge upon the tabletop. In the middle of the liquefied remains, a small hard crystal shone.

There were seven-sided columns; high-groined ceiling; naves and alcoves: all stippled with strange white-and-bronze illumination cast by spike-encrusted glowclusters. Their sculpted, intricate forms concealed micrograser arrays, ready to be turned upon the populace at the Liege Lord's command.

The chancery contained some seventeen or eighteen shaven-headed commoners at prayer. Pale pink smoke drifted from a thurible, and caught in Tom's throat.

Where are you, Trevalkin?

The followers of the Finite Computational Path had split from the Church of the Incompressible Algorithm in a schism that remained bitter (though unbloody), stemming from minor differences of interpretation. A preacher was declaiming on their holy mission, and Tom strove to look interested while casting glances in all directions.

It was five hours since the glassbird had come to a programmed suicidal end in Tom's conference chamber.

Now, militiamen were walking past. Their uniforms were silver and green, suggesting a festive spirit at odds with their stone expressions and purely functional graser rifles. Realm Buchanan's reputation had always been that of a friendly, tolerant realm, open to outsiders.

Tom's thumb ring was wrapped in nul-gel and concealed inside his belt. A ruby ID stud in his left ear proclaimed his merchant trader status: a cover that gave him freedom of movement.

He was not alone here in Realm Buchanan. Doria Megsin, Academy-trained like Tom, led one support team of six paramilitaries dressed as civilians; they were a klick away from this position. Her lieutenant, Grax Tegoral, led Team Beta, also in mufti; he was keeping an eye on a fallback escape route. Doria and Grax were security officers (based in Axolon Array) whose advice Tom had finally taken. They would not let him go in alone, unsupported and with a suicide implant; they wanted to keep him alive.

So where the Chaos are you, Trevalkin?

Tom backed away from the praying folk—some were penitents, lying face-down on the cold stone floor—and spotted a purple hanging which led to a small shop containing crystals and sacred statuettes.

He slipped inside, nodded to the shaven-headed youth who tended the shop, then checked the wire racks. Tom allowed his gaze to slip unfocused over a sequence of Laksheesh epics: they looked fascinating, but fluency in the language was inconsistent with his cover.

Instead, Tom picked up a locket which, when pressed, displayed the current ruler's family tree (using a patrilineal line) back to the first Earl, with a sidenote about a Terran called Sean Buchanan, proto-logosopher and twenty-first-century "direct ancestor."

"Five minims, good sir," murmured the youth.

Tom shook his head, hiding a smile. Forty generations back, *assuming no interbreeding*, meant a million million "direct ancestors" alive at that time, which was impossible (as well as ridiculous: any one ancestor would account for a minute fraction of inherited genome). Since Terra had never supported that many inhabitants, the assumption was wrong: the entire human race is inbred. There has never been a genetic basis for aristocracy; can never be, since the ancestral genes are scattered throughout the populace.

"Three minims," Tom offered, in keeping with his cover: a trader always negotiates.

Glumly, the youth nodded in agreement.

Tucking the locket inside his belt, Tom left via a second exit, and found himself in a clean, well-kept tunnel. He walked past trestles loaded with goods; behind them, the vendors stood patiently.

Got to be here somewhere.

Then Tom was standing beneath an archway soft with moss, between walls in which reptilian heads were graser-etched. In front of him, floating lev-steps led to a balcony where people sat. One of them was lean and composed.

Trevalkin.

His hair and clothes were different, but Tom recognized him immediately. Nerves tightening with the possibility of betrayal, Tom climbed the steps slowly. Silver leaning-frames rather than chairs ringed each table. Tom took a table far from Trevalkin's, and muttered his order to the house system.

On the wall, orange fastsnails slid, whistling their eerie mating songs. Some diners reached out to the trails of hallucinogenic slime, dipped their fingertips and sucked them.

Tom's daistral arrived and he drank it quickly. As he finished, Trevalkin was already rising. After counting to fifty (in Laksheesh), Tom followed.

Puffs of sporemist rose above mossy boulders, metamorphosed from grey to apricot, then drifted off. Iridescent green patches flowed across the corridor walls.

Below the landing on which Tom and Trevalkin stood, silver-foamed water swirled in a decorative pool. In the mossgarden beyond, a lone mother grabbed her toddler by the arm, looked fearfully up at Tom, then half-ran from the garden, was gone.

The gardens were deserted.

Treachery?

Then three men appeared, walking in unnatural synchrony among the soft moss-covered boulders. At their throats, bright scarlet cravats were strangely luminous in the pale light.

Absorbed.

Tom had seen their kind before . . .

Trevalkin tugged at his sleeve, and they slipped out of sight.

After walking along an empty tunnel, they reached a public thorough-fare where quiet crowds were moving. They blended in, and Trevalkin leaned close to Tom, keeping his voice low.

"Memetic engineers among the colonists," murmured Trevalkin, "created a society where even lowborns could ascend to the highest ranks."

For a moment, Tom thought Trevalkin must have access to the old Pilots' tales. Then he reconsidered, and muttered: "What are you talking about?"

"Only that you're the proof, Corcorigan, that one who receives all the benefits can turn out to be an ungrateful snot."

"*What?*"

An argument was developing between them, but there were mili-tiamen up ahead, so Tom quelled his anger. He and Trevalkin kept their heads bent forward, and walked on quietly.

Suddenly, off to their left, the air seemed to waver and darken, and then black flames were burning, becoming a whirlpool of ink and shadow. Tom was frozen. The Blight's other name had been Dark Fire, and the Anomaly must manifest itself in similar—

Trevalkin pulled him onwards.

The creature which moved out of the darkness was formed of metal: black iron talons and bronze flanges, and razor-edged predator wings. It seemed too heavy to fly, but it lifted into the air and sailed quickly over people's heads, heading for an exit corridor, then passed silently out of sight.

No-one among the passers-by even blinked. Their stares were fixed ahead as they went about their business.

Trevalkin. What have you got us into?

The general population was not fully Absorbed; but the people were no longer normal, either. Just walking among them was risky. Still they continued, with Trevalkin leading the way onto a wide concourse; and here the atmosphere lightened, though the environment was thronged with people.

"I prefer this place," Tom murmured.

Trevalkin nodded, then stepped onto a spiral ramp. It did not flow as expected—perhaps the occupying Anomaly considered such capabilities frivolous—so they walked up in the plebeian way, into a square-edged tunnel where people seemed normal. Most were headed in the same direction; Tom and Trevalkin tagged along.

"You tried to provoke me deliberately, Trevalkin. Why?"

"To keep your emotional focus. We can't stay here for long without being affected."

As the tunnel narrowed, pedestrians were forced to walk more tightly packed together, so Tom could not ask Trevalkin to explain fully. Was there some general hypnotic malaise surrounding them, trying to infect them?

Then, as they passed through an archway, Tom heard two burly tradesmen talking.

"I'm a bit bloody old," said one, "for going to the bloody circus."

"S'posed to be great," replied his friend. "You'll bleedin' love it."

Tom looked at Trevalkin, whose mouth twitched in the suggestion of a grin.

They came out into a thirteen-sided piazza where festive bells were chiming, passed beneath floating streamers announcing a holiday, and joined the slow-moving crowds. On raised platforms to either side, bands of mummers were performing masques and oddly solemn skits at which no-one laughed.

Jugglers and sword-dancers drilled their routines, the clash of blades and showers of orange sparks sounding in counterpoint to the love-poets' murmurs. People stood aside as a group of pilgrims crossed the piazza, crawling on their stomachs instead of walking. They were either very holy or insane, Tom thought, but their discipline was admirable.

Freemen and women were wearing orange and yellow armbands around their sleeves, brightening up the drab browns and greys of tunics and robes. Trevalkin and Tom had tuned their cloaks to a lesser sheen as they walked; still, they looked like travelling traders rather than local folk.

While Tom's poignard remained sticky-tagged at the small of his back and out of sight, Trevalkin wore long bodkins, as he had in Realm V'Delikona, enclosed in obvious forearm sheaths. The style offered interesting possibilities in augmenting forearm strikes and facilitating cross-draw attacks from unusual angles, but Tom did not approve.

"Never use a weapon to intimidate," Maestro da Silva had taught Tom. *"You'll get killed while waving it around, by someone who's more direct than you are."* In phi2dao, a weapon was drawn in order to kill, preferably without the enemy's having seen it.

Even so, Trevalkin's blades should have been a warning to thieves. It was a surprise when a hand came snaking out of the crowd towards Trevalkin's belt, then froze. Tom and Trevalkin both stared directly at the miscreant's face: it was a girl, aged thirteen SY or even less. Then the girl broke away and merged back into the swirl of passers-by, surely unaware how close she had come to being skewered.

Trevalkin's right hand was upon his left forearm, ready to draw and throw.

"No," said Tom.

"I can hit her from here. She's in my sight."

"*No.*"

"Too late, now. She's gone."

Blade-throwing is mostly for show; only a tiny percentage of knife-fighters have ever been able to work the techniques in the messy reality of combat. Trevalkin had a certain sadistic flamboyancy, but his goals were realistic and deadly.

So where's he leading me now?

Then Trevalkin was handing cred-slivers to a vendor in return for two piezo-wafer tokens. When Tom accepted his token, it shone holo tigers and dragons: mythical beasts from the distant past.

The crowd flowed through a portal into a heptagonal auditorium with rough stone benches. Tom and Trevalkin descended to the middle tiers where they took their seats, one either side of a sloping aisle.

At the rear of the stage lay a stone block, pushed into the shadows, bearing discolorations the colour of old rust which made Tom's face tighten in understanding. But these were relics of other, less festive occasions.

A child nearby asked his father for a drink, and the fresh innocence and simple demand cheered Tom a little.

"Me, too," murmured Tom. "Can I have a drink?"

"Only if you behave yourself," said Trevalkin, surprising Tom.

Before the sweetmead vendors with their racks of squeeze-bulbs could reach the cheaper seats, cymbals clashed and streamers of light curled through the air as glowclusters dimmed. People sat upright, their voices fading to murmurs.

The show began.

Cartwheels. Spectacular jumping kicks. Steel whips and glass blades which moaned through the air and left gleaming tracks delineating dangerous trajectories. Monomolecular edges cut dangerously close to skin.

Two female warriors, clad in orange like the male fighting-monks, whipped their swords so close to each other that fine wisps of dark hair floated to the stage.

Tom watched in awe. He saw exactly the meaning of each move, knowing the limitations as well as the athletic qualities of what he was seeing. Choreographed combat fails to deal with the Chaos-laden truth of actual conflict; without seeing the monks under those conditions, he could not tell whether they were trained to adapt.

It was the second time Tom had seen such a wu shu demonstration. On the first occasion, he had been at the Ragged School, soft and unschooled in any physical discipline, and simply awed by the spectacle without understanding what he saw. That was when he had met Zhao-ji's uncle, and learned a little of his austere family history as part of a secret society whose history reached back through the centuries.

"Chaos," muttered Trevalkin, at the spectacle of a seventy-SY-old monk lowering himself into splits.

That'll be me some day.

It was the best Tom could hope for. At that moment he remembered the dream of his own death, the dream which had visited him only once, two Standard Years before. Tom shivered as memory swirled like cold fog: *Winds beneath a lemon sky, mu-space vessels dripping fire reflected from the rising sun, before shadows press in from all sides and squeeze the universe from existence.*

Tom brought his attention back to the moment. A full-scale battle, carefully arranged, was taking place on stage, but Trevalkin was rising from his seat. He began to climb up towards the auditorium's rear, and after a moment, Tom followed.

At the rear, a short corridor led to the men's toilet chambers. Trevalkin was standing in the main chamber's centre, alone. "The contact's not here." Stress tightened his voice. "I think we should—"

Grasers spat through the air outside. The electric sound froze Tom, as beams lanced through the auditorium. It was a second before someone screamed.

"Chaos!"

A wave of coldness pulsed through the air. Tom did not need to look out into the auditorium to know what was happening. Great metallic winged shapes were forming amid rotating black flames as the audience faced the sudden realization that their quotidian lives had ended, not just for the duration of an hour's entertainment but for ever.

Then a panel at the chamber's rear liquefied and both Tom and Trevalkin spun, crouching, blades at the ready. The man who poked his head inside was orange-clad and shaven-headed, a Zhongguo Ren monk who said: "Hurry, please," and ducked back out of sight.

Without hesitation, Trevalkin tucked down and rolled through the permeable membrane. Tom gave him half a second before following.

They were on their knees in a half-lit duct while the panel vitrified in place, leaving no sign of their passage. Already, the monk was crawling quickly but silently ahead of them, leaving Trevalkin and Tom to do likewise or stay and die.

They stopped at an intersection of crawlspaces, and Trevalkin hunched over on one side, tapping his finger-ring until an intricate schematic holo hung in the gloomy air.

"The red points"—Trevalkin made a gesture, and the indicated highlights flared brighter—"are my support team. Where are yours?"

"We agreed," said Tom, "to come alone."

"And . . . ?"

"Here. I've a team here." Tom's fingertips flickered as he amended the holo. "The backup is here."

"My people will make contact. What's the parole and counter-sign?"

Tom stared at him for a long moment, then decided this was a time for trust, and told Trevalkin the greeting/response code.

And if I've just betrayed them, you die first, Trevalkin.

Trevalkin merely nodded and turned to the monk: "I fear the

Amber Tigers may be impossible to reach now. If you journey with me, I can put in a good word with the Strontium Dragons."

Even in the cramped space, there was an uncanny serenity in the monk's bow.

"My thanks, sir," the monk said. "The Strontium Dragons are an honourable society. However"—glancing into the shadows—"when I'm sure that you are safe, I must return to help my brothers."

"No-one's safe," said Trevalkin, as a pale shape approached along the shaft, slowing rapidly. "But here's our transport."

It was a cylindrical maint-drone whose natural habitat was the crawlspaces and access shafts of this stratum. The carapace cracked open.

Tom's teeth rattled together and he clung on with eyes squeezed almost shut, tense-chested and taking minimal breaths as he bounced inside the drone. They swung through another crazy turning, and Trevalkin let out an insane laugh as they accelerated into a long dry duct.

Buffeted by stone topography and the drone's unheeding speed, Tom's thoughts were with the nameless monk whose uncompromising honour had not allowed him to abandon his brothers.

Fate be with you, my friend.

The drone was slowing.

I hope you take down many of your enemies before the end.

Then they were scraping to a halt, blood-rush in Tom's ears, and he realized he was half-deafened from the Chaotic ride. He rubbed his face, hard.

The shaft wall was softening, glowing.

"It's not a trap," said Trevalkin.

"What choice do I have, either way?"

Tom rolled sideways, through the softening membrane and into chill pure air, and fell to hand and knees on a polished quartz floor.

Behind him, Trevalkin crawled through the membranous panel, his face caked with sooty grime and heavy sweat.

"Why are you looking at me, Corcorigan? Wait till you find a mirrorfield."

"Right." Tom wiped at his face and his hand came away black. He looked up. "And who are *they?*"

A group of nondescript men and women was approaching. Only their lean, relaxed bodies and watchful eyes gave them away as more than civilians.

"My people." Trevalkin nodded to a bearded man. "He'll look after you." And, to the team: "This is Lord Corcorigan. His safety is your top priority."

"Sir. This way, please."

One by one, they stepped through a solid-looking arras, a tapestry depicting the Founding Lords' first Convocation, and found themselves in a darkened, dank tunnel which smelled like rotting rags. Pale-blue handheld beacons shimmered, grew brighter.

"It might be better if we ran."

24
NULAPEIRON AD 3426

It was a raw cavern with long, pale vehicles whose like Tom had never seen, hanging by tendrils among bulky stalactites; but it was the people who drew his attention. His own teams, headed by Doria Megsin and Grax Tegoral, were standing in a loose arc, their expressions tense, facing more of Trevalkin's people. Their hands hovered near sticky-tagged weapons.

Tom's agents had formed a protective shield around a cowering family who swallowed continually and could not look at the men and women who threatened them.

"Witnesses, by the look of it," said Trevalkin.

"The kind of people we're trying to save." Tom dug cred-slivers from his belt and crossed to the family group. "Stand up." It was the thin-faced woman who looked most composed, so he gave the cred-slivers to her while pretending to address the husband: "If you have relatives you can stay with, go there. Leave the demesne if you can. Right now."

"Thank you, sir."

The woman took her husband's arm, and the family of six slunk away, while Doria moved to stand between the retreating figures and Trevalkin's agents.

Trevalkin looked up at the hanging vehicles, then down at Tom.

"My people are more valuable than the dubious gain of eliminating witnesses. And we don't have the time."

"So you're not sending anyone after that family." It was not a question.

"No, we're getting out of here. This minute."

Tom sat between Trevalkin and Doria on a bench-seat at the rear bulk-head, while before him the two pilots readied their phase-space displays. The control cabin was like that of an arachnargos, but the vehicle itself—

"Ready to go, sir."

"Then do so." Trevalkin's voice was flat, eyelids flickering as he scrolled through tactical displays only he could see. "Quick as you can."

"Sir."

Acceleration hammered Tom back into his seat, then banged him against Doria as they swerved through a tight arc before speeding up again. Through the forward view-membrane Tom watched rockface rushing past, chiaroscuro-play of light and shadow as they swung sideways over a wide vertical shaft filled with ink-solid darkness . . . and paused.

For a moment, they hung above the abyss.

Then dropped.

They fell headfirst. A gossamer, ghostly sheet grew closer, filled the shaft, and then they were through the membrane. The other vehicles kept formation as they fell. What interested Tom was a small rear-view display which showed the shaft's tattered protective membrane re-forming: there would be nothing left to betray the vehicles' passage.

Such membranes were designed to shriek in alarm when penetrated, and to deliver massive doses of hydrofluoric acid from glass arteries. This vehicle's ability to subvert the membrane was impressive; so was the quiet professionalism of its crew.

"Hold tight." Trevalkin sounded almost amused. "This is where it gets interesting."

They plunged into black water.

"Nether Ocean," Trevalkin added. "We're in our element now."

Streamers of bioluminescence hung in the surrounding darkness, playing their ghostly light across the small submerged fleet. Then, one by one, each vessel unfurled great flexible wings like manta-rays. Their finer sensory tendrils remained, testing the environment, while the greater manipulative tendrils pulled back into the central bodies.

"Mantargoi." Tom stared at the displays. "We're in a mantargos."

Then one of the pilots turned, and her face was familiar.

"First time, my Lord?"

"Feltima." The hurtling manoeuvres before hitting the ocean had been familiar. "I should have guessed."

The fleet swam on with movements which seemed clear and graceful but cut through the darkness of Nether Ocean with surprising speed.

"So, Trevalkin. What next?"

"You'll see. The voyage will take some time."

"What are we going to talk about? Childhood reminiscences?"

"Ah . . . My parents knew I was different," said Trevalkin, "when a Palace servitor found me vivisecting neko-kittens."

Tom grew cold.

"Only people," he said to Trevalkin, "deserve to be tortured to death. *Some* people."

Trevalkin smiled, and pitched his voice towards Feltima, now busy at the controls.

"See? My Lord Corcorigan and I have so much in common." His long features grew serious. "And I've done you a favour, Corcorigan. The terraformer log-records no longer look the way they were."

It took a moment for Tom to parse the information from Trevalkin's words.

"You mean Axolon Array no longer exists, officially?"

"Oh, it exists. It's just not the particular sphere you live in, is all.

It's one of the other seventeen thousand or so floating around up there. Until such time as the enemy can take down *every* sphere, your place is safe."

"For that, my thanks."

"But for the rest, we're still enemies? You're priceless, Corcorigan. You really are."

Then Trevalkin leaned back in his seat, crossed his arms and closed his eyes, and appeared to sink instantly into carefree sleep.

Hours later, they were travelling deeper than Tom had thought possible, far below the Ultimum Stratum of any demesne he had visited. Those black waters knew nothing of the tiny fragile interlopers whose bodies would be crushed to pulp in seconds should the hulls fail.

"So, Corcorigan. How do we defeat the Anomaly?"

Tom shook his head. "We need Avernon. No-one else has the expertise to—"

"He doesn't know how to defeat the thing."

"What?" Tom stared at Trevalkin. "He *is* working for you."

For some time, Tom had been trying to locate Avernon. Even Avernon's sister Renata claimed to have no knowledge of his location or current work.

"For all the good it's done. 'You can't fight something as big as that,' Avernon says. It's what he believes, and he's never going to achieve a thing in that state of mind."

Tom looked away. Outside, along the ocean floor, startling lambent orange glowed inside a long fault: molten magma, cooling where it impinged on cool waters, spewing gouts of smoke-like steam.

"If you had a small infestation of strange bacteria . . ." Tom began slowly, "or maybe fungi in your realm . . . what would you do?"

"Eradicate it, of course."

"What if it was located in some tiny, out-of-the-way shaft, which was closed off by rockfall and quite inaccessible. Then what?"

Trevalkin slowly smiled. "I *might* leave it alone, if it's not worth the bother."

"To the Anomaly, I don't think we're of any more importance than that. If we could shield the world from its influence, that might be enough."

"A *shield* . . ."

"And no," said Tom, "I don't know how to build such a thing. But I know what to aim for."

He remembered his conversation with Eemur, after she had hauled him back from his traumatic trip to the hellworld.

The way is blocked. I cannot reach Siganth again.

"*Fate. Blocked by the Anomaly? Because it knows I was there?*"

It knows somebody traversed the Calabi-Yau geodesics.

If the Anomaly could block the crawlspace beneath the universe . . . perhaps humankind could do the same.

"Chaos."

"You disagree, Trevalkin?"

"No, Corcorigan. I think you've finally proved your worth. But there's so little time."

Tom remained silent, unwilling to agree, but seeing nothing in the shadow ocean outside besides the blank face of predestined defeat.

25

TERRA AD 2165

<<Ro's Children>>

[7]

Aberdeen has always been Seagull City. Flocks of gulls spread across dour granite buildings draped with guano, ignoring the robot freighters nestling at the docks. While other species perished in the hard-bitten winters that followed the Big Chill, the gulls survived. In the century since other oceans warmed and the North Sea convection cell tipped, Arctic conditions had brought coldwater fish and even land animals: the Scottish Highlands were now home to polar bears.

There were other species the Big Chill failed to eradicate: pub landlords and the hardy folk who frequented their premises. Right now, in one such snug establishment, a bulky weatherbeaten man who looked like a lumberjack or fisherman but whose name was Professor Iain McLean was giving Dirk salient advice on local customs.

"The thing to do, laddie, is spot the biggest person in the room, awright?" Then, tapping Dirk's shoulder with one big finger: "And ye shout out: *That great numpty over there is gonna pay for 'em.* Have ye got that now?"

"That's the friendly thing to do, is it?"

"Aye, absolutely. It's a hospitality thing, like the Arabs."

"Hmm." Dirk turned to the young woman who sat between them. "Orla? Does he expect me to believe that?"

"Probably. But, to be fair"—with a sly smile—"you may not be as daft as you look."

"Thanks, I think." Dirk stood up. "Same again?"

"Aye, laddie. You learn fast."

But, as Dirk threaded his way through the babbling crowd towards the bar, his preternatural hearing picked up the words which McLean, leaning close to Orla, whispered: "*Watch who you're making eyes at, sweetheart. Remember what his job's going to be, when his student days are over.*"

Dirk blinked, feeling the contact lenses, as the fun faded from the convivial atmosphere, and left behind regret.

"—to drink?"

"Oh, sorry. Same again."

The barman nodded, his infostrand providing him with the information and directing the pumps to pour.

"You having a good time here, son?"

"Yeah," said Dirk. "Sure I am."

When the drinks came, he carried them back carefully, managing not to spill a drop.

Their aircab skimmed above the ground, throwing up swirls of snow, then settled in a quiet street. Dirk felt giddy as he stepped out into the clear night air, and saw an aurora billowing scarlet near the horizon.

An iron gate clicked open; Orla led the way up narrow steps to a stained-glass door. It, too, opened at her approach, and in a minute all three of them—Dirk, Orla, McLean—were stamping snow from their boots, then pulling them off in the stifling warm narrow hallway.

In his socks, Dirk crept into the cosy sitting-room where Claude Chalou, hands crossed over his stomach, lolled back in an easy-chair, an old-fashioned hardcopy Braille book open on his lap. At his feet, barrel-chested Sam lay; the black retriever opened one dark eye, gave a small twitch of his tail, slipped back into sleep.

Holoflames danced in the fireplace, cast bright reflections across Chalou's silver eye sockets. Dirk turned just as Orla mouthed the question—*Coffee?*—and pointed towards the kitchen. McLean nodded first, then Dirk.

Tiptoeing, they began to leave the room.

"*Et un petit café crème pour moi, chère Orla. S'il te plaît.*"

"Uncle Claude, you old faker."

"The UNSA review board"—Chalou's gravelly voice was full of disapproval—"is tightening its restrictions on matter compiler shipments."

McLean nodded, knowing the blind Pilot (or ex-Pilot) could detect such gestures. True matter compilers, if they ever reached their full potential, would change economic systems for ever. A compiler's owner could create anything from food to a house; they could even build another compiler. But that was in *theory*. Current devices were nowhere near that level, and they consumed vast amounts of energy. If you wanted a building, it was cheaper to grow it, not compile it.

The compilers turned energy into matter, whereas most people found it more useful to make the transformation go the other way: matter into energy.

"You'll still get the Elleston 9000 we talked about," said McLean. "But—"

"*Oui, d'accord.* It would be impossible to hide your tracks if we try again."

"Scanners at every spaceport. SatScan tracking every vessel."

Orla said: "It's a kind of defence, isn't it?" Coffee mug between her hands, sitting cross-legged on the beige rug, she looked up at the others. "Personal weaponry is already obsolete, just because it's always detectable. I'm writing a paper on it."

"Right." McLean put down his coffee, took a sip of the Laphroaig he had poured himself. (The drinks cabinet was well stocked.) "Maser pistols will soon be as outdated as swords and daggers."

Real wars would be fought by smartmiasmas and killmists, at

dimensions invisible to humans. The coordinating generals would be AIs reacting faster than people could think. That was the popular view.

"No-one's going to hand over the reins to machines," said Dirk.

"And the first time an AI applies for membership to a church . . . ?"

"Then we'll have some interesting debates."

"Which side would you be on?"

"I don't think an AI has a soul." Dirk, sitting on the rug near Orla, clasped his knees. "But then, I don't think anybody here does, either." He half-consciously echoed his mother's usual argument in this regard: "Can *anyone* spell 'emergent properties'?"

Chalou's rumbling tones lent his voice a natural gravitas. "I'd fight on the AI's behalf myself."

Dirk tipped his head to one side, seeing reflected flames dance like devils in Chalou's silver eye sockets. "Sir? I thought you insisted on Darwinian processes being sufficient to explain consciousness."

"And linked AIs, if they form an environment where memeplexes like religion can propagate, should have the same rights as us, *n'est-ce pas?*"

"*Ouais, bien sûr.*"

"But then, it is unwise to discount the mystic experience . . ."

"Oh, good." Orla shifted on the floor. "Is it time for ghost stories?"

In the half-lit room where holoflames danced in the fireplace, sitting around in a cosy half-circle with Sam the black retriever curled up at Chalou's feet, it seemed the perfect moment for it. Only the chill winds outside were inaudible, the modern house insulating them from the snowbound winter night.

But, "This is no story," said Chalou. "Every word is true."

Rivulets of energy in a sea of golden light filled with black spiky stars. The seedpoint: an insertion from another continuum. Whorls and loops of energy spiral, tighten, and then replicate.

Selection acts within the pattern. Dendrimers branch, seeking energy: it is perception, and a form of tropism: blindly searching for survival; learning coping strategies; absorbing others of its kind, lesser patterns that are helpless before its burgeoning capabilities.

Call it alive, but not self-aware. Not conscious:

Not yet.

"Such patterns still exist in mu-space," Chalou added in a lighter tone. "Nowadays, we know to avoid them."

"This pattern," said Orla, ignoring Dirk's frown. "What did it do?"

Karyn stares at the black lightning-flash decal on his cheekbone, at his muscular, ugly/attractive face. Dart Mulligan, her sensei's son. Hand in hand, they walk across the green campus, and she feels more alive than she has ever done.

Two weeks, and UNSA surgeons will be removing Dart's eyes.

"What's it like?" They stop beside a silver birch.

As they sit down on the grass, Dart says: "Almost normal. Everything looks a little flat, a little grey, you know? But the viral insertion was only three days ago."

"Another few days"—suddenly Karyn can hardly look at him—"and perspectives will start shifting."

"Yeah. But"—Dart grins, and everything changes back to being exactly right—"you'll still look beautiful, babe."

Orla sensed the change in atmosphere.

"What is it, Dirk?"

"My grandparents." Dirk nodded in Chalou's direction. "He's talking about my grandparents."

"That," said Chalou, "is exactly correct."

It spreads, a fractal web of recursive patterns, hovering on the verge of self-organized criticality. Something new is happening. Through golden space, streamers of scarlet and purple blaze.

A tiny copper form, born of unnaturally smooth geometry, is trapped at the pattern's centre. Offshoots struggle to pierce the event membrane surrounding the intruder.

The vessel manages to loose a buoy into realspace, broadcasting its endlessly repeated message.

*** MAYDAY, MAYDAY. Pilot Dart Mulligan requesting aid . . . MAYDAY, MAYDAY. ***

In mu-space, the pattern brings all its attention to bear.

"It was his maiden voyage." Chalou shook his head. "His only voyage. And yet, he will always be remembered."

I ought to leave.

Dirk tensed his legs, ready to stand; but something kept him in place, to hear more of a tale garnered only in fragments from his mother.

They lead her in darkness—only the cool air, with a hinted scent of distant mesquite, tells her that this is true night, not just the endless dark: it is a full day since they removed her eyes—to a waiting TDV. A short drive, breeze tugging at her hair, takes her across the runway.

Then strong hands guide her to a lift-chair, and she is hoisted up, then lowered through the dorsal opening, into her vessel's control cabin. Fibres click into her eye sockets. A faint mist of mathematical spaces, of shadowy geometries, lies just beyond sight.

It takes two more days of lying there, while the diagnostics run and technicians adjust and monitor, before phase-spaces billow in her awareness, and someone touches her shoulder.

"Ready to fly, ma'am."

"All that wheeling and dealing at UNSA." An ironic smile creases Chalou's hard face. "Not to mention blackmail. Karyn got what she wanted: a ship, and the means to extricate her trapped lover, or so everyone thought."

"*Merde.*" Dirk had not meant to interrupt.

"*Exactement.* She was already pregnant when the cortical rewiring commenced. The medics should not have performed the viral insertion . . . unless someone had ordered them to. Now, we'll never know for sure."

"But Grandmother knew she was pregnant when she entered mu-space."

Chalou's voice was grave.

"Yes, my young friend. That much is certainly true."

Scarlet-analogue flashes across Karyn's non-vision as proximity sensors blare: **Destination achieved.** *In golden mu-space, his ship still shines bronze.*

++ COME IN, DART. COME IN. ++

Bronze, impaled by fractally branching tendrils of scarlet and purple lightning: they coruscate across the hull's event membrane, beginning to bore through.

KARYN? IS THAT YOU, BABE?

++ DART! ++

If she had eyes, she would have wept.

Karyn has hurtled through mu-space as fast as possible . . . from Dart's point of view. In the counterintuitive relativity of fractal spacetime, her voyage has lasted thirty-three subjective weeks.

There is a stirring in her womb.

I DON'T WANT YOU HERE.

++ TOUGH. I'VE COME A LONG WAY. ++

She brings her enhanced field generators online. The event membrane shivers.

Black light pulses across their conjoined vessels: the tiny silver form of Karyn's ship, the massive bronze of Dart's. The ships bond, interface. It will need both their efforts to throw off the energy pattern.

JESUS CHRIST!

Inside her Pilot's cocoon, Karyn laughs.

The infoflow has been fast and deep; he has seen all her internal status-fields. He knows she is pregnant.

YOU SHOULD HAVE TOLD ME.

Scarlet tendrils brighten, tighten around both hulls. Questing: not blindly, but algorithmically driven. Shifting frequencies, searching for pseudo-quantum tunnelling across the event-membrane barrier.

IT'S NOT GOING TO LET ME GO.

Boring deeper.

++ THE HELL IT ISN'T. ++

Lightning gathering, tendrils flaring with energy.

KARYN. YOU HAVE TO LET GO.

++ NO CHANCE. ++

Glowing figures, highlighted: Dart pinpoints the intensity manifolds and sends the data back to her. Intensifying . . .

A contraction ripples through her.

KARYN. ARE YOU ALL RIGHT?

Their ships are **very** *closely interfaced: he senses everything.*

++ TOO EARLY, DAMN IT. IT'S TOO EARLY! ++

Op-codes stream through her input buffers. What do they—?

Dart has control.

I LOVE YOU, KARYN.

Waves oscillate across the black field.

++ DART, NO. I—I LOVE YOU, TOO. ++

Datastreams freeze.

Event membranes pull apart.

LOOK AFTER OUR DAUGHTER. I—

Separation.

Dart's vessel explodes into a million fragments. As Karyn triggers reinsertion she glimpses a cloud of sparkling bronze motes, and then it is gone.

Black cold realspace slams into being.

Orla took hold of Dirk's hand, then glared up at Chalou, at McLean, as though daring them to say she should not touch him.

"It was a long time ago," said Dirk.

But he continued to clasp her hand.

Realspace. Drifting.

Too soon. *The baby should have waited.*

Her ship's systems were never designed to help a pregnant woman give birth. Sensors trained on her swollen womb, where the baby is pushing her organs away from their ordinary location, reveal the problem: Karyn's daughter-to-be is sideways on to the cervical opening, and no amount of painful muscular pushing will allow a normal birth.

With Karyn's mind raving from pain, it is impossible for her to track her position among the stars, or to decide how many light-years she might be from the nearest surgeon capable of delivering by Caesarean section.

Crisis . . .

There is only one thing which comes to mind, and then it is happening. Internal robot arms pull cocooning material back from Karyn's abdomen, and then she screams as the lasers bite through skin and muscle, an explosion of heat and pain.

Before her consciousness disintegrates, the robot arms' co-processors complete the intended action, gently lift the struggling baby from her opened womb: a baby with eyes of glistening jet.

She will be named Dorothy, after the astrophysicist on watch at Metronome Station on far orbit around the pulsar known as Delta Cephei. That Dorothy will hear the beacon broadcast, the pre-recorded message as well as the realtime audio of a newborn baby's wailing, and direct a retrieval shuttle to find mother and daughter.

Of course, with a teenager's wilfulness, the girl will later refuse to be known by any other name than Ro, though Pilots will refer to her as Admiral.

"But that's not really a ghost story," said Orla.

"Does it matter?" McLean took a swig of whisky, and blinked. "I was riveted."

"How"—Dirk stopped, swallowed—"how does it end?"

"Well, the official records show that mu-space voyages rarely ended in mysterious disappearances after that date. You could put it down to experience, and techniques of avoiding any patterns that might be waiting."

"Or . . ."

"Or," said Chalou, "I can tell you what happened when my ship was caught in a geodesic maelstrom, and I was minutes away from death."

On the floor, Sam picked up his ears and softly growled.

"I think he's heard this one." McLean raised his glass in mock toast. "Sorry. Go on."

"It sucked my vessel in, beginning a sliding chaotic trajectory which would last literally for ever, and I fought for as long as I could but in the end I relinquished all system control and just . . ."

"Just what, Uncle Claude?"

"I prayed. Aloud, on open channel."

"Oh, God." Dirk turned away.

"Perhaps. Or something very like Him. At any rate, a strange band of stillness passed across the maelstrom and carried my ship to safety."

"Just a freak—"

"And a feeling of calmness and warm amusement settled over me. As if a benign presence was watching out on my behalf."

"Sounds like pure relief, Uncle Claude. Emotional reaction."

"Except that a geodesic maelstrom never behaves like that . . . Unless you broadcast a prayer to Dart."

You prayed to my grandfather? My dead grandfather?

It was a concept Dirk could not quite connect to reality.

"The thing is, Orla"—Chalou smiled—"that is the only ghost story I know. But every single word is true."

Holoflames flickered in the grate, though nothing burned.

Dirk stood with Orla in the kitchen, while a small machine labelled *Plasmonic Barista* flash-heated lattes.

"You grew up in a convent?" asked Orla, pretending not to notice the drinks were ready.

"Sort of. It was fun, but . . . It left me a bit institutionalized, I think. Mother always makes fun of the Holy Rollerettes."

"And she's away most of the time. Your mother, I mean."

"Yeah, but . . . She's an awful lot more fun than most older folk, y'know? What about your—?"

"My parents died. Uncle Claude helped raise me after the—Afterwards."

"Is that why he retired?"

"Part of it. But he no longer had the reflexes, apparently . . . It's not fair!"

The sudden depth of feeling surprised Dirk.

"What isn't fair?"

"Here, he's just another old blind man, right? But in mu-space . . ."

Her voice trailed off.

In mu-space, he was a fearless explorer who communed with a god.

If you believed in that sort of thing.

"Orla, I think your uncle is a—"

But Orla's hands were on Dirk's shoulders, and she was raising her lips to his, and her kiss was a soft explosion of sweetness which pushed aside old tales and misery, a soaring promise of an elated future where things could never fall apart, grow old or die.

<<MODULE ENDS>>

26

NULAPEIRON AD 3426

Tom was surprised to see asymmetric forms loom in the darkness: buildings constructed on the ocean floor. A comma-shaped building, softly luminescent, grew large as Feltima directed the mantargos towards a wide membrane.

If the Anomaly manifests itself here, there'll be no escape.

Anywhere else, there was at least the faintest chance of running. But at the bottom of Nether Ocean there was nowhere to go.

"Gently now," Feltima murmured, and her co-pilot nodded.

Then they were through the membrane and surfacing in a docking-bay pool, floating flat-winged. On the ceiling above them, graser batteries swung to bear.

"Just precautions." Trevalkin made a control gesture, and the control cabin's ceiling furled open. He called out: "It's only us."

There was no response from whatever system or human being controlled the weapons. The dock itself extruded a nest of tendrils. One of them elongated, extended itself to the mantargos, dipped inside and wrapped itself around Trevalkin's waist.

"See you in a moment," he told Tom.

The tendril lifted him across the pool, deposited him on the platform and released him.

At least he's *safe.*

It begged the question of what these people intended to do to the renegade Lord Corcorigan in their midst. Was the Anomaly his only enemy now?

Elva. I ought to be with Elva.

If these were the final days—

A tendril plucked Tom from the cabin, and hauled him up into the air. It placed him down gently beside Trevalkin. Then more tendrils lowered, reaching into the mantargos for the remaining passengers.

All of them, Tom and Trevalkin and Doria and Grax and their operatives, assembled before a bank of drop-tubes. Then the whole party descended together to a waiting antechamber, where a solitary grey-uniformed soldier bowed in salute.

"Welcome back, sir."

"Good to be here," said Trevalkin.

"The . . . emissary will be here shortly."

Doria and Grax took up opposing flanks, guarding Tom: a small gesture in the midst of another organization's stronghold. Whether that organization was an ally or an enemy remained to be seen.

"Safe." Trevalkin looked around at the solid walls. "Thank Fate."

Grax laughed shortly.

"Does that mean," said Trevalkin, "that you don't believe we're—? Ah, welcome, honoured sir."

A modest lev-chair slid slowly through a door-membrane. On the chair sat a pale, drawn man of Zhongguo Ren ancestry. His moustache was long and narrow.

"Zhao-ji!"

"Hey, Tom. How's life?"

A subtle palsy kept up a constant shaking of Zhao-ji's bony left hand.

"It's called Oracle's Dreams, old chum." Zhao-ji had seen what Tom was looking at. "If you're exposed, however hard you fight . . . eventually, it gets you."

"Fate." Tom remembered the flash of sapphire he had glimpsed earlier at Zhao-ji's wrist.

Years before, when they were both at school, their friend Kreevil had been convicted of theft. They had visited Kreevil once—and only once—after he had begun his sentence.

Inside a vast chamber filled with fluorescing blue fluid, strange shadows had been clumped. The convicts moved slowly in the fluid, breathing it and subsisting on it, their bodies linked by tendrils to the unknown shadowy forms.

At the time, Tom and Zhao-ji had been frightened off by the custodians of that place; but it came to Tom now that Zhao-ji had touched Kreevil, and been burned—or chilled—by that blue glowing stuff. Had it been working strange changes on him all these years? Another thing: why was it the exact same hue that Tom associated with Oracles and Seers?

"Kreevil must be dead by now." Zhao-ji spoke with a stone-cold finality that chilled Tom. He had known just what Tom was thinking.

And how long do you *have to live, old friend?*

Zhao-ji's dark eyes were giving nothing more away. Behind him, through the still-softened membranous door, shadowy outlines were visible: 49s, footsoldiers of the Strontium Dragons who would sell their lives—hard—to ensure Zhao-ji's safety.

These aren't our schooldays any more.

Around the oval conference table, three small groups sat. Doria had made sure that her and Grax's team members were being cared for, in a comfortable chamber equipped with food and drink and couches. Now Doria took the seat on Tom's left, while Grax sat on the right.

Zhao-ji, in his lev-chair, positioned himself beside another Strontium Dragon officer. This other man was no mere footsoldier. Nevertheless, his elbow-length sleeves revealed white hairless forearms that were bulbous with muscle; and dark oval calluses covered his swollen knuckles.

Zhao-ji introduced him only as Lao.

Tom bowed to Lao and said: "We are honoured to have a Red Rod in our presence. And my old friend has surely advanced to *pak tsz sin*, White Paper Fan. Perhaps I do not go too far in suggesting he might someday be considered worthy of *heung chu* status?"

There might have been amusement in Zhao-ji's eyes when he answered: "My Lord Corcorigan does me too much credit."

Lao, the Red Rod, *might* have been quietly impressed. Though his rank was Zhao-ji's equal, he was still an enforcer, with little hope of further advancement; but a White Fan was an Incense Master in waiting, and that was powerful indeed.

At least I know one party we're negotiating with.

As for the other group: Trevalkin sat with Feltima on his left, and she bore herself with a watchfulness that suggested she was more than just an arachnargos (or mantargos) pilot. An unnamed man dressed in grey sat on Trevalkin's right.

Did Zhao-ji speak only for the Strontium Dragons, or for allied Zhongguo Ren secret societies as well? Was Trevalkin representative of all the reactionary Action Leagues, or just his own small group of associates?

And was this a negotiation? With what goals?

The Anomaly is in our world, and we're not even talking yet . . .

Then Feltima made the introductions for her party:

"You all know Viscount Trevalkin, of high standing as a Liege Lord, adviser to the Circulus Fidus, and a prime architect of Fire Watch, begging my Lord Corcorigan's pardon."

Tom inclined his head, conceding the right to argue.

"He is also a member of the Grey Shadows High Command—"

"*What?*" Tom half-stood, hand going to his hip; but his poignard was not there.

"—whose alliance with the former LudusVitae in no way indicates that social revolution is our primary goal."

Trevalkin's smile was cold.

Grey Shadows?

Slowly, Tom sat back down. Grax and Doria had pushed themselves back from the table but not risen.

"*You* want revolution? Equality for all?"

Trevalkin shook his head. "It won't happen in my lifetime. I'll enjoy my privileges while I can, thank you."

The Grey Shadows were an ultra-secretive organization that remained a mystery to Tom. Elva had been raised to their cause, by common-born parents willing to sacrifice their daughters to achieve the Grey Shadows' goals . . . which had *not* been to keep people like Trevalkin in power. (Elva had not been in contact with the organization since the war . . . as far as Tom knew.)

"The thing is," said Feltima, "our objective has always been to guard Nulapeiron from its enemies."

Tom leaned back in his chair.

But the Blight and the Anomaly are the first external *enemies the world has faced.*

These people were representatives of hidden networks of power which had evolved over centuries: networks which had taken on lives of their own, and would cooperate only when threatened, in order to achieve goals unknown to the world at large.

Grax broke the tension, hoisting a daistral jug and a beaker from a tray.

"Does anyone else feel thirsty?"

Some twenty minutes later, they were deep into discussions of communications routes. Over the table hung a web of glowing holographs, arcs and nodes brightening as indicated whenever someone made a point. Analyses appeared and disappeared in briefly blossoming subsidiary tesseracts: a morass of confusing and conflicting details.

Doria was amending Feltima's model of compromised Fire Watch cut-outs—trying to work out which realms' Fire Watch contacts could be trusted, and which ones had already been subsumed by the Anomaly— when something shifted and clicked in Tom's mind. In an instant, some internal barrier fell down inside him, and he knew that everything he was doing was wrong: not just this meeting . . . everything.

Tom pushed himself back from the conference table.

Maintain solidarity.

It is a primary rule of negotiation in teams: never betray a difference of attitude within the group, for it denotes a weakness, a fault line which an experienced opponent will crack open.

Elva. I need you here with me.

Not just as a former Grey Shadows operative, but as a tactician in her own right, Elva would laugh at the notion of negotiations without defined objectives.

I thought I was protecting you.

Tom had failed. Elva was in Realm Strelsthorm (the former Demesne d'Ovraison) and he was in this place; and they were likely to die apart, never seeing each other again before their universe ended.

I'm a fool.

"—Lord? You don't agree?"

"Sorry, Feltima, I . . . It doesn't matter."

Tom rose to his feet, feeling dizzy.

This is the moment.

Everything was spinning away from him, from everyone, in a world which might fall to the Anomaly in days. *Win or lose.* None of this talk was helping. *Right now. This has to change.* Tom took a deep breath and looked around the table, locked eyes with each person in turn, including Doria and Grax. Including Trevalkin.

Do it.

"This is not working," he said.

"What do you mean, Corcorigan?"

"Misdirection and obfuscation and unfocused goals and crossed purposes. *None of it helps.* This is an alliance of confusion."

Feltima rocked back in her seat.

Someone gestured the holodisplays out of existence.

"Everyone here," Tom said, "knows the mechanics of phase transitions. It's like heating a block of ice: it shifts into the liquid state just like"—snapping his thumb—"*that*. Given a critical mass of people Absorbed into the Anomaly, the effects will cascade through the world in a matter of days, maybe *hours*. Does anybody disagree?"

The others sat as though punched in the stomach.

None of them, not even Trevalkin, had a reply. They had been acting as though they were planning a long campaign; but time had already run out.

"That being the case," Tom continued, "I am assuming command of this alliance. Right now."

There were widened eyes, audible intakes of breath.

"You will need to discuss this. I'm going to leave the chamber for ten minutes, so I suggest you decide quickly."

Tom's cape swirled as he turned away, and strode from the chamber with his heart beating hard, a paradoxical cold heat flooding through his body, experiencing the joy and fear of risking everything for a cause which he knew, finally and for sure, was right.

For Elva.

He stopped outside in a long chill corridor whose transparent panels looked out into the deep: into black waters where strange luminous predators swam.

For everyone.

Ten minutes later, Tom re-entered the conference chamber. He was half-expecting Chaos and shouting. Instead, the atmosphere was silent, but charged with adrenaline. Fear and anger pulsed in the air.

"We can't say yes or no," said Trevalkin.

"Then I suggest you—"

"Because it's not our choice. There is someone else"—Trevalkin's features were unreadable—"you have to see. Alone."

"No." Doria was standing. "My Lord Corcorigan travels nowhere without—"

"It's all right." Tom looked at Trevalkin. "This time, we trust each other, or nothing can save us."

Trevalkin stared back, then nodded.

"Fate help us all," he said.

27

NULAPEIRON AD 3426

Tom travelled almost alone, in a slugtrain which slid surprisingly fast through utilitarian tunnels fashioned beneath the ocean floor. For a while, Tom stood at the rear carriage's end panel, looking out at the slime trail which glistened then faded.

He returned to his side-facing bench seat, and sat down opposite a blue-robed man whose white hair had been teased into short spikes. Tom looked up. Droplets of moisture beaded the carriage ceiling.

"Just condensation, my son." The man was a priest. "We're safe from the ocean overhead, Fate willing."

"Thank you," said Tom.

The small priest pulled out a holobreviary, and bent forward, muttering prayers.

As the train entered a series of switchbacks, Tom clutched his armrest. The priest continued his orison without pause, swaying in his seat. Then the train straightened out, and Tom became aware that the air was warmer than it had been, almost stifling.

He leaned back and closed his eyes.

As the carriage rocked, Tom slipped into a dream.

It is a long, concave-walled laboratory furnished in black and dark grey where strange shapes swirl: peripheral, subliminal . . . Not quite there.

The chamber is—and yet is not—one that Tom knows: located deep in the interior of Axolon Array. It is a lab where the best researchers Tom could recruit work hard to decipher time's true nature. Yet this place is subtly different, distorted . . . Just how, Tom cannot tell.

He stands on the solid jet floor, and the air is sharp in his lungs. At the same time he is disembodied, incorporeal. Tom cannot move; yet he feels calm and liberated.

In the chamber's centre, blue lightning dances. It tears the air apart but the electric dance of energy does not stop. One moment, it sounds like a tsunami crashing upon a shattered shore; the next, the sound is a gentle shush of white noise and distant breakers.

It is cold. It is hot.

Sweat springs out upon Tom's skin. Or perhaps he is not here at—

Sapphire lightning.

At the centre of the chamber, a floating figure screams. The trapped Pilot? But that was on the hellworld known as—

No.

The figure is Tom Corcorigan.

Not me.

The floating man waves his arms in supplication—his two arms—and then the blue fire grows brighter and the world lurches—splits—this Tom waves his one *arm—yelling out his agony to anyone there—but the Tom who observes is frozen by the knowledge that this suffering is self-inflicted. This Tom had two arms, but severed one.*

A trial of pain.

By which he will regain Elva and defeat the—

No.

None of it makes sense.

His eyelids half-opened, to the bright swaying carriage and the nodding priest who muttered, "Auguries like the tide," amid the overpowering warmth.

Sleep welcomed him back.

As Tom Corcorigan watches, the split occurs.

Time without time, attoseconds or aeons, the duration of an electron jump or a red giant's birth and death . . . He suffers, the Tom who is trapped, for an unknown time, until a brilliant nova-burst, electric blue, whose flash obscures the laboratory.

When it has passed, a figure lies at the foot of the wall, and groans. Slowly, as a disembodied Tom watches, the bruised Tom Corcorigan pulls himself to his feet.

"I guess it worked."

The Tom who observes aches to speak: Are you addressing me?

"I guess it did."

The voice comes from behind—no!—then another *Tom Corcorigan faces the one who looked in pain. They wear identical cloaks, each with a whitemetal poignard tagged at the hip.*

"The one nearer the drop-exit—"

"—gets Elva. That'll be me. And you—"

"—will see another universe."

"Destiny go with you, my brother."

"Destiny."

The two Tom Corcorigans leave by different exits, each heading towards his own Fate, tricking the Destiny which thought just one path could occur.

Is that what I must do? *the Tom who observes can only wonder.* Do I harness the trick of parallel time?

A scraping sound brings all his senses whirling round to bear on one spot: a shadowed alcove behind a buttress.

"I wonder why," says the third Tom Corcorigan (not counting the one who observes), "everyone assumes a bilateral *symmetry. Even me."*

The smile which twists his face is lupine: a predator with prey in sight.

What? There's always another alternative?

The new Tom, too, gathers his cloak around himself, checks his weapons, walks from the lab chamber, is gone.

And the dreamer who observes . . .

. . . finally woke up.

What have I just seen?

In an empty carriage.

Bulky, blue-skinned figures were waiting at the landing platform. They were fighting Kobolds, kin to the greystone warriors, likewise melding flesh and living stone so deeply that a simple boundary could no longer be drawn. Oil-slick light slid across their hardened craggy forms as they snapped to attention.

"Where's the . . . ?" Tom hitched his cloak tighter against the chill which swept across the platform, and looked back at the slugtrain. "There was an old priest aboard with me. Where is he now?"

The officer appeared to speak into his clenched stone fist. Then: "There was no-one else aboard. The train has made no stops since picking you up."

"I don't—" Tom shook his head. "It doesn't matter."

Strange eyes regarded him. Tom remembered the myth: that Kobolds could submerge themselves inside solid rock, move through it as if through viscous water.

"Welcome to Surturheim, Lord Corcorigan."

Beneath Tom, the platform glowed orange, started to melt. He began to sink.

"Where am I—?"

"To see the Lady."

The Kobolds made a strange gesture of respect, fists to forehead, then disappeared from sight as Tom sank into glowing ooze.

Surturheim?

And continued to descend.

28

TERRA AD 2166

<<Ro's Children>>

[8]

The final draft of Deirdre's dissertation was entitled "Sequencing the Memome," and it owed nothing to UNSA funding or Rand-Miti intervention. Her wit shone clearly, even through the academic language, and Kian chuckled as he read the final chapter, his infopad's display bright enough to read beneath the morning sun.

They sat at their usual outdoor table on the Athenaeum Café patio. The Caltech campus stretched away to one side. Deirdre, clutching a tall iced latte, vibrated with anxiety. After the blaze of creative energy in which she had written, a deep uncertainty enveloped her.

"Yes," murmured Kian, reading. "I like that."

Beside their table, the olive tree's dark leaves rustled in a short-lived breeze, grew still. A bush with downturned violet flowers cast a subtle scent on the hot, clean air.

"You like it?"

"Come off it, Deirdre. It's marvellous, and you know it."

She shrugged, sipped her latte, then gave a tiny smile.

"I *thought* it was, when I started. But now—"

"Now you've only got to sit and wait for job offers to come flooding in."

"Job offers?"

"Every faculty in the world will want you on board." Kian raised his iced tea in salute. "And I can't blame 'em."

He drank a toast, and Deirdre blushed.

"You need to publish it as a popular science book. You have to—"

A shadow fell across them: a slim man standing in the sunlight.

"You've finished the dissertation." It was Nikolos Vlessides, who was working on a master's in plant design. "Already."

Kian waved him to a vacant chair. "And it's amazing."

"Amazingly good"—Nikolos's variable English could be surprisingly colloquial—"or amazingly bad?"

Deirdre rattled off a curse in rapid Greek.

"My mother," said Nikolos, "is not inclined like that."

Kian shook his head.

"You can be a real moron, Nick. What do you want to drink?"

"A real espresso would be nice."

"But you'll make do with what they serve here, right?"

Kian placed the order using the table's microphone; less than a minute later, a dog-sized robot came whirring across the patio. Nikolos removed his cup and saucer from its back.

"You know . . ." Nikolos gestured at the olive tree. "This reminds me of home. Very much." He reached across and picked up Deirdre's infopad. "And this looks like one of my plants' root systems." He highlighted the fractal diagram of propaganda channels. "How you say . . . *Apeiron?*"

"Boundless." Deirdre grinned. "Like the poet: 'To see a World in a Grain of Sand / And a Heaven in a Wild Flower—'"

"'Hold Infinity in the palm of your hand,'" said Kian, "'And Eternity in an hour . . .' Or Hamlet: 'I could be bounded in a nutshell yet count myself the king of infinite space, were it not that I have bad dreams.'"

Deirdre took the infopad from Nikolos's hands. She tapped it, and the text of *Auguries of Innocence* hung above the table.

"See here? 'The Babe that weeps the Rod beneath / Writes Revenge in realms of Death.' In Will Blake's time, 'beneath' must have rhymed with 'Death.' Isn't that great? Makes you wonder what our speech would sound like to a TwenCener. Y'know, to a Victorian gentleman, 'civilization' was pronounced in English just like the Français."

Kian grinned.

"You *are* brilliant."

Nikolos nodded solemnly. "One smart cookie, Deirdre Dullaghan."

"Come on," said Kian when Nikolos had gone. "Let's grab boards and find some waves."

Deirdre started to shake her head, then stopped.

"All right. But you drive."

The ancient car was hers, but the onboard AI was bug-ridden—it had a recurring fixation for Anchorage, Alaska, and occasionally spun in circles until someone hit the override—and she considered manual driving a chore, not a pleasure.

"Deal."

Twenty minutes later they were at the beach, removing their boards from the back seat. They trudged across hot powdery sand.

"That," said Kian, looking back, "is a very buggy buggy."

"Jesus. Give me peace."

"Well . . ." A breaker crashed. "Surf's up, dudette."

"Race you, dude."

They caught a tube, and rode it pure. Yelling with fear and pride, they crouched beneath a curling glass-like wave, borrowed its power, cutting the gradients.

Afterwards, they sat on floating boards, watching the sun splash orange and crimson across the sky as it neared the horizon. The night grew cool.

"The sea engenders life, tugged by the moon. Always."

"Poetic, Deirdre Dullaghan. Very poetic."

"I'd like to know what's wrong, though."

Gentle wavelets lapped around them.

"'Sequencing the Memome' is bloody perfect."

"I doubt it. But that's not what I'm talking about."

Kian sat silently on his bobbing board.

"Come on, Kian. I've been self-absorbed, but I'm still on the planet. What is it?"

"I'm . . . I'm scared."

"Jesus. Scared of what?"

"You know Dirk's arriving tomorrow? Well, we're going on to PhoenixCentral together."

"The spaceport."

"Well, what other—? Yeah. Right. For a kind of, um, fitting session."

"For a suit?"

Kian splashed water in Deirdre's direction; but in the fading light his face was serious, not playful.

"For a ship."

Borges Hills had been a residential area before Hot Strike Sunday. Now it was a fused plain on which JLB Shuttle Port stood like a glass confection gleaming in the sun. Every Sunday night, when there were few passengers to be disconcerted by rapid morphing, the architecture reconfigured itself; afterwards, it remained static for another week.

The car's AI attempted to argue with the parking garage, but the greater system won and forced the car into the designated slot. Kian and Deirdre walked away while the microwave buzz of machine communication continued.

They passed through skin-tingling scans, were carried by pedistrip along a maze of glass corridors, and reached the sun-drenched Arrivals concourse three minutes early. Kian stopped beside a weeping, embracing family group.

"Dirk's here."

Deirdre tapped her infostrand. "Landed early. How did you—?"

"That way."

They were at the gateway some thirty seconds before Dirk came into view, grinning broadly, and strode towards his brother. They hugged tightly.

"Bro."

"Good to see ya."

After a minute: "Meet Deirdre."

"Heard all about ya." Dirk shook her hand.

"Shit. I was hoping to make a good impression."

Kian clapped his brother's shoulder and grinned at Deirdre. "Too late for that."

They left with Kian carrying Dirk's bag, passing near a coffee booth where a pale young blonde woman, dressed in a grey suit, watched them walk by.

"I think," said Kian as they reached the exit corridor, "she was looking at me."

"She fancied *one* of us, for sure." Dirk glanced back. "But I could've sworn—"

"Jeez, you guys." Deirdre shook her head. "What makes you think she wasn't falling in love with me?"

"Er . . ."

"No reason."

They stepped onto a vacant pedistrip.

"Right. That must've been—"

"—what she was—"

"—up to. Absolutely."

"Absolutely."

The strip beneath their feet slid into motion.

<<MODULE ENDS>>

29

NULAPEIRON AD 3426

Orange pillars of flame rotated in the hall, forming twin lines receding down a wide aisle of clean-lined blue-grey stone. The hall was cathedral-like, designed to intimidate.

Tom finished shutting down the story in which he had been immersed—having for the first time learned the origin of his world's name—and stepped further into the long hall. Then he shivered.

Were there figures dancing, trapped inside those flames? The closer Tom drew, the harder it was to see inside the hot, bright conflagration.

Perhaps flickering fingers reached out as he continued past; perhaps they did not. Tom was both chilled and sweating by the time he reached the hall's far end, and stood before a hardened membrane wall. Behind him, the flame-pillars crackled.

"Why the Chaos doesn't—?"

Off to one side, a patch of wall began to glisten. Head down, Tom pushed his way through the softening membrane before it fully liquefied.

He came into what could only be a prison cell, with a captive who turned at Tom's entrance and jumped back. The man's hair was white and cropped short, his jaw square; his blocky body had lost weight. His face was lined in a way Tom had not seen before.

"Sentinel. Is that you?"

"*Tom!* Oh . . . They've got you as well."

"No, they—"

Tom's voice trailed off.

Perhaps they have *got me.*

It occurred to Tom that he was here because he trusted Trevalkin, of all people; and this was Sentinel, whom Tom knew only by his code-name: once a senior officer in LudusVitae, later serving in the intelligence service attached to Corduven's Academy. For an outsider, it was hard to tell where Sentinel's core loyalty was situated . . . but then, the same might be thought of Tom.

Sentinel sat down on a soft dark-grey cubic block (which blended into the rest of the cell: the furniture and walls were matching monochrome). "Five tendays, I've been here. Maybe more." There was a tremble in Sentinel's voice that was very different from before.

"What happened, my friend?"

That was a misnomer, for their relationship had always been professional, edged with mistrust. But Tom needed *information*, so he sat on the edge of Sentinel's bunk, facing him, matching body language to establish rapport: legs splayed in the same fashion, hand on knee to mirror the position of Sentinel's left hand.

It was basic psych manipulation and the Sentinel that Tom had known would never have fallen for it; but Tom had already sensed that Sentinel was different now.

"Infiltrating an Action League got me here. I found that another organization had already penetrated them, and when I followed *that* trail . . ." Sentinel blinked away tears. "They lace my food, I think. Not with logotropes, but . . . something else. Or perhaps it's just the . . ."

Sentinel gestured at the blank walls, the rank hole in one corner of the floor, the wall-mounted spigot above it.

"Fate," said Tom. "I'm sorry. I don't know if I've any influence in this place."

Sentinel scowled. "You're not a prisoner?"

"I don't know."

"Hmm." A sly look descended on Sentinel's face. "Tell me something only Tom would know."

"I beg your pardon?"

"It's not as if they lack holos in this place. How do I know you're really . . . ?" Sentinel turned his face to the wall, shivering. "I don't know what to believe."

Tom stood up.

"If they let me, I'm going to leave now. Whatever I can do, I will."

The membrane softened at his approach and allowed him through. No thump sounded from behind him. Sentinel no longer had the will to try to batter his way out.

Tom turned left, and continued walking.

Rotating flames, a hushing sound; then a new opening formed in the blue-grey wall. Tom stepped inside, then held himself still as, with a great sucking sound, *the stone flowed* and formed a spherical chamber all around him, sealing off the hall outside.

An oddly liquid squeal sounded. The bubble-like chamber lurched, rotated, and began to slide. The motion continued, as a patch of stone grew partially transparent; outside was a white-orange blaze. Tom realized he was trapped in a floating bubble in a magma sea.

There were white-hot ellipses and hexagonal flukes within the molten rock. Lifeforms, close to the heart of the world.

Darkness gathered as the sphere grew opaque. For a while, it continued to move. Then it scraped to a halt, there was a long pause, and the stone split neatly open. Tom stepped out into a basalt chamber adorned with fractal trees of quartz. Behind him, the stone bubble sealed up.

Here, the air was lilac-scented and cool. The chamber was largely triangular, formed of interlocking slabs. There was detailed knotwork carved at random—or apparently so. Tom took a step back, reappraising, then chuckled: the chamber delineated the inverse of a static tricon, like a mould of the original, which combined the motifs for *Strength* and *Stealth* to form a more complex ideomeme: *Warrior Observing Silently.*

A doorshimmer sparkled, white and silver; then a Lady stepped through.

Destiny.

A Lady formed of living crystal.

A blue cape was draped around her shoulders; the rest of her feminine form stood revealed in flawless diamond perfection. Her voice was a song more than words, beyond sound.

—*You are most welcome in this place, Thomas Corcorigan.*

A tear coalesced in Tom's eye. "I don't deserve to be here."

Microstructures danced with vermilion light inside her, washed with violet and cobalt and fiery scarlet. —*Your form belongs in this place.*

Tom did not understand, but he could not question her. He was in awe. Tom was a child; he was thirty-six Standard Years old.

What happened next he could never clearly recall, for the Lady sang her questions in tones which would melt a statue's heart, and his soul responded without words, honest in its faults, without embarrassment before the purity of her regard. Almost incidentally, he learned—some-how—that Sentinel would be cared for until it was safe to release him.

Then the Lady was gone.

It took a while for the realization to sink in; then Tom dropped to the flagstones with a whooping sob of regret and pain and old wounds and the dirty, scratching knowledge of unworthiness.

He was sobbing like a child when the Kobolds came to fetch him.

At the platform where the sluglev train stood waiting, the Kobold platoon saluted Tom, fists to foreheads. One-handed, Tom returned his version of the gesture.

"You have allies now"—their officer's bluestone face was craggy, hard with experience—"my Lord Corcorigan. Both Viscount Trevalkin and *pak tsz sin* Zhao-ji will obey your orders. They are already journeying back to their respective bases."

"Yes," said Tom, not questioning how the Kobolds had established this.

"This crystal"—blue, square-ended fingers held out a violet dodecahedron—"allows you to contact the Grey Shadows *in extremis*."

There was a warning in the Kobold's voice, and a question.

"I would die, sooner than betray her." Tom accepted the crystal.

The Kobold warriors bowed.

"Fate go with you, Lord."

Some ten minutes later, Tom was riding the otherwise empty train along deserted tunnels, wondering what had occurred. Had he been dazzled and manipulated? Or had he gained an ally greater than the Grey Shadows or any human organization?

And what kind of being was the Crystal Lady?

It was hard to imagine that she might represent a presence that pre-dated humankind's arrival in this world, or that she somehow reflected the will of Nulapeiron itself.

Destiny. What other hope is there?

Perhaps there was none, besides the ability to stare unflinchingly at overwhelming odds, and the determination never to back down or betray a sign of weakness, in conditions where giving way meant death.

30

NULAPEIRON AD 3426

It should have been the second Corcorigan Demesne. Instead, it was Elva's original family name which designated this place: Realm Strelsthorm.

I shouldn't have waited so long to come here.

As Tom's jade-shelled levanquin passed along luminous halls and broadways, he saw how the populace, both freedfolk and servitors, stared at the strange noble who was visiting them: with curiosity, not fear. That told him all he needed to know about the openness of conditions here. It highlighted one simple joyful fact: the Anomaly held no dominion in the realm where Lady Elva Strelsthorm-Corcorigan ruled.

Masked children chased each other, laughing, across an aqueduct. Bright sashes were draped across millennium-old statues of the Founding Lords. Perched on a high gargoyle, a black neko-feline gazed down on Tom and blinked her lazy oceanic eyes.

As Tom's floating levanquin passed into an Outer Court, two squadrons of Chevaliers sprang to attention, then bowed. Tom stepped down, and the Chevaliers escorted him on foot to a marble waiting-hall. The hall was adorned with woven platinum drapes and drifting air-plants, which trailed tantalizing scents on their graceful meanderings.

"Her Ladyship is conducting formal audience, my Lord, with Ambassador Lord Khaliran and others. We'll take you straight—"

"I don't think"—Tom looked down at his travel-stained clothes—"I'm dressed for the occasion."

The officer scarcely blinked.

"No problem, sir. Give me a moment."

Ten minutes later, clad only in training-tights, Tom was being fitted for a formal tunic by one Ferdinar Twilbodin, an angular, ebony-skinned alpha servitor, whose twittering and fussing almost concealed the precision with which he executed his craft. "For most, it is the clothes who wear the man. But for you, my Lord, it is most certainly the man who wears the—"

"Yes, all right," said Tom.

"Hmmph. Well, if I might suggest the additional golden pleats—"

Tom frowned.

"—will of course *not* be required. You two"—Ferdinar Twilbodin gestured to a pair of helpers standing by with handheld smartfabric-configuration modules—"will get on with this at once."

The Chevaliers had left, but they had been replaced by Adam Gervicort. Now he stood leaning beneath a holoportrait of the late Chancellor Xalteron (whose ethical calculus still survived, and was taught at the Sorites School). Adam gave a short, ironic laugh.

"Old Ferdie here is the best smartfabric designer around."

"Well thank you, I suppose, Captain Gervicort."

Since Adam had become Realm Strelsthorm's chief of security, he had bulked up a little, but from the gauntness of his face it appeared the additional mass was lean muscle. "Ferdie programmed the Chevaliers' chameleoflage to perfection."

"Shame I couldn't redesign those hideous control-cabin interiors. Simply eyesores . . . Right, good." Ferdinar Twilbodin snapped his fingers, and his two helpers removed sections of fabric which had been draped around Tom. "We'll just be a short while."

Carrying the fabric carefully on their forearms, the assistants left the chamber with Ferdinar Twilbodin, and the exit vitrified behind them. Tom picked up his old and somewhat shabby tunic, and pulled it on.

"There was a man just like Ferdie," said Adam, "in my battalion in Dilvin Secteur. His name was Libron."

Tom nodded. Adam had won his first award for bravery in Dilvin, at the Battle For Kithin Blŵr.

"Libron called us all 'dears,'" Adam continued, "even while he was ranging parashrikes against incoming minemists. Kept us almost laughing, when half our men were dying there."

Adam had known of Corduven's proclivities. Did he think that Tom and Corduven were other than just friends?

"Is there a point to this?"

"After the war was over, I tried to track Libron down. He was a minor Lord-sans-Demesne, and his family had been apprised of his, er, off-duty wartime activities."

"Fate."

"Right. They found Libron hanging from a gargoyle. Used his dress-uniform's lanyard just to make the point."

There was an edge to Adam's tone, which made Tom ask: "Why are you telling me this?"

"Permission to speak freely? I hate to see the bravest warrior I know being betrayed by the person who ought to care for her the most."

Obviously he was referring to Elva. Tom had seen the way that Adam looked at her.

There was nothing Tom could say.

"I . . ." Adam shook his head. "I've an ordnance inventory to complete. Sorry . . . Tom."

Tom could only nod. His stomach felt sour.

At least someone knows the meaning of loyalty.

"I'll see you later, Adam."

"Yes, I . . . Yes, of course."

Drapes of opulent vermilion furled back as Tom approached the Receiving Court. Servitors bowed deeply. Tom ignored them, walked through the small knot of freeborn suppliants waiting for an audience—they drew apart to either side—and brushed past an ambassadorial entourage.

One of the ambassador's bodyguards, a hulking housecarl with a black spade beard, appeared about to step in Tom's way. Then the carl stopped, looked closely, and gave a tiny nod of respectful acknowledgement which had nothing to do with Tom's noble-house status.

Well met, my brother berserker.

Elva, in her raised throne of quartz and parafur, sat very still. Then she stood up, throwing aside her white surcoat to reveal a plain grey jumpsuit without insignia, and half-ran down the steps to meet Tom.

"My Lord."

Tom took hold of her left hand, pressed it against his chest. "My Lady."

Her grey eyes held no accusation, merely love tempered with a hint of caution.

In the official visiting entourage, the ambassador—whose name Tom had forgotten—executed a courtly bow. "Perhaps Lady Strelsthorm needs a private meeting at this time."

At that, a majordomo clapped his hands and announced: "The audience will be postponed until tomorr—"

"For two hours," said Elva.

"—until Sunbloom Hour today. Thank you, my Ladies and my Lords, and good freepersons all."

There was one freedman near the back who began to mumble; he was quickly hushed by those who surrounded him. Among the others, solemn faces mixed with smiles as they left, staring back at the one-armed Lord who had interrupted their audience.

In three minutes, the chamber contained only Tom and Elva, and a cage full of fluttering blindmoths whose odd fluting music formed a fitting accompaniment to the Corcorigans' fiery hot kiss.

The universe lurched back into its rightful position.

Later, he said: "I spent some time with a strange Lady recently."

Cradled against him on the quartz throne, Elva tensed.

Expecting betrayal?

Tom swallowed, then: "She was all of crystal. Do you know who I'm talking about?"

"Fate." Elva drew back. "You met *her?*"

"Yes . . . It was some kind of miracle. But if you want to know what we discussed, I can't tell you. It's like a . . . dream."

Elva blinked, and Tom knew she was reviewing conversations stored in her perfect memory: remarks her parents might have made when Elva was young; hints her superior officers dropped when she was a Grey Shadows operative.

"That's consistent," Elva said after a while. "Some people have been known to break down after such a meeting. That's part of the reason why it—she—is considered a myth."

"What, or who, is she really?"

"Shh." Elva's finger pressed against his lips. "Only you can determine that."

She slid her fingertip down his chest and reached his stomach. Something liquid and vulnerable, like a pool disturbed by deep movement, shifted in her eyes.

"Isn't it time I met the ambassador?" murmured Tom.

"He can wait."

Lord Khaliran was dark-skinned and very thin, and his clasped fingers were like spiders' legs as he considered his opening remarks. Aides sat on either side of him, facing Tom and Elva across a conference table formed of diamond.

"Svadini-ihm-Kaltrin Gestalt," he said, using the collective name for four large realms which formed a significant federation, "is concerned by the lack of Fire Watch reports around our borders."

A tactical display hovered near Elva, but she did not need to look at it: the disposition of Enemy forces was in her mind, and she would not forget.

"Conversely," Lord Khaliran continued, "we have suspiciously rosy descriptions of life in Realm Tangori and Hilkin Demesne. These are reports which cannot possibly be true."

Tom gestured, rotating the display. Too many hotspots bloomed around the sector's edges.

"In one sense," he said, "the reports are probably correct. It was one of the signs, when I was in the Aurineate Grand'aume during the occupation. Normal crime dropped to zero. It was the *lack* of disruption, the inability to raise a dissenting voice . . . There was just something in the air that told you immediately something wasn't right."

Tom's deputy had been Tyentro, hot-headed and aggressive, but a good man to have beside one in a crisis. Tom wished Tyentro had survived.

"I fear, Lord Corcorigan, we will be requiring advice on setting up resistance groups very shortly. Any assistance you can give on optimal communication channels and operative training, that sort of thing . . . would be very welcome."

Tom noted the yellowish tinge to Lord Khaliran's eyes, the sagging skin beneath.

"How long," he asked gently, "did it take you to travel here?"

"Two days. I could not be sure of Fialangin Fault: it's an easy place to ambush. We took a roundabout route."

Tom understood the trembling weariness which lurked behind

Lord Khaliran's every gesture. "You think your own realm might already have fallen."

"Or been infiltrated. How does it start? My daughters . . . No matter. A whole sector is at stake. More than that."

"They matter," said Elva. "Everybody matters."

"As for how it starts"—Tom stared into his own dark memories—"no-one knows how the Anomaly works. Does a mental influence reach through spacetime, Absorbing victims? Or does the Anomaly first manifest itself, transporting some of its component entities into place?"

Tom's stomach rumbled, and something sour moved inside him.

"Excuse me." He stood up. "I'll be back in just a minute."

"My Lord."

Elva was already opening up a network diagram showing resistance cells and how they might communicate. "You'll notice in this holo that the internode coupling varies according to—"

Tom stepped through the nearest membrane door, and froze.

There's something odd here.

Guards came to attention.

"Relax," Tom said. "Um, can you show me where the ablutions chamber is?"

"My Lord." One of the guards gestured and the opposite wall liquefied. "The nobles' facilities are down the corridor, but . . . just through there, is where *we* go. If you're, er, in a hurry—"

Ah. A door there. Right there. That's right. I remember . . .

"This is fine," said Tom. "Thanks, my friend."

Five minutes later, Tom was cleansing his face and hand with wood-scented smartgel. As he scraped it off, it crept back into its pewter container, leaving him feeling fresh. A mirrorfield shimmered into existence, allowing him to check that his tunic was in order, his half-cape hanging straight.

Then Tom noticed that there was another way out of this place, a door directly opposite the way he came in, and he knew that he should step through it.

Elva can handle things.

Maybe it was a subconscious desire to see more of the realm his true love had made her own. Perhaps Tom could not bear, for the moment, to return and see Lord Khaliran's strained fatigue as he worried about his daughters' Fate. There had been too many families split up by—

A hand outstretched on a flagstone, cold and unmoving.

Then Tom shook his head and the image was gone.

They're dead. Khaliran's daughters are dead.

Tom could not know that. How could he? Yet . . . he was certain, as he walked through the membrane, that the young women had fought back, choosing to die rather than to be Absorbed.

What am I doing here?

In front of Tom, an iron grille set in a circular opening swung back, revealing steps formed of alternating green and blue minerals. They led down to a piazza paved with chequered quartz and lucite blocks, where a small group of fit-looking men and women had congregated at the centre. They drew Tom's attention: all dressed similarly (though not identically) in dark, sober, functional clothes.

Other people were moving around, rushing on business, buying minrasta cakes from a floating vend-stall—this place must lie beyond the Palace proper—but the dark-clothed group was different.

Elva's people?

There was a conspiratorial closeness to the way they stood, but not overtly so. Something was bothering Tom . . .

A tingling spread across his neck, rose up between his shoulder blades.

Down in the piazza the group was breaking up, splitting away in ones and twos into the crowd, making their way to exit corridors, while the lean young man who was the leader turned and—

Sweet Fate no.

—revealed, in one easy athletic movement, the abbreviated left sleeve which depended from his left shoulder.

Then he was striding fast towards the widest exit.

Who are you?

Was gone.

By the time Tom recovered enough mental equilibrium to move, there was no point in trying to follow the one-armed man. Besides, it was irrational. The pure coincidence of someone whose Fate had been hard and similar to Tom's own . . . was no reason for pursuit or confrontation.

And yet, and yet . . .

He was their leader.

It looked so very much like a clandestine cell. Not of the Absorbed. Maybe not even an intelligence organization. It just felt like—

Tom shook his head.

I don't know what it felt like.

As he retraced his steps, with the iron grille swinging shut behind him, weird thoughts and odd emotions twisted inside Tom's mind. What had impelled him to visit this place, at just the right moment to catch that unsettling glimpse of someone so like himself? And why did it seem so familiar, when he had never been in this realm before?

It doesn't matter.

Elva looked up and smiled as Tom entered the conference chamber; and everything was perfect.

31

NULAPEIRON AD 3426

They made love and slept and made love again, and in the morning, Tom and Elva went shopping; but there was more to the walkabout than procuring a few goods. Elva, as Liege Lady of this realm, could have ordered her servitors to acquire anything she wanted; strictly, no-one could force her to pay within her own borders.

As they passed through airy arcades and trading halls on the Secundum Stratum directly below the Palace, Elva exchanged greetings with merchants and ordinary freedfolk, all the while gauging the mood of her populace. It was something Tom should have done, back in his brief period of rule in Corcorigan Demesne. Yet he had always felt uncomfortable with old manipulative techniques which reinforced the status quo.

Some revolutionary I am.

Tom had wanted individuals to be free, not treated as chattels. Now they were to be Absorbed into a vast entity which would consider them to be no more than microscopic cells among the trillions which formed its distributed self.

"I'm going to visit the armoury." Elva touched his arm. "Why don't you head down to the Tertium Stratum? Ginvol and Arkin can accompany you."

Elva made a subtle head movement, and two Halberdiers in civilian clothes came out of the crowd and stood before her.

"Downstratum?" said Tom.

"There's a place called Voort's Warren. I don't know how many dramacrystals they have in stock, but it's a vast number. Thousands."

"Ah." Tom smiled.

There's no time for frivolity.

Yet this was what made people human: the small, civilized things.

And there's no danger imminent.

Tom was growing to trust his instincts, and in any case he knew that Elva needed time to think about how they were going to conjoin their forces, and where they were going to live. He nodded to the two Halberdiers. "Show me the way—"

Yes. This is right.

"—and I'll try not to stay browsing too long."

Elva smiled. "You'll bore them rigid, but that's all right."

The Halberdier called Ginvol gave a discreet bow. "The floor hatch is this way, my—"

Tom was already headed in the right direction, as if he were intimately familiar with this realm, though this was his first time here. He found his way among the trading hall's pillars and aisles with a certainty whose origin he could not have named.

Two hours of browsing musty racks in low-ceilinged chambers lit by mutated crimson fluorofungus: that was Tom's idea of a good time. As he paid for the small sack of crystals—the store's owner raising his eyebrows at the breadth of Tom's interests—one of the Halberdiers sighed, then reddened as Tom looked at him.

"Beg your pardon, sir. I didn't mean—"

"No problem. Why don't we go somewhere where we can sit and have some daistral?"

"Er . . ."

The other Halberdier spoke up: "There's a good place nearby. Mad Molly's Meeting Mall, though I don't know who Molly is, or was. Probably died decades back."

Tom looked at the storekeeper, who shrugged. "I don't know who Mad Molly was either," said the man, "but it *is* a good place to eat."

"Well then," said Tom. "That's decided."

There was a bustling energy in Mad Molly's Meeting Mall which Tom enjoyed. Occasionally, faint scents of ganja escaped from membrane-sealed booths at the rear, but airplants quickly swallowed the vapours, cleansing the atmosphere.

Tom sat with Ginvol and Arkin at one corner of the noisy, twenty-sided chamber, while servitrices moved among the tables, taking orders and delivering food. There were no tabletop terminals or house drones here: this was the personal touch.

When the food came, Tom poked at his Mad Molly's Mycoprotein Pie with his blue tine-spoon. Hot pastry crumbled, smelling heavenly.

"Good," he said, noticing that the other two were already tucking in.

Among the clientele were rough-clad runners—couriers whose area of coverage was within the demesne, but covered many strata—who had their own dress code and slang, from the few sentences Tom managed to overhear.

But he was hungry, and it was the pie and vegblock which held most of his attention until one of the runners called out a greeting— "Hello, young Jissie!"—and Tom's mouth turned dry as the tine-spoon slipped from his fingers and clattered against his plate, spilling lumps of pie, though he hardly noticed it.

"Hey, Jissie," said a second runner. "How's it going?"

The girl led a group of dark-clad young toughs, streetwise teenagers who looked older than their years. Jissie grinned back at the runners, raised her forefinger in a victory salute. The boys accompanying her walked with a swagger which would have amused Tom under other circumstances.

No . . .

Silver chains hanging in catenary curves across the youngsters' tunics were not just decoration: they were steel whips sticky-tagged in place, ready to be ripped off and used as weaponry. Still, Tom hoped they were more for show than actual use.

But that was not the realization that drew steel talons down Tom's back.

Instead, as Jissie turned to exchange a greeting with a green-haired female runner, she revealed . . . the sewn-up remnant of a sleeve which covered the stump at her left shoulder.

Elva.

How could Elva allow this in her realm?

After what the tribunal did to me—

Tom was on his feet then, and the girl turned at the movement. When she caught sight of Tom her mouth opened, unable to speak, face growing bone-white as she took a step back.

Then Tom drew his cloak around himself, and brushed between two crowded tables where conversation stopped at his approach. He stalked with icy rage from the eatery, leaving the two Halberdiers to pay the bill, abandoning their half-finished meals.

They caught up with him at the ceiling hatch, as the helical stair's treads slotted into place.

"My Lord. Are you—?"

Fate. Tom slipped on the first step, caught the rail for balance. *What am I going to do?*

The Halberdiers' hands steadied him, then they withdrew quickly, their faces growing blank. If a noble-house Lord had taken offence at their familiarity . . .

Tom was shaking.

"Not your fault," he said, noting the way his voice trembled. "Not your fault. There's no need for *you* to worry."

"Sir?" Ginvol looked concerned. "I'm sorry. I didn't realize she'd be . . . that there'd be someone like her there."

"No." Tom turned back to the stairway.

Behind him, Arkin muttered: "I don't know how they can do that to themselves."

Tom froze, feet rooted to the steps. Slowly, he turned back, and descended to the floor. "To themselves? They do this to *themselves?*"

"Yes, sir." Ginvol swallowed. "It's right across the sector. I'm afraid . . ."

Arkin took a deep breath, swelling his chest.

"Always gang leaders, my Lord. The more hardcore do their own cutting, instead of getting their friends to do it. Young Jissie . . ."

No. Tom's head reeled.

". . . is definitely hardcore. I've known her for years."

Ginvol nodded quickly. "I've heard it's spread to other sectors, too. Not just gangs as such, but any kind of . . ."

He let his voice grow silent.

Tom did not know what expression was on his own face, but Arkin, too, became quiet and took a quick step back when Tom looked at him.

"How long has this been going on?"

The two Halberdiers shrugged, though whether it was ignorance or fear which prevented them from answering, it was impossible to tell.

When Tom reached the Palace core, he found Elva in her training chamber, inside a transparent-walled tank whose constant-convection aerofluid allowed her to swim suspended in one place. She was working hard against the current. As soon as she saw Tom, Elva stopped the flow and hauled herself out, dripping.

"What is it?" She descended the steps, her gymnast's body moving easily, the wet fabric of her costume tight against her skin. "What's wrong?"

"Nothing. You know . . . In Realm V'Delikona, there's a strange propensity for people to group together in fives. It's a deliberately planted meme, an ancient throwback. And then there's fashion in general, which is where memetic engineering really comes from."

"Tom . . . You're worried about the way people *dress?*"

"Sometimes, you get waves of teen suicides. It happens in every culture. All sorts of self-destructive behaviour spontaneously arise, spread through a population and last for years, then just die out. It's always been that way."

"Fate." Elva placed her damp hand against his chest. "What's got into you, my love?"

Tom shook his head.

"They're cutting their own arms off. Did you know that? Because some mental image is growing in their consciousness. Lord One-Arm! But that isn't *me.* Destiny damn it—"

Elva clasped his face between her hands, let out a long breath, and said: "Tom, I love you, but you're wrong in this."

"What—?" Tom started to back away from her, but that clear grey gaze held him. "What are you talking about?"

"You're the man I know, the one who cares about poetry and logosophy. But you *are* Lord One-Arm also. The icon people need to follow now."

"*No* . . ." It came out as a whisper.

"Yes. That's how it has to be."

Tom took hold of her hand, kissed her palm, stepped back. "I can't allow it."

"You can't control it."

"I—"

But whatever his answer might have been, it was drowned out by a klaxon wail which cut through the chamber, accompanied by a sudden ozone charge upon the air. The blood drained from Elva's face.

"*Fate.* It's here. The Anomaly . . ."

Tom spun round, as three Chevaliers ran into the chamber, weapons drawn, and turned away from Tom and Elva, forming a defensive arc to protect their Liege Lady and her husband.

". . . is here."

32

NULAPEIRON AD 3426

It took three hours for Realm Strelsthorm to fall to the Anomaly.

In the outer chambers of Elva's apartment, more Chevaliers took up formation, and in their midst stood someone whose appearance jolted Tom.

"I know you," Tom said to the one-armed girl.

Wide-eyed, she stared back, and said: "Lord One-Arm."

One of the soldiers moved to clamp his hand over her mouth, but Tom stilled him with a raised finger. "You're . . . Jissie, is that right?" When she nodded, he continued: "What are you doing here?"

"We saw 'em. Things with metal-like wings and, and . . ."

"She warned Sergeant Ygralk," said a Chevalier. "Before he stepped into an ambush. Downstratum. Saved his life."

"My gang." The girl, Jissie, blinked. "They're gone."

"Black flames, sir. Ma'am." Another Chevalier made his report. "They appeared in the air, revolving, and creatures of some kind just . . . flew out. Directly below the Palace. Don't sound right, and scan-watch systems ain't confirming, but that's what the witnesses—"

"I don't think, Corporal Druvan," said Elva, "that they're making it up."

"Um . . . No, ma'am. There are *people* appearing too, not just creatures. But some of our own folk are . . . changing."

"Being Absorbed."

There was a distant crack of graser fire, and a high-pitched scream, suddenly cut off.

"Move it." From somewhere, Elva had gained a graser rifle. She ejected the hafnium core, checked its status bar—ninety-five per cent—and snapped it back in. "Druvan and Biltwin, you're point. E-and-E pattern beth-3. Got it?"

"Ma'am."

With hand-signals, she directed the troopers.

"Yes, ma'am," the officers answered.

"Then go."

And the designated team leaders were directing their teams: "*Go-go-go.*"

Time to get out of here.

Choking dust billowed in the corridor outside. From the Chevaliers' collars, protective membranes grew slick and shiny across their faces. They ran crouched, Tom and Elva and the girl Jissie in their midst, heading through the confusion with desperate determination.

Faster now, as the dust cleared, they sprinted along a marble corridor while behind them the rearmost troopers went down on one knee and opened fire, just as a percussive *thump* sounded. The shockwave knocked everybody flat.

Shapes moved in the roiling clouds of dust and floating debris.

"Move it." Elva was standing up alongside Tom, dragging Jissie upright. "Come on."

Grasers spat behind them.

"Right." Druvan pointed. "Go right."

There was a cross-tunnel and the group went right. Three men broke away, digging at their equipment belts, one of them climbing up a toppled statue to reach the ceiling.

"Setting booby-traps," muttered Elva. "Bastards'll get a nice surprise."

If they don't just materialize in front of us.

Tom guessed that the Anomaly could not manifest itself just anywhere: that there were constraints in the geometry of the Calabi-Yau crawlspace beneath ordinary reality.

Graser fire sparked and cracked.

Elva had ordered escape-and-evasion, not stand-and-fight. "We haven't lost them yet," said Tom.

One of the troopers spun around, then collapsed, inert. Dark blood spilled from his nostrils and ears.

"Fate damn it." Elva turned to Druvan. "Are there any lev-bikes *not* in barracks?"

"In the Outer Courts, near the crypto chambers. But the barracks are a lot nearer. We could go down the—"

"What if the Enemy has plans of the Palace?"

"Impossible."

"Not if Ambassador Lord Khaliran was something other than he appeared." Elva hefted her rifle. "And I think he was."

"No, not him." Tom remembered his vision of the ambassador's slain daughters. "One of the aides, maybe."

"Surely not . . ." Elva's eyes blinked rapidly. "Ah, damn it. The one who sat to Khaliran's left. His body language . . . I didn't see it at the time."

As a group, they shifted again into a diagonal corridor, while the sounds of fighting grew louder behind them; but it was simply fiercer, not closer.

"None of us saw it," said Tom. "We didn't know."

But I should have done.

The floor trembled, and half of the Chevaliers tumbled over.

"The Inner Courts," said Druvan.

"Breached from beneath." Tom's gaze met his in sudden under-standing. "*That's* why it manifested downstratum first."

They picked themselves up and broke into a staggering run.

In the Outer Courts it was quieter, and they tumbled onto silver lev-bikes, Tom and Jissie each taking a place behind a Chevalier, while Elva mounted an armoured bike of her own.

They rose like silent hunter bats and skimmed through long brownstone tunnels where they caught glimpses of people running for cover, panicked by the distant screams and bangs. It was tempting to think that fast lev-bikes meant a better chance of getting away, but such reckoning was dangerous.

This was the first phase of escape-and-evasion. Academy training had drilled into Tom the following dictum: that most people get caught because they shift into the second phase too soon. It is point-less to pick up speed if the Enemy knows where you are or can follow your trail or predict your route. They will surround you before you reach reinforcements or a pickup rendezvous.

"Before you evade the bastards"—Tom remembered the rasping voice of his instructor, Lahfti—*"you gotta bleedin' disappear, right?"*

They skimmed down a long ramp, moving fast. Slipstream tugged Jissie's red hair around her face. Tom's own breath was whipped away and his eyes watered as he tried to focus, checking her safety: her small hand was wrapped in the rider's equipment belt. Safe enough.

The chamber flickers.

Tom shook his head. The memory-remnant formed the start of a koan, a Zen paradox learned during his stay in the monastery where monks' zentropes had reacted so very badly with the logotropes in Tom's mind.

The flame is still.

It seemed real, that vision of stone walls and candle and a perspec-tive very different from normal; then a lurch brought Tom back to the moment.

En masse, the bikes hurtled without a sound through a tight banking turn and were flying down a broken slope, heading for a wider cavern system. Tom glanced over. Stamped on young Jissie's features was a fixed mask of determination.

Snowy edelaces drifted high overhead, too disturbed by the lev-bikes' sonar disruption to consider dropping down to hunt.

The lev-bikes slowed, close to the ground.

"Drop Tom here," commanded Elva. "And the girl."

"What are you doing?"

Tom clutched at the rider but the saddle shifted, morphing, and it bucked Tom off. He hit the ground rolling—shale, not great to fall on, but he had experienced worse—and came up to his feet. The girl, Jissie, took the hint and slid off.

Then the entire troop of Chevaliers ascended, their lev-bikes hanging too high up for Tom to leap.

"I need to set a false trail." Elva stared down. "Sorry, my love. But I'm good at this."

"Destiny. I *know* that. But we have to—"

"I'm not abandoning you. Run that way"—Elva pointed into a broken tunnel—"for three klicks. You'll find a docking area. If it's not been compromised, there are submersibles that will get you away."

"No."

"Fate, Tom. I'll *be* there. But we have to make it look as though we've gone another way. The Enemy knows what it's doing . . . So we're going to track wreckage and induction signatures in the conductive-ore deposits in Voelsing Cavernae. It's a false trail, all right?"

"And then you're doubling back."

"Yes. *You* have to go on foot, just in case. But you'd better run, or I'll be there before you. Have you got that, my Lord?"

Tom stared up at her.

"Yes, my Lady. And you know I love you."

"Of course you do. Right." Elva turned to her troopers on the floating bikes. "Ready? With me."

The bikes wheeled overhead, then shot off in formation towards a far tunnel. Tom continued watching even when they were gone from sight.

After a time, Tom felt a tug on his sleeve. A smudged face with wide eyes was looking up at him. "We have to reach the . . . rendezvous."

"Yes, Jissie." Tom squeezed her shoulder. "Yes, we do."

Together, they moved off at a brisk walking pace, heading towards the tumbledown scree which led to a narrow tunnel and perhaps to safety.

Along the way strange visions assaulted Tom, knocking him aside with the force of physical blows. Seconds later, he was unable to recall exactly what he had seen or felt.

What's happening to me?

Tom stumbled.

"I'm sorry . . ." His voice degenerated to a mumble.

He ought to make Jissie go on, but she was young and might not survive alone.

"Lean on me, sir."

There was a kaleidoscopic flash of red and black and sapphire, and Tom fell again.

"Get *up*, my Lord."

Forcing himself to his feet.

It was an age before Tom and Jissie came out at the head of a ramp, and stared down at the docks and the dark confusion which swirled there; and Tom knew they had made the trek in vain.

Refugees thronged the wharf, tens of thousands of people whose lives had shattered in an instant, trying to board a tiny fleet floating on dark-green placid waters beneath raw stone cavern ceilings. There was no possibility that more than a tiny fraction would leave this realm before the Anomaly subsumed the entire populace into its hungry, spreading self.

Too late.

It was like a swarm of glistening, mobile ants: a long dark column stretching down the broken grey stone path which led to the dockside, where a controlled pandemonium reigned. To either side, a dark plinth extended upwards to form a tall pedestal. Atop each one stood a squat, bronze-armoured figure. Suddenly it was obvious why the refugees had not resorted to violence to get aboard the boats.

Jacks.

The two bronze figures were Jacks, each with the firepower of a regiment built into his body, capable of sniffing the air and spectroscopically detecting mood-pheromones or toxins, able to filter out subvocalized thoughts from a babble of noise . . . except that now, the sound was the Chaos-stirred susurration of ten thousand chests breathing, of muttered prayers. There was no shouting; even the children were shocked into silence by the drawn, bloodless masks of their parents' faces.

There were older people in the crowd—here, a frail figure simply sinking to her knees; there, a large man leaning against the rockface, his blotched face soaked with sweat—and Tom wondered how many would even reach the gangplanks.

Mantargoi and other submersibles floated on the waves, using small boats to help the loading process. As Tom watched, one large grey rotund vessel sank down, followed by another.

And how many refugees will other realms accept, Tom wondered, *before they close their borders?*

Then lev-bikcs swooped over the crowd, strong hands reached down to Tom and Jissie, swung them up. They coasted over a myriad heads—upturned faces following their progress with fatalistic jealousy—before alighting on the wharf's edge, in a clear area where platoons of Halberdiers with interlocking mag-shields held back the jostling mob.

Elva was not among the bike riders, but just then her voice called out from inside a small vessel floating at the wharf's edge. Tom helped Jissie climb down, then flicked off his cloak and vaulted down in one easy motion.

Nausea hit him as his feet touched the deck inside the cabin, and he stumbled as kaleidoscope images flashed through his mind. Then he was on his knees, vision clearing. Jissie was nervously scanning the vessel's interior just as the hatch solidified shut overhead.

There was no sign of Elva.

"Elva . . . ?"

Then her disembodied voice said: "*Sorry, my love. I'm a little delayed. What you once called 'salting the ground,' as I recall.*"

"You recall everything perfectly."

"*So I do, darling. So I do.*"

Tom sat back on the soft flooring, leaned against a bulkhead, and tried not to vomit as the vessel lurched into motion.

"What's your . . . situation?" he managed to say.

"*We made contact with the Third Battalion.*" The comm hissed. "*There's a Jack down and—*"

Silence, save for an internal thumping of the vessel's systems.

"Elva!"

Tom coughed.

"*—little delayed. Tom? Are you all right?*"

The visions were closing in again.

Dead man's hand, severed and lifeless amid broken furniture and licking flames.

Tom blinked. There was a drop of fluid on the back of his hand, electric blue and glowing . . .

"No."

. . . which sank away, absorbed into his skin. It left him wondering if there had been anything there besides an artefact of blurred vision and sickness.

Then a vertiginous shift took hold of Tom and *black-and-bronze figures rear their talon-hooked wings whose leading edges carry rows of targeting eyes, and tear liquid bodies asunder with a swipe. They leap aside as more of their kind materialize in the Dark Fire where black flames spread wide and—*

Tom squeezed his eyes shut.

"*Jissie? Look after him until—*"

Shift, and *the screams of children as the Absorbed men with scarlet scarves at their throats move in unnatural synchrony, bringing their grasers to bear.*

"Yes, ma'am. I'll do everything I—"

Then the shards of scenes which surrounded Tom became a blizzard of impressions born of Chaos, fragments of a world under siege, spinning round him like a pack of ravening beasts whose maws were open to devour his sanity while the fetid stench of rotting corpses rose from their throats and overwhelmed him.

When Tom's head cleared, some hours later, the sickness was gone as if it had never clutched his body. Tom felt weak but clean, and he smiled as Jissie fetched him a squeeze-bulb filled with indigoberry daistral.

"Thank you," he said. "I'm feeling much better."

"That's good, my . . ." Jissie, kneeling in front of him, looked down at the deck. "Sir."

"Hey." Tom, still clutching his drink, raised her chin with his forefinger. "Call me Tom, all right?"

"Yes, sir."

Tom let that slide. Instead, he squeezed hot daistral into his mouth where it exploded with sweetness and warmth. It slipped down inside, silk-soft and spreading energy.

"Good. Ah . . . Where are we?"

Jissie gestured towards a small display. They were alone in the humming vessel, which was guided by its onboard AI.

"Close to where my Lady bade the machine go. They'll have a, um"—Jissie glanced at Tom—"an autodoc all ready for you. She said."

"That's good," muttered Tom. "But I'm all better now."

Tricons shifted in the holo. They were travelling along a submerged tributary of the Hypotubule Way, just passing through another realm's border. Sensors indicated neither scanfields nor weaponry to delay their progress.

Tom put aside the empty squeeze-bulb, and lay back against the curved bulkhead. It felt warm, hard against his shoulder blades. His eyelids drooped, opened.

"Sir? Tom . . . ?"

"I'm just tired, but I won't sleep just yet." Tom reached inside his tunic, pulled out the stallion talisman. "Are you interested in historical stories?"

Outside the vessel, black waters which rarely experienced visible light slipped past soundlessly, without revealing the tiny fragile forms that lived and fought and died inside its fluid, nurturing, yet treacherous medium.

33

TERRA AD 2166

<<Ro's Children>>

[9]

Blinding sunlight sparkled from the great glass spheres, the long walkways which angled into the sea or carried holidaymakers between the restaurants and the sightseeing-globes high above the warm, dancing, lapis-lazuli waves.

There was an official name but no-one used it. Gerbil Heaven stretched out across the sea, enabling pastel-dressed tourists to spend time in its submarine restaurants and gift shops, while allowing a few precocious schoolchildren access to study centres where grinning researchers carried out real marine biology.

"Last time I was beneath the sea," murmured Dirk, "it was black and choppy and I thought I was going to die."

"This was with McLean?" said Kian; and, unspoken: *Along with Orla? Smuggling matter-compilers?*

"Right."

With Deirdre, they rode a spherical lift to a high bubble-shaped restaurant where, she assured them, they could take lunch while watching the dolphins play below.

"You're the expert." Kian looked at Dirk. "She's been here at least, well, once before."

"Hey . . . I *thought* about coming back here at Christmas."

"But you didn't."

"It was shut." Deirdre looked from one twin to the other. "Is it true that people can't tell you apart?"

"Well of—"

"—course they—"

"—can't."

Deirdre stepped right back, staring hard. "Thicker neck, heavy shoulders . . . Narrower features, lean . . ."

The twins looked at each other.

"You look like a wrestler," Deirdre told Dirk. "And you, Kian, are a long-distance runner. Easy."

For once, the brothers could find nothing to say.

"Come on, guys." The lift-sphere stopped, and Deirdre waved the doors open. "Stop worrying about your spaceships, and let's all go eat some smelly fish."

An hour later, they were drinking lattes, slumped back in their chairs around the detritus of lunch, happy with the buzz of their own conversation and ignoring the families surrounding them.

"—learned more about the exercises in this weird old book," Dirk was saying, "called *Zen and the Art of Programming* by this Buchanan guy. Old website-derived thing that foresaw the merge between evolving software and formal specifications. Grainy bitmaps. Weird stuff about self-defence as a branch of physics, and Lord knows what."

"And your buddy Rajesh taught you these *baithaks* and *dands*? Combat conditioning?"

"Yeah, and some takedowns you'll really like. There's a pickup where—"

Deirdre shook her head. "Am I going to enjoy this bit?"

"Never mind. Anyway, the original site was described as 'the mingled thoughts of Borges, Pirsig, and Dijkstra, as produced by the bastard intellectual love-child of Feynman and Bruce Lee.' That's verbatim, pretty much."

Deirdre laughed, and Dirk looked at Kian.

Not many people would have caught those old references.

"I see what you mean," said Dirk.

"Yeah. Pity," said Kian.

"What?" Deirdre looked from one to the other. "What?"

That was the moment a strange woman approached their table, pulled out an unused chair without asking and sat down.

Her suit was pale-grey and elegantly cut, her coiffed blonde hair was short, and though she looked eighteen at first glance, it was obvious from her calm self-possession that she was actually much older.

"My name is Zoë, and I'm a friend of Ro's. I need to talk to you. All three of you."

She was also the person who had been watching them back in the shuttle port's Arrivals lounge.

"What," said Deirdre, "do you want to talk about?"

"Well . . . Did you know some people still hold to the idea of parallel universes? Every time an electron has a choice of two ways to travel, there are two entire universes, as if our own wasn't unimaginably vast already."

"That's nonsense." Deirdre's voice was flat, unfriendly. "And why are you talking physics to complete strangers?"

Neither Dirk nor Kian responded. There had to be a second level to this conversation. And there was one kind of entity which seemed to exist in many superimposed states—maybe overlapping realities—at any instant in time.

The Zajinets.

"Time is weird, too. Two centuries of looking," said Zoë, "and there's only one low-level process that appears to know the difference between past and future: neutral kaon-antikaon decay. Otherwise, there's no telling past from future in any fundamental equation."

"If they're neutral," began Deirdre, "how can there be an *anti*—?"

"It's the strangeness number—"

"—not the charge—"

"—that's opposite."

"Decoherence," said Zoë. "Definite past to fuzzy present to unknown future . . . Are the concepts meaningless? It's probably one of those unanswerable questions, like whether everything has to proceed from a first cause, *prima causa*, like that." Zoë stood up, pushed her chair back. "A thousand years from now, scientists and philosophers still won't have a clue, y'know?"

Zoë's attention rested on Deirdre just for a moment; then Zoë turned and walked away with a side-to-side sway that captured three intent gazes until she entered a lift-sphere and transparent doors slid shut and she dropped from sight.

"What the bastard hell," said Deirdre slowly, "was that all about?"

Kian turned to Dirk.

"They can't be watching now, otherwise—"

"—she wouldn't have talked to us, right."

"What? D'you two have any idea what she was talking about?"

The twins looked at each other. The woman, Zoë, had been using oblique and surreal language because she was *almost* certain that they were not currently under surveillance, but not entirely sure. However, the twins had the advantage of nameless preternatural senses which could detect sensor devices trained upon them. Right now, they felt nothing.

"She was talking about quantum weirdness, and how particles behave differently depending—"

"—on how you observe them. It was a hint that we should behave differently, ourselves. Not too clear a hint, obviously."

Deirdre leaned forward on the table. "Are you two trying to tell me something? Or just playing games?"

"She's UNSA Intelligence and we're in danger from Zajinets and we're under—"

"—surveillance. You as well. That's what she was telling us."

With a long sigh, Deirdre closed her eyes, opened them, then gave a tiny smile.

"You're forgetting the most important part."

Kian and Dirk simultaneously raised their right eyebrows, in a synchronized gesture which would have scared most people witless. Deirdre was unmoved.

"I mean," she said, "that young, or not-so-young, Zoë just fancies the pants off me. Or didn't you notice?"

"Um . . ."

"Er . . ."

Dirk coughed. "Excuse me? Could we—"

"—have the check, please?"

Particles under observation might or might not behave differently than they would otherwise, but people under surveillance are certainly constrained.

That night, they sat cross-legged in a circle on the rug in Deirdre's candle-lit room, taking it in turns to sip from the fat bottle of Drambuie which Dirk had brought from Aberdeen. Their conversation remained subdued and morose, encouraging them to drink.

"*Uch* . . ." Deirdre shivered at the sweet/sharp taste, and passed the bottle to Kian. He drank, grimaced—"Likewise"—and handed it on to Dirk.

Outside, small lights twinkled in a broad tree, unmoving in the breezeless California night.

"Come on," said Deirdre. "We should all get some sleep, ready for our trip to Arizona. All right?"

"*Our* trip." Dirk nodded, as if he had expected this all along.

"Naturally," said Kian. "We're hardly going to go to DistribOne—"

"—without our best pal, are we?"

"Come on, boys. Scat. I want sleep."

The twins hauled themselves to their feet, Dirk snagging the bottle as he did so.

"'Night, dear."
"'Night, dear."
"Goodnight, boys."

<<MODULE ENDS>>

34

NULAPEIRON AD 3426

The vessel surfaced in a wide oval lake in the Umbral Caverns of Realm Rinsenberger. On the brass-coloured dock, green-uniformed Dragoons helped Tom from the subaquargos, while Jissie clambered out by herself and skipped ahead.

Though the atmosphere was warm and humid, the Dragoons betrayed no signs of discomfort, even in their dress uniforms with heavy polished helmets. The officer bowed and introduced himself as Lieutenant Hixent. Then the whole platoon wheeled, forming an escort.

After they had walked only a few metres, the platoon halted, and it took Tom a second to realize that he and Jissie and Lieutenant Hixent were standing on a wide silvery disk, one of many inset in the brass wharf. The disk detached itself and rose into the air, carrying all three of them aloft.

"A moment, my Lord . . ." Lieutenant Hixent made a gesture, assuming control. "OK. Now, we have an arachnargos waiting for you."

Tom looked down at Jissie. Her eyes, widened, took in everything.

"We should move quickly," Tom said. "If that's possible."

"Of course, sir." Lieutenant Hixent caused the disk to slide through the air, while the escort marched below to a jogging cadence, matching the lev-disk's speed. "Would you and your daughter care for refreshments, or should we get you straight aboard?"

Jissie flinched then reddened.

"We'll eat on board," said Tom, "if that's all right. My compliments to Lords Draxon and Traquinal, but I should not stay to make their acquaintance. My presence here is a liability."

"Sir."

They wheeled into an airy, cathedral-high hall, filled with high arches and intricate friezes and centuries-old mosaics. At the hall's centre, a functional-looking arachnargos was poised: long and low, its upper carapace a dark, shining green, its lower thorax pale-grey speckled with brown. The tendrils were hunched and angular, ready to thrust into motion.

"It's the fastest we have, my Lord."

"My thanks, Lieutenant. My profound thanks."

It was only as tendrils were lifting Tom and Jissie aboard that Tom saw relief soften Lieutenant Hixent's square features. And Tom wondered whether it was a spirit of solidarity or a desire to remove a prime target from a fearful realm which motivated the Dragoons' assistance.

Five hours later, after a journey which Tom spent worrying about Elva while Jissie stood in the control cabin watching the pilots, they reached the border with Valkeu Demesne, another realm which Tom had never visited. No longer ruled by the eponymous Count Valkeu, it had become a demesne whose reputation was for innovative technical products produced by an isolationist culture which grew increasingly . . . strange.

The arachnargos lowered Tom and Jissie to the ground. Then, before the oddly etiolated Valkeu guards had time to verify Tom's credentials, the dark-green arachnargos sprang across broken ground, ducked low to slither through an abandoned colonnade, hauled itself past the border checkpoint, and raced out into raw cavern: interstitial territory that no-one wished to rule. In seconds, it was out of sight.

Then one of the guards blinked in a way that made Tom step back: with a sideways flicker of nictitating membranes. Their leader spoke in a dislocated, fluting voice.

"Transport for you is readied."

"Er . . . Thank you."

Tom and Jissie, with their narrow-limbed otherworldly escort, passed through a gateway formed of polished white stone, while faint vapours slid across their skins.

No lev-disks awaited them here; they had to walk. The tall soldiers had stilt-like legs and a jerking motion which allowed them to eat up distance with no sign of fatigue. By the end of their trek, Tom could remember only a succession of identical white halls, of strange-looking people who paid no attention to two strangers in their realm, and gleaming arcades and mazes formed of glass and diamond, their purpose impenetrable.

At some point, when Jissie could walk no more, Tom swung her up onto his back. She rode in silence, fingers clutched in the collar of Tom's cape, her small stump hooked over Tom's left shoulder, her legs looped around his torso.

Finally they stopped and Jissie slid down, and stood beside Tom on a balcony. Beneath, on a wide elliptical floor, five white dart-shaped shuttles stood. Overhead a vertical shaft led upwards into shadows. High above, invisible, was the night-shrouded opening to the planet's surface and its clear, waiting skies.

Tom might have convinced himself that free humanity was collaborating to remove him to safety, were it not for his final conversation with the guards of Valkeu Demesne.

"Thank you," Tom said. "Thank you very much."

"Not required." A wave of a long, skinny hand. "This individual performed task on track."

"Er, yes. But you didn't have to help us. I was just—"

"False-to-facts that must be, since these individuals *did* perform such." The spokesperson (for the hard-looking asthenic soldiers looked sexless to Tom) pointed with a loose-jointed forefinger that seemed too long to be human. "Path followed, therefore Destiny is manifest."

Jissie moved closer to Tom, her lips squeezed shut.

"Quantum predestination," said Tom, "doesn't mean you can't—"

"If only one path, then no choice. If many paths and randomness, still not *choice*: only randomness. Free will not required."

The individual Tom had thought of as an officer bore no insignia or markings. Perhaps any one of the group might have been nominated as the one who spoke with strangers.

"But when did you stop believing in it?" Tom asked. "In free will?"

"Seven Standard Years ago, this realm renounced idea."

"*Renounced* it? But, but . . ."

Impossible . . .

Yet Tom wondered if a concept so fragile that it could be destroyed merely by professing its non-existence could ever form a fundamental truth.

They have no free will because they stopped believing in it.

Then Jissie tugged at his sleeve.

"They're calling us from below."

The shuttle launched.

Acceleration and the hand of fear squeezed Tom and Jissie back in their seats. The vertical shaft's walls raced past in darkness. Sensor displays scrolled fast as the IR-scanned circle up ahead grew from a dot to a wide, protective membrane. Then they were almost on it, about to—

Impact.

—fly through and break into a silvery night lit by all three moons. The landscape fell away beneath.

Jissie laughed.

It was a startling reaction. No-one faced the agoraphobia-inducing skies without a programme of deconditioning; but she was fearless, that was all.

Then the blood drained from Jissie's face.

"What is it?"

Jissie pointed into an image of the ground below, at a wide shadow sliding from the field of view. "I thought it was the . . . lake. You know."

Ah, Fate.

"You mean"—Tom's scalp tightened—"the Lake of Glass."

"Mother and Father are there."

Tom squeezed his eyes shut.

Just two of the quarter-million people I killed.

Jissie touched his stump, in a matter-of-fact way no-one else had ever done.

"You freed their souls, my . . . Tom."

Her face was serious.

"Did I?"

"They were Absorbed and you freed them."

"Sweet Fate, Jissie." Tom's voice was a dry whisper. "I hope you're right."

Still, Tom and Jissie had a long flight ahead of them. As the shuttle whispered above moonlit clouds, Tom closed his eyes and allowed sleep to claim him. Then suddenly—

<Greetings, my Lord.>

The voice booming through the comm system punched him out of his dreams.

"Uh . . . Axolon? That you?"

Hours had passed. Tom felt drugged.

<Of course. You are well?>

Tom blinked, took in a deep breath. Beside him, Jissie was wide-eyed but not afraid.

"Yeah. I have a . . . friend with me. Her name is Jissie."

<Lady Elva is on her way. I'm monitoring her flight.>

Tom placed his hand over his eyes, and stayed very still for a moment.

Elva . . . Oh, my love.

"Thank Fate."

Jissie stared into the view-images as sunlight brightened post-dawn skies to a creamy apricot-and-yellow mix. Tom tried to compose himself: dream-fragments briefly surfaced then spiralled back into the subconscious depths. A strange, reedy voice said:

"The kaon persists."

It was the old abbot who spoke to him.

"The universe decays."

Strange, curlicue particle tracks across the blankness of sapphire vacuum: a pattern flicked across Tom's mind, was gone.

Then Axolon spoke once more:

<I'll prepare breakfast.>

The everyday world clicked back into place, though the term *kaon-koan*, *kaon-koan* continued to whisper in Tom's mind. The great stone sphere grew larger in the forward display, as the shuttle decelerated on the final approach to Axolon Array.

To home.

35

NULAPEIRON AD 3426

Tom and Jissie ate breakfast outside, at a small table on the ring-shaped balcony, while creamy gases spewed from the terraformer's apex and the air blew cold and clear around them.

"How have you been, Axolon?" Tom sipped his daistral.

Jissie was tucking in to her third boljicream pancake.

<I was destroyed by a space-enfolding detonation yesterday evening.>

Tom put his cup down, stood and crossed to the balustrade. He leaned over and stared down at the convex bulging stone surface which hid the equatorial rim where Axolon's head was melded with the sphere, his nerves and sinews and cables splayed and rooted across the terraformer.

"You're looking pretty good," Tom called down, "for a burst of gamma rays."

<I'm quoting the official logs.>

Tom walked back to the table. Jissie looked up briefly without a pause in her eating.

"Ah," said Tom. "The other sphere. After Trevalkin swapped identities in the system."

<Exactly so.>

Picking up his daistral cup, Tom paused. "I don't like feeling indebted to that man."

<He did us a favour.>

"Precisely." Tom replaced the cup without drinking. "And I wonder what he'll want in return."

But if the Anomaly fell across the world, there would be no human debts to repay. Before Tom could follow that thought further, Axolon caused a small holo image to appear above the breakfast table, low-resolution and blurred against the day's brightness.

<Ten shuttles approaching.>

"Are they—?"

<My Lady Elva is in command.>

Tom leaned closer to the holo, as though it brought them nearer in reality.

<There are wounded. Two of the shuttles are badly damaged.>

"What?"

<They lost two other shuttles during the escape.>

"Is there any sign of pursuit?"

There were small fighter-darts aboard the terraformer, ready to launch; but if the Anomaly or its suborned forces knew where Axolon Array was—

<No pursuit. The shuttles laid decoys.>

Tom whirled away from the table, ignoring Jissie's concerned expression, and strode inside to the hemispherical conference chamber where a lifetime ago he had slain an Oracle.

Even as Tom brought up his tactical displays, he had time to wonder why Elva had not tried to talk to him directly. He called his lieutenants, ordered autodocs to be made ready, and braced himself for bad news as the ragged formation drew near.

But Elva had been busy tending to the wounded. Charcoal-smeared and with blood across her swollen lip, escorting a lev-stretcher, she came out of the docked shuttle at a jog. She smiled at Tom before returning her attention to the moaning patient. This was the reality of war: whimpering and screaming, the stench of burned flesh, of blood and faeces, and the awful stares of those who saw death coming for them now.

"Outlying parts of the realm, and the lowest strata, won't hold for more than three days. The rest is already gone." Elva stepped back and wiped sweat and slick blood from her forehead, as medics took over the stretcher. "Realm Strelsthorm is lost."

At that moment, one of the wounded soldiers shuddered, turned away from her and died.

"Fate."

"How many people"—Tom pulled her back from the incoming flow of injured—"did you bring?"

"Two hundred and fifty. Maybe more. Maybe . . ."

Maybe fewer, depending on how many survive.

"Fate, Elva. I love you."

"I love you, Tom."

Then Axolon announced: <There are more vessels lifting off. I'm tracking via encrypted SatScan.>

Axolon meant that the Anomaly's forces might not be aware of the vessels.

"Are the vessels shielded?"

<Yes. And broadcasting Fire Watch codes.>

"You'll have to give me details."

<They're the codes least likely to have been compromised.>

Tom stared at Elva.

"Look," Elva said. "If comms or SatScan are breached, these are Anomaly fighters, and they've no need for subterfuge. I'd say they're genuine free forces, come to join us."

"Ah, Destiny."

In that moment, Tom knew who was aboard the new shuttles: the Action Leagues, the natural enemies of the LudusVitae movement to which Tom and Elva had once belonged. He did not know whether to cheer or sob.

"It's Trevalkin." It was the only explanation. "He's spreading the word, through the Leagues that remain secure."

And I wanted to be in charge. I'm a fool.

Elva looked around, at the medics and ordinary staff still carrying in the wounded. "How many people can we support?"

"Not even this many."

It was two hours amid the Chaos-laden process of getting refugees on board, and docking shuttles, and beginning repairs to the damaged craft, before Tom could stop to think. Two of the shuttles had torn or twisted flight surfaces, and would not have been able to make it this far without heroic feats of piloting which would never be told. Scarcely any craft was untouched by graser fire.

Shuttles continued to rise from the surface.

The motley armada of refugee vessels was growing larger. On every continent and from beneath the oceans, they rose into the air, broadcasting their encoded signals of despair and hope, as darkness consumed the realms they left behind.

So few among the population.

Axolon Array was already full.

Yet too many for us to cope with.

Suddenly, incredibly, Tom laughed—the act surprised even him—and people turned shocked stares in his direction.

"Axolon! Are you there?"

<Obviously. Where else would I be?>

It was comforting to Tom that his floating stone fortress was alive and powerful, a kilometre-wide sphere with a mind and armaments of its own.

"*Exactly* how many terraformers are there? I know it's thousands . . ."

There was a pause.

<Over seventeen thousand. Some four thousand two hundred are probably habitable, with effort.>

"Ha. You're way ahead of me. What state will they be in? How many already have people living in them?"

<Some recluses have lived this way for years. Seven for sure. Two other spheres . . . maybe, if the owners still live. That's all.>

"And the other spheres? What about food?"

<I'm already budding the gel-sacs in my kitchens. Rations will be short for a while, but we can begin growing supplies immediately.>

"Axolon . . . You're a bloody genius."

Tom turned away, heading for the conference chamber which had become his command centre. A bloodstained man in the torn uniform of a Halberdier captain was standing; he had obviously heard the conversation.

Now, he went down on one knee.

"No, my Lord, with respect," the Halberdier said, bowing his head. "There is *one* leader now, one genius, and we all know who it is. Sir."

When Tom reached the command centre, Elva was pointing out arcs and nodes within a tactical holo while the men and women around her, mostly in uniform, nodded agreement. When Elva saw Tom, she said: "Give me a moment, people," and crossed over to him.

"The place is crowded, Tom. I've moved our stuff into a smaller bedchamber, and I mean *small*. I think it used to be a storage cupboard."

"It'll be better when the other spheres become ready."

"Yeah . . . And I've made room for a third person, too. Not much privacy."

"Um, all right."

Tom looked over at the display. More vessels were rising to join the floating armada; some were already headed for other spheres. That was Axolon's doing.

"Oh, and . . . Nice thinking, Tom, about the terraformers."

At that, a junior trooper came up carrying something dark and supple, and bowed to Elva. "They're ready, my Lady."

To Tom, Elva said: "This is for you, my Lord."

It was a tunic she held out, black and with a red circular knot-design upon the chest, formed of interwoven tricon-facets denoting Courage and Determination. A military leader would have worn such a garment during the Founding Wars, at the beginning of Nulapeiron's history: it was the kind of thing no-one had worn for centuries. There was no left sleeve.

Held across the trooper's forearms was a second one-sleeved tunic, nearly identical save that the red design was missing and it was a fraction of the size.

"The spare one," said Tom, "doesn't look as though it will fit."

"It's not for you, my love."

"Ah." Tom leaned over and kissed her. "Excellent, my Lady."

Most of Nulapeiron's ten billion inhabitants kept to the same diurnal cycle, following a single timezone which had been established more than a millennium before. On the terraformer, where they floated in the open, that cycle bore little relationship to the hours of light and darkness: a cycle that continually changed as Axolon Array drifted through the skies.

There were other problems besides disrupted sleep-patterns and the anxiety of those who were terrified of open spaces. In the midst of darkness, Tom jerked awake, and realized that the images of encroaching forces blowing terraformers apart in the nightbound sky were from his dreams, and not reality.

Two pairs of eyes were gleaming in the darkness. They had been using lased-in displays while he was sleeping.

"All right," he said. "Lights."

The chamber brightened.

In the bed beside him, Elva blinked three times rapidly, and the membrane coating her eyes cleared. From the smaller makeshift bed laid across the far wall, Jissie gasped, then made a control gesture which stilled the game she had been playing.

"*Sorry . . .*"

"You didn't wake me up," said Tom.

Elva sat up properly, tucked her pillow against her back. "I've been keeping in touch with SatScan comms—"

"I guessed."

"—and Adam Gervicort got away."

"Good."

"And Zhao-ji took Paradox to safety, apparently, from his base." Paradox was a neko-feline, very old and grand, whom Tom and Zhao-ji had looked after in their school days. "And his latest-generation offspring: Fawn, Constantia, and Antinomios."

Thank Fate.

"Ah, Destiny." Tom rubbed his eyes, wiped the back of his hand across his nose. "With all that's happening, worrying about the Fate of a neko and three kittens—"

"I'd think less of you, Tom, if you didn't."

Tom swallowed and shut his eyes.

"If we're not fighting for the three of us," added Elva, "then what are we fighting for?"

"Um, right." Tom cleared his throat, looked at her. "Things happen fast in war, don't they?"

Jissie, in her makeshift bed, looked from one to the other. "Three?" she asked.

"If that's what you want, of course," said Elva.

"Oh," said Jissie.

Then she lay back down, curled on her side, and slipped into peaceful sleep.

"Lights off," said Tom, and lay back, knowing that nothing awaited him but nightmares. Perhaps the dreams were prescient, or perhaps they were like the truecasts of Oracle Gérard d'Ovraison who once lived in this place, dreaming of life, until the day Tom murdered him.

36

NULAPEIRON AD 3426

Tom and Elva, along with most of the senior officers, were already grouped around the conference table when Axolon interrupted, displaying an image of dart-shaped shuttles flying in tight formation.

"That's Adam's group, is it? How is he doing?"

<He has several hundred people aboard. One of them wants voice-to-voice, claims to know you. A carl called—>

"Kraiv!"

Axolon took that as assent.

"Greetings, old friend. By Axe and Blood, we made it."

"Fate . . . Kraiv! Is that really you? Where's Draquelle?"

"Here, with the children, and thirty per cent of the Manse Hetreece. Are we welcome in this place?"

"Ha." Tom looked around the table. "One third of such a fighting clan is welcome anywhere . . ."

"Aye, my Lord."

"Definitely."

". . . and my colleagues agree."

"We'll see you in twenty minutes. Till then."

Tom waited for a second to ensure the comm link was ended.

"Axolon?"

<My Lord?>

"Make weapons ready, all the same. An AI could fake that voice, given the right surveillance material to work from." It was unsettling, but they had to face the possibility. "Sooner or later, the Enemy will find out where we are."

There were grim nods around the table.

"But it will cost them"—Elva placed her graser pistol flat upon the tabletop—"to take us down. That's for sure."

It was not just nightshift: it was real night outside, with dark clouds scudding and chill winds in the air. Inside the terraformer's command centre, the white and blue tiles showed track-marks of boots. The chamber was quiet with the odd feel of a workplace when everyone has left.

Tom stood watching the empty space where his mother's sarcophagus had stood. Someone had ripped out the equipment before he took possession of the terraformer; still he could almost see her near-dead body, if he tilted his head a certain way.

Behind him, someone coughed.

"Oh." Tom turned. "Hi, Adam."

"Tom." The scar on Adam's face rippled in the half-light as he nodded. "I hear my Lady Elva is safe."

"As much as any of us." After a moment, Tom gestured for a drone. "You need a drink?" A small drone rose, and hovered at shoulder height. "This one's got daistral and juice."

"What I need is something stronger. But . . . All right, a daistral. Command: bring—"

"Cancel that." Tom stopped the drone before it could float over to Adam. He gestured the carapace open and reached inside, and drew out a steaming cup. "Here you are."

"Thanks." Adam accepted the drink. "That's the second time I've been served by you, my Lord."

"It won't become a habit."

"I know . . . I hear you've a new tunic which no-one's seen you wearing."

Tom raised his own cup in a toast. "You've just got here, and your spies are reporting already. Not bad."

They clinked their cups together.

"I rescued some new 'tropes," Adam said. "From the labs. My Lady ordered a research programme some time back. The logotropes work for anyone who's not had desensitization against all that." Adam gestured to the night sky outside. "Works in ninety-nine per cent of cases."

"What about the other one per cent?"

"That's the thing. Adverse reactions range from nosebleeds all the way to haematoma or anaphylactic shock."

"Chaos. All we can do is offer them around and explain the risks."

"I . . . Right. I didn't think you'd agree, Tom. They need more testing and development. You've got *children* on board this thing."

"No, what we need is more time, but we're not going to get it. If things get bad, we'll have to evacuate via drop-bugs to the surface. Anyone who can't function in the open . . ."

Tom let his voice trail off, as Adam carefully placed his cup down on the conference table.

If you're going to attack me, now's the time.

There was tension in Adam's shoulders. He blamed Tom for Elva's stress over the past two years; that was understood. Perhaps now he had nothing to lose by attacking Tom, since their whole world was gone . . . and he was Academy-trained like Tom, and just as dangerous.

Then Adam straightened and looked Tom right in the eyes.

"Tom. Sir. I need to tell you . . ."

Tom held his breath.

". . . that we need a commander . . ."

Right. It was a shame Corduven was not still alive, is that what he wanted to say?

You think I'd disagree?

". . . and you're the right man. We need you, Tom."

Tom could only watch as Adam bowed in formal salute, spun on his heel, and left.

After three hours of immersion in tactical displays, it seemed that the only thing Tom had accomplished was reading about the successes of others; and those were limited to the practicalities of survival, not victory. Dispersed shuttle groups were entering the first eighty terraformer spheres to begin the task of recommissioning.

We're hiding. Hoping the Anomaly won't notice.

Grimly, he looked through hanging stacks of tesseracts delineating the Anomaly's absorption of realm after realm below.

While the world dies.

From inside his belt, Tom took out the violet crystal which the Kobold officer had given to him. It would allow him to contact the Grey Shadows, and perhaps whatever forces the Crystal Lady herself might command. Tom's tech analysts had decided it used a Calabi-Yau bridge, which allowed the comms-beams to bypass the kilometres of solid rock between here and the Crystal Lady's deep dwelling, by sliding through the hyperdimensions.

The problem was, such a broadcast would almost certainly produce resonances which a hungry and expanding Anomaly could detect and pounce on.

"I can't use it," Tom muttered, "until I know what I'm asking for."

He was talking to himself: harmless in an academic logosopher; fatal in an intelligence agent, as Tom had been back in the occupied Aurineate Grand'aume. Then he thought of the young girl, Sadia, in Realm V'Delikona, writing poetry at Corduven's funeral, and wondered how she and her father had fared.

So long since I wrote poetry.

Now was the time to fight.

Tom looked again through the displays which pulsed in the dark-

ness while everyone else in the overcrowded terraformer sphere slept—
all but a few night-duty sentries and obsessive researchers . . . plus the
wounded who suffered despite the autodocs' morphitropes and delta-
inducers.

"I can't do this."

Tom pushed himself back from the table and stood.

Unclasping his cape, he cast it across the chair. His belt, with the
Grey Shadows crystal, went on the table. *We're lost.* Tom considered a
moment, then bent forward, tugged his tunic over his head, and threw
the garment aside. *Lost* . . . The tunic fell through the holo images and
lay spread across the tabletop like a fallen soldier.

Bare-chested, with the stallion talisman and its hidden crystal
hanging round his neck, Tom crossed to the window. Membrane slid
wetly across his skin as he stepped outside.

Chill night air encircled him.

Step and smear.

And lean out, *for Fate's sake.*

Traversing with his fingertips brushing the stone, walking almost
upright, using the sides of his slipper-like shoes for greater friction,
Tom moved along silvery stonework rendered treacherous by moonlight.

Sliding shadows and odd perspectives made him constantly review
the basics. The smallest mistake would spring him outwards from the
sphere, betrayed by his own tension and the basic laws of physics, only
to topple into a void filled with darkness.

The wind was fresh. The wind was freedom.

Thank Fate I'm here, now. Breathing.

For there were, as one of the ancient proto-logosophers pointed
out, many more ways to be dead than to be alive.

Then the going became more difficult, and both rational and
whimsical thinking disappeared as the cerebellum brought the

climbing problem into his forebrain: jamming his fist inside a wide crack, extending down for a foothold—*missed*—and scrabbling, looking for a knot of stone where he might hook his heel—*got it*—and continue his descent.

Wind buffeted his ears, flailing at his bare torso, as Tom perched gargoyle-like upon the narrowest of ledges, at the equatorial rim of the kilometre-diameter sphere. Moonlight caused clouds to whiten as though from internal fluorescence, painted the sky dark-blue and purple, occluding the stars.

The ground, far below, was scarcely visible, save as half-glimpsed patches of grey heathland plus, once, a tiny spark of orange flames. Refugees.

You're safer down there.

Tom would order a drop-bug, filled with supplies, to be flung back in that direction.

<What are you thinking about?>

The face was mostly stone now. The one faceted eye that Tom saw was a silver shard of moonlight.

"Oh, you know . . . Time passing like a cloud. Life dissipating like a morning mist. That kind of thing."

Seconds slid by.

<In what regard? Whether there's a purpose to it all?>

Chill movement of wind.

"Yeah, but teleology ain't in fashion, my friend."

<Though Destiny is?>

"You've got me there."

Silver-grey, the distant glimpses of land below.

"What about you, Axolon? What do you think of as you float up here?"

A shining lake moved past below. Soon it was gone, hidden by nimbus and distance.

<Time. Life. Clouds. Like that.>

Tom chuckled.

"Let me know if you come to some conclusion."

A dark gap appeared overhead, split by the major moon's white disk.

<Likewise, my friend.>

Later, in the depths of the terraformer, Tom opened the small cupboard he sought. Someone who could explain his random visions and what they might mean: that was what he needed.

Her flensed head was glistening with blood, and her lidless spherical eyes somehow appeared to widen; and Tom realized he was interrupting what should have been a private time.

Nutrients swelled striated strips of tissue.

"Sorry, I'll . . . Later, OK?"

The cupboard door vitrified shut and Tom stood there for a moment, face flaring with embarrassment and something more. Then he turned away, looking for the helical stairway which led back up to the level where the Corcorigan family chamber was, where he might attain a few hours' rest before the morning crowded in on him.

At mid-morning, Elva beckoned Tom from a briefing session after he had called a short break. Leading him down to the lower levels, she stopped at a clear internal window and nodded.

"I'd say she gets it from you."

"What do you—? Well."

Inside a storage bay which had been refitted with old matting on both floor and walls, a silver-haired, hard-looking carl was instructing some twelve or thirteen children. In the front row, a stern-faced Jissie stamped and whirled her way through a phi2dao beginners' fighting form.

Part-way through, she became aware of Tom watching her, but her ferocity only increased, all hesitation evaporating as she gouged and struck imaginary opponents crowding in upon her.

Tom was very careful not to smile. When the form was finished, he gave a long slow nod, while Jissie stood to attention and appeared to be watching only her instructor.

"Come on," said Elva. "There's someone else you need to see. Arrived a few hours ago."

In the next level down, in one of the many chambers that had been transformed into a sick-ward, they found Lady Renata bent over an autodoc. A maintenance drone floated overhead, just below the ceiling, beaming control codes into the autodoc's processor blocks at Renata's direction.

"Right," she said after a minute. "All done, I think."

"Very good." Tom smiled as Renata jumped. "Sorry. All that stealth training."

"Right. How are you, Tom? Hello again, Elva. Are . . . ? Look, drone, put the 'doc into restart mode, and I'll check it myself, OK?"

The drone hung in place for a moment as though in reproach, then slowly slid from the chamber.

"Sorry about that, Tom."

"Our fault for interrupting. You're doing good work."

"Maybe . . . You've a question you need to ask me. I can tell."

"How about a statement first? I've seen a . . . Lady. One whose substance is like nothing I'd ever heard of. Though there are people who've heard certain . . . stories."

"*You've met her.* The Crystal Lady."

"Yes, though I've no way of proving that." Not without revealing the comms crystal, and that Tom did not want to do. "It seems quite a coincidence, that your investigative field is magma studies and indigenous lifeforms—"

"Pretty much the same thing, as it turns out."

"—and that Trevalkin ends up being associated with an organization that somehow links to the native species' . . . what? Representative?"

The Grey Shadows were old. Tom wondered how many of the nobility were members. Yet Renata made no mention of them as she explained: "According to legend, the Crystal Lady is *ancient*. Some say one of the Founding Lords constructed her. There are more mystic tales . . . The planet's core manifesting itself in dreams, stuff like that."

"But the Lady is a construct?"

Renata shrugged. "You're the one who's met her, not me."

Tom had read some of Renata's technical papers. Their academic language failed to disguise her enthusiasm for the creatures she studied: not just thermidors, but huge entities that moved deep inside the magma, swimming in schools and emitting long-harmonic vibrations that might be a form of singing.

"We need Avernon," he told her. "Do you know where he is?"

There had been no word from Trevalkin.

"One man can't save the world." Renata shook her head angrily. "Avernon can't be expected to pull out some miracle that will destroy the Anomaly."

"Destruction is too grand an aim." Tom explained that his techs were working on ways to shield the world, to close off the hyperdimensions so that the Anomaly could not reach into Nulapeiron from its other locations thousands of light-years away . . . before Nulapeiron became a hellworld as bad as Siganth or the legendary Fulgor.

Then Renata rubbed her eyes, bit her lip, and thought hard about what she was going to say next. "The thing is . . . I heard from Trevalkin, but I don't know whether to trust him."

"You can trust him." Tom surprised himself with the certainty of his feeling. "He hates the Anomaly more than any of us."

"Then . . ." Renata looked at Elva, then back at Tom. "Trevalkin was in the Aurineate Grand'aume, but will have left by now. Gone to fetch Avernon, his message said."

"Bifurcating Chaos." Elva turned away. "The Grand'aume's sur-rounded by Anomalous realms. They're trapped."

"That's not what Trevalkin thinks. He called it an exercise in exfiltration."

A chill wind seemed to blow through Tom's heart, cold and hard. He never, ever, wanted to descend to Nulapeiron's inhabited strata and enter an occupied demesne again; but in his mind was a clear image of himself, rappelling down a shaft with another figure at his side . . . and he knew that the laws of Destiny trapped him, Tom Corcorigan, as much as an ant or an Oracle or a morning mist which swirled, and dis-sipated, breaking apart at sunlight's touch.

37

TERRA AD 2166

<<Ro's Children>>

[10]

It was blazing hot in Arizona. Deirdre, who had visited the state before, had never known it otherwise. A sky like unblemished lapis lazuli, clear and blue, stretched overhead, beyond their flyer's membrane cockpit. Below, their shadow flitted across a tan landscape; the rust-and-icing-sugar strata of the empty Painted Desert; scattered green saguaro cacti, five metres tall and more; straggling mesquite.

Tiny beige dots were ground squirrels, like little meerkats, standing upright on sentinel duty by their burrows. Kian wondered what they made of the big white flyer coasting overhead like some predatory bird with four human beings held in its stomach.

"Ow!"

Clear air turbulence bucked the flyer, but the AI compensated and the human pilot merely tipped back his Stetson and grinned at his passengers. Deirdre, stony-faced, returned a hard stare.

Then the desert over which they flew was Martian red in all directions, sere and stark. Its harsh beauty did not conceal its true nature; if the flyer went down for any reason, this was an environment that could kill.

"Home, sweet home, folks."

Far from anywhere, stood a cluster of blue glass pyramids; near them, black-and-silver structures formed hangars and administration blocks, while a baked yellow runway shaped like an elongated question mark angled out into the desert.

All around, the clean red sand and hot still air crackled with latent energy.

"Goin' down."

They swooped in to land.

Their guide was an amiable, soft-looking man called Solly, pear-shaped, dressed in a short-sleeved shirt with a bolo tie. Solly revealed a habit of wiping his high forehead with a forefinger as he led them through the visitors' registration process. He watched as Dirk, Kian and Deirdre downloaded encrypted parole-and-countersign routines into their infostrands; then he showed them where the restrooms and the drinks machines were situated.

"This w-way."

Solly led them into the hushed, grey-carpeted expanse of the Human Engineering Department, where analysts worked quietly over pulsing holosimulations of control systems and Pilot/ship interface processors.

"Th-this is where we'll be monitoring your f-fitting session tomorrow."

Solly flicked a hand in the direction of a wide console, currently unmanned, where diagnostic displays pulsed and billowed, checking and re-checking transponders and i/o buffers. It was automated, triple-AI verified (no test was passed until all three independently evolved systems concurred), ready to pass the buck to humans the moment a potential fault revealed itself.

"Is that our ship?" asked Dirk.

"Oh, y-yes." Solly beamed. "Ready to fly."

Deirdre looked at Kian and shrugged.

"What?" he asked her.

"Seems thorough enough," Deirdre said, neutral-voiced. "Would you like me to check the deduction chains, maybe the interface den-drimers?"

Offering to check UNSA's system was provocative, but Dirk and Kian could see that Deirdre was uneasy. They had expected arguments when the twins tried to sign her in as a visitor with them, but the security people had immediately accepted her presence: almost took it for granted that she would be there.

It made the twins wonder whether Security had expected her. Perhaps the mysterious Zoë had told the truth when she said—obliquely—that they were being watched.

Dirk answered: "I guess we ought to trust them."

"Yes, of course."

Kian grinned at Solly.

"She's got our best interests at heart."

"Um . . . Yes." Solly wiped his forehead once. "We *are* a little behind schedule. Can I sh-show you your q-q-quarters?"

"How far behind?" asked Deirdre.

"T-tom-morrow m-m-morning?" Solly's reply sounded like a question. Then a look of relief passed over his face as a slim, crop-haired young woman walked towards them.

"Oh-ten-hundred," she said, matter-of-fact. "Ready to interface. I'm Paula, by the way. Assistant controller. I'll be monitoring."

"In which hangar?" asked Kian.

"Right out there"—Paula pointed—"on the main runway. No-one else will be using it."

Dirk frowned. "It's just a static session, right? Fitting interfaces. No flying."

"Part of the delay was that flight control integration came in *ahead* of schedule, thanks to Solly here . . ."

Solly blushed. His forehead shone with sweat.

". . . so if you want to take a little spin overhead, feel free . . ."

Kian and Dirk grinned in unison.

"... but only in this universe, mind you. We're not ready for mu-space y—"

"Hey! We get to—"

"—fly! That's—"

"—outstanding."

Deirdre looked at Paula and shrugged.

"I apologize for my friends. They're very grown up, really."

"No apologies, please." Paula's smile was directed at Deirdre. "I'm really pleased to be working with you all."

They spent the evening playing Go, having discovered—in a lounge set aside for Pilots' use; there were no other Pilots here at this time— a traditional wooden table and two porcelain bowls filled with the polished ellipsoidal pieces known as stones.

Cross-legged, staring down at the nineteen-by-nineteen grid etched in the low tabletop, Dirk laid down the first black stone with a *clack*. Deirdre, playing white, responded by occupying one of the pivotal intersections at the other side of the board.

"You don't want to know," said Kian, "how long she's been playing."

Deirdre smiled. "I know the rules, is all."

"Ha." Dirk picked a stone from the bowl. "I've heard that one before."

The initial stages proceeded quickly, as black and white stones swirled across the board, increasing territory at each other's expense. Then a strong envelopment from Deirdre's forces caused a collapse in Dirk's strength, and it was only through cunning play that he managed to deploy "eye" formations which could not fall to the enemy.

Dirk began to lay down counteroffensives, penetrating white territory. Deirdre fought back; but Dirk merged with the flow, became calm, and used a deft series of feints before enveloping her stones to achieve victory.

Dirk's body, when he brought his mind back to normal awareness, was coated with sweat.

"So ... How long *have* you been playing for?"

"A whole year." Deirdre looked at Kian and wrinkled her nose. "I thought I was going to win this one."

"We're pretty much neck and neck these days," said Kian. "Evenly matched."

"After a year. Just one year."

"Right."

"Jesus Christ."

Both twins had been playing since the age of four, a form of tutoring which Ro had considered as vital as physical martial discipline. Though they held no formal dan ranking, they had beaten strong players who did.

"You're a scary person, Deirdre Dullaghan."

"Well, Jeez . . . You two should talk."

After that, they switched to an in-house holosystem which would allow them to play 3Go, a new variant that added red stones to the other two sides, and allowed them to wage a three-way campaign which, when applied to political situations more complex than a single battlefield, was a truer simulation of real-life complexities.

They wondered, as they played their first game with lighthearted banter and no conversation of deep import, whether Security was monitoring them even now, analysing voice tones and measuring body responses, constructing psychosomatic profiles. Perhaps UNSA techs were already implementing manipulative systems whose gameplay affected the fate of countries and even offworld colonies, and whose pieces were myriad; and every single one was a person.

Later, the three of them went outside at sunset, walking across sand that glowed with vermilion warmth. Crimson sun dragged spectacular violet across the sky, before slipping below the empty horizon with a rapidity which disconcerted Dirk.

"That's the way it happens round here, bro," said Kian.

"Amazing."

It was the lack of high mountains nearby, or human habitation besides the UNSA field at their back, which made the night sky magnificent: black velvet in all directions, a vast hemisphere over the world. Stars were silver points of light but gathered in a profusion such as neither twin had ever seen.

"You'll be going out there." Deirdre stared straight up. "Hard to believe."

A faint sharp scent drifted on the air and Dirk sniffed.

"That's mesquite," Kian told him.

"Right." Dirk turned. Out in the desert, in shadow, stood a fat alien shape bristling with spikes. "And what the hell is that?"

"Er . . ."

"A boojum tree." In the gathering gloom, Deirdre looked from one twin to the other. "What? You think I'm kidding? I swear on my mother's grave, that's what it's called."

Kian sighed. "Your mother lives in Portland, Oregon."

"Does that mean she can't have a grave? She's got a nice little plot all marked out."

"Jesus, Deirdre. You're one—"

"—sick woman, that's for—"

"—sure."

The twins' conversation and examination of the desert night concealed a deeper vision, a mode of analysis they could not share with Deirdre while being monitored . . . and they *were* being watched. They knew it for sure.

Low across the sand, a microward boundary glimmered invisibly. Scan-waves pulsed; bats turned back in the darkness, disturbed by the vibrating barrier only they and the desert mice and two young men who were almost human could sense.

"Does the emptiness," asked Deirdre, "seem frightening to you?"

"Sometimes," said Dirk.

He shifted his shoulder minutely.

There. Below the sand.

Kian's answer was a subtle mouth movement impossible for others to read even in daylight.

I see it.

A bunker, or a . . . launch silo, that was it. Covered by a hatch or membrane over which sand lay. There was the faint sense of ducts and fans—or perhaps a polymer spray of some sort, capable of transforming dry sand to manageable sludge—waiting to suck the desert away and clear a path for defensive fighters to launch.

"There's another universe beyond that one." Kian spoke as though only the surface conversation counted, turning to gesture at the night sky while scanning further along the nightbound sand.

Another silo, there.

There was a subliminal answering sound from Dirk.

Got it. And there.

They had the pattern now. Laid out in a ring, spaced every klick around the perimeter, submerged fighters waited for the "go" signal, in permanent readiness. Mother had never told them that the base was so heavily defended. Perhaps she had not known, or perhaps it had not been this way the last time she was here.

"I wonder why the Zajinets," murmured Dirk, "are our enemies? Not that any of them's been seen since Mother and the others evacuated Beta Draconis."

Deirdre inhaled quickly, surprised that they should raise the subject: she could not sense the surveillance devices, but assumed they were there.

"That was our settlement, a human settlement," she said, "on the Zajinet homeworld. Beta Draconis III, is that right?"

"Yeah, BD-3. Except"—Kian turned again, still scanning—"it turned out not to be their homeworld, after all. Subsequent reconnaissance flights showed wasteland, nothing more. Just a colony which they abandoned as soon as we caused trouble."

"Some kind of internal politics, Mother thought." Dirk shrugged in the near-complete darkness. "She and the other humans witnessed a gathering that was something like a court case, yet utterly different. The thing is, Zajinets are *alien*. Not just in two minds about everything: more like a thousand minds, for each individual."

"And," said Kian, "the majority disapproved of the ones who were killing humans. At least, that's what Mother and UNSA analysts *think* was what happened."

Deirdre looked at them, deciding whether to say what she was thinking. Then she nodded. "You said the Zajinets could enter mu-space, right? Had ships like yours?"

"Like the one that's going to be ours."

"Perhaps they wanted to guard their trade routes and such. You know, like Dutch and Spanish and English fleets going to war over who controlled the oceans, five or six hundred years ago."

"Maybe. But ya gotta wonder why, in that case—"

"—they seem to have vacated mu-space, too, which is—"

"—vast, in any case. Loads of room for everyone."

They were silent for a minute. Then Dirk said: "Want to go back in?"

"Yeah, I think we should."

But, as they headed back, boots padding mutely on the cooling powdery sand, neither Dirk nor Kian could prevent a small, dry chuckle escaping.

"What?" demanded Deirdre.

"Nothing."

They could not tell her how their infra-red sensitivity enabled them to detect the targeting beams that swung through the still air, or the way a night-sighted sentry inside a near-invisible bunker was tracking their movement with his cross-hairs centred firmly on the moving target formed by Deirdre's perfectly curved buttocks.

"Nothing. Really, dear."

✧✧✧

· At 5:13 a.m. the twins' eyes snapped open. It was still dark in their shared room. Their heartbeats rose, then deliberately slowed as they remembered the surveillance bead-cameras embedded in the walls and ceiling, one trained over each of the two beds.

Dirk mumbled and turned to one side, as though he were still asleep.

Outside in the hallway, a man was coming closer, and the pheromones he was broadcasting in the air were like a screeching siren, a transmitted chemical fear that would have had guard dogs yowling had there been K9s stationed here.

Coming this way. To this room?

Kian twitched minutely: a gesture of agreement.

One man, Dirk subvocalized. *If he enters, I'll attack low and left.*

A grunt from Kian. *I'll go high, right.*

Kian would use the bed as springboard, leaping high with a knee-strike as the primary technique, aimed at the man's throat if the threat appeared deadly. Dirk would probably go for a leg takedown, snapping his hands against kneecap and heel as his shoulder struck the thigh. Kian's attack would complement the throw . . . but the situation was fluid and could change in a tenth of a second, which was why they were prepared to—

". . . *the danger they're in. But I can't* tell *them.*"

It was not just each other's subvocalized murmurs that the twins could detect; this was the fearful man outside, muttering to himself without realizing, as he stopped in indecision directly outside the door.

". . . *don't deserve to die. But if I, if I tell, then they'll know, everyone will know* . . ."

Though they could not see him, the twins knew from the rustle of cloth, the stink of noradrenaline, what was happening in the corridor. The hesitant hand reaching for the door-plate; the profuse sweating; the hesitation. The trembling.

A sob, almost silent and probably unconscious.

Then the withdrawal, both hands jammed into pockets and the shoulders slumping as he turned and slouched away . . . he was crying mutely and without tears as he gave in to cowardice and demeaned himself still further.

Yet he could not know that he *had* delivered the message, despite the shivering fear. And he had not needed to enter the twins' bedroom for them to know who he was. The scent-signature he transmitted was blaring at the chemical equivalent of top volume.

His name was Solly. He was the engineer who had shown them around the facility, and he seemed convinced that anyone who tried to fly the new ship today would be torn into oblivion.

At 5:45 the alarm beeped.

"Ugh." Dirk sounded like someone who had just woken up. "Shut up."

There was one last defiant beep, then silence.

"'Mornin'," Kian mumbled.

Dirk used the adjoining bathroom first, and came out drinking a long glass of water. He pulled his tracksuit from a drawer as Kian brushed past him.

Ten minutes later they were outside, breathing deeply in the pre-dawn air, drawing energy as they stretched and turned. Then they moved off in a slow jog across the sand.

"One circuit of the base?"

"That should—No, look."

They slowed to a walk, then stopped. One of the big hangars was opening.

White light flooded out, revealing the huge predatory bird cast in gleaming bronze, banded with blue-green ceramic which gave off its own quiet glow.

"Oh, my God."

"You got that right."

Like the attendants of some mighty deity, small vehicles guided the delta-winged vessel out into the open. They made a long slow arc as it moved onto a purple track which led to the main, dark-yellow runway.

"I can't believe they'd trust us with this."

"The numbers, the cost . . . It's *real*."

Later, when they had graduated and been through the final training, Dirk and Kian would each have a vessel configured to their own body and nervous system. For now, for the purposes of interfacing and initial flights, the twins were so similar that one ship would suffice for both.

Yet the expense, the sheer size and weight of the vessel and the knowledge that it had cost millions to build, would cost millions more to maintain . . . it was real.

It was theirs.

For the first time they began to accept the enormity of the path that was laid out for them.

But what did Solly mean?

As the twins began to jog once more, this time heading towards the open hangar, their heavier breathing concealed words no eavesdropper could detect.

A bomb on board?

Maybe.

Still, they could not help smiling as they upped the pace, ran towards the bright solid polished ship.

Could be a weapon out in the desert.

Ready to launch when we do.

Pre-dawn gave way to dawn.

A liquid golden blaze slid and dripped along the great polished ship, bronze and powerful as it pointed towards the rising molten sun, filled with the hope and energy of the thousands of men and women and machines who had designed and constructed the vessel.

And if there was a price to be paid by young Pilots submitting themselves to the machiavellian systems of the vast organization which dared to trade with the stars, then it was one they could not help paying in their eagerness to fulfil their bounding ambition: to leap forth from the home planet, into a universe filled with golden space and black spiked stars.

For they were young, and they were proud.

Ready to fly.

<<MODULE ENDS>>

38

NULAPEIRON AD 3426

Tom had an abiding interest in the true nature of spacetime, in the logical rigours of exploring the structure beneath the surface illusion of reality. But this was not the time for cosmological thinking. Now, he had to pull together everything he had learned about minds and emotions, cognitive strategies and modes of perception, and the thousand subtle ways in which thought and body and environment were linked.

Today, Tom would have to manipulate people with an expertise he had never attained before. It was a very different approach to the logosophical disciplines.

Tom remembered his first day at the Sorites School: turning up as directed, where the tall, white-haired Lord Velond waited in an otherwise empty tutorial chamber. Tom was young and a servitor still, and he expected to be serving drinks or moving furniture. But Lord Velond's words shifted his life onto a very different track.

"We need your brain, laddie. Not your brawn."

When Lady Sylvana and the other noble students filed in, Tom took his seat as if he were one of the privileged élite, and not a delta-class servitor whose role in life was menial and whose legal status was little more than that of chattel.

Vistas of logosophical knowledge began to open up that day.

But Lord Velond was not the only person who taught at the Sorites School. Tom could never forget the famous Rhetor Primus, Lord Linski, who taught the pyschomanipulative arts as part of rhetoric. Linski's ability to transform a person's emotions and deeply held beliefs with or without the use of logotropes was legendary.

After the first hectoday under Linski's tutelage, an unspoken conspiracy spread among the students during a particular lecture. They tried to turn the tables and subtly manipulate Lord Linski by minute nods or shakes of the head, using the language of posture and gesture to reinforce or dissuade his movements. It was a form of feedback, and they intended to control Linski so that he would end up standing where they wanted him to.

Just when they thought they had succeeded, and Lord Linski stood on the spot they had been guiding to, smiles broke out upon the students' faces. That was Lord Linski's cue. He made a grand, sweeping gesture that caused a long-prepared tricon to display itself: *I predict the whole class will be facing this spot*—the correct location relative to the chamber's walls was denoted in the tricon's geometry—*and smiling at me, at two minutes before Snapdragon Hour.*

The class gasped, then broke just as a musical tone sounded, denoting Snapdragon Hour. Time for a new class to begin.

Yet the most profound lesson that Tom received in manipulating another's will occurred not when Lord Linski was teaching, but when Linski was absent from the Sorites School, attending a conference in Sektor Grayleim. It was Lord Velond who replaced him.

The students always began tutorials by opening up their infopads, causing blank phase spaces to blossom by each chair. This time, Lord Velond clapped his hands to interrupt them. The unexpected sound reverberated through the chamber.

"You know that induction and deduction are my fields." His elegant voice rang. "So, since my colleague, Lord Linski, is both Rhetor Primus and absent, I would not presume to teach in his place."

A couple of young Lords laughed politely.

"Instead," continued Lord Velond, "I believe we should all go shopping."

Tom's head ached.

He had been learning the Laksheesh names of colours, and how they related to triconic representations, and it was harder than expected. In formal intercourse, there were sixteen thousand hues identified, and their names related not only to electromagnetic frequency but to historical and cultural references unfamiliar to Tom.

The modern term for teal-green, *Vakdosh*, rhymed with the Old Laksheesh term for death. If you did not know that teal was the archaic colour of mourning, it made no semantic sense.

Tom was about to raise his hand and ask for permission to remain behind and study alone, when he saw something the other students (he thought) did not: the dance of amusement in Lord Velond's normally unreadable eyes.

Tom shut down his display. Chairs slid silently back as students stood. Tom took his place among the rest.

Going shopping?

He did not think so.

Before descending, the tutorial group stopped in an antechamber where servitors took their discarded cloaks and half-capes. The noble-born students pulled on surcoats which made them look like young freedmen and freedwomen: apprentices, perhaps, to the white-haired man in the faded green ankle-length coat, for Lord Velond had adopted the appearance of a down-at-heel trader. Velond left his platinum cane in the care of Malgrix Groshe, the alpha servitor who acted as chief caretaker for the School.

Even Tom, though he was not dressed as a Lord, pulled on a drab orange vestment which obscured his black-and-ivory tunic in the house livery of Palace Darinia.

Then Lord Velond led the group to a brown stone chamber where a round steel door was set in the flagstones: a floor hatch leading down to the Secundum Stratum, in a location where no-one would expect it.

Lord Velond himself, when the door had rotated open and the

descending slats had clicked into place to form a spiral stairway, was the first to go down, exuding an air of devilish mischief. The chamber below boasted a second floor hatch, allowing them to descend again.

"No thumb rings," he said, when they finally gathered in a chamber on the Pentium Stratum, four strata below the Sorites School, but a universe away from the world in which the Palace aristocracy lived.

Lord Velond removed the noble-house ring which denoted his rank and inserted it inside his belt. Those among the students who had thin fabric gloves pulled them on; the others followed Lord Velond's lead—save for Tom, who had no need for subterfuge in order to appear a commoner.

They trooped out into a jade-lined broadway, and followed Lord Velond to the nearest mall. From carts and modest boutiques, vendors plied their trade. More than one of the young Ladies—Sylvana among them—paused at a stall where bolts of exotic fabric and racks of subtle bottled fragrances were on show. Lord Velond walked on, tall and straight-backed and as vigorous as a man half his age.

They passed a tavern, then an antiques shop where several of the Lords, including Qizan and Shrolikin (who were among the least prejudiced when it came to having a lowborn studying in their midst), could not help admiring the stained old short-swords and bucklers. Qizan was on the point of picking up a battered vibe-gun when Lord Velond cleared his throat. Qizan took the hint, snatching back his hand as though a narl-serpent had tried to bite him.

"Sorry, sir."

They passed through a wide circular chamber of raw stone whose bulging pillars were adorned with holoflames, while the floor space was set out as a temporary market. It reminded Tom of home, of the smaller marketplace in Salis Core where Father had sold his carved statuettes and talismans. But that was many strata lower than this, and there was no way to contact anyone there.

Did Trude Mulgrave, their old neighbour and family friend, ever wonder what had happened to Tom? Had she learned of his abrupt departure from the Ragged School, his swift involuntary entry into servitude?

Tom shook his head, and hurried to rejoin the group.

They stopped in a tunnel beyond the marketplace, and gathered around Lord Velond.

"There was a garment vendor back there," Lord Velond said, "by the cracked pillar. No, don't look round, Shrolikin, there's a good lad."

"Sir."

"I trust you'll all believe me when I say, I've never set eyes on the proprietor before, and he certainly does not know who I am. Are you prepared to take my word on that?"

"Yes, sir."

"Of course, sir."

"Good. Then follow me, and let's see what occurs."

The young nobles looked at each other. There were shrugs and a few giggles before they followed Lord Velond between the stalls and congregated near the garment seller.

The cloaks hanging from the racks looked like discarded fabric that Malkoril, in the Palace kitchens, would have decreed should be used only to wipe floors, and only then after a drone had done the major cleaning work.

"Do you remember," said Lord Velond to the vendor, "that you sold me a tunic two tendays ago." It was worded like a question, but the intonation said something different.

Lady Sylvana, in her peasant garb, was round-eyed with surprise, and scarcely noticed the two common-born youths at the far side of the market who had stopped to stare at her perfect face. Instead, Sylvana turned round to Tom and whispered:

"Didn't Velond say he'd never been here before?"

Tom nodded. Viscount Humphrey, who had been frowning at them for not staying silent, looked thoughtful, then grinned.

What is Lord Velond up to?

Lord Velond, despite his faded green surcoat, appeared commanding as he straightened, and looked the vendor in the eye.

"W-what?" said the vendor.

"I'm not saying you will have to pay me the full dozen minims." Velond tilted his head a little. "The garment was unsatisfactory, but credit where credit is due. I know you are an honest trader."

The vendor's hands trembled as he reached behind the stall. Then he stopped and stared at Lord Velond. "I don't . . ."

His will was already crumbling when Lord Velond issued the final hidden command: "These twelve or so folk will see you return my minims. You will feel so much better, I'm sure, when you've given me my refund."

As though afflicted with palsy, the vendor shook as he dropped the cred-spindles into Lord Velond's cupped hands. Then he gave a sick, weak smile, and backed off, wiping sweat from his face.

"And good day to you, sir," said Velond.

He commanded *the stallholder.*

Then Lord Velond gave a short bow, turned and walked away through the group of students. They parted as if repelled by a magnet, then followed along, drawn into his wake.

Forced him to hand over the credit.

Tom remained for a moment, regarding the vendor who had been cheated of his credit. The thing was, Lord Linski had talked about the theory which they had seen Lord Velond applying here.

"Use different intonation in the key words," Linski had told them. "Embed a directive inside what *appears* to be an innocuous sentence, even a sentence whose surface meaning is the opposite of your intended meaning. Be subtle in your use of posture, sparing in your use of touch."

Rationally, Tom knew which of the words must have been commands: *will, pay me, dozen minims,* so forth. But Lord Velond had not

even had to tap the vendor on the shoulder—a common technique—
in order to shock him into a different state of mind.

I couldn't hear a difference in the tone.

Tom knew what Velond had done. He did not know *how* he had
done it.

The rest of the group was following Lord Velond, drawn along by
his personal magnetism, or a desire to be like him . . . or perhaps in
response to a hidden command which made sense only to a Lord, to
someone whose noble-house upbringing brought a certain sensibility
to attitude and intonation.

By study and hard work (solo at first, then under Mistress
eh'Nalephi's tutelage), Tom had accumulated merit-points. Each new
accreditation earned merit-points which allowed him to access more
eduthreads. But since starting at the Sorites School, he no longer had
to use merit-points, save for additional study modules purchased from
the Palace AIs. Recently, Tom had converted some of his bonuses into
cred-spindles.

He spent them at crystal shops whenever he could, buying ancient
dramas and logosophy texts and anything else that snagged his
interest.

Now, Tom dug inside his waistband, found four spindles, checked
their values. Four spindles, containing three minims each. The vendor
had handed exactly twelve minims over to Lord Velond.

Is that a coincidence?

The hairs prickled on the back of Tom's neck.

Or is Lord Velond playing a manipulative game with me, too?

Either way, it did not matter. Tom walked over to the garment
vendor, who was staring into space and ruminating. He jumped a little
at Tom's approach.

"Did you really," Tom asked, "owe credit to that tall man who was
here just now?"

"I . . . Yes. No . . . Well, I don't think so."

"But you handed it over."

"He . . ." The vendor swallowed. "He expected me to, like."

"Even though the credit wasn't his. You hadn't sold him anything."

"Well . . ."

"And if he had bought a garment from you, and wanted a refund, he would have brought the original tunic back, wouldn't he?"

"I . . . guess so."

Tom waited, then realized he was torturing the poor fellow with uncertainty and self-doubt. "My Lady Darinia"—Tom adopted the patrician tones he heard every day in the Palace—"will be pleased to know she has such a loyal subject. And of course you should not be out of credit. Here."

Tom handed over the cred-spindles, all twelve minims' worth.

Then he strode quickly away, heart beating fast as he sped up, knowing he was in trouble if he did not rejoin the group before they reached a ceiling hatch and ascended to the next stratum . . . But somehow he doubted that Lord Velond would leave him behind.

Tom found them sitting outside an eatery, sipping daistral and eating boljicream cakes, all purchased with Lord Velond's ill-gotten minims. As Tom joined them, Lord Velond snapped his fingers, and a servitrix brought Tom a goblet, handed it over with a polite curtsy, then withdrew.

The others, young Lords and Ladies all, were laughing, enjoying the joke they had seen played out in the marketplace, talking over the high points, trying to work out how Lord Velond had accomplished it.

Tom raised the goblet in a silent toast, and the gleam in Lord Velond's eyes was both mocking and understanding as Tom, still standing, drank the daistral which in some sense he had paid for himself. He did not expect Lord Velond to reimburse him for the twelve minims.

But you, my Lord, have given me the greater gift.

On another occasion, Sylvana said to Tom: "To you, logosophy is a *weapon*."

And neurolinguistic rhetoric was the most subtle weapon he could possess.

That was seventeen Standard Years ago.

Now shadows shrouded the empty conference chamber. Night winds whispered in empty skies that bore the terraformer aloft, and perhaps Tom heard the spirit of the Oracle he had knifed to death in this place. Then, he had thought that Gérard d'Ovraison, an Oracle who could bring his consciousness into normal timeflow and wield considerable charm, was scarcely human. Now, the Oracle's words were haunting him.

"*If you could remember*"—Gérard d'Ovraison had spoken in ice-cold tones—"*the moment of your own death, your outlook, too, would change.*"

For Tom *had* seen his own death, and no longer knew whether it guaranteed victory or defeat in a world that had already fallen to the Enemy.

Tactical models hung over the table, cast a muted glow, denoting comms-webs and military dispositions; fallen realms; regiments who still fought back, on the surface and far below. Holo images failed to show the hard reality of hand-to-hand struggles in half-lit tunnels: epic battles which history would never record but which for the participants were mortal.

We're losing.

There was no other interpretation.

One hundred and thirty-seven terraformer spheres now housed refugees: some were civilians, others were trained military. Many were broken and defeated, their families abandoned in realms that had already been subsumed by the Anomaly. Everyone they had known was now merged into that single, dark entity whose cognitive processes were as far removed from human thought as logosophy was from a microbe's chemical tropisms.

Some of the refugees—too few, perhaps—burned with the need for vengeance.

It's time.

Finally. If there was a purpose to life, if Destiny was anything more than a single sloping path down which time tumbled, this was it.

It's my time.

The weapons of manipulation which Lord Velond had allowed Tom to glimpse so long ago were what he needed now.

The routed military forces, desperate to regroup, had their own commanders, each with his or her own ideas on what should happen next. The shuttles had continued to rise from Nulapeiron's surface, and no-one had been turned away.

The Anomaly had not yet directed its attention to the rag-tag army gathering in the sky. Now was the time for someone to take control. Someone who knew what must be done to save the world.

What if I'm kidding myself?

The answer was obvious: Nulapeiron would be no worse off than it was right now.

And if I'm right—

Tom walked around the chamber, planning. He would stand on *this* spot to deliver the difficult information. He would stand *there* to make light-hearted interjections when he needed to lift the attendees' mood.

Every off-the-cuff remark Tom planned now, knowing he would deliver it with an apparent spontaneity that even Lord Velond or Lord Linski would applaud. He rehearsed the full sequence of tactical displays in his mind, knowing how the chamber's lighting and his stance would shape the attendees' perceptions: the thoughts and feelings of those who commanded the last free forces in the world.

I have to get it right.

Again.

From the beginning . . .

Tom rehearsed the whole presentation through, over and over. Then he waved the display out of existence, sat on the tabletop, and waited.

And waited.

While the hours passed.

Finally, as morning brightened the chamber and hard sunlight splayed across the blue-and-white floor, Tom looked up at the ceiling and said: "It's time."

A welcome aroma drifted from a side-chamber.

<Daistral. A block of clean-gel, too.>

"Thank you, Axolon."

Tom slid off the table, onto his feet.

"Summon the commanders now."

39

NULAPEIRON AD 3426

Polite murmurs did little to hide the tension as the various commanders and delegates took their places around the long conference table. Others took seats among the rows which spread out to either side, leaving a space clear from which Tom could address them.

He smiled and nodded, just a little, as they filed in.

Trevalkin. I wish you were here now.

At that thought, a sardonic laugh echoed inside Tom's mind, though he kept his expression blank. Trevalkin was too treacherous to trust; but his support in this could have swung things Tom's way.

So I'm on my own.

That was the way it had always been when the crunch came.

Until I get these people behind me.

Tom wore his black tunic with the red insignia emblazoned on the front. Later, he planned to stroll around the terraformer sphere with Jissie beside him, if the day was a success; but for now there was business to transact. The terraformer's upper levels were clear of children.

In the skies outside, flyers hovered, and that was a danger: that Anomaly-controlled forces might notice the activity and grow curious. It could not be avoided: this was something that Tom had to do in person, as Lords Velond and Linski had taught him so many years ago.

I hope I live up to your teachings, my Lords.

At the table's far end, Elva was seated with Adam Gervicort to her right, Kraiv on her left. Next to Kraiv sat a narrow-bodied man with long arms roped with muscle: Volksurd, cousin to Queen Lirna and ruler of Clan Hetreece . . . of those who survived. Both Kraiv and Volk-surd bore copper helms thrown back across one shoulder, hanging from straps. Their morphospears stood against the wall.

Around the main table, in addition to the carls, sat the commanders that Tom considered most valuable to the cause. Some were natural allies; others were here to pursue agendas of their own. Already, cliques had been forming in private meetings in the halls and docking bays outside.

Beside Volksurd, Captain Goray took his seat. Goray's Liege Lord, Count Dvalkin, had died before his privy council's eyes when metallic *others* appeared from nothingness inside the Star Chambers and cut down the highest ranking nobles first.

Tom mentally reviewed names and biographies at lightning speed: Goray, who, slim and soft-looking, had led a team of battle-hardened Dragoons who cut and blasted their way to freedom; Vintranne Zhoframinova, tactician and combat instructor for the Rohlmay Spectaculars; Lady Xamila, wide-eyed and trembling, but commanding an impressive regiment of Palace Guards; Truholm Janix, bearded Lord and Academician, an unknown quantity; and a brother and sister of the House A'Vinsenberg, noble-born but gazing at Tom with worshipful eyes; finally their aide, angular-bodied and ebony-skinned, Lieutenant Xim eh'Gelifni.

Then there were key players whom Tom could not be sure of manipulating, such as Lady Flurella: white-haired and crimson-eyed, most malevolent. Her burning desire for revenge was directed at the alien *things* which had despoiled her realm. (Tom would not want to number among her enemies.)

Ankestion Raglok was purple-skinned, his black eyebrows formed of graphite crystals, his eyes green with horizontal slits. Two of his clone-brothers stood near the wall. Twenty-three separate clone-clans had escaped the realm known as Druvogue Fastness.

And then there was General Lord Ygran.

The general was white-moustachioed, a senior officer who had served as a colonel under Field-Marshal Lord Takegawa during the Rikoshine Revolt, promoted to General on the battlefield. Ygran was experienced in the enormously complex politics of melding disparate allies into a joint fighting force, despite differences in protocols and command structures and the diverging goals of their separate realms.

Corduven had admired him.

Tom knew enough military history to realize that wars had been lost because a commander-in-chief was unable to organize mixed forces under one aegis. Of the military leaders that Tom knew about, only Lord Takegawa, Corduven's mentor in military logosophy, was better qualified than Ygran.

But according to Fire Watch reports which Tom had no reason to doubt, Field-Marshal Lord Takegawa had recently taken a battalion into action in the former Realm Boltrivar, destroying significant sections of the encroaching front line, until Absorbed components that had never been human materialized amid swirling black flames, and tore apart the senior officers one by one. Takegawa, just as the Anomaly reached into his brain and began Absorption, turned his graser pistol upon himself, blasting his own head out of existence.

Perhaps we're the best of what's left.

Elva. Adam. Kraiv. Volksurd, the carls' leader. Pale Captain Goray. Vintranne Zhoframinova, capable and professional. Lady Xamila, afraid but commanding strong forces. Truholm Janix, intellectual, character unknown. The A'Vinsenberg siblings and the tough-looking Lieutenant eh'Gelifni. Lady Flurella, the malevolent albino. Ankestion Raglok and his clone-brothers: Academy-trained members of an élite long-range penetration squadron. General Lord Ygran.

You're the key, Ygran.

There were nearly two hundred others crowding in now: tactical officers, aristocrats with little to offer by way of military force or com-

petence, technical researchers, experienced partisans who had already fought
in Anomaly-dominated demesnes. Lady Renata had a seat near the door.

Hovering in the background on her silver lev-tray was the glistening flensed head of Eemur, which so disconcerted those who did not
know her that they looked away, unable to process the sight.

**You're different now, my sweet Lord. Stronger. More deter-
mined.**

Tom inclined his head. That was the truth.

But are you determined enough?

He smiled.

We'll soon find out.

Then he nodded to Elva, who rose to her feet and addressed the
assembled nobles and officers. "It's time to make a start."

Tom was resourceful. He was *inspired*.

"—one great chance to survive is our strongest means of victory—"

Using every trick of rhetoric, the hidden commands in speech
backed up with subliminal directives of body posture which went
straight to hardwired primate behaviour . . . and in some cases all the
way to the ancient reptilian mind situated deep inside every human
brain.

"—the Enemy is concentrated below, but we have freedom of the
skies and near-space beyond—"

Tactical displays whirled through their sequence of messages:
designed not just to build up a subtle emotional impact but to hit
beats and rhythms in synch with the electrical cycles of the visual
cortex, as Tom controlled the chamber's mood.

At one point, as that mood became too sombre, Tom stepped to the
floor-tile which he had already stood on to make appropriate jokes. The
hairs rose up on the back of Tom's neck as the commanders—sub-
consciously conditioned—straightened in their seats and smiled before
he had even begun to make his lighthearted aside.

It's as if I'm controlling their emotions with a slider switch.

Tom knew now why dictators fell victim to their own adrenaline rush. Imagine the god-like power you would feel addressing a thousand, or a hundred thousand people in this fashion!

It was possible. In fact, it might be easier: a vast crowd automatically grew a collective mind of its own, one with fewer psychological defences than individuals.

"—certain it is *not* our Destiny to fall before a different kind of life-form. We may be more complex than bacteria, but bacteria still exist! They are the *dominant* biomass, and if they can manage to find niches in which to live, then I'm damned sure that human beings have the guts and determination and foresight and will to—"

Volksurd was nodding. Anomaly be damned: if it truly were unstoppable, he would still go down fighting. Lady Xamila, who had been so afraid she trembled, was looking stronger by the minute, as if strengthened by the mental force broadcast by Tom.

Not so much force, Tom thought, *as resonance.*

Locking their thoughts in synch with his.

"—we can fight and run, merge back into the forests and wastelands of the surface—"

Lieutenant eh'Gelifni smiled. This was a concept he cared for.

But that was when Tom paused, and General Lord Ygran coughed. And Tom knew he would have to let this renowned soldier take the floor, and deal with the consequences afterwards.

"There." Ygran pointed at the chamber's floor. "Is that the spot where you slew the previous owner of this sphere?"

Tom blinked.

Ygran's words drew a reaction among the commanders. Intakes of breath. Some jerked back in their chairs, losing their subconscious rapport with Tom.

"You know," Tom said, "I was declared innocent in that matter."

General Ygran began to speak, but Tom continued: "Yet if we are to fight together, we must trust each other. So, yes . . . I slew the Oracle. I had reason to."

That's done it.

General Ygran stared at Tom for a long moment. Then:

"Well said, sir. The exploit is legendary." General Ygran's white moustache bristled as he smiled. "According to our élite forces who analysed the scenario, the only way in was a free-climb from the very bottom of the sphere up to the top. Entering right there." Ygran pointed at the membrane-window leading to the balcony. "With no smart-tech whatsoever, since internal scans would have picked up the microwave resonance."

"Just so."

"And you killed an Oracle whose sworn truecast indicated his eventual death of old age, decades from now."

"That's right, General."

So now they knew.

Try me now, if you want.

There must be a way of finding Tom guilty despite the document signed by Corduven . . . but General Lord Ygran was standing up, hands at his sides.

Making a formal bow.

"Then you are the right man, Lord Corcorigan, to lead the free forces of Nulapeiron against the Anomaly."

There were murmurs, there were nods, and then every one of the two-hundred-and-more nobles and freeborn rose to their feet and cheered. All of them . . . save for the albino Lady Flurella, whose scarlet eyes glowed in a way Tom had not seen before. Suddenly tricons were floating before him: virtual images, lased directly into Tom's retinas, invisible to everyone else.

You manipulated them with finesse, my Lord.

Flurella could ruin everything.

There was a long delay while the commanders and aides continued cheering, but Tom was sure that his schemes were in ashes. Then Lady Flurella gave a cold, slow smile.

Don't worry. As Ygran says: it proves you're the right person for this job.

She did not mean it as a compliment.

No matter. So long as we bring down the Anomaly.

Tom wondered how many other autocrats had thought the same thing as they took control for selfless reasons.

"What kind of actions," said General Ygran as the approving sounds died down, "do you propose, my Lord?"

"Here." Tom pointed into the holo. "And here. There are large armies already encamped, not allied to us, but fighting against Anomalous forces." He looked around the chamber, at the enraptured gazes. "We strike around the Enemy's flanks, extract as many free forces as we can."

General Ygran nodded. There had to be more, but he understood that this was too large a forum for Tom to share detailed battle plans.

"I'll tell you one thing right now," said Tom. "This is going to be a war not only of courage, but of *intellect*."

"And the legendary Lord One-Arm"—General Ygran smiled— "known also as The Oracle Killer, is *exactly* the right person to lead us."

Tom took a deep breath.

The kaon-koan. A shield around the world.

In the end, that was his only strategy.

There was a final rousing speech Tom had planned to make, but before he could step back to his earmarked position on the floor—Lady Flurella, seeing his intention, gave a sardonic smile—General Ygran pushed his way to the front of the gathered audience.

Ygran. You can take the power.

General Ygran turned to face the commanders.

They will follow you.

"You know who I am. Perhaps you don't know"—and here he moved to the area of the floor from which Tom had made his few jokes—"that old soldiers like me are mostly history buffs, who'd rather be at home wearing slippers immersed in old crystal tales"—there were chuckles; then Ygran shifted, echoing Tom's most commanding posture: he possessed skills of neurolinguistic rhetoric in his own right—"and I tell you now, this world has never been in such danger since the Founding Wars. Perhaps not even then."

The smiles faded.

"Accordingly," General Ygran continued, "I propose that we rein-stitute a precept from the *Codex Belligerens*."

He gestured a holo into being.

In the time of greatest danger, appoint a single leader over all.
That person's decision shall be the final word in every dispute.
Their orders will be obeyed unquestioned, without delay.

Tom shook his head.
This was not my plan.

In the chamber the air was still, as though the whole of Axolon Array had inhaled a communal breath and held it.

"I propose," said General Ygran, "that Lord Corcorigan should *not* be nominated as Commander-in-Chief of the freedom forces. Instead we must—"

Blood-rush washed in Tom's ears. He was about to stagger.
Control.

Breathe, that was it.
Steady.

General Ygran had the floor. For now, the audience was his.

"—appoint him Warlord Primus, supreme military commander, and more: ruler of Nulapeiron."

Stunned silence expanded in the chamber.

No . . .

Then Volksurd, the carls' chieftain, sprang to his feet, fists high in the air.

"We offer the Enemy . . . *Blood and Death!*"

Kraiv leaped up beside him. "Hail to the Warlord Primus!"

You can't do this.

They were all standing now, raising their fists and joining in one tumultuous roar:

"Warlord Primus!"

Then Tom bowed—

"*Warlord Primus!* WARLORD PRIMUS!"

—accepting the title they bestowed—

I will do it.

—and in that moment, became the acknowledged ruler of the world in which he lived.

"*WARLORD PRIMUS!*"

I vow to save you all.

Adrenaline still charged the atmosphere as the officers and nobles and tacticians left the chamber in twos and threes, chattering excitedly as they went down the spiral stairs to the terraformer's core levels, pulsating with the sure knowledge that they had a chance for victory.

If I don't let you down.

Soon there were only a few left: General Lord Ygran, sitting with his hands on his knees nodding to himself at a job well done; Elva and the two carls, Kraiv and Volksurd; several others chatting in small groups.

On a lev-tray which had not moved during the whole meeting, but now lifted a few centimetres from the shelf on which she had parked herself, floated the bloodied, striated head of Eemur, wearing her black moirée cap.

Warlord Primus, no less.

Tom could only nod. No-one else in the chamber had the ability to hear her silent words, much less the ironic tones that embellished them.

Who would have thought it?

He remembered sitting in an alcove near a small, poor marketplace in Salis Core, writing poetry on an old infotablet. From there to here was such a journey that the fourteen-year-old Tom Corcorigan scarcely seemed the same person.

Ruler of all Nulapeiron.

Of a world, Tom reminded himself, where the greater part was under the control of a massive powerful entity that did not belong here.

Kraiv said something to Elva, who nodded.

I'm going to do my best.

It was all that Tom could do.

But you know they'll turn against you—

Tom snapped his head round to stare at Eemur.

—when they see you're not human any more.

For a moment Tom felt paralysed. Then he answered her aloud:

"Maybe. But by then it will no longer matter."

Elva's eyes widened as Tom's words revealed the depth of the link between himself and Eemur's Head, a Seer beheaded centuries ago but living still. Tom felt the innocent days of his childhood ebb further and further into a peaceful past which could never be reached again.

Tom's one hand tingled.

Then sapphire flames glowed, licked across his fingertips, and were gone before anyone besides himself and Elva noticed.

40
TERRA AD 2166

<<Ro's Children>>
[11]

If it were not for Solly, and the way he had stopped outside the twins' bedroom broadcasting his fear through the closed door—warning of sabotage or attack or *something* which threatened Dirk's and Kian's lives—this would have been a day of triumph. Instead, the twins sat with Deirdre in a chill air-conditioned lounge while their nerves twitched and jangled.

Deirdre used her infostrand to set up a random integer generator. An odd number meant Kian; even meant Dirk. "Guys, this is the simplest function I've set up since I was five."

When the call came through from Human Engineering, they recognized the voice of Paula, the crop-haired young woman who had smiled at Deirdre.

"We're ready for you now, Dirk or Kian. Take the down-slide to bay seventeen, where a TDV is waiting."

"OK."

"Got that."

Still sitting, they turned to look at Deirdre, who tapped the strand wrapped around her wrist. A number glowed in front of her.

"Seventeen," she said. "I guess that means you, Kian, good buddy."

"Always the lucky one." Kian looked at Dirk.

"Right." Blood faded from Dirk's face. "You're always lucky, bro."

The lounge door opened, and an automatic holosign pointed the way to the waiting ground vehicle. Kian stood.

After Kian left, Dirk turned to Deirdre.

"I want to watch from outside."

"But we're both supposed to go to the control—"

"I know."

Deirdre blinked.

"Right. I'll . . . I'll tell Paula you're in the john. Bad case of the squits, as my sainted mother used to say. It happens when you're nervous."

"Didn't Kian say your mother lives in Portland?"

"Does that mean she can't be a saint?"

"Ha." Dirk leaned forward and kissed her cheek. "Thanks."

"Good luck."

But Deirdre's eyes were damp as she left, as though she, too, sensed the threat.

Come on. Dirk's heart beat faster. *The danger must be outside.*

The ship's control cabin smelled new, a mixed scent of organics and metal. The seat, adjusting itself to Kian's form, felt both solid and oily as it morphed.

I'm not scared.

Status displays billowed: phase spaces and graphs, number-grids and vector-arrows enumerating a myriad subsystem values. And that was merely the top-level overview of an immensely complicated craft.

I'm bloody terrified.

Diagnostics scrolled through a dozen holos. Kian shut his eyes.

What does my blood pressure look like now?

If he asked the question aloud, someone in the control tower would answer him. They could probably say how likely he was to piss himself before take-off.

"How long is this going to take?"

The answer came back straight away: *"Not long now, Pilot Candidate McNamara. Hold on to your horses."*

"Yee-ha, roger that."

And I hope to Christ Dirk works out what's happening.

The scent of Kian's sweat strengthened in the cabin.

In a ground-level bay, heavy outer doors were sliding shut.

"Hey! You can't—"

Golden sparks glimmered in Dirk's eyes.

The doors screeched, halted, leaving a narrow gap.

"What the goddamn hell?"

He squeezed through.

The hot air was hammering down. The great ship was gleaming.

Dirk ran towards the runway.

Up in the control tower, Deirdre stood next to Chief Controller Bratko. From here, through blue-tinted windows, the poised ship was deep-bronze banded with darkness: the green-blue ceramic appeared almost black.

"—clearing you to go," said one of the controllers.

At the ship's rear, the engines increased power—pale flames expanding into nova-white brightness—while the vessel rocked on its undercarriage, straining against the brakes which kept it bound to Terra.

"My God," breathed Deirdre. "Will you look at that."

"Makes my heart thud"—Bratko touched his bulky chest—"every single time."

Then he was leaning forward as two of the controllers rose from their seats, pointing at the small figure streaking across the tarmac, running towards the ship.

"Who the hell is—?"

"Dirk." Deirdre's voice was unnaturally calm. "Something's wrong."

Bratko spun fast despite his heaviness.

"Shut down. Immediate shut down."

There was a moment's silence as fingers danced in control displays, voices muttered commands. Then a young-looking controller rotated her chair and looked at Bratko.

"No response. Main thruster's still burning."

"Shit."

At the control room's rear, Solly was shaking, wiping large runnels of sweat from his forehead.

Come on, Dirk.

Deirdre's attention was all on the running figure below.

Come on.

In the ship's control couch, Kian closed his eyes.

"Pulse engines are go."

The great roar, however muted by protective insulation, was deep and massive behind him. Status displays brightened as the ship gathered its power, strained against the leash.

Then something shifted at the edge of Kian's awareness, in the twilight between subconsciousness and thought.

Dirk?

It was a kind of distant movement that he could not see but *felt.*

"Control? Come in, control."

No reply.

"Onboard command: shutdown-shutdown-shutdown."

Nothing.

Behind him the engines' power continued to build.

Dirk could sense it, where the starboard delta-wing met the fuselage: a tugging against the natural flux, a warp in the rising energies that overrode system commands while blazing starfire brightened at the vessel's tail.

Hang on, Kian.

Running faster along the runway, getting closer.

I can feel you now, you bastard.

It was a definite presence inside the wing. Insulated in the Pilot's cabin, Kian would be sitting above the huge energies growing in the vessel, shielded from the tiny malevolent presence that did not belong on a well-ordered ship.

A bomb?

Getting closer.

I can see the access hatch.

But the roar was palpable, shaking the air, and it was hard to breathe this close to the titanic engines.

No.

Percussive waves slapped Dirk to the ground.

Damn it . . . No.

On hands and knees, he hung his head, blood dripping to the tarmac. Then he looked up at the wing, where the device was hidden, and began to concentrate. Golden lights danced in the blackness of his eyes.

Where are you?

It was not enough to sense its presence: he must go inside, parse its internal complexity and hold the thing in place.

There?

Questing.

Yes, there.

Now Dirk's eyes held a steady yellow glow like a wolf caught in headlights.

Got you.

The device had intelligence. Its counteroffensive modules activated, trying to regain control, but Dirk's focused power beat them down.

Got you, motherfucker.

A hatch popped atop the vessel. Kian clambered half out, stopped with one leg dangling against the hull.

Jesus, Dirk.

Concentrating.

I'm with you.

But Kian was still interfaced with the ship. Even as he joined forces with Dirk in containing the device's murderous system commands, he pulsed internal directives through the control cabin's emergency processors, activating catastrophe-procedures in sequences that had never been envisaged by the engineers who built the vessel, executing protocols that should be impossible while engines were firing up.

Underneath the wing, an access hatch snapped open.

I've got it, Dirk.

His grip tightened against metal as he sensed his brother move.

An emergency TDV, orange lights flashing, came hurtling from a maintenance bay.

Behind it, fire tenders and other stragglers followed.

The wing was too high to jump at but Dirk could see the thing now, a white boxlike presence that did not belong, fastened by electromagnets to the main conduits; and that was no problem at all. A tug, a redirection of power, and the magnets became inert.

The white box dropped.

Got you.

Dirk caught it—damn, it was heavy!—but he held on, not dropping it, sensing that there were internal pulse-explosives ready to blow: the saboteurs had not relied solely on the ship's own engines blowing apart under misdirection.

The TDV screeched to a halt beside him.

The driver, a round-faced man stained with grease, poked his head out. "Hey pal, you OK?"

"Get away!" Dirk swung the white box and himself onto the TDV's flat bed. "Get us the hell away from here!"

"*Bozhe moi*, you got it!"

The vehicle spun on the spot, accelerated at a forty-five-degree angle away from the runway and control tower both, heading for the boundary and open desert.

Moved faster.

Kian's first impulse was to slide down from the ship and try to get to the ground, but the TDV with Dirk aboard was two hundred metres away and still accelerating.

And there was a faint uneasiness born not of natural senses but his interface with the ship's long-range sensor loops.

"Sweet bleeding hell."

Kian frowned, concentrated.

Below the wing, the access hatch snapped back up, locked into place once more.

"Move it, move it."

Kian pulled himself back into the cabin, not needing to see the scarlet ellipse flaring in the display to know that something big was coming. Something from the sky.

Two ellipses.

"Oh, God."

The overhead hatch thumped down and his chair was morphing, grasping him like a gloved fist as the brakes came free and the great bronze ship began to roll.

At the boundary the TDV braked, its thermoacoustic motor whining to a halt. Dirk stood on the flat bed with one foot on either side of the white box, squatted down to grab it, back straight.

"You all right up there, pal?"

Dirk braced himself . . .

"If you want, I could—"

. . . lifted and swung, and the box made a short arcing drop, thudded into the ground.

In Dirk's obsidian eyes, the yellow lights shifted, formed complex patterns.

"Take us back," he called down to the driver. "Don't hang around."

"*Bozhe moi!*"

The sudden lurch toppled Dirk so he fell on his side, but the glow remained in his eyes, and his gaze stayed fixed on the white box receding in the TDV's wake.

In the control tower, Deirdre and the crew were frozen, staring at the events taking place below, only half-understanding them.

Then something—a rustle of cloth, the scent of fear—caused her to turn and see Solly backing away towards the exit, jowls trembling, mouth open like a landed fish, his face layered with shining sweat.

"I . . . I d-d-didn't w-w—"

Deirdre took two long silent strides forward.

And swung her foot into Solly's groin.

In the rattling TDV, Dirk judged the distance was great enough.

He lowered his head.

BANG!

The flat hard sound smacked the air. Screeching, the TDV curved to a halt.

Black, stinking smoke belched from the twisted white remains: the bomb.

But Dirk was staring up into the sky, to the small dark point high above the horizon that grew visibly larger as he watched its diving trajectory towards the runway.

He snapped around to see Kian's bronze ship begin to move.

Get out of here.

The strange vessel was more than a point now. Its configuration was alien, growing larger.

A Zajinet?

Come on, Kian. Get out of here.

The younger controllers sat on top of Solly's squirming bulk until security officers came and fastened his wrists and ankles with smart-rubber bindings, while Bratko gave Solly's ribs a kick which everyone pretended not to see.

But the alarms that sounded next indicated a new ship coming in high and fast, and there was no reason to expect an UNSA vessel. Sabotage had failed, and someone or something was shifting to the direct approach.

Deirdre stumbled back towards the tinted window.

The bronze ship with Kian inside was moving faster on the runway, gathering speed for take-off.

Too late.

Growing huge in the sky, the intruder let rip a beam of energy in front of Kian's vessel. Kian reacted fast, spinning the great bronze bird off to one side as the alien hurtled overhead.

The strange vessel had blasted a smoking trench across the yellow tarmac.

"Oh, Christ. Kian!"

But the bronze vessel was stuck in sand, unable to back up or reach a clear length of runway.

While in the sky, the intruder was arcing around.

Ready for a second strafing run on a big heavy target that could not move.

"Shit shit shit."

Kian fought through the interface, knowing there was no time to leave the ship and run, desperate to use those immense engines, feeling the whole vessel lurch as sand enveloped half the undercarriage.

"No."

The display whirled in urgent primary colours, and *both* intruders rendered as blood-red ellipses arced in for the final approach.

Two of them.

From the halted truck, Dirk could only watch the Zajinet fighting vessel dive towards Kian's halted ship.

No. Please God, no.

Then a silver delta-winged vessel burst out of the sun, and its graser gatlings split the air with a hundred sun-bright beams and swung towards the intruder.

At the last moment the Zajinet tried to evade, in a daring sideways dive.

But the silver vessel tracked the move and the blazing beams struck and everything was over. The Zajinet intruder blew apart in a cacophony of fire and light that no observer that day would ever forget.

The silver ship arced upwards into the blue sky, glowing with brilliant light.

Was gone.

Only emptiness, the desert, and smoking wreckage remained.

The TDV driver helped Dirk down onto the tarmac, kept hold of his upper arm. Dirk wavered a moment, then pulled himself upright.

"Thanks."

"Huh." The driver wiped grease from his forehead, turned to stare at blackened debris strewn beyond the runway. "Who was that?" And, looking up to the empty sky: "And what the Devil was that silver ship?"

Dirk's laugh was weak but proud.

"That was my mother."

"Oh. *Bozhe moi.*"

"And it's a good job she didn't get *really* mad."

<<MODULE ENDS>>

41

NULAPEIRON AD 3426

Warlord Primus Tom Corcorigan began his war of retribution.

You will not have my world, Anomaly.

For the first phase, nothing would be different. Avernon's whereabouts were unknown (except possibly to Trevalkin, who was out of contact) and Tom's researchers had gone as far as they could without extra guidance. They needed the spacetime-manipulating technology that existed only in the Collegium Perpetuum Delphinorum. The weaponry available to the freedom forces—whether launched from terraformer spheres in Nulapeiron's skies or fighting on the surface or in the occupied strata—was conventional.

The Anomaly retained all the advantages: able to materialize forces (both human and alien) without warning, subject only to geometric restrictions impossible to determine; Absorbing human components into itself in a process no-one could get close enough to observe without falling prey to it (and some two dozen volunteers had tried); and its mentality was so far beyond its minuscule opponents that its purposes remained unknown and unpredictable, the power of its advance overwhelming wherever it chose to concentrate its forces.

And yet, perhaps one thing had changed.

For now the human freedom fighters had a single commander: co-ordinating through many layers of delegation and imperfect communication, but still with a single mind and a single purpose.

Humanity had a Warlord Primus.

You will not take my world!

A Warlord who could See.

◇◇◇

Slowly, communication webs strengthened, extruded finer tendrils into the world. Tightened.

In the command centre of Axolon Array, tactical displays now shone constantly, attended by teams of planners and advisers relaying advice and instructions to those who fought the war below.

Most of the senior officers put their emotions to one side as they disposed forces in fraught situations, measured gain and loss strategically and expressed them as numbers: topographically vital tunnels and broadways held, percentages fallen and wounded. At night, they could only imagine as they tried to sleep what the human cost of their decisions might be: the screaming of a wounded resistance fighter with her leg shorn off as graser beams spat overhead; the courier's terrified run through dank tunnels as the Enemy closed in; the dark insidious rape as a force beyond humanity entered a soldier's mind and turned a man into a component.

But Tom did not need to imagine these things.

Blood glistens on the stump. Above, her thigh is creamy and unblemished, her garments burned away, the skin untouched. The graser has half-cauterized the severed arteries and she scratches at the stump, far beyond pain, praying she can squirt her life-blood onto rubble before the Anomaly comes to take her.

Tom could See them.

Splash as his boot goes into a puddle. Echoes up ahead where shadows fill the tunnel but there is an opening to his left and he ducks through. Crawls, rolls, is on his feet once more.

Cold and shivering. The soldiers are closer now.

Run.

Gathering new insight.

The air crackles as the man's eyes roll up and there is a lick of darkness which is symptomatic of tunnelling through spacetime, neural links conjoined through the rat-infested crawlspace which lies below normal reality as he becomes one microscopic cell in the great Anomaly and his mouth lolls open then stretches in a madman's smile.

Tom could See them all.

Tom grew confident in his ability to control and direct the visualizations which so directly reflected the abilities of his Enemy. Once, when he established contact with research labs deep within the Collegium Perpetuum Delphinorum, he watched (from his terraformer base, thousands of kilometres away) the painstaking work they performed, the complex logosophical model built using intricate holodisplays . . .

Pain, and the Dark Fire shimmering.

. . . and then saw the alien incursion, heard the screams, regarded the bravery of Collegiate researchers who contrived to release the zero-point vacuum energy from their spacetime manipulators. Normally they used it to drive their hypergeometric transformations, their bending of the universe, in the same way that a water mill might draw power from a river's flow; but now, the devices erupted in a cascading tidal wave of blazing light and sound that split air and rock, creating a sequence of flash-explosions that ripped the heart out of the Collegium, killing every human (and former human) and metallic being within the inner boundaries.

"*Chaos*, no . . ." Tom withdrew whimpering from the trance. "The Collegium . . ."

The Collegium was gone. The researchers had destroyed it, and themselves.

But we needed them.

He was on a couch in their family chamber, and Jissie was looking scared. Then the membrane door softened and Elva stepped inside.

"Jissie, why did you call—? Tom, are you all right?"

"The Collegium. I just Saw it . . . They killed themselves. Took the Anomaly's people and . . . things . . . with them."

"But we need their tech." Elva looked pale. "You said yourself, we can't drop a shield in place without their techniques."

Jissie spoke up. "Which one was it?"

"Sorry?"

"Jissie, dear, we don't have time for—"

"Was it the Collegiate site near Realm Buchanan," said Jissie, "or the one in Rigay Larn, or the one in Strehling Suhltône? Just wondering."

Tom and Elva stared at each other.

"Near Realm Buchanan." Tom sat up on the couch. Sweat trickled either side of his nose, and his eyes stung. "The one where—"

The one where Elva had served undercover, as Commander Herla Hilsdottir in a Blight-controlled death camp, for far too long. Where she and Tom had broken free.

Where on the surface, the great glass edifice used by the Blight to contact the Anomalous hellworlds had exploded, undergone a heatless phase transition to produce the Lake of Glass that encased two hundred and fifty thousand people whose minds had formed a small yet significant component of the Blight.

And where Jissie's parents lay entombed.

So many dead.

Elva knelt down at Tom's side and took hold of his hand.

"We will get through this." Then she turned to Jissie. "And how were you aware, young woman, that the Collegium spans—spanned—three sites? That's not common knowledge."

"Renata told me. She's nice. We chat a lot."

Elva clapped Tom's thigh and stood. "Looks like we need to recruit two new strategic command officers."

"Two?" said Tom.

"Well, Jissie, obviously. Maybe Lady Renata will make the grade as well."

Jissie's smile was the first good thing Tom had seen for days.

In a translucent hologlobe representing Nulapeiron, dark sectors continued to expand like spilled ink. Only at high magnification did the small bright lines of the freedom fighters' flying columns grow visible.

It took local-scale diagrams to denote the acts of sabotage and assassination of a desperate resistance movement fighting against a power that would not stop growing.

Spreading darkness.

And, where three specific locations had been picked out in blue, one had been blackened from existence. Crescents of Anomaly-controlled territory curled and tightened around the remaining two.

Tom Saw:

A raiding party creeps through a ruined banquet hall, clambering over fallen blocks of shattered marble, into the heart of a former Palace. Some of them stop to admire the marble-and-jade, platinum-inlaid bedchambers of the fled nobility. They grin or shake their heads.

And stop dead.

There is a whisper of sound.

Blindmoths explode in a flurry from a crack in the wall, flutter near the diamond-mirrored ceiling, and fingers tighten on firing-studs before someone breathes out, mutters a profanity, and the fighters' shoulders relax.

Then something scrapes against broken stone. The fighters whirl, unable to raise their weapons as the air shivers and darkness manifests itself.

His vision shifted:

A lone courier runs across the surface, silver grasses clinging at his ankles while the cold wind buffets him, whips up waves on the Argent Sea, where a tiny three-person aquabug awaits.

Muttering, he reviews the specific command sequence that will activate his thanatotrope should the Enemy capture him. It is almost as if he wants *to commit suicide.*

Tears track unnoticed down his cheeks as he runs.

Shifted:

Angular grey blocks of stone, thrust up by geological upheaval over ages, form a cluttered slope. Pink and crimson algae coat their tips. Nearby, in the air, near-invisible glassmoths slip and slide. While below, linked together by smartrope, the commandos continue their dangerous climb.

Again:

Circular pools of light dot the grey stone plain. Here and there stand worn columns: statues of Founding Lords whose features have been scoured to smoothness by the harsh atmosphere of early times, and the corrosive oxygen-rich winds of recent centuries. The circles shimmer like water but are membranes, covering vertical shafts which lead down into the federated demesnes known collectively as Strehling Suhltône.

A membrane parts as pulse engines fling a big orbital shuttle vertically towards the clouds. Then, like a fast-healing wound, the membrane grows whole once more.

And on the plain, immobile beneath her grey camouflage blanket, the observer mutters into her comm-ring, then thumbs it off. Only a ceramic knife is sticky-tagged to her uniform: otherwise, she is unarmed. A graser would only tempt her into fighting, and that is not her purpose.

She settles down to wait and watch.

Some part of Tom raised a question: was it possible to See too much?

A deserted galleria, where broken statues lie, and only ciliates move, rustling. Small orange beetles feast upon a dead girl's eyes.

Again:

In the tavern, they swing their tankards and sing, as though the war and the final calamity are but distant things or tales to frighten children.

While in one corner, the air grows dark, begins to twist.

Alone on his couch, Tom shuddered as the visions took him deeper:

Infiltrating a realm far from home, the narrow-shouldered man moves among well-dressed men and women, stops at the buffet tables, selects a red confection and chews as though he is used to such luxury. Then he moves to the edge of a conversational group. He can learn much from their speech-patterns, by the topics they choose not *to discuss. But he is after specific information.*

Standing by a pillar, a security officer dressed in purple and black turns, and the expression in those cold eyes is one that no human being should ever witness.

Tom. Reach out to me, Tom.

Again:

The interrogator's fingers squeeze her breast hard, and she cries out.

"No . . ."

Again:

Lungs burning as they run from the conflagration but then black flames burn and the things are in front of them as well, and metallic talons slice the air.

Slick and blue, intestines slide from their bodies.

Tom! Don't let the Chaos take you.

Again:

Gouts of superheated steam as grasers pierce the water and the infiltrators boil alive.

"Leave me alone!"

Again:

Lev-bikes arc, spitting fire, but the armoured ground troops are too many, and the things behind them rear and spread their wings. The team leader cries out as her bike tips, spins, is gone.

And Enemy rifles come to bear upon the remaining Chevaliers.

Let me help, sweet Tom. Let me help you.

It was as intimate as a lover's hand sliding inside his garments, fingertips touching him and moving lower.

"Eemur?" Tom half-raised his head.

Then fell back into the maelstrom.

Ozone stink as the air splits apart . . .

No, Tom. Keep control. Like this.

Shift:

A swimmer, masked, moving through black water in an arterial channel enwrapped by solid basalt, then broken light ripples on waves overhead, and he surfaces. The things that move upon the dock are not human, and never were.

Something cold trails across the swimmer's leg.

Leave it.

"No! I can't . . ."

Leave it now.

Tom flung his arm around. He screamed.

You have to disengage, my love.

But the visions pulled at him, dragged him down.

Yes, but I have you.

"Eemur?"

Stay with me.

Tom slipped away.

Stones sharp beneath his belly as the sighting mechanism focuses, the scarlet-clad officers spring into sharp relief and he squeezes the—

No. With me.

Armoured levanquins sliding over the—

No.

Finger on the—

No.

Darkness and—

I've got you.

Fading.

I've got you now, dear Tom.

"Eemur?"

The darkness that slid down next was ordinary exhaustion, a heavy sleep, while Eemur's Head, on her lev-tray separated from Tom's chamber by three distinct layers of stone and steel, used the talents and abilities she had honed over centuries of life and non-life to keep the roiling visions at bay.

42
NULAPEIRON AD 3426

Tom's first significant success was the rescue of Duke Karalvin's army. It reinforced his commanders' determination to fight for their Warlord Primus; it also made Tom realize the limitations of his own powers.

The operation started with a small event, a sudden movement in a holodisplay over the big conference table, and Elva pointing at the shift in colour. "What's that? Something in Tulgrin Vastness?"

Wind howling past broken pillars, while men in cobalt-blue uniforms with crossed silver sashes flee from clawing metallic wings . . .

Tom maintained focus.

Are you all right?

Yes, so far.

Eemur was floating somewhere behind Tom's head, but he did not turn to look. Instead he asked General Ygran: "Which force has a uniform of cobalt with crossed silver, do you know?"

"I don't . . . Karalvin's Halberdiers. Why do you ask, Warlord?"

"Because that"—Tom nodded towards the display—"is the force the Anomaly's attacking in Tulgrin."

There were glances among the tactical planners around the table. But Elva merely rubbed her chin, considering, then said: "They would be worthwhile allies. Karalvin's got quite a reputation."

General Ygran nodded.

Truholm Janix, the logosopher who was beginning to prove his mettle, ran his fingers through his untidy hair, stared at the image, then shook his head. "Duke Karalvin passed up on a chance to join us before. And *look* at his position."

"It is bad," admitted Elva.

"But not impossible." Tom looked at General Ygran. "What do you think?"

"I don't like it. The Anomaly's forces are sweeping in from three directions on that stratum, and look . . . A fourth battalion is going to rise from directly beneath them, if the Enemy can cross Beeling's Gap fast enough."

"You don't think a rescue is possible?"

"I think a relieving force would be destroyed, *unless* they could extract Karalvin's forces en masse before all the Enemy forces can come together. But such an extraction . . . Damn it, Warlord. I don't think it can be done. Not in the time available."

On her floating lev-tray, Eemur's Head circled the chamber, close to the ceiling. Elva glanced up, her face expressionless, then dropped her gaze to the tactical schemata.

"If only the Alstern Abyss wasn't occupied—"

Tom rocked slightly on his feet.

Black flames form a portal, as men and winged beings move into *it, deploying elsewhere, leaving behind five platoons of men whose eyes no longer reflect human thoughts, their graser rifles held at port-arms. They stand centimetres from the edge's lip. They have no more fear of the sheer drop than a single blood cell is afraid of ceasing to exist.*

Tom smiled.

"Perhaps," he said, "the Enemy is not as powerful there as you think."

Six holovolumes opened.

Count Uvril, bearded and glowering. The ferret-faced Lord Vandon. Square-featured and professional: Major Elksin. Lady Liranda, her hair prematurely white, her eyes shining with a psychopathic need for vengeance. Young Alvix, his empty left sleeve tugged by the wind. A brown-skinned woman wearing a golden torc who refused to give her name, but whose partisan group had wiped out three Anomaly-held supply depots.

Every one of them commanded forces still fighting in tunnels and halls and caverns down below.

"Alvix?" Tom addressed the most loyal man first. "You see the target. Will you take your force downshaft to this location?"

Subsidiary holos flared at Tom's gesture. Alvix and the other five commanders looked to one side, seeing the same display replicated.

"Aye, Warlord."

"Action in two hours and twenty minutes."

"Sir."

Alvix's image winked out.

The other five forces were located at varying distances from the target areas. Coordination was going to be the greatest problem. Tom sent schematic images to Major Elksin, whose band of experienced mercenaries was closest to the target.

"Can your people deploy quickly?"

"Five minutes' notice, and we're moving, Warlord."

"Thank you, Major. Out."

Tom addressed the remaining four commanders: "The key issue is transportation. We want to get as many of Duke Karalvin's people away from the pincer-trap as we can. But—"

"Question, Warlord."

"Yes, Lady Liranda."

"How critical is the timeframe? We can mobilize more lev-plat-forms if we—"

"Absolutely critical, I'm afraid. The Enemy will be able to concentrate huge forces in the area if we let the schedule slip."

"Then we go with what we have."

Tom nodded. "Other questions, my friends?"

There were none.

"Then Fate be with us all."

$$\Diamond \Diamond \Diamond$$

In the command centre, no-one quite dared to ask how the Warlord Primus knew things that strategists and SatScan logs and intelligence analysts had no knowledge of. They stared at him when the briefing was over, then found things to do, busying themselves at their displays, talking in low-toned voices over comms-links: all the myriad tasks that kept a war machine functioning.

Eemur floated on her lev-tray, spherical eyes trained upon the tactical holos.

Speaking as a non-expert . . . Aren't you cutting this rather fine?

Tom looked up at her.

You know I am.

Her lev-tray bobbed once in acknowledgement.

It was a rout.

Liranda's group made better time than expected, and laid down covering fire throughout the Giraltae Cavernae. Karalvin's beleaguered forces, finding unexpected reinforcements, acted sensibly: instead of switching to the attack, they executed a sequence of sweeping moves that cut along the periphery of the Enemy positions, falling back and regrouping in a series of fast manoeuvres that caused command staff in Axolon Array to gasp at their audacity and timing.

A worthwhile ally.

One-armed Alvix attacked Enemy ambushers from the rear, taking down most of them before they knew an attack was under way. But the fighting after that was fierce, and a third of Alvix's troopers were wounded or killed by the time he reached Duke Karalvin's positions.

Then Major Elksin's tough-disciplined soldiers discovered that even the fiercest black-bronze metallic creature will die when twenty graser beams are trained upon it at the same time.

Amid clouds of choking stone dust and the cries of wounded men and women, lev-platforms bore Karalvin's forces away, beating a hard-fought retreat before the main mass of Anomaly-controlled forces could enter the region and envelop them.

Hundreds were left behind, broken or dead.

It was a rout, but it was not a disaster. Ten thousand fighters escaped, and spread the tale of Duke Karalvin's Retreat that became a victory in the face of an Enemy that had seemed unbeatable.

In Axolon Array, as planners totted up the figures, the engagement's true worth became known. Within hours of the first reports, their comms-webs received tentative queries from scattered groups of freedom fighters that had not dared to affiliate themselves with anyone, preferring to hit and run from hiding.

To the Anomaly, Tom suspected, the setback was no greater than a servitor missing a spot when he scrubbed out a dirty processor block. But to free human beings throughout the world, Karalvin's Retreat became a symbol of defiance, a hint that the all-powerful Enemy was not the irresistible juggernaut it appeared.

By the day's end, thirteen new groups had sworn allegiance to the Free Alliance, as people had begun to call the growing resistance movement. They pledged fealty to the Warlord Primus. Duke Karalvin was the most prominent warrior to proclaim his devotion to the cause, as he knelt before Tom in person and accepted Tom's leadership.

The next day, twenty-three more resistance groups, including a full battalion of Drusigan Dragoons, signed up.

Strike and fade.

That became the unofficial motto of the Free Alliance over the next tenday, as Tom directed a series of daring attacks against Enemy-controlled targets. One of the missions was a disaster that ended when the Dark Fire simply enlarged and swallowed half of the attacking force, and the others were forced to flee beneath a barrage of superior fire from Absorbed humans who had once been élite troops of the Brildakov Brigade.

But other raids were successful, with few losses as they swooped in from directions the Enemy had not foreseen and took out strategic targets.

By the end of the tenday, three hundred and twenty-two separate outfits from throughout the world had joined the Free Alliance, their liaison officers reporting aboard one or other of the four hundred terraformer spheres that were now home to the resistance forces.

"Now," Tom told Elva, "it's getting critical."

"If the Anomaly starts attacking the terraformers—"

"Then we won't have much time left."

"Which means you need the Collegium techs right now, Tom."

"But Avernon . . . We need him, too."

Elva turned away, not answering.

She agrees. But you put too much faith in one man.

Eemur's Head floated outside the command centre.

"Avernon," said Tom, "is a bifurcatin' genius."

That was the moment that Lady Renata came bustling into the chamber, holding up a crystal. "I know," she said. "And we know exactly where he is."

"Where, for Chaos' sake?"

"As you might expect . . . In Strehling Suhltône. We have Pathfinder observers on the ground."

"Around the Collegium?"

"Right."

Elva swore quietly. Then: "They could have told us. We've beamed messages to the Collegiate defence squads, in Strehling Suhltône and in Rigay Larn, and got *nothing* in reply."

"That's because," Renata said, "they don't trust anyone. You could be Absorbed for all they know."

"We . . . Right."

Tom looked at them, then dug inside his waistband, pulled out a violet crystal.

"The Crystal Lady," he said, "gave me this. I can call on the Grey Shadows for help. The question is, should I? And is now the time?"

Elva, whose contact with the Grey Shadows was long lost, said: "Most of their people are probably already with us, in Free Alliance groups. I don't see it making much difference. It can't hurt, but I don't see it changing anything."

Renata was thoughtful.

"You're wondering what the Crystal Lady herself can do, is that it, Warlord?"

"There may be forces other than human that she can command. You're the expert on native lifeforms. What can *they* do?"

"I don't know. I mean . . . They live in the magma. Perhaps they can control it. But I don't *know* at all."

"There's only one way to find out," said Elva.

"Yes, but . . . I want to hold something in reserve, my love. Maybe they're it, or part of . . . What is it, Elva?"

She was staring into space, in a way Tom knew well: searching through minutiae in her memory—a memory that could never stop recording what she saw and heard and felt.

"The *bastard*." Then Elva looked at Tom. "I've been trying to figure out what he's up to, because he's been moving fast, all over the place. He's sent indirect reports, but other groups have observed his whereabouts . . . Some of them have been Grey Shadows-trained: I recognized the protocols."

"Who are we talking about?"

"Your old friend Viscount Trevalkin. If he's not already in the Collegium, then I'll eat your socks. And believe me"—Elva turned to Renata—"I've no intention of eating *those* alien lifeforms."

Tom's attention was turned elsewhere, in a way that only a Seer could have understood, as he Saw and experienced: *a supercilious laugh, and the Magister known as Strostiv nods in agreement. To one side, a lattice of pure white light shines, its purpose not apparent.*

"*All right, Trevalkin,*" says Strostiv. "*But I don't see how—*"

Then Tom was back in the chamber, where Elva and Renata were staring at him.

"You're right," he said. "It's time we pushed this into another phase."

43

TERRA & MU-SPACE AD 2166

<<Ro's Children>>

[12]

"Don't you two ever fuckin' scare me like that again."

"We'll try—"

"—not to."

Kian looked at Deirdre. "After the way you kicked Solly's nuts up into his throat, we wouldn't dare."

"Yeah? Then just you remember that. Play with bombs again, and I'll show you both an explosion you won't . . . Ah, shit."

"We love you too, sweetheart."

"I've got something in my eye, that's all."

They were in the Pilots' waiting lounge when Paula, who had introduced herself the previous day as an assistant controller, came to see them. She used a jargon filled with abbreviations and acronyms, but not the ones expected from a flight engineer.

"BID"—she pronounced it as a word: *bid*—"are talking to Solly. The bio-intel boys. We've already sussed out his rdv procedures and dead-letter drops. With a bit of luck, we'll take out his whole cell before they know what's happening."

"I thought," said Deirdre, "you were coming to apologize."

"No, I wouldn't presume. I *am* sorry, but why should you accept that from me?"

"Yeah, why would I? Don't you have any fuckin' vetting procedures in this place?"

"It's all right, Deirdre," said Dirk.

"No it isn't."

Kian blew out a breath, and shrugged. "Perhaps not. But it *will* be all right."

"Maybe . . ." Paula hesitated. "Maybe you'd let me buy you all a beer. On me, not UNSA."

"Why would you want to do that?"

"Well." Paula was trying not to smile. "To celebrate the sweetest kick in the *cojones* I've ever seen, for one."

"I'm up for that," said Kian. "Provided you spill the beans a little. What kind of cell would this Solly belong to?"

"The Zajinets have used humans before. Your mother would have told you that, surely."

"And who exactly"—Dirk leaned forward, intent not just on her words but on heartbeat and skin tone—"did you say you work for, again?"

"We're all on the same side."

Deirdre shook her head. "Hard to see evidence of that."

"Has anyone ever told you," said Paula, "you're drop-dead gorgeous when you're angry?"

"I . . ." Deirdre stopped.

Dirk and Kian looked at each other.

"I do believe—"

"—she's speechless."

"Screw you, boys."

The twins did not attempt even subvocalized communication. If UN Intelligence was involved, their devices would be orders of magnitude more sensitive than any available to the space agency's security branch. Or so they guessed.

Pride filled them at the thought of Mother's swift, decisive counterattack on the alien ship. But they worried that she might have revealed her hand to those within UNSA who were already uneasy at the Pilots' potential for unauthorized, independent action.

In mu-space, a drifting cargo-pod was broadcasting its distress signal. There was a general mayday and a more detailed log which any Pilot's ship could read; but this pod came from Ro's own vessel. She had left it here deliberately.

Abandoned it. With VIPs aboard, in coma.

"Damn. I'll bet it's the senators who spend the next three days throwing up."

As Ro's ship slid through golden space, she browsed the pod's transmissions. There were fifty-three passengers on board, most of them rich or politically prominent or both. And she had left them drifting here too long, while she had flown back to Terra to protect her sons.

I could've kept the passengers on board while I fought the Zajinet.

But Ro's objective had been to save the twins, and if she had revealed her intelligence source—Zoë—then that was too bad. Her dumping the passengers, if it came to a tribunal, would be icing on the prosecution counsel's cake.

Thin end of the wedge, though.

In many ways it was guilt that had made Zoë open to persuasion. Zoë's intelligence team had used Ro as bait back in Moscow, and it resulted in Ro's abduction. She had awoken on Beta Draconis III.

Fun times. Not.

"Come on."

Ro manoeuvred her vessel closer to the pod.

Any non-Pilot who woke up inside mu-space was liable to have their mind torn apart in a psychotic episode which would last until death. That was why passengers travelled inside delta-coma.

But Ro had left her passengers drifting here for so long that some had started to waken, fighting off the delta-band-induced sleep. The pod's automatic systems had injected them with antipsychotic deep-narcosis drugs.

Which meant they would not come round naturally. Medics would have to revive her Very Important Passengers at their destination: Vachss Station, in orbit around the Haxigoji homeworld, Vijaya. And those passengers would be cursing her name for every vomit-filled hour it took their bodies to regain normal equilibrium.

"It doesn't matter." Ro's voice echoed, a snowstorm of fractal parasound inside the cabin. "So long as the matter compilers function OK, we'll be all right."

Bravado.

She was years from bringing her plans to fruition. For now, every Pilot was dependent on UNSA completely. Ro was the only true-born Pilot—meaning one who did not require viral rewiring and the eye-removal surgery—to have her own mu-space vessel.

"Damn, damn, damn."

Then the cabin's rear door opened, and Claude Chalou entered. A blocky visor covered his metal eye sockets and enabled the ageing Pilot to interface with the ship's systems. To see in mu-space. After years in Oxford, guided by sound and touch and his trained dog Sam, he was no longer a stumbling old man: he was in a sea of golden light once more.

It was not just outside the ship. Amber pervaded the control cabin. If you let your concentration go, you could drift into fractal vastness for ever.

"The pod," he said, "is safely aboard, *mon amiral*."

"*Merci*, Claude. Vachss Station, here we come."

It was 4 p.m. when Dirk, Kian, Deirdre and Paula walked to the flight officers' mess, crossing the tarmac towards the black glass recreation dome. Around the base of the control tower was a small fleet of armoured TDVs, while overhead slow-moving flyers kept watch.

On foot outside every entrance, mirrorvisored guards held lineac rifles at the ready.

Inside the mess, the bar was open but quiet: it was an hour before the first officers would come off duty and look to relieve the tension by socializing and drinking. Paula marched up to the bar, and ordered four beers from the corporal in charge.

"Here you are." She carried the round to the booth Deirdre and the twins had picked. "Bottoms up. Isn't that what they say in Old Blighty, Dirk?"

"Sure. Here's mud in your eye."

"*Kampai*," said Deirdre.

Dirk raised his glass. "*Sláinte*."

They downed the first beers in one.

"I've a feeling," said Paula, "this will be a long evening."

She was right.

But even at her merriest and most abandoned, Paula kept her back to the wall and the increasingly crowded bar in full sight, covering all vectors so she could never be surprised. It was a behaviour pattern the twins noticed and approved of.

Deirdre and Paula went their separate ways at the night's end, but they both cast backward glances as they left.

"Just the kind of person—" Dirk murmured from his bed later on.

"—Deirdre needs to keep her safe." In the other bed, Kian rolled over.

"Right."

Kian was the first to begin snoring, followed three seconds later by Dirk.

Next day they went shopping in Flagstaff.

Chief Controller Bratko granted the twins special leave for two, maybe three days—all reasonable expenses paid—while investigations proceeded and their ship was serviced and triple-checked. There was no sign of Paula.

An airtaxi coloured pale pink, emblazoned with a flamingo and the words *Fiona's Flying Cabs*, came in to land.

"You kids go play," Deirdre muttered as she boarded with the twins, "while the grown-ups take charge."

Kian and Dirk remained silent. Perhaps the headaches were part of that.

Their faces whitened as the taxi's nose pointed upwards and the engines kicked in.

The taxi banked right, taking them down.

"You know that turning *right*," said Deirdre, "and having a legal *right*—say, to demonstrate—are obviously homonyms."

There was a crowd below, despite the Arizona heat, outside the mall. They held placards, and might have been chanting: in the airtaxi it was impossible to tell.

"So what's the word in Français?" she asked. "You two are linguists."

"What?" Dirk pinched the bridge of his nose.

"I beg your pardon, dear?" said Kian.

"What's the Français for *right*?"

"*Droit.*"

"For which meaning of 'right'?"

"Um . . ."

"Both, OK? Isn't that weird? You'd expect two different words. See, there's a very tangled history between Anglic and Français, complex linking, with different core vocabulary but centuries of parallel—"

"Darling?"

"Is that a polite way of saying shut up?"

"Or *ferme la*—"

The taxi touched down, and the gull-door swung open. The crowd's noise swelled inside the cab.

"Shit," said Deirdre. "Boys, I'm not sure we ought to be here."

The bobbing signs read *Keep Arizona Human*, along with *Kill All Aliens, Let God Sort 'Em Out.*

"We'll just circle around them."

"Yeah, they're not inside the mall, looks like."

"All right." Deirdre slid out. "Come on, what are you waiting for?"

But as they took the walkway towards the polished glass entrance, the parking lot with its noisy demonstrators to their right, Deirdre pointed to the left.

"Interesting cloud forms. *Look at them.*"

"Um . . ."

"Right."

There were faint wisps of white vapour in an otherwise limpid sky. It was true that the clouds were tugged into shapes one would not see elsewhere; but the only reason for looking in that direction was to avoid the demonstrators' seeing the twins' faces.

When they drew close to the mall entrance, and the chanting crowd—"*Xenos out!*"—was some two hundred metres behind them, the twins stopped.

"What," said Kian, "was all that about?"

"You two have forgotten something. I should've noticed earlier."

Dirk shook his head. "Deirdre, you've got to stop—Oh, bugger."

"Exactly right."

The twins looked at each other, each seeing the other's obsidian eyes, sparkling jet in the sunlight.

"We forgot our contact lenses."

"But we're not aliens."

Deirdre gestured with her chin towards the noisy crowd. Two police flyers were coming in to land.

"I'm not sure they've the brains to tell the difference."

Sensibly inside the air-conditioned mall was a quiet counter-demonstration, formed of four glum-looking people at a picnic table. Two signs were propped against the wall: *Teachers for Rationality* and *Xenos Are Our Friends.*

Dirk looked back to the parking lot, where police officers were descending from the flyers. Only one did not wear a helmet; he had cropped grey hair and looked to be in charge. He kept his officers well back from the demonstrators. As a white cargo flyer descended, he made no attempt to stop the crowd from surging forward, thumping at the hull when the flyer had landed.

"Look," said Kian.

Several doorways along inside the mall was Offworld Delights, a curio and educational store, with a steel barrier across its entrance.

"They're picketing a delivery," guessed Dirk. "That's why they're demonstrating here and not city hall."

"And the cops," said Kian, listening hard, "are standing by and doing nothing."

"Come on." Deirdre took his sleeve. "I'll see if I can buy some old-fashioned sunglasses for the two of you. *Très* retro. Then we'll go find some—"

But that was the moment when low comedy intervened in a way that neither Dirk nor Kian would ever laugh at. A huge woman came out of a doorway marked Ladies Restroom, tucking her shirt into too-tight pants, a placard saying *Kill Zeno's* tucked under her arm.

"Ought to see those teachers," murmured Deirdre. "Get some hints on spelling."

Then the woman raised one pudgy hand, pointed at the twins, jowls wobbling.

And screeched: "They're here. *The aliens are here!*"

There was a thin-chested man with lank hair and a brown bag in his hand, standing near the entrance. He was the one who stumbled out into the open, and yelled to the crowd: *"In here! Aliens!"*

The teachers rose from their table, then stopped helplessly as the first of the angry mob reached the doors and burst inside.

"Shit," said Deirdre. "Let's get the hell out of here."

They turned back into the mall.

Walk slowly, subvocalized Kian.

Got it, answered Dirk.

Had the place been more crowded, the tactic might have worked. But there was no crowd for them to blend into: this early on a weekday morning, the bright-lit space was mostly empty, soft muzak playing to a few older shoppers and lone parents with babies.

An old-fashioned glass bottle sailed over their heads. It burst into blue flame as it shattered on the floor.

"Jesus Christ!" said Deirdre. "An ethanol bomb."

"Run."

But the crowd behind them was already metamorphosing into a mob. Up front, a second group was spilling into the main arcade from a different entrance, blocking their way.

"Here."

The twins ducked into the nearest store, dragging Deirdre with them.

"Where the fuck," she muttered, "are those cops?"

Running along aisles that were a kaleidoscope of colour, ignoring the startled faces of shoppers, *feeling* the pursuers behind them, the twins and Deirdre ran to the store's rear. Dirk's eyes sparked as the doors clicked open and then they were through.

There was a store-room but as a hiding place it was a trap. They ran through, and Kian kicked open the fire-door. It banged back against the wall.

Then they were in the open, in the hot morning air. Angry voices shouted inside.

"Round to the parking lot."

Moving fast, Kian propelled Deirdre as Dirk tapped his infostrand, contacting Fiona's Flying Cabs and hoping the airtaxi they had used was still free, ready to circle round and fetch them.

Cops still stood in the parking lot, but they had made no attempt to stop the insurgence of angry demonstrators. As the twins skidded round the corner with Deirdre, the police commander spun in place, startled.

"Come on." One of the officers gestured to Deirdre. "Get away from them."

From the demonstrators? Or from the twins?

Deirdre kept hold of Kian's sleeve.

"Protect us!" she yelled.

Two of the officers started forward, but in that moment two things happened simultaneously: the commander held up his hand to stop his officers, and the first of the angry demonstrators came pelting around the corner. Stragglers in the parking lot, beer-bellied men who had not attempted to run into the mall, strode forward now with mob-courage and madness in their eyes.

"Come on, xeno-lover." A big bald man grabbed Deirdre. "Better get you out of here."

There was a kind of concern in his voice, and that just made it worse. Deirdre kicked out, connected with his shin, and his hands dropped away.

"*Kill the aliens!*"

And then it went to hell.

The crowd rushed over them in a tidal wave of scratching and yelling and sheer body momentum. Kian snapped his fist and a man's nose exploded in a gout of blood, then something struck the back of his head and he spun, arced back with his elbow, connected, and his attacker went down beneath the mob's feet.

Dirk kicked once, protecting Deirdre, before a mass of flailing limbs closed in. Fingers clutched his clothes, and he roared as he tried to shake them off.

"Look out!"

The sound of glass shattering.

Someone stabbed a broken bottle at Dirk's eye and he twisted at the last moment. Glass ripped his forehead and blood spattered. Deirdre yelled out.

Something dark came out of nowhere, shattered against Kian's head and he went down on one knee.

"No. Kian, no!"

Deirdre tried to push her way through but the bald man grabbed her.

Smell of ethanol.

A sparking sound.

Then flames enveloped Kian and the crowd fell back. Kian screamed.

And burned.

The crowd stood in silence, frozen by what they had done, as Kian writhed in flames on the ground. Dirk reacted first, pulling off his jacket and throwing it across his brother. Desperate, he rolled Kian along the ground, smoke pouring from his brother's body with the roast-pork stench and Kian yelling in agony.

Deirdre screamed at the police commander—"Do something!"—
as she tugged her shirt off and dropped to help Dirk with Kian,
beating the last of the flames out, rolling Kian onto his back.

Half of Kian's face was a ruin of glistening black and reddened
meat.

"Oh, no. Oh, Jesus, no."

Deirdre, on her knees, clutched Kian's smoking clothes. Dirk
slowly stood up, and looked at the silent gathering.

From the rear, someone muttered: "Kill the aliens," but no-one
moved. Even the police officers remained still, shocked by the sudden-
ness of the violence or their own inaction; while the commander's face
was like a clenched fist, as he attempted to process the way his day had
just fallen apart.

"You think we're different?"

Dirk's voice was cold and pitiless. Deirdre looked up at him.

"You think"—gesturing at Kian, who shuddered and gave an
unearthly whimper—"you should be *afraid* of us?"

"No." Deirdre, shaking, rose to her feet. "Dirk, don't. Please don't."

The commander moved at last, pointing at Dirk.

"Arrest him."

"But sir—" One of the officers shook his head.

On the ground, Kian moaned.

Dirk took hold of Deirdre's shoulders.

"You think you can get away—"

Dirk spun Deirdre towards him, then clasped her head.

"—with *this*?"

He buried Deirdre's face against his chest.

Golden fire rose inside his eyes.

"*No, Dirk . . .*"

Something changed in the air and the nearest demonstrators tried
to fall back, but their own comrades were in the way and then it was
too late.

"*Dirk* . . ."

Yellow incandescence ripped through the parking lot.

DIE!

Exploded.

The roar echoed in Dirk's mind.

DIE, YOU BASTARDS.

And then it was over.

He released Deirdre, who stumbled back.

All around, stunned survivors lay on the tarmac, clutching at their ruined faces while their friends lay dead. Deirdre looked for the police commander.

Smoke rose from ruined eye sockets that would never see again.

<<MODULE ENDS>>

44

NULAPEIRON AD 3426

Tom stilled the display, let it minimize and hang off to one side. He leaned back against the bulkhead, staring into nothing.

Kian, burned. His hand ruined.

Tom rubbed his own face, as his missing left arm blazed with non-existent fire.

"It *was* you."

There was no-one in the chamber; Tom's voice had a strange flat echo, as if uttered by an ancient machine. But in his mind's eye he could see only the poor tortured Pilot on Siganth, flensed inside the vivisection field tended by alien components of the Anomaly. A Pilot with a half-ruined, silver-scarred face, and a right hand hooked into a claw.

"Kian McNamara."

Tom took a deep breath, then immersed himself again in the centuries-old tale.

45

TERRA & MU-SPACE AD 2166

<<Ro's Children>>

[13]

Deirdre called Paula. She wept as she begged for help, unable to look away from Kian's ruined face and the taut, charred remains of his right hand. All around, scattered across the parking lot, blinded demonstrators and policemen moaned and whimpered. Some clutched the bodies of the fallen dead.

Dirk stood silent, unmoving.

Stub-winged UNSA ambulances accompanied by unmarked armoured flyers came hurtling down from the sky, two minutes before the civilian authorities arrived. No-one argued as medics rushed Kian aboard the nearest ambulance. It rose immediately, its crew not waiting to help anyone else, and headed back towards the base.

"Oh Christ. Oh Christ."

Deirdre could only watch as security officers mag-cuffed Dirk and led him into one of the unmarked flyers. Paula took hold of her.

"Come on, Deirdre. Let's get out of here before those bastards start arguing jurisdiction."

Green-uniformed cops of some kind were jumping down from a sky-blue flyer, mouths grim, eyes hidden behind mirrorvisors.

"All right. Is Kian going to be . . . ?"

Deirdre let her voice trail off.

"Come on." Paula's arm encircled Deirdre. "I'll look after you. Promise."

But they both knew, as they climbed a ramp and took their seats in a too-cold passenger cabin, that Kian was close to death, and that even UNSA would not be able to keep Dirk from captivity and subsequent trial in the local court.

Deirdre was sure Arizona had the death penalty.

"Oh, my boys . . ."

The ground dropped away beneath the flyer.

The cell had a narrow bunk and a tiny chemical toilet which stank of ozone. Dirk sat on the bunk, staring at the door's triple mag-locks. He had said nothing as the medic dressed his forehead wound, or when the guards removed his cuffs and offered to bring him water.

Kian. What's happening to you?

Some part of Dirk felt that his brother must still live: that no-one as close as Kian could die without the universe shrieking as the bond between them ruptured. But perhaps that was a delusion brought on by an awareness of the things that made them different from ordinary human beings . . . from folk who outnumbered Pilots by millions to one.

UNSA can get me out of this. They've invested too much money to let the mob take me down.

But the mall had security systems, bead cameras that would have recorded everything. Maybe UN Intelligence could swoop in and take over the logs, *if* they moved fast enough. *If* no-one in the local police or newsNets got there first.

And if UNSA had the political will to bury the case. Perhaps they did not.

Perhaps they, too, would turn against him.

Against all our kind.

Deirdre, her arm in a silver cast, stood beside Paula, watching through the glass wall while robotic arms and human surgeons toiled over Kian.

"Are you all right?" Paula touched Deirdre. "Want a drink of water?"

"No."

"OK."

They stood together. Deirdre's arm throbbed inside its cast. She did not know when it had broken. Perhaps when the bald man grabbed her.

Perhaps when Dirk took hold of her and—

Oh, sweet Jesus.

And—

She turned and buried her face on Paula's shoulder.

At 3 a.m. the door slammed open.

Dirk jerked up, expecting burly men to rush inside with batons upraised. But there was only one guard visible, and he remained standing in the doorway while his colleagues waited around the corner.

"They told me to tell you . . . Your brother's condition is now severe. No longer critical."

"You mean he's—"

"Going to live, they think."

"Thank—"

But the door was closed before Dirk could finish what he had to say. Inside the mag-locks, coils hummed with energy as they drew the bolts into place.

On the waiting-room couch, Deirdre jerked awake. She felt cold. Paula's warmth was gone.

"It's all right." A young nurse, her eyes bruised with fatigue, held out a cup of hot chocolate. "Drink this. Your . . . friend had to attend to something."

Too weary to protest, Deirdre accepted the chocolate.

"Thank you." She sipped, and shivered as the warmth slid down inside her. It revived her, just a little. "Is Kian . . . ?"

"Doing well. The doctors will tell you that things could still go wrong, and it *is* still early days . . ."

"But?"

"But some people are natural-born fighters. You get a feel for it. And Mr. McNamara is one of them."

Deirdre nodded. She understood that intuition was based on more information than rational procedures coped with. She could have modelled it mathematically. But, "Thank you," was all she said. "That helps a lot."

"Good. Perhaps you should get to bed. Get some proper rest."

"I'll try." Deirdre's cup was empty, and she looked around for somewhere to bin it.

"Here, give that to me."

"Thanks . . . Um, do you know where my friend went?"

"I'm not sure." The nurse shook her head. "Something about checking on a prisoner?"

"Right."

Deirdre hugged herself and shivered.

The runway was a pale ghost in the darkness. Paula stopped for a moment to stare at the silvery shape—moonlight on polished bronze—of the mu-space ship that stood outside its hangar.

"It could have been so different. A simple test flight."

One of the MPs beside her put a hand on his holster: an unconscious gesture.

"Ma'am? Is everything all right?"

"Not really, sergeant. Come on."

At the steel-armoured security building, Paula held out her pass, stared into the retina-scan, and submitted her infostrand for resonance-inspection. The MPs passed quickly through the gates.

"You want to see Prisoner McNamara?"

"Yes, please."

"Disturbing his beauty sleep, ma'am?"

"Maybe. Do you care?"

"Not after what that bastard did to dozens of innocent civilians and law officers."

"Right."

Triple-armoured doors slid open.

"This way," said the chief escorting officer.

Five burly MPs with armoured vests and mirrorvisor helmets, lineac rifles powered up, kept pace with her along the polished titanium corridor. When they stopped outside the cell door, they took careful aim.

"Ma'am? You can reconsider, still."

"I want to see him in person. My responsibility."

"Be careful. OK . . . Hit it."

One of the MPs touched a lock-plate then quickly stepped back, positioning his weapon. Paula stared into the bright-lit cell. It was stark and bare, designed to prevent a captive from falling asleep unless the custodians wanted him to.

"Is this the right one?"

"What—?"

The MPs stood frozen in place, unable to comprehend the blank walls, the made-up bunk, and the lack of any sign that the cell had ever been occupied. Then the officer slapped his throat mike into life.

"General alarm. Escaped prisoner. Sound it now."

White fire brightened the night.

A lineac cannon banged and sent tracer fire and explosive rounds screaming low across the runway, spattering harmlessly off a shining hull designed to withstand the worst that two universes might throw at it.

The ship turned, straightened up, pointing dead straight along the runway. Jury-rigged metal sheets already covered the trench blasted by the Zajinet ship.

"*Aim for the undercarriage*," came the order, and the cannon lowered its barrel as soldiers ran from the buildings, took kneeling stances, and joined their rifles to the fusillade.

Nova-bright, the white flame shone.

And the ship began to move.

The cannon swung its beam low but hit the temporary metal sheeting after the ship had rolled past, and the fragments blew apart, shielding the vulnerable undercarriage just for a moment, and then it was too late. Night air wavered as the ship slammed horizontally along the runway, covered its length in seconds, and its nose tipped up into the air.

The vessel rose.

Then it was arcing fast, turning starboard and upwards, becoming a streak too rapid for even automated weapons to follow; and there was a burst of light as the air itself tore apart and a new, ephemeral aurora formed.

By the time the accompanying crack of thunder reached the ground and UNSA's fighters were rising to launch, the ship was already gone from realspace, flying into the golden vastness of a fractal continuum where few could follow—into a place where Dirk McNamara might remain unharmed, in a universe where he could make his home.

<<MODULE ENDS>>

46

NULAPEIRON AD 3426

Sun blazed through the membrane windows, caused the blue-and-white tiles to glow with an odd sharpness as if today the world was in stronger focus. A handful of the most senior commanders sat around the polished conference table. No holos shone.

Tom's voice was sufficient to hold them captive.

"General Lord Ygran." He nodded to the general. "You will be in charge during my absence. In the event of my failing to return . . . you will assume command."

General Ygran ran a thumb along his white moustache. "I'd rather not have to do that, Warlord."

"In that case, I'll try not to let it happen."

Lieutenant Xim eh'Gelifni's ebony face cracked in a bright smile. "That's good, sir."

There were a few light laughs around the table, then serious expressions once more.

"You're the historian, General. Remember the Battle of Agincourt? Sometimes the ruler has to lead a strike force into battle."

General Ygran could probably have come up with a dozen reasons why the analogy did not apply. Instead, he silently bowed his head.

"Ankestion?" said Tom. "Did you check in with Volksurd and Kraiv?"

"Aye, Warlord." Ankestion Raglok's slitted green eyes dilated, then narrowed, and his graphite eyebrows bristled. "The drop-bugs are already fitted, ahead of schedule. My clone-brothers are ready to go."

"Excellent. Xim? Did you complete your inspection of spheres ten through fifty?"

They had tried using separate names for the other terraformers, but there were too many. Instead, the planning staff resorted to simple numbering: chronological sequence as freedom fighters took possession.

"Yes, Warlord. Shakedown flights of the shuttle squadrons went well."

"Then, with General Ygran's approval, I'd like you to coordinate the squadrons. Assume command straight away."

General Ygran nodded, and Lieutenant eh'Gelifni sat up straighter.

"*Aye*, Warlord. My thanks."

"Good."

Tom looked around the table.

"That's all. Thank you."

Captain Goray had chewed at his moustache during the entire briefing. His pale face and mournful eyes looked more worried than ever.

Tom leaned close to him as the others were filing out.

"Don't worry. There's going to be a ruckus when we make our break from the Collegium. You're going to have one Chaos of a fight on your hands, soon enough."

Goray smiled, relieved.

"Thank Fate for that, Warlord."

"In the meantime, come with me. There are some tac-displays you need to see."

They took the spiral stairs down to the next level. Tom stopped before a sealed doorshimmer, which swirled in place until scanners confirmed his identity; then he and Captain Goray stepped through.

"This," said Tom, "is forbidden tech. VLSI."

Eemur's Head floated before a holo network which Elva was manipulating. Tom found their cooperation unsettling.

"Never heard of it, sir." Goray rubbed his moustache. "Won't mention it to anyone."

"The Oracle who lived here used it to interface with installed systems. The devices are original, left inside the terraformer at construction."

"*Old* tech, then, Warlord."

"They date back to the Founding."

Elva halted the display, and looked at them. "Want to know something funny? There's a theory that this tech is what enabled the Anomaly to grow in the first place, from a mind distributed across plexcores—pre-logotrope enhancements—on the hellworld of Fulgor."

Tom watched Eemur. She floated on her lev-tray, looking intent.

The display remained static.

"I read Xiao Wang's *Skein Wars* when I was a kid," Tom said. "That's the story it told. Fulgor was a paradise, not a hellworld, when it started."

In one corner of the chamber a translucent hologlobe rotated, stained with darkness representing the Anomaly.

Will people someday talk about the hellworld called Nulapeiron?

No they won't. Because you're going to succeed.

Tom smiled at Eemur, and bowed his head. Suddenly, the display swirled with random colours.

"Well done!" Elva checked a subsidiary holo. "You've got it, Eemur."

The lev-tray bobbed a curtsy in the air. The interface was a glistening strip woven around the dangling remains of Eemur's left carotid artery and disappearing into her flesh.

"How long," asked Captain Goray, "before the Seer can establish full conscious control of the holodisplay?"

"I *thought* you were quick on the uptake, Captain." Tom placed his hand on Goray's shoulder. "I'd like you to work with Elva and Eemur, to liaise with General Ygran and the command staff. Relay questions and answers in both directions, between this chamber and the planners upstairs. Interpret intelligently."

"Sir?" Goray clasped his hands behind his back. "I don't truly understand."

Tom looked at Elva and Eemur, took a deep breath, slowly expelled it.

"Have you noticed, Captain, that I seem to be more aware of the

Enemy's movements than I ought to be? That the planners blindly accept what I tell them only because I've been proved right?"

"Yes." A faint smile tugged at Goray's lips. "Yes, sir. I've noticed that."

"Then . . ."

Don't worry, lover. You will come back.

". . . If I don't make it, my Lady Elva has the strategic training and Eemur has the ability to . . . Let's just say, between them, they can do as good a job as I can."

Tom could not help looking at Elva then, seeing the depth of fear in her grey eyes before she blinked and resumed a professional expression.

"I'll leave you to it," said Tom.

Wearing the grey jumpsuit he needed for the drop, Tom made one last stop before joining his team. In the labs situated at the terraformer's heart, Truholm Janix oversaw teams of workers, a mixture of logosophically trained Lords and Ladies—the young Lord A'Vinsenberg showed a particular aptitude—and Academy-trained freeborn, even three of the techs that Tom and Elva had recruited years ago in the original, short-lived Corcorigan Demesne.

"How's it going, Truholm?"

"Um, well, my . . . Warlord. My Lady, ah, Flurella was looking for you." *And she can fluster anyone.*

Hiding a smile, Tom asked: "What about the work?"

"Oh, right. We're reviewing models. Also, some of them"—he waved a hand; A'Vinsenberg looked up and nodded—"are improving the anti-agoraphobia logotropes. We have one that produces agora-*philia*, in fact."

"Overcompensating," said A'Vinsenberg. "But I'm bringing it back under control."

"Good, good." Truholm wiped his desktop display. "It seems too strong, but the point is that this version has no side effects. Besides an excessive longing for the great outdoors."

Tom was frowning. "Why are you working on logotropes at this time?"

"Because, Warlord, it's where femtotech reaches its apex. There's a nicety of design when artificial atom construction meets computational theory meets biochemical pathway. We're engineering subatomic particles in order to influence human thought."

"And . . . ?" said Tom, thinking: *I know what a logotrope is, for Fate's sake.*

"And when you bring us the Collegium's devices, we're going to be collapsing spacetime using attotwistors none of us here have practical knowledge of. This is the nearest we can get."

"Hmm. Good answer."

"Thank you, Warlord."

Lady Flurella caught him in the corridor. Her crimson eyes shone like blood-filled orbs against her bone-white skin.

"You're attempting to penetrate Strehling Suhltône, Lord Corcorigan."

"That's right."

"And you're extracting . . . what? The Collegium's devices? Or their people?"

"Both, if we can manage it. The equipment comes first."

"And Lord Avernon."

"Yes."

If he's there.

Tom had tried to See into the Collegium again, but Anomalous activity in the Calabi-Yau dimensions was blocking him. Trevalkin *had* been there, and Magister Strostiv, the last Tom had Seen. But that was days ago.

"What about Trevalkin?"

"He may," said Tom, "be the one person who can keep Avernon safe until we get there."

"And you trust him?"

"Trevalkin? He's extremely capable."

"Mmm. Be careful, Warlord. Don't turn your back."

Then a surprising thing happened. The albino Lady Flurella reached up on tiptoes, leaned forward, and kissed Tom on the cheek.

"Good luck."

She bustled away, while Tom could only watch.

"Thank you," he said finally, addressing an empty corridor.

Then he checked the equipment tagged to his jumpsuit, nodded to himself.

Time to go.

Elva and Jissie were waiting outside the shuttle bay.

"Tom . . ."

They hugged, kissed, and pulled Jissie into their embrace. Then Elva released him, stepped back, her hand on Jissie's shoulder.

"Give them Chaos, my husband."

"Yes, my love. I will."

As Tom was stepping into the shuttle, silent words rang in his mind. He jumped.

Don't lose your head, lover.

His laugh caused fourteen heads to turn and stare, fourteen pairs of horizontally slitted eyes to dilate and contract. Fourteen purple-skinned faces each raising a graphite eyebrow.

"Ankestion." Tom nodded to Ankestion Raglok—or at least, to the clone wearing the narrow red armband of leadership: if Ankestion had swapped places with one of his clone-brothers, Tom would never be able to tell the difference.

"Warlord."

The hatch sealed shut as Tom took his place on the bench seat.

"*Launch in thirty seconds,*" came the pilot's voice.

And finally Axolon himself spoke into the shuttle.

<Good luck, Warlord. Warriors.>

The shuttle slid forward.

Ten minutes after they were airborne, a strange change came over the clone-warriors. One by one they closed their eyes, and their faces grew not just still but solid, as if turning into stone. Only Ankestion Raglok remained watchful.

"May I ask—?" Tom began.

"It is how we prepare for battle. I expect they're doing likewise in the other shuttles."

There were no windows or holodisplays depicting the five other craft flying alongside. Instead, Tom concentrated and Saw:

Twenty carls raise a cheer. Kraiv thumps morphospear against bronze shield, and Volksurd yells a curse upon their enemies. The single non-combatant, a specialist they are taking into battle, stares around at the carls, disbelieving what he sees.

Then the whole group launches into a rousing battle hymn.

Tom withdrew, blinking, just as the five shuttles banked away, following their own trajectory, engaged in their own mission.

"Something like that," he said.

"Good."

I wish you luck, Kraiv.

Tom would have preferred that Kraiv remain on Axolon Array, but to have suggested it would have been a grave insult to his old friend.

Beside Tom, Ankestion Raglok closed his eyes, and slid into trance like his brothers; while on Tom's skin, sparkling drops of sapphire sweat formed, shone for a moment, and then soaked back in, vanishing from sight.

47

NULAPEIRON AD 3426

"Ten minutes to drop." The pilot's voice was clear inside the shuttle hold. *"Take your positions."*

It had been bright daylight when they left Axolon Array, but they had flown for hours and into darkness. Tom did not use his Sight to check—in case the Anomaly could detect such spacetime twisting—but he knew it would be night outside.

"Ready," called the first clone-warrior, as he clasped his arms in front of his chest.

Gelatinous morphglass emerged from the deck, rose to envelop him. Within seconds, its exterior hardened, formed a polished egg-shape enclosing the warrior.

"Ready," called the next man.

Two minutes later, everyone but Ankestion Raglok and Tom was ready for the descent.

"After you, Warlord."

"Ready."

Tom closed his eyes as soft material rose around him and covered his face.

The world went silent in his cocoon.

And drop.

Empty stomach. Tumbling, over and over. Sheer fear flooding the body.

Then a bump as though the air itself had thumped him with a giant fist.

Sweet bleeding Fate.

Tom gasped.

Night grew visible, stars between the clouds. Then the drop-bug rolled, straightened, as the morphglass around his head cleared to complete transparency. Facing towards the silvery ground that slid past far below.

To either side, stubby wings elongated.

"Oh, yes!"

His drop-bug's wings stretched, snapped out, flared back. Tom laughed, and swooped through the night like a raptor hunting prey.

Years of climbing had never taken away Tom's fear of heights. But the air felt solid, supporting, and moonlit heathland moved smoothly below. There was no longer a sense of falling. Only a faint whistling sound, audible now that he had calmed down, accompanied his flight through darkness.

Once, he glimpsed something, perhaps another drop-bug: a glint of moon-white reflection, a banking motion. But then it was gone.

I hope you're all safe.

The long night-glide continued.

Finally, it was laughable. There had been crude toilet facilities aboard the shuttle and he should have used them. Instead, Tom's bladder felt swollen by the time his drop-bug's wings altered curvature, and he banked down for the final approach.

Don't lose control.

The ground suddenly whipped into rapid magnification, silver grasses hurtling past just metres from his face, a stand of trees—shadows against night sky—growing large impossibly fast.

Hold on.

Just centimetres now, and the grass was a blur close to his face.

Then the bug's wings cupped, braking.

Hold it.

And the belly struck the ground.

Hold . . .
Shaking now, and he gritted his teeth to save biting his tongue.
Hold.
Slowing.
Made it.
And stopped.

For a moment Tom lay there, cocooned.

Then the morphglass rippled, pulled away from him, dissolved. It left him face-down in long grass, the woody soil-scent filling his nostrils.

First things first.

Slowly, he rolled onto his side—not wanting to present a silhouette by standing upright—and pulled at his jumpsuit's fastening, and urinated as quietly as he could. Then he adjusted himself, and crawled forward on forearm and knees until he reached dark undergrowth and raised himself to a kneeling position.

Someone tapped Tom's shoulder.

Enemy? Adrenaline jolted through his system.

"*Warlord.*" The whisper was close to his ear.

Tom tapped Ankestion's shoulder in reply.

It took three hours to make the rendezvous, at a stony outcrop overlooking a deep valley. The bugs' drop pattern had spaced out their landing positions in a precise arc centred on this point. Following the protocol, the clone-warriors gathered in twos and threes—as Ankestion Raglok had rendezvoused with Tom—then proceeded to the central rdv.

But when Tom counted identical purple faces, only thirteen pairs of green eyes shone back at him. One of the warriors leaned close to Ankestion and whispered. Ankestion nodded, then crawled over to Tom.

"Zakedion didn't make it." He kept his voice to a low whisper.

"Did the—?"

"The bug dissolved. Too soon, but it dissolved."

Which meant there would be no traces left in the open. That at least was good.

"And the body?" Tom had to ask.

"Disposed of."

"I'm sorry."

Ankestion Raglok did not reply. He looked up at the horizon, now touched with pale turquoise. Fewer stars were visible.

He made a patting gesture with one gloved hand.

Moving as one, in silence, the clone-warriors and Tom dispersed, crawling across the ground. It took only a hillock or even just a thick clump of grass to break up a prone man's profile. Each man unwrapped chameleoflage from his thigh pouch, spread the gossamer-thin sheet over himself, and settled down.

They would wait unmoving until it was night once more. Both bead cameras and human beings could be equipped to see in darkness, but as a matter of course they were not. Tom and the clone-warriors needed every small advantage.

As the sky lightened to a smoky amber against pale grey, Tom's breathing became almost imperceptible, and he slid into logosophical trance.

General Ygran had designed the approach phase, using techniques proved during Academy missions when Corduven was in charge. The required personal attributes were based on the ultra-hard endurance training that élite squadrons underwent: emphasizing patient determination and a capacity for sneakiness. A notice in the recruiting colonel's office declared: *He-men and heroes need not apply*.

Ankestion Raglok and his clone-brothers fit the profile exactly. So did Tom Corcorigan.

It's time.

As darkness descended and the stars became diamond points, fourteen figures rose and slipped across the nightbound land like shadows.

48

MU-SPACE AD 2166–2301

<<Ro's Children>>

[14]

Ro's ship hung off Vachss Station, drifting in orbit around Vijaya, the Haxigoji homeworld. There was an awful fuss ongoing in the station, to do with a return visit from Rekka Chandri, the UNSA solo observer who had made first contact. That time, she had involved herself in the indigenous culture in a major way. Her return visit, as far as station staff were concerned, was controversial.

The chattering local newsNet, lively even for a community of two hundred opinionated researchers, was full of analyses and contradictory predictions of the continuing intellectual rise—or possibly the imminent decline—of the intelligent native species, who had leaped from something like a Babylonian culture to medieval Renaissance in two short decades.

"Interesting." Chalou was using an ear-plug, browsing audio. "*Cannibalism*. That's a new one."

"What?" Ro was immersed in feedback displays.

"No matter. Just filling in the gaps that old public news items managed to gloss over."

The pod which Ro had abandoned and then retrieved from mu-space was now aboard the station, clamped inside a docking bay. Remote view showed station medics wheeling passenger couches from the open pod: taking them to med-wards where autodocs would revive them. Other passengers were staggering out: some by themselves, others leaning on station staff who had come to assist.

"Breaks up the monotonous routine," murmured Ro.

"Are they safely onboard?" said Chalou.

"No disasters yet. Looks like eight of them have gone to the med-wards, which matches the pod's log. The same eight folk. Deep-drugged to hell."

"Hell is what they'll raise when they wake up, *amiral*."

"What can I say, Claude? *Merde alors*. I should've taken a different geodesic."

Relativistic effects were even more pronounced in mu-space than in realspace. Ro's chosen route had maximized time dilation, while minimizing the subjective duration. A gentler trajectory might have been easier on her passengers' constitutions.

After Ro's firing on the Zajinet interloper over the Arizona base, UNSA controllers would already be backtracking, trying to calculate her movements since her previous official stop on Ganymede. The fact of her little side-voyages could not remain a secret. But so long as their purpose and destination remained hidden, Ro would weather the polit-ical storm.

Zajinets tried to kill my son.

The action had been too fast for Ro to determine whether it was Dirk or Kian aboard the ship that lay vulnerable on the runway. The Zajinet had been already setting up its strafing run when she inserted into realspace—*almost too late*: the thought caused her to tremble yet again—and there had been no time for communication.

Perhaps they had both been aboard.

"Are you all right, Ro? You fired on a ship."

"A Zajinet ship. And they were asking for it."

"Obviously. But why? Why would they attack a Pilot?"

"*I don't know.* I . . . No-one does."

Chalou nodded, and returned to browsing the station's newsNet.

✧✧✧

It was perhaps an hour later when Chalou stopped humming softly to himself and turned to Ro. "Look . . . This explorer, Mam'selle Chandri, who has caused so much trouble . . . If you slip away quietly, there will be little fuss. She's all they're interested in."

Claude Chalou had a life—perhaps a twilit half-life—to return to in Oxford.

"What if one of the passengers," said Ro, "fails to wake up?"

"And what if station personnel demand to scan the holds? Standard procedure in an accident."

"They won't find any malfunction."

"But they might find the matter compiler which McLean and I stole for you."

"Goddamn it, Claude. The passengers are my responsibility."

After a moment, Claude Chalou nodded. *"C'est ça. C'est exact, bien sûr."*

Something faint pinged in a display, was gone.

What the hell was that?

Ro could make no sense of it. Increasing the sensors' gain, while simultaneously reviewing the log and attempting to analyse the signal, she searched for the source.

"Electromagnetic flare." Chalou, though blind in realspace, had heard the tone and guessed what she was doing. "From the star."

"Yeah. Maybe."

She could find nothing to suggest otherwise.

Then a message request shone, high priority from Station Control, and Ro waved a holo open. A lean, grey-haired woman looked at Ro, eyes widening in surprise.

"Excuse me?" said Ro. "I believe *you* called *me*."

"Yes . . . But you look, um, different from the last time I saw you."

"I'm sorry? Have we met before?"

"Actually, I held you in my arms. Half of me is surprised to see a strong, capable woman. The other half of me can't get over how young you look."

Ro did not want to get into a discussion of time-dilating voyages through mu-space. She was going to be in enough trouble anyway, in that regard.

"Were you a friend of my mother's?"

"Eventually. But I heard you, before I ever met Karyn." The woman's face dimpled, and the smile removed decades from her features. "My name is Dorothy Verzhinski. Forty-three years ago—objective—I was based on Metronome Station, in the Delta Cephei system."

Ro wondered if the woman had undergone time-slowing travels of her own. Then she realized what Verzhinski was telling her.

"You're the one who picked up Mother's distress beacon. Saved the both of us."

"If I hadn't, someone else onboard would have heard you. Not just the auto-beacon, but the realtime audio channel: a baby wailing in deep space . . . I'll never forget that day."

"You're the reason I was christened Dorothy."

"What? You don't like the name?"

"Let's just say, there's a reason why they call me Ro. But I am really pleased to meet you. I would love to come aboard, but only for a short—"

Verzhinski shook her head, looked off to one side as if reading a display.

"Perhaps some other time. I'm happy to report, all your passengers have woken up *physically* healthy."

"But psychologically?"

"Well . . . It might be better for you to leave before Senator Margolis reaches a comms terminal. I'll say that I informed you of their waking up OK. That should cover both our backsides."

Ro grinned.

"That's another huge favour I owe you."

"Come back someday, and we'll catch up. In the meantime . . ."

"Right." Ro concentrated, and her cabin displays rippled with system changes. "Thank you, Vachss Station. Ready to depart."

"*Bon voyage*, Pilot McNamara. Vachss Station out."

The comms-holo was gone.

"Well, Claude. Looks like we're going."

"No more strange signals?"

"None that I can detect."

"Then, *mon amiral*, I would be grateful if I could see Labyrinth, just once before I die."

"In that case, *mon ami* . . . Labyrinth, here we come."

Ro could have flown directly along a minimum-duration geodesic. But this was Claude Chalou, a Pilot grown too old to be entrusted by UNSA with an expensive mu-space vessel. A man who deserved more than a blind existence on Terra.

So Ro took him through crimson nebulae, across great tracts of golden light where no stars showed, and through a scintillating tree of fiery life whose rustles and whispers persisted in the ship's cabin long after they had left the formation behind.

"*Ah, mon Dieu.*"

All the beauties of the mu-space vastness, she showed him.

Then Ro turned her ship along a familiar trajectory, and a fractal universe slid past as they flew further and further from anything an unaltered human being would term reality.

The ship slowed, in a region filled with amber light where spiky black stars massed. In realspace, it would have been the centre of a galaxy; in this continuum, one might dive into lower dimensions that opened up entirely different features: endless sheets of blank golden space, or—conversely—dense bracketed spongiform blackness. In a sense, a ship might remain in one spot yet explore an infinite variety of surroundings for ever.

"Is it here?"

"Just around the corner."

A twist, a ripple in the continuum which Ro navigated with skill.

And then a vast construction was hanging before them: silver and black, smooth and jagged, its complex architecture both self-similar and varying, in a geometry far beyond humanity's ability to grasp.

"It's . . ." Chalou's voice trailed off.

"Yes, it is, isn't it?"

There were endless halls, some open to golden space. There were arches and towers and turrets, pointed in every conceivable direction, worked at every conceivable scale from mountain-sized to microscopic . . . as near as such terms had meaning in this place.

Seven—no, eight—ships were visible, hanging before various portals. As Ro and Chalou watched, another ship slid from an opening surmounted with an impossible triangle—braided in perspectives that *almost* made sense—and arced away into the depths of mu-space.

"Are Pilots living inside?"

"Not permanently," said Ro. "Not yet. But there are those who spend more and more time here, not just helping with the construction, but resting and meditating among the Courts. It's interesting . . . Sometimes, you come across a square or a building that no-one claims responsibility for, as though it has come into existence by itself."

"Perhaps you have wrought more than you expected."

"Maybe." In the cabin, Ro patted his arm. "I think you've brought us the last matter compiler we'll ever need. We've passed a critical point."

"You mean, the city's growing by itself?"

"It's more than just a city."

She urged the ship forward through amber space.

Closer. Chalou gasped at the detail.

Amid the infinite complexity that was Labyrinth, a welcoming portal opened. An event membrane slid over Ro's vessel as they passed inside.

Into the only home a Pilot could require.

Walking in the space known as Hilbert Hall, they met another Pilot and exchanged greetings. Like Chalou, Pilot Sandberg wore a visor clipped across his metal eye sockets; Labyrinth shone with energies that resonated in just the right way for the visors to decipher.

"I wonder, Admiral"—Sandberg's words formed ghostly shimmerings in the air, faded—"whether you perceive this place in quite the way we do."

Ro looked around at the infinite planes which formed the Hall. Silver reflections slid across her obsidian eyes.

"It's like two people on Terra agreeing to call an apple red. Whether they're experiencing the same thing, no-one can say."

Chalou turned in a circle on the spot.

"Whatever we see, we can agree this place is magnificent. It is heaven."

"That it is, sir," said Sandberg. "Will you stay long?"

"I think"—Chalou sighed, turned to face Ro as golden ripples passed across his visor—"that Sam will be missing me. My dog," he explained to Sandberg.

"Ah. Then I hope to see you again sometime, Pilot Chalou. Admiral."

Sandberg turned in a certain way, planes of light that had not been visible now rotated like doors, and he slipped into another level of Labyrinth and was gone from sight.

"Such a marvellous place," said Chalou. "I would like . . ."

"When the time comes," Ro told him, "I'd be honoured to bring you back here to stay, for good."

Around them the hall's majestic walls seemed to expand and contract as though in a sigh. The air, or what passed for it in this place, transmitted an intoxicating shiver.

You are most welcome here.

Chalou's mouth dropped open.

"My God, Admiral. It's like the wind talking."

"What wind? Talking?"

"Ah."

Beneath his visor, Chalou smiled.

On the journey back to Terra, Chalou said little, and Ro respected his silence. But finally, in a pale stretch of amber space, they were nearing the insertion point.

"Almost there."

"Thank you, Ro."

They shivered into realspace, into its blackness, with white stars as pinpoints in the void, and the fluffy white and blue globe of Terra that only Ro, now, could see.

"Proximity alert. Proximity alert." Flaring holos.

And the fast approach of three ships, headed straight for them.

"Zajinets."

There was an infinite number of ways to re-enter mu-space from anywhere, but each point had its own quickest route: the least-action path. That was the one Ro took.

"Hang on, Claude."

They screamed back into golden mu-space, with three attacking vessels on their tail.

Violet lightning streaked past—some Zajinet weapon that operated in mu-space—and Ro took her ship through a shuddering series of turns. Golden space and black stars became a blur.

"Shit."

The Zajinet ships, all three of them, were still behind them. Ro spun the ship through a helical manoeuvre, hesitated over a possible trajectory that would hook them back into realspace some thirty years after they had left it, then broke off and levelled out.

"My niece Orla will take care of Sam." Chalou's voice was grim. "Do what you have to do."

The ship shuddered as backlash from enemy weapons washed against the hull.

"Damn it. They don't even have to shoot us straight on." Ro's own ship carried armaments, but the main weaponry was the graser-gatling arrays that worked only in realspace . . . but in realspace, the Zajinets would catch her in seconds. *This* was where her ship came alive. "Come on . . ."

Turn, and turn.

In his seat, Chalou arched back, fingers hooked like claws on the arm-rests; and Ro realized anew that Chalou was no longer a young man.

"I *will* get us out of this," she said.

Crimson turbulence gathered up ahead.

Here we go.

Ro accelerated. The Zajinets followed.

Through a tunnel in the crimson nebula they flew. Then they burst out into a region of clear amber space. Far ahead hung one of those fractal shining trees that might be lifeforms whose distances spanned light-years measured by least-action geodesics.

Everything is relative in mu-space.

Ro flew hard, knowing that if she could reach the scintillating pattern in time, her three pursuers would never—

"What's that?" Blood trickled from Chalou's lip where he had bitten it.

"I don't—Oh, sweet Jesus Christ."

She banked the ship, desperately, knowing the pattern was unreach-able now. *There are thousands of them.* An entire Zajinet fleet was looping towards them: too many vessels to count. *Tricked me, the bastards.*

"Ah, Claude, I'm sorry. I ran just where they expected me to."

"It's been my honour, Admiral."

"Mine also, Pilot."

Ro turned to join battle.

"Weapons armed."

Knowing she could not win.

The fleet was vast and unbeatable, but the trio who had chased her here
. . . Perhaps Ro could take at least one of them with her.

Best I can do.

In the seat beside her, Chalou gasped and wheezed, fighting for breath.

It's over for both of us.

Ro bowed her head, deep into interface. Her vessel leaped forward
and accelerated. Violet lightning flared so Ro—*avoid!*—slammed her
ship to one side and Chalou groaned—*again*—and then something
came out of the golden void moving faster than she would have
thought possible.

##Hi, Mom. How's this for a role reversal?##

"Dirk?"

The bronze ship blasted the centre Zajinet vessel before the alien
pilot had registered the new ship's sudden appearance. The other two
Zajinet craft peeled off to either side.

##Hang on!##

"No. Shit . . ."

Ro enabled ship-to-ship transmission.

++Dirk? What the hell is going on? Get out of here!++

Desperate, she glanced at the Zajinet fleet. Impossible to fight.

##Bastards had a trace on you. But *I* was tracing *them*. Ha!##

Up ahead, the tree-like pattern scintillated. Dirk's ship was glowing.

##Stand by for grappling.##

++No! I've got a . . .++

Impact.

I've got a passenger on board.

The shock hammered into her.

No . . .

An awful choking sound rose from Chalou's throat. Darkness pressed in on Ro, and she struggled, as her vision tunnelled, to retain consciousness. Dirk's ship, locked to hers, was using its momentum to carry them both along a fast geodesic, confounding the enemy fleet but not for long. Heading for the glowing pattern.

"Damn . . ."

It was too late to fight it.

Claude, my friend.

Too late for him.

Ro concentrated, joining her ship's energies to those of her son, as they screamed through extreme trajectories neither vessel had been designed for. Then they struck the pattern. Their ships twisted and turned, were hurled aside by unseen vortices within a maze of turbulence, and fell endlessly through a trajectory no sane being could hope to follow.

Hang on.

Automated systems screamed warnings neither Ro nor Dirk paid attention to.

Hang on . . .

They burst into a region of open space.

"All right . . ."

Began the insertion sequence.

"At last."

Slid into black realspace, and floated among the stars.

No-one, no Zajinet, followed from mu-space.

They waited some hours just in case, but not even a suicidal Zajinet could have followed every twist and turn of the madcap geodesic they had followed.

There was no sound inside Ro's vessel.

She welcomed the delay, giving her time to process her vessel's flight log, to assess and calculate and see just where and when they were. Finally, she sent a question to Dirk:

++Have you worked out the date?++

##Sorry, Mom, but no. I've been plotting geodesics to a certain mu-space locus.##

++You mean Labyrinth.++

##Right. You thought I wouldn't find out about it? ##

Ro let the question ride. Floating here in darkness, there seemed little point in arguing.

++Try plotting a least-action geodesic, Dirk. Back to Terra. And check the arrival date.++

##All right, I can . . . Oh, shit. ##

++Oh yes. ++

Everything in realspace as well as mu-space is relative. But, by the most sensible method of performing the calculation, their ships' processors could nail the date back on Terra precisely, the earliest date they could possibly arrive there: July 11, 2301.

Their hell-flight had lasted one hundred and thirty-five years.

When the two vessels approached Labyrinth, the place was far greater than before: an immense spreading construct whose infinite architecture was spellbinding. Two Pilots—physically older than Ro, yet with eyes as obsidian as hers—entered her ship's cabin and bowed, and greeted her in Anglic that sounded well-rehearsed more than fluent.

"Welcome, Admiral. This is a signal day for us all."

In a daze, Ro followed them to an antechamber where perspectives slid and curved, and where Dirk was already waiting. He gave her an uncertain smile.

"Hey, Mom. Looks like you created an entire world."

Maybe even more than that.

"Could be."

One of Ro's escorts gestured in the direction of wide doors that revolved out of existence, revealing Hilbert Hall . . . but not as she had left it a few subjective hours before. Then, it had been infinitely complex. Now, it seemed also to stretch for ever in all directions, even—as Ro and Dirk stepped from the antechamber—back the way they had come.

Before them stood a massed gathering—parade was too small a word—a huge ordered crowd of ten thousand people or more standing in straight ranks. Every man and woman wore a black jumpsuit and black cape trimmed with gold. Each one watched with glittering black eyes.

My God.

While behind Ro, as she had promised, Claude Chalou returned to the magnificence that was Labyrinth, his coffin borne by six solemn Pilots.

<<MODULE ENDS>>

49

NULAPEIRON AD 3426

Under the chameleoflage sheet, Tom came out of sleep slit-eyed, and realized first that he was hot. Sweat layered his face, and he was breathing open-mouthed, taking shallow breaths.

Everything reduces to basics.

Perhaps it was some kind of paradox, that to fight for humanity meant relinquishing the civilized mind which made the battle worthwhile.

It was the second day "in-country," as the clone-warriors termed it, and the ground was hard beneath a baking mid-morning sun. But Tom told himself to remain still, ignoring discomfort until he knew why he was awake. Was it natural, or had a rasp of sound dragged him from his fading dream?

Swirl of dark-blue cloaks and shining copper helms. The screams of dying men . . .

In his fist Tom held the story crystal. Yet it was not the old tale, but something else, that he had dreamed of.

He moved minutely, took a peek with one eye from beneath his draped chameleoflage. Some fifty metres away on the ground, a membranous circle, ten metres in diameter, looked pale and sticky. All around, the surface was broken, with uneven bumps and depressions in the hard clay. Some of those bumps concealed clone-warriors, as unmoving as statues or preying reptiles.

Morphblade singing through the air . . .

In that moment Tom remembered the contents of his dream, and knew that it was more than random electrical waves sweeping through his brain. He had Seen while he was dreaming; and every man who screamed inside his mind had perished in reality.

"Yours is a deep penetration mission, Warlord." That was what Ygran had said during final briefing. *"The territory is occupied but not Absorbed, not a pure hive mind. Ideally, you'll be in and out with no enemy contact, no-one even realizing you were there."*

Then Ygran had pointed to a different location in the holomap.

"Volksurd's carls, however, will be conducting an all-out commando assault, with overt advance-to-contact in the final phase, and holy bloody Chaos once the thing kicks off."

Now Ygran's words returned like a fulfilled prophecy.

Nestled amid a bowl of purple grassland (Tom remembered from his dream) something like a wide lake shone—but the sunlight glistened on glossy membrane, not water. What lay hidden underneath was not a placid marine ecosystem but a single vast cavernous space remade centuries ago by human-directed drones.

In his dream, Tom had Seen five suborbital flyers hurtling through the yellow sky. They screamed to a halt above the wide membrane, turned and hung in formation, then their grasers stabbed downwards.

Shining membrane bubbled and blackened. Great rents appeared. Within a minute, only burned tatters remained. Then the grasers fired onto selected targets as the lateral hatches opened and twenty smartropes snaked down from each hovering flyer. One hundred carls, bronze shields and jade morphospears slung across their backs, launched themselves downwards.

Return fire spat upwards, knocked three carls from their ropes. The remaining ninety-seven warriors and five non-combatant specialists slid down. Some of the bigger carls fired heavy magzookas from the hip. Thirty seconds later, they touched ground. Ropes fell away, and the flyers turned towards home.

Down in the pit, the battle began.

There *was* something. Tom held his breath. Listened.

Then a black-armoured ciliate the size of Tom's thumb rustled past, on its random hunt for grubs buried in the clay. Nothing untoward. Tom closed his eyes, and his dream came flooding back.

The objective was clear. Three great stubby pillars stood in the caverns: cones with the tops sheared off level. On each one perched an orbital shuttle with a bulging hold and strong, angled wings.

The carls, laying down heavy magzooka-fire, spread in coordinated teams across the cavern's polished floor. Many of the grey-uniformed men and women that fell back before them were unarmed. Others returned fire, untrained in countering surprise attacks but still dangerous: their response was unpredictable.

Kraiv, leading his team, slowed down as two big hostile civilians with grapplers in hand—engineering kit as deadly as any purposebuilt weapon—stepped from behind a processor block. Kraiv drew back his lips and gave his berserker roar.

"Blood and Death!"

Morphospear still slung across his back, he leaped for the two men with his big hands coming up, reaching for their throats. They died.

Off to Kraiv's right, Volksurd's team was fighting. Volksurd's morphospear moaned through the air, bit into an Absorbed man's neck, and there was a liquid crunch. The head dropped and rolled, its eyes already growing opaque.

"By Axe and by Blood, we take what is ours!"

Deep in berserker rage, the carls howled, and threw themselves into the half-determined, half-panicked mass of fifty or more soldiers and engineers who faced them. The carls' weapons swung and twisted, sang and altered shape from one deadly form to another, while their massive owners roared with blood-lust, white spittle-foam caking their lips as they took the battle to the Enemy.

In minutes, it was over.

Designated carls used magzooka-fire to collapse the entrances, while their comrades moved among the dying, dispensing *coups de grâce* with quick thrusts. The strongest climbers pulled on gekkomere gauntlets and began to ascend the pillars, Volksurd and Kraiv among them.

Seventy-nine carls survived.

The three shuttles, resting on their massive plinths, were theirs. Now, the carls had only to wait.

As Tom lay still, sweltering beneath his chameleoflage sheet, he heard a tiny sound. Perhaps it was just another small ciliate, but he could not take the—

A small round hole appeared in the membrane, and a human hand reached through. Then a turban-wrapped head followed, as the man hauled himself up, onto the hard ground. On hands and knees, he pulled small silver gadgets from inside his tattered robe, and set them down.

Then he sat back on his heels and giggled, while the silver objects clawed and crawled their way across the hard clay. The man watched, slack-mouthed, and a thin line of saliva drooled from his lip.

The gadgets were toys. Tom watched from beneath his chameleoflage, wondering who the man was, and who had looked after him before the realm below fell to the Anomaly.

"Bright." The man mumbled incoherent words, then: "Bilgon like."

All around the nearby ground, Ankestion Raglok and his clone-brothers were as still as stones, none of them presenting an outline that might suggest a human presence. Like Tom, they waited.

For half an hour, the man—Bilgon, presumably—watched his glittering, crawling toys. Then his attention seemed to drift, and he stared unfocused into nothingness. More time passed.

It was not Bilgon's lack of intelligence that rendered Tom and the clone-warriors invisible to him. More intelligent observers would have been *less* likely to notice the hidden warriors: people see what they expect to see.

If Bilgon had not gone by nightfall, Tom and the clones would melt away in the darkness, then proceed to an alternative shaft ten klicks away. But that was not going to happen . . . Already, Bilgon was gathering up his toys, muttering as he tucked them back inside his robe.

Then he paused. Tom could not see if Bilgon was staring in his direction.

I am invisible.

For a long moment, Bilgon did not move.

I am clay. I am natural ground.

Then Bilgon was crawling back to the shaft. At the edge, he hunkered, murmuring. He hummed a small tune, then stopped.

He's missed one . . .

In that moment there was a flash of silver, then the wandering toy's pincer took hold of Tom's chameleoflage sheet and tugged it. Just a few centimetres, but enough. Tom stared into Bilgon's widened eyes.

Bilgon's mouth dropped open.

Then he stiffened. A dark shape launched itself through the air, hands wrapped around his chin and the crown of his skull, and twisted. The backwards hip-throw was overkill.

A clone-warrior looked down at Bilgon's corpse, then went down on one knee and plucked something from the body's neck. It was a thin black needle, retrieved from between cervical vertebrae, which the warrior pushed back into place above his own eye: just part of his graphite eyebrow.

Two more warriors took the corpse away, while Tom and the others resumed their earlier positions, hoping no more innocents would blunder into their way.

✧ ✧ ✧

Nightfall was not enough. Darkness on the surface was good cover; but they would need nightshift in the realm below, and that was not in synch. They had to wait until two hours before dawn.

Then they moved.

Five metres from the shaft's edge, working by the moons' silver-white light, the clone-warriors screwed simple titanium bolts into cracks in a rocky outcrop, and wove a web formed of rope among the bolts. Tom and Ankestion Raglok tugged at the web and nodded their approval.

They strapped on safety harnesses. Each man checked his neighbour's harness. Then they attached fourteen separate ropes to the support web, let the ropes slide down inside the shaft, and checked the ropes hung freely. Almost ready. Ankestion Raglok took small vials from his belt pouches, and clipped them onto the supporting web.

There was a tiny squeak of sound as Ankestion twisted each vial's calibrated cap to a precise angle, allowing a precisely measured chemical reaction to begin.

Now the team moved quickly, laying rough fabric covered with clay over the web. When they stepped back, they saw only a clump of ground from which fourteen ropes mysteriously extruded like black serpents upon the moonlit ground. In one hour, hydrofluoric acid would spill through the vials, split the casings and attack the hidden rope-web, disintegrating it in seconds.

At that point, the fourteen attached ropes would snake down the shaft and drop from sight. On the surface, no obvious sign of interlopers would remain. Down below, it would be *rather a good idea,* as General Ygran had put it, if Tom and the clone-warriors were no longer dangling from the ropes when the hour had elapsed.

They descended in darkness, rappelling down the shaft. Their harnesses were attached to the ropes via squeeze-beeners—intricate carabiners fitted with triggers—which slid freely when gripped with medium strength, but locked when released or squeezed hard in panic.

Tom descended in the pitch-black shaft.

Neither he nor the clone-warriors carried smart tech: no corneal smartgel to see into infra-red; no smartropes to lower them under control. The chameleoflage sheets were minimal tech, now buried beneath twenty centimetres of clay upon the surface.

Something hard struck Tom's ankle, a rocky protrusion, and he bit back an exclamation—*bifurcatin' Chaos!*—as he spun away from the shaft wall, dangled helplessly in darkness—*heisenberging harness*—straps digging into his crotch—*who the Fate designed this?*—before taking control once more.

Tom continued the descent, with his ankle sending pain signals: a little distress beacon all of his own.

They reached a balcony inset against the shaft wall. Bright light shone from a tunnel of the Quaternium Stratum, and voices drifted from it. Tom and the clone-warriors hung in place.

Come on. Go talk somewhere else.

Minutes were sliding away and soon the webbed support up on the surface would tear apart under acid attack and the ropes would come snaking down.

Come on . . .

Then the voices faded and the nearest clone-warrior slithered over the stone parapet and dropped to a low crouch. After ten seconds he gestured, and the next warrior swung in a pendulum action until he could reach balcony's side and grab hold. As the second man went over the parapet, the third was beginning his own swing.

Then the next, and the next.

As the eleventh man hooked onto the balcony, Tom got ready. Releasing the squeeze-beener, he trusted to the harness and lock as he ran *away* from the balcony then back, swinging back and forth in increasing arcs until he could hook on with his one hand.

Ankestion Raglok hauled Tom over the parapet. Tom rolled aside just seconds before the next man grabbed hold and clambered onto the balcony. One more to come.

The last man fell.

It was two minutes early, but a severed rope tumbled past, and Ankestion reacted fast, throwing out his hand to grasp the last warrior. For a second Tom thought they were going to make it, but then the remainder of the acid vials must have released up above as the other ropes fell and the warrior plummeted from sight.

Tom leaned over the parapet. Below him, the falling clone-warrior flung his hand out towards a small ledge on the shaft wall—*hook it, come on*—making contact, but torque spun his body, bouncing him off—*no*—and then he was done for.

The clone-warrior fell in silence.

Fate.

A yell would alert the Enemy, but the man kept his discipline even as he tumbled into darkness, shrank to a spot of grey against black, and was gone.

50

NULAPEIRON AD 3426

In occupied territory, read the Academy's Infiltration Manual, *assume the enemy's appearance*. Like all good military manuals, its precepts were simple enough to work under extreme stress, and were best learned in dangerous conditions, with adrenaline.

Tom and the twelve remaining clone-warriors crouched in hiding places high up in a natural cavern. The cavern was unaltered by humankind, save for a small decorative fountain off to one side, where water tinkled from copper nozzles beneath a stone dragon's wings.

There were no locals in sight.

Initial rendezvous, the manual warned, *is fraught with danger.*

Finally, two warriors lowered themselves from their positions. It took ten minutes for them to examine the environs and satisfy themselves that no booby traps or alarms lay in wait. Still, the Enemy could have left devices too small to be detected without sophisticated tech: exactly the kind of hardware that infiltrating warriors could not carry.

Come on . . .

Then the two warriors slid back a panel in the fountain's side, and hauled four green sacks of supplies out of the cache. One of Trevalkin's agents-in-place had readied the cache; so far, everything was in order.

The warriors descended in twos and threes to shuck off their jump-suits, pull civilian clothing from the protective sacks, and tug the garments on. They used simple theatrical make-up—no smartmasks here—to turn their purple skins to ebony. Contact lenses disguised their eyes. With their soft caps and tunics of brown or grey, they looked like typical freemen-artisans of Strehling Suhltône. Their features were almost identical, but that was no problem: they would not travel as a group.

Tom folded up the discarded jumpsuits, wrapped them in the green sacks, and secreted them inside the fountain. He sealed the panel up; it looked untouched.

The clone-warriors performed a final check on each other's appearance. Graphite needles protruded from one warrior's brow; a clone-brother adjusted the glued-on false hair. Then they stared at each other, looking for signs of dismay or overwhelming stress, and nodded: their minds were also in order.

"All right," said Ankestion Raglok. "Chain-sequence rdvs, over-lapping contacts. First objective is the dead-letter drop in Horstmann Pentangle. Likardion, you'll make the pick-up. Tom"—he nodded: no-one would use ranks until the operation was over—"and I will cover you. Everyone else . . . You'll be nowhere in sight, until rendezvous gamma. Understood?"

There were nods all round.

Then Ankestion Raglok surprised Tom by giving a farewell and benediction whose wording came straight from LudusVitae, from those who had plotted revolution:

"Go in freedom, my brothers."

Tom walked with Ankestion Raglok, while the others faded into side-corridors to make their separate ways through the beleaguered realm.

At first, Tom and Ankestion were in square-edged residential tunnels that bore all the marks of armed resistance: scarred ceilings and broken pillars; tunnels where the air tasted of soot. They passed through dead zones, chests tightening, as the charred remains of ceiling fluoro-fungus struggled to replenish the atmosphere. In communal squares people were waiting in food queues, or going about their listless business with drawn faces and sunken eyes. No children laughed.

After a while, they reached clean, unbroken boulevards, with the architecture peculiar to this sector: low, almost oppressive blue-grey ceilings covered with angular knotwork, yet stretching wide. Rows of square pillars stretching out on every side. Among them, people walked, looking subdued.

"This way." Ankestion subtly changed direction.

"What . . . ?" Then Tom noticed the sentries taking up position. "I'm with you."

Militiamen were forming a checkpoint, blocking off the aisle along which Ankestion's clone-brother Likardion had been headed. Tom hoped Likardion was far ahead, out of the troopers' sight.

They followed a convoluted route to Horstmann Pentangle, before coming out into the busy plaza. Most of the crowd were civilian, but here and there military officers walked with purposeful strides, or sat drinking in front of daistral houses. (It was the prettiest servitrices who brought food and drink to the most senior officers, Tom noted.)

Head down, Tom pretended not to notice the flat-faced woman who scanned the crowd from behind a café membrane window, or the three nondescript men bracketing the main exit tunnel. As pedestrians passed the window, the woman made a subtle gesture.

And then, as the people continued walking, one of them, a man with foppish hair, suddenly jerked upright as he sensed danger, yet disbelieved his own perceptions, for he did not run in those few seconds when he had the chance.

Then there was a short scuffle which would have gone unnoticed in any realm, never mind one whose subjects had little incentive to pay attention to the dark things happening around them. Within seconds, the three agents—or policemen—had dragged their victim through a membrane wall and were gone.

It was so swift that—

Something brushed against Tom's hand.

Danger.

But the person walking past him was Likardion, and the hard object clutched in Tom's fist must be whatever Likardion had retrieved from the dead-letter drop. Tom watched for the woman in the window, to see if she had spotted Likardion, but she had already turned away: she had her target for today.

Ankestion headed for a quiet corridor, and after five minutes Tom followed. They came out into an angular hall where a mag-water pool floated above them, its lower surface only a metre overhead.

Tom held out his hand and opened it. On his palm lay a polished silver teardrop.

"We came all this way"—Ankestion plucked the silver object from Tom's hand—"for a holopin?"

Tom shrugged.

"Can you see anything strange about it?"

"No." Ankestion looked in every direction, but they were alone. "Not a thing."

He handed the holopin back to Tom.

"Thanks, I suppose. We should—Ow!"

Something had pricked his hand. The holopin . . .

Fate.

. . . was unfurling, as it tested Tom's DNA and confirmed his identity, knowing he was the right person to see the map it bore. The image was ghostly, transparent, and their current location was marked with a small scarlet sphere.

The route through to the edge of the Anomaly-occupied territory was marked in faint amber; the Enemy's forces were shown as massed, bruised purple clouds, blocking off the main tunnels, on all five strata depicted in the holomap.

Someone's coming . . .

Ankestion moved away from Tom, drawing a punch-knife from his belt—the only weapon he was carrying here, to maintain civilian cover—and Tom's hand went to his own knife. But the figure moving out of the shadows was a clone-warrior, and Ankestion nodded and said: "Likardion," for Tom's benefit. Although Tom had memorized all fourteen clone-warriors' names, he had found no way of telling them apart.

"The holopin," said Likardion, "was in the dead-letter drop, exactly where it was supposed to be. There was no surveillance."

All three of them looked at the entrances to the hall. The mag-pool hanging overhead cast strange silver ripples across their faces, lending them an eerie aspect.

No Enemy forces were coming with grasers drawn and inhuman determination in their dead eyes.

"I took a long route here," Likardion added, "but I had no problems. The locals, the ones who haven't been Absorbed, are too afraid to pay much attention to strangers."

"Good." Tom pointed into the holomap. "This is our rendezvous gamma"—the place where all the surviving clone-brothers were due to meet up—"and this is the route that Trevalkin's local agent has surveyed for us. We're not too badly situated."

Ankestion's voice was a growl as he asked, "Do you trust him, this Trevalkin?"

"I—" Tom shook his head. "Our personal history is . . . complicated, the Viscount and me. Why do you ask? Any particular reason?"

"Just that this tunnel here"—Ankestion pointed into the map, and a section glowed soft blue—"is a more direct route."

"Aye," said Likardion, "and I walked past it on my way here. There were only two guards."

Tom frowned, for the map indicated a well-guarded post. If the map's information could not be trusted—

"Let's go," he said, "and take a look. What d'you say?"

Ankestion's stone features hinted at a smile.

"We're with you."

Square blue pillars stood in rows along the broad hall. At the far end, where a square-cross-sectioned tunnel opened, stood eight troopers wearing identical dark uniforms of the Anomalous forces. All of the troopers bore graser rifles.

Out of sight behind a huge pillar, Ankestion and Likardion exchanged unreadable glances. Likardion had reported only two guards, not eight. Tom did not dare ask Ankestion and Likarion what they were thinking: even a faint sound would carry in this place.

Then something caused the air to change, and a faint scent of ozone drifted in their direction. Tom slowly put his head around the pillar's corner, and looked towards the hall's far end.

Sixteen troopers stood in the entranceway, and they were exactly identical. Beside Tom, Ankestion and Likardion stiffened, but this was not a clone-group that the Enemy had deployed. Tom had seen this kind of thing before.

Before Ankestion could stop him, Tom rolled away from the pillar and crossed the gap to the next one. Again, he moved with silent steps one pillar closer to the entrance; and another pillar, and then one more.

Close enough to feel strange energies on the air, Tom crouched with his back against hard stone, closing his eyes, trying to recall his mental state the last time he had seen this.

The air ripping apart as nine scarlet-clad fighters become eighty-one, advancing on Tom, but he has kissed Eemur's Head, swallowed her sapphire tears, and somehow he can take the momentum of their reality-splitting energy flow and subvert it for his own use. As the geometric proliferation continues, the arena fills with hundreds and then thousands of Absorbed fighters, but Tom is not outnumbered.

For he, too, has become Legion, and there is one of him for every enemy, and then he strikes with focused intent, each fight a solo duel, the whole forming a battle he will remember as a dream when it is over and he has won and become singleton once more.

Eemur was not with him now, but sapphire fluid sang in his veins as Tom breathed deeply, feeling the dark forces moaning in the air. He raised his clenched fist, concentrating, merging with the flow—

Come on. I need to split apart.

But nothing was happening.

Fate. Chaos. Destiny damn it. Come on . . .

Whatever the mysteries of parallel times, whatever strange abilities he had gained in the past, making use of the Blight's power to split reality . . . none of it was working now. Tom might have become more Seer-like, but something had been lost.

I can't do it.

Defeated, he slid down to a sitting position on the cold floor, back against the pillar.

Can't . . .

Then Tom risked a glance around the pillar, and saw hundreds of troopers—two hundred and fifty-six he guessed, by sheer logic—and pulled back before any of them (or any of *him* . . . it was one man doubled, eight times over) realized there were intruders here.

No go.

Ankestion's face peered around the rearmost pillar. After a moment, Tom rose to his feet, and made his way quietly back, trembling inside, sickened with defeat.

He could not take out even one small checkpoint manned by a single Absorbed component. What hope had he of destroying the trillions-strong entity as a whole? Here, in the midst of occupied territory, it came home to Tom for the first time that Nulapeiron was already lost.

51

TERRA AD 2166

<<Ro's Children>>

[15]

And so, the life and times of Kian McNamara.

What happened after Dirk stole the ship and disappeared?

UNSA closed ranks. Within the organization, few learned the full story; most accepted that grief over Kian's burns had caused temporary insanity. A PR campaign focused on Kian's suffering meant that UNSA management did everything possible to treat him with compassion.

Then there was the matter of Ro McNamara's disappearance and presumed death.

No-one involved in the Flagstaff mall riot ever saw a courtroom. Two cops who had remained conscious throughout, and gave damning evidence against their own commander, found themselves taking early retirement in Florida. There, they took up part-time roles in a small consultancy that never advertised and paid exceptionally high salaries.

As for members of the public blinded in the freak electrical storm that had struck during a perfectly legal demonstration . . . they received generous out-of-court settlements, and none of them was foolish enough to rock the boat after their discharge from hospital.

During their hospital stay, every one of the victims had received extensive hypnotherapy to help them see the truth of what happened, and allow them to recover from the trauma of being caught in such a storm.

SpyMotes Inc., by chance a wholly owned subsidiary of UNSA (via several layers of corporate indirection), upgraded the mall's security systems free of charge. In the process of replacing every component, engineers quietly removed the old crystal logs to a safe location.

By the time the first witnesses were available for interview, the Atlanta Archipelago, a linked series of morphing artificial islands for rich tourists, had undergone catastrophic failure—terrorists were blamed for the virus—and newsNet journalists were more interested in cataloguing the dead in a high-profile disaster than in an odd, no-longer-newsworthy incident at a Flagstaff mall.

The chief architect of UNSA's PR campaign was a soft-faced man called Ben Winrod who had learned to lie to his parents at an early age. It was sheer coincidence that he visited the Archipelago two days before its tragic collapse.

One week later, UNSA medics pronounced Kian fit to walk.

No cameras or journalists recorded Kian's exit from the hospital. Disfigured face half-hidden by a hood, his claw-hand pulled up inside his sleeve, he walked with a limp which would diminish over the years but never disappear.

Only Deirdre was there to see him. She walked beside him, escorting him across the parking lot without touching. Kian stopped at the hire-car's door, looked up at the sky with an unreadable expression, then hauled himself inside.

"Take me home please." The soft tones were unlike those of the brash young man who had arrived in Arizona twelve weeks before.

Later, some would say it was the voice of a saint.

There was a small memorial service, held in the tiny Church of the Holy Trinity on a Wicklow mountainside, in whose leafy cemetery earlier generations of McNamaras lay buried. One of the attendees was an astrophysicist called Dorothy Verzhinski, who pulled in favours to get a voyage home. She was the one who had dredged through Vachss Station's scan-logs to find the faint signature of a Zajinet vessel.

It had lain in wait, followed Ro into mu-space . . . And no-one had seen Ro since.

"I'm sorry," Dorothy told Kian. "So very sorry."

"Thank you for coming," he said. "It's good that you're here."

Later, as Kian stood alone in drizzling rain before his great-grandfather's worn brown headstone, the infostrand round his wrist beeped. The message was urgent, text-only, from Ilse Schwenger. She had served in the highest echelons of UNSA management, and had helped Ro, years earlier (and Grandmother, before that).

My profound sympathies, the message read. **UNSA will be holding an official ceremony of remembrance next week, on Wednesday in Saarbrücken Fliegerhorst, at 10:00 local time. I'll confirm your flight arrangements shortly.**

Kian held out his wrist. Silver rain drifted like tears through the holo.

"Come on." It was Deirdre, her face long with sadness. "Let's get you back to the hotel."

"All right."

Kian allowed her to lead him along the wet gravel path, his right arm hooked in her left, the twisted claw-like ruin of his hand visible to anyone who cared to look.

A sputtering log fire filled the hotel's snug with heat and a smoky tang. Kian and Deirdre sat on opposite sides of the fireplace. Deirdre's infostrand displayed the official UNSA invitation to next week's remembrance service.

"The subliminal message is: *We look after our own.* What they mean is, we look after our own *interests.*" Deirdre rotated the holo so he could read it. "See? It's for Dirk as well, the service. Or that's what they're implying."

"Dirk's not dead."

"No . . ."

"Who's the other message from?"

"What other message?"

"Deirdre, I can see the icon from here. Is it Paula?"

Deirdre shut down the display.

"She works for them. For UNSA."

"As my mother did. And the father I never knew. And my grand-mother."

"As you will, Kian?"

"Yes . . . Yes, I think so."

The fire popped and a small piece of smouldering wood landed on the rug. Deirdre pulled a poker from its stand and shoved the wood onto the tiles. There were iron tongs on the stand also, and she used them to fling the lump back into the grate.

"I think you should reply to her message, Deirdre."

"Even after everything they've . . . ?"

Kian nodded. "Even after everything. You may only get one chance at love."

"Ah, Kian."

Deirdre's room was at the apex of the old building. The ceiling sloped in from either side, and three-century-old oak beams spanned the gap. A faint draught moaned from a small leaded window.

After a night of fitful sleep, she woke in a blue-grey dawn, padded on bare feet across the cold wooden floor, and peered outside. The Wicklow Mountains were majestic. Down below, on the lawn behind the hotel, a figure was moving.

"My God."

It was a dance.

Such grace.

And then again . . . there was a warrior's intent behind the flowing motion.

Deirdre could only watch as Kian moved like a swallow, swooping through graceful movements that were like tai-chi, like aikido, and yet were something new and different. There was a phrase she had always found stupid: *becoming one with nature*. But now . . .

Now, for the first time she knew what people meant, and she continued to watch as Kian's dance brought the dream to life.

Twenty spellbound minutes later Kian finished. He cupped his right hand over his left and bowed. And looked up at Deirdre's breath-fogged window, his black eyes glittering.

Then he retrieved his walking-stick from the tree it had leaned against, and limped back into the hotel, no longer magical, with his right hand a claw and his face half-covered in glistening scar tissue.

Over the years, Kian would refuse reconstructive surgery until the medics grew tired of offering it. But after seeing that more-than-dance in the dawn, Deirdre could never think of Kian as anything other than a supremely complete being who had already evolved to a level beyond the most daring aspirations of Zen mystics.

Yet he was also simply her friend.

It rained over Saarbrücken, too.

Ranks of young Pilots-to-be, each wearing the new dress uniform of black edged with golden braid, stood on emerald grass in the open-air sports stadium and listened to the eulogies. Older Pilots attended, their metal eye sockets beaded with rain, with sighted helpers to guide them.

The music was solemn. Stravinski's melodic *Rite of Spring* was the least mournful. Monsignor Edwin Grayling, SJ, stood at the podium and read from Psalms: "Though I walk through the valley of death, I will fear no evil . . ."

Ro would have hated it.

At the end, as Frau Doktor Ilse Schwenger delivered the final tribute, a thunderclap sounded overhead. Three thousand heads tipped back, ignoring the rain, as thirteen mu-space craft crashed through into realspace, screamed past in perfect formation, and were gone.

Every one of two thousand fledgling Pilots looked towards the podium and snapped a perfectly synchronized salute.

"*The Admiral is dead.*"

They spoke in unison, unrehearsed. Every non-Pilot in the stadium felt their neck-hairs rise.

"*Long live the Admiral.*"

Kian bowed his head.

When the service was over, there was largely purposeless milling. Among the senior UNSA management, a politically minded observer would have paid close attention to who leaned close to whom and talked in low tones. With such powerful figures in one place, it was inevitable that the day's alleged purpose became merely an occasion that brought people together, not the only reason for being here.

Deirdre watched it all with sour amusement. She had not known Ro, but she knew Kian and had begun to know Dirk, and they were not the kind of people to wheel and deal at a time of mourning . . . except that Kian had been assured as well as modest in the way he took the young Pilots' tribute and bowed back from the podium.

"Deirdre?" The tone was uncertain.

"Paula. I wasn't sure . . . you'd be here."

"If you'd read my—Never mind. Have you seen Zoë?"

"Who?"

"Blonde hair, petite, looks a third of her actual age. You've met her."

"Yes," said Deirdre. "I didn't realize you had."

"She used to be my boss." That was the clearest admission yet that Paula worked for UN Intelligence, not UNSA. "She told me . . . something. Something Kian ought to know."

Deirdre crossed her arms.

You're using me to reach Kian.

Paula read the gesture correctly. "So here it is, and you can just tell him or not, OK? Zoë accessed the interrogation logs for Solly. You'll remember him"—with a trace smile—"as the one whose testicles squished on the toe of your boot. Er . . . Where are they all off to?"

Young Pilots were moving past them. Some were children of seven or eight, leading their even younger colleagues. All were in black uniform.

"I don't know. I do remember Solly."

And I wonder if Zoë needed to access the logs.

Someone had to perform the interrogation, after all.

"Solly knew he was working for Zajinets."

"Um, right." Deirdre stared at Paula. "Wasn't that obvious?"

"Not really. From past experience, many of their cell members are recruited by other humans. When you join a shadow organization, particularly a small one, it's pretty hard to be sure who it is you're working for."

"I suppose so."

"Anyway, Solly knew the truth, so they pushed the questioning further than the usual: what's your contact's name, how do you meet up, that sort of thing."

Deirdre shivered.

Perhaps it was the cold rain that was falling more heavily now. But Paula showed no sign of wanting to head for shelter.

"They asked the question," Paula said, "that no-one's been able to answer: *Why do the Zajinets hate humans?* Why have they targeted Pilots, specific Pilots?"

She paused.

Deirdre gave in. "So why? What's the answer?"

"Solly said: '*They'll allow the darkness to be born. It will spread across the galaxy, and they won't fight back until billions have perished. I've seen it.*' That's what he said. '*The Zajinets showed me the future, and I've seen it.*' It may sound insane, but Solly believed. He was in no fit state for joking by that time."

"You're using the past tense," said Deirdre.

"He did not survive the interrogation. A pre-existing medical condition, they said."

"Oh, Jesus."

"I don't think He was there that day. Deirdre . . . Things are different now. I don't like the way the organization is going. I'm not sure I belong here."

After a moment, Deirdre said: "Well, here's a thing. I *never* liked it."

In a huge near-empty hangar, designated Flugzeughalle Zwei and vast enough to hold three mu-space ships at once, the Pilots-to-be convened. They were children and young adults with obsidian eyes and solemn expressions, and they stood in rows on the cold concrete floor and waited for Kian to speak.

None of them had flown a ship. Not a single virally rewired adult Pilot was present.

This was a gathering of Ro's Children.

All two thousand of them, near enough: only a few had been kept away by minor disasters or administrative snafus. In Tehran, fifteen youngsters were trapped in the spaceport while anti-xeno demonstrators picketed the buildings and prevented landings and take-offs. But enough of them were here.

Two of the older youths dragged a wheeled platform into place. It was designed for engineers who needed to work underneath a mu-space vessel's wing; it would do for what they had in mind. They locked the wheels in place, and nodded.

From the hangar doors, Kian limped—still using his cane—along a natural aisle with a thousand young Pilots ranked on either side. When Kian reached the platform he paused, as though reconsidering. Then he handed his cane to one of the young men who had positioned the platform.

"Thank you, Carlos."

"No problem, boss."

Kian hooked his bad hand over the steps' rail, and climbed up to the platform.

And looked down upon his brothers and sisters.

In the flight base control tower, Paula used her ID ring to open a steel door, and ushered Deirdre inside. In a half-lit room, surveillance holos flickered. In them, shone scenes of a large hangar and the two thousand young Pilots gathered there.

"Does Kian know he's being watched?" said Deirdre.

There were twelve men and women observing. One of them turned at Deirdre's question, mouth opening.

"Is there a problem, Browning?" asked Paula.

"Er . . . No, ma'am."

"Good."

Deirdre was shaking her head. "This is not right. You can *not* do this."

But one of the observers was frowning.

"There's, um, something going on."

"What?"

In most of the displays, the scene was as before. But one of the holos showed a close-up of Kian's face, as if he were looking directly into the observation room.

And smiling.

Deirdre shivered. For a moment, she thought a faint glimmer of gold crossed his black eyes, and she remembered the Santa Monica PD drone that had fallen from the sky.

In the observation room, every holo winked from existence.

This was the speech that Kian gave:

"We are a family, my brothers and sisters. We mourn our mother, the first Admiral. And our brother Dirk who is lost, perhaps for ever.

"There are armoured flyers overhead. You've seen them. Soldiers surround the base, guarding us. Protecting us.

"For UNSA we are resources. Of course! Millions are invested in our training, in the construction and maintenance of great ships that we will come to think of as our own. We cannot blame them for fearing that we will go astray, or that public opinion will be swayed by paranoid minorities.

"If we upset them, they will be like children whose toys have been stolen. It is *we* who must be the adults here.

"Some people fear what is different. But they should not fear us, for we are humanity. UNSA need not fear us, for we will do their bidding, and they should know that.

"My brothers and sisters, we pledge to humanity unwavering service and total dedication. And you know what? *We're* the ones who get the best side of the bargain.

"We're the ones who reach the stars."

For a moment there was silence.

Then a roar filled the hangar, echoed back from those stark walls again and again in affirmation:

"Admiral. *Admiral. ADMIRAL.*"

Three separate audio pickups remained intact inside the hangar. Later, UNSA management and analysts would replay Kian's speech over and over, listening for strange tones or internal contradictions, finding none.

After that day, every young Pilot in training would redouble his or her efforts. When natural-born Pilots began to take their own ships into mu-space, they would be fearless and reliable, committed to UNSA and performing every single operation with determination.

Only one thing would worry the most astute analysts: that they heard Kian's words, but could see nothing of his gestures and body language, or the odd hints of golden light that holo images occasionally captured in Pilots' eyes.

But those worries were tentative, and few people dared record them in official reports. Over time, vague suspicions would fade and be forgotten.

✧✧✧

Yet one more thing happened that day which Deirdre would *never* forget. Before she and Paula could leave the observation room, the steel door clanged open and a bristle-haired man wearing a braid-draped uniform strode in.

"What the bloody hell"—he stabbed a finger in Deirdre's direction—"is *she* doing here?"

"I signed her in, General."

The general scowled at Paula.

"That's *how* she entered, not what she's doing."

"She's a civilian observer, who knows the surveillance subject and might have shed some light on what was going on. That is"—Paula waved towards the blank spaces where the holo images should have been—"*if* your people hadn't bollixed up their jobs."

The lines on the general's face deepened.

"I'll look into that, mark my words. But as for your attitude—"

Paula was already tugging the ID ring from her finger.

"You have my resignation, sir, and this is not spur-of-the-moment. I've thought about it."

"Not acceptable."

"And if you allow my friend and me to leave quietly, then we won't need to raise a fuss about what happened here today. Or rather"—with a malicious smile—"what *failed* to happen. Do we have a deal?"

The general clenched his fists and for a moment Deirdre thought he was going to lash out. But his voice when he spoke was calm.

"Get out. Get out of my friggin' sight."

Ten minutes later, they were outside, watching the young Pilots dispersing to the shuttles which would take them to their various homes.

"Look at him." Paula nodded towards Kian, who was walking among his young kindred. "I'd swear he has an aura about him."

Her hand touched Deirdre's, as if by accident.

"It was only in medieval paintings," Deirdre said, "that artists started showing halos as disks around saintly heads. Before that, they were thought to surround the body with a faint glow."

"Right." Paula shivered. Then she rubbed her face with both hands, and stared up into the cloudy sky. "At least it's stopped raining."

"You're not really worried about the weather."

"What? Just because"—with a shaky laugh—"I've destroyed my career, in the only environment I've ever known. Why should I be worried?"

"I know what you did." Deirdre touched her shoulder. "And I admire you for it."

"Really?" Paula looked into her eyes. "I'm jobless. Christ, I'm homeless. I've been living in barracks."

"You mean, you can't find a bed for the night?"

"Um . . ."

"Is this happening too fast for you?"

"No. Yes. I think so. Go slowly, would you. I'm feeling fragile."

"Don't worry, dear. I *will* be gentle."

<<MODULE ENDS>>

52

NULAPEIRON AD 3426

Tom stumbled along, led by Ankestion and Likardion, scarcely processing their route through blue-shadowed, square-edged tunnels and darkened halls, or the way that three shadow-figures—more clone-brothers—joined them one by one as they proceeded in the direction of the rendezvous.

We're lost.

Elva was on the terraformer sphere, on Axolon Array with Jissie and the senior commanders. He should be with her—

They came to a halt, Ankestion dragging Tom down into a crouched position. Tom was about to whisper a question, then stopped: not so much from stealth as from the realization that he no longer cared.

Elva, my love. I'm sorry.

Everything was formed of blue-grey stone. Before Tom and five clone-warriors, a straight narrow footbridge of that same stone led to a dark cross-corridor beyond. The bridge spanned a kilometre-long hall, close to the flat ceiling.

There were sounds of movement from below, the sense of breathing, yet no voices spoke. Mixed aromas of food arose: fleischbloc and a fruity tang, overlaid by something else that was sour and unpalatable. Ankestion looked grim.

Absorbed components, feeding in the hall.

Nothing else could account for the presence of hundreds, maybe thousands of human beings out of sight in the hall below, carrying out their actions without speaking. But even as Tom came to this conclusion, a single educated voice said: "This is outrageous! My family are innocent."

Ignoring a tug at his tunic, Tom crept forward and slowly looked over the footbridge's parapet, down into the hall. He saw row upon row of long tables, at which five hundred or more uniformed soldiers sat spooning some viscous liquid broth out of deep bowls. Off to one side was a vast food processor block, bigger than anything Tom had seen as a kitchen servitor. Attendants stood ready to dish out more food.

But it was the silver-haired man with the elegant goatee who caught Tom's attention, and the woman with him. She was too scared to speak, but clutched the back of a small lev-chair inside which a young boy was sitting. The boy looked pale and infirm, his breath coming fast and shallow in panic; he was obviously in the chair for medical reasons, unable to stand.

"Please . . ." The elegant man pleaded with one of the Absorbed components standing in front of him, as if the component were still a person, with a human being's sensibilities. "If you could allow my wife and son to go past, I would be happy to stay as guarantor of their . . ."

His voice trailed off.

Tom's skin tightened.

No . . .

There was nothing he could do.

For Fate's sake, get out of there.

But the air was already blackening, roiling, and then the man's eyes rolled up in his head. His wife's stare whitened as her eyes also rolled. In the lev-chair, the young boy opened his mouth as if to yell at his parents, but his vocal cords were frozen.

What happened next was almost too swift to perceive.

Unnatural synchronization meant that the man and his wife and two of the waiting attendants moved simultaneously. The man hauled the useless boy out of the lev-chair; the woman helped swing the boy to one side, then throw him.

One attendant caught the boy as the other flipped open a hatch, and the boy went sailing inside the processor block before he could scream. The hatch banged shut.

Oh, Fate . . .

The boy's corpse, hidden from view, was already sliding apart, dissolving and merging with the broth inside, before Tom could even understand what had happened. Then horror clenched him.

No. He was your son.

But the beings who had sacrificed the boy were no longer capable of seeing their son as anything other than damaged organic matter, whose only use could be to provide nutrients for the operating components of the greater whole: the Anomaly of which they were part.

Clone-warriors pulled Tom back from the edge before his gagging reaction could betray their presence. A stone hand clamped across his face. Then they were half-carrying him across the bridge, moving bent over but fast, until they reached the cross-corridor beyond.

Two more clone-warriors were waiting at a seven-sided junction which was otherwise deserted. They stared at Tom as he tugged himself free of Ankestion's grasp, leaned against a wall, and gave spewing vent to sour vomit, spattering onto blue-grey stone.

Oh, Destiny.

Another paroxysm took hold of Tom, and then another, as the remainder of his stomach contents hurled themselves outwards, beyond his ability to control.

After several minutes, he stepped away, wiping his lips with the back of his hand.

"Warlord?" Ankestion used Tom's title, though it broke the mission rules. "Are you all right?"

Tom looked back at the mess. One of the clone-warriors had already pulled off his surcoat and was using it to mop up the evidence. Another joined in.

"No." Tom turned to Ankestion. "No, I'm not."

Clone-warriors would continue to fight or operate flyers or carry out any task even as they vomited, if they ever did: that much was clear. But they did not expect that level of determination in people who were not of their kind.

The boy didn't even scream . . .

"I won't be all right," continued Tom, "until the Anomaly is out of our world. For ever."

The clone-warriors looked at each other.

"Come on," said Tom. "We have work to do."

They met at rendezvous gamma without incident. Then all twelve clone-warriors, along with Tom, made their way to a natural cavern where a small opening was hidden in shadow. One by one, they crawled into the borehole on hands and knees.

It took them most of an hour to make their way along its twisting length. Their progress was slow because of hard effort and the need for silence, but eventually they came out onto a ledge overlooking a vast cavern, almost as big as the caverns of Realm V'Delikona.

Below them, an entire army filled the cavern floor.

Troops moved around large blocks of equipment: heavy weaponry, mining devices, basic supplies. Perhaps a thousand Enemy soldiers were encamped.

Ankestion pointed. A strip of black water, a service canal, ran through the cavern. Automated cargo-bugs floated on the canal, moving in a slow steady train.

After a moment, Tom nodded. The Enemy troops were near the battle-front and therefore alert, but no army expects to be infiltrated from *behind*. And no-one could move more silently than Ankestion's clone-brothers, or an Academy-trained infiltration agent like Tom Corcorigan.

One at a time, the clone-warriors descended—slowly, so very slowly—from the ledge. Tom followed, spidering from one hold to another, holding very still when he rested. Their clothes were the right colour to blend with the brownish-grey rock: Trevalkin's agent had thought carefully before leaving the garments in the supply cache.

You train your people well, Trevalkin.

Finally, Tom and the twelve warriors were hunched behind a tall container on the cavern floor, almost within touching distance of a full regiment of Absorbed troops, waiting for Ankestion's signal.

The warriors slipped from container to stone outcrop to container, un-noticed by the milling soldiers. Soon, they were just metres from the canal. To their right, it disappeared back into a tunnel in the rockface they had descended; to their left, it arrowed through the Enemy camp.

The clone-warriors moved off at five-minute intervals. As each man reached the water's edge he crouched very low, reached into the dark waters, and rolled silently into them. When it was Tom's turn, he concentrated on breathing, taking huge quiet inhalations, then one last gulp as he tipped forward and went down, cold waters closing all around him.

Tom went deep, until his fingertips touched the bottom, and then began to swim.

After three minutes submerged in water, yellow fluorescence was pul-sating in Tom's eyeballs and he was desperate to breathe. He could not rise, unless he wanted graser fire to blow his body apart. There was a whole army up there.

Swim.

Tom hauled himself onwards.

Just swim.

Desperate to inhale . . .

Ignore.

No. Absolutely imperative that he—

Not there yet. Ten seconds more.

Swimming. Still swimming.

You said ten seconds.

I lied.

Again. Another ten seconds.

Can't swim any further. Breathe now.

No. Push it. Ten seconds more.

Now.

No. Push . . .

Now?

Yes.

And Tom rolled to the surface, face into the air, inside a tunnel away from the cavern, burning with primeval joy as he sucked in life again.

At the edge of the canal in a deserted tunnel, the clone-brothers washed off the remainder of their disguises. Most of the theatrical make-up had failed to survive the swim. Soon, they were purple-black in the dim light, their graphite eyebrows invisible.

They made their way forward, until they came out into another cavern, where microwards were deployed upon the ceiling, and the main Collegiate defences were arrayed: graser cannons and armoured troops, dug into the heavy emplacements.

It was almost nightshift, and neither Tom nor Ankestion had any intention of being shot by the people they were trying to help. They settled down out of sight, and waited for the darkness.

Two hours later, half a regiment of Collegiate Dragoons failed to spot thirteen shadows flitting through their lines like ghosts. Within minutes, Tom and the twelve clone-warriors were past the first defences, and into one of the Collegium's Outer Courts.

At the centre of the Court stood a glistening membranous tent, framed with narrow ribs: a commander's tent. The clone-warriors slipped inside, and Tom followed. They found empty chairs set up around a briefing table, and no-one in sight. They looked at each other, grinned, and sat down.

It was twenty minutes before the commanding officer, his uniform draped with silver braid, entered his own tent and stopped dead.

"How do you do." Tom remained sitting. "My friends and I have an appointment with Viscount Trevalkin, in Chronos Court. To save misunderstandings, perhaps your people could escort us?"

For a long moment, the officer could not speak. Then he went down on one knee and bowed, and greeted Tom in a way he had not expected.

"Warlord. Thank Fate you're here."

53

NULAPEIRON AD 3426

Instantia Hall was long and spacious, a right-angled triangle from whose polished walls slender buttresses protruded. The ceiling arced, light and airy; but despite the clean lines, the overall shape suggested broken symmetries and odd intrusions.

Be on guard in this place.

Tom was alone. General Ivlon of the Dragoons had invited the clone-warriors to his chambers, along with his own staff officers. An escort had left Tom here.

A doorshimmer evaporated. In the archway, Magister Strostiv bowed.

"So you got out of Realm Buchanan," said Tom.

"Aye, my Lord Corcorigan. Or should I say *Warlord?*"

"Perhaps you should."

"Ah . . ." Strostiv took a pace forward. "You wonder how I escaped intact."

"The Anomaly descended quickly."

"You don't need to tell *me*, Warlord. I was there."

Tom blew out a breath. This was getting them nowhere. "My apologies, Magister. How did you escape?"

Strostiv's laugh was short and cynical. "An old friend of yours got me out."

Tom looked around the hall, hiding his thoughts. Odd glass flanges and panels reflected strange, sliding combinations of unsettling hues.

"Trevalkin," said Tom. "I should have guessed."

"As a strategist and organizer, he's extraordinary. If we survive . . . this . . . then I expect we'll offer him the Chancellorship."

"Good for him."

Strostiv gestured. "This way, my . . . Warlord."

But as they walked past one of the strange glass panels, a vision moved inside it, and Tom could not look in any other direction but inside the illusion.

Around the table, in a raw stone chamber, a family laughs. There is a fleshy man, in his mid-thirties but with the heaviness of middle age that often envelops non-athletes, and for a moment Tom jerks in recognition—Father!—but he is mistaken. The man turns and Tom sees . . . himself.

A bulkier version of himself who lifts a bowl of broth in both *hands to drink. Opposite him, Elva, likewise softer-looking than he has known her, drinks and compliments the woman standing over them, whose red hair is streaked with grey.*

"That was marvellous, Ranvera," Elva says. "You've excelled yourself this—"

Mother!

Tom ripped himself away from the shimmering glass.

"What did you see, Warlord? The past or the future?"

"I saw myself"—Tom surprised himself by revealing the truth—"the same age as I am now. Poor but happy, living out life in Salis Core. A *different* life, Strostiv."

And Elva was there.

But Elva had lived in the same district, working as a member of the astymonia patrol. If Tom had never met Pilot deVries, then the Oracle would not have descended to their humble stratum, would not have taken Mother . . . but Tom might still have met Elva. Life *could* have turned out that way.

Strostiv sucked in a breath. "That's . . . unusual. To see a different Fate."

But the man I saw, thought Tom, *wasn't me. He was soft and useless.*

If he wanted to save Nulapeiron, Tom Corcorigan would have to be a very different kind of man.

"Chronos Court," added Strostiv, gesturing towards another door-shimmer, "is through there. The Viscount will be waiting for us."

"Marvellous."

Other visions swirled in Tom's mind as they entered Chronos Court.

Dead carls litter the floor. Fighting men and creatures of the Anomaly swarm through the vast hall, despatching the wounded of both sides. And on those three gigantic plinths—

On one of them, the wreckage of a destroyed shuttle belches black toxic smoke. But the other two plinths stand bare.

Tom moaned, squeezing his eyes shut, feeling Strostiv grasp his sleeve. "Are you all right, Warlord?"

In one of the two escaped shuttles, Kraiv is in the cockpit behind the pilot's seat, staring down at the receding ground. His face is half-covered in glistening blood. Outside the membrane window, another shuttle is visible, flying along-side, matching speed.

Tom brought his attention back to the moment.

"I'm fine."

The carls had just taken their captured shuttles into the air, without waiting for Tom's signal. Tom's vision suggested that Anomalous forces had mounted a counterattack, trying to recapture the shuttle bay, and the carls had been forced to take off early.

None of this helped.

And Tom wondered, as he sat down to face Trevalkin, whether Collegiate sensors could detect the flow of information through the Calabi-Yau dimensions of realspace, and knew that the Warlord sitting here was no longer just a human being, but something similar to the Seers which Oracular engineering programmes occasionally produced.

"Greetings, Warlord."

"Viscount. How interesting to see you."

"I can see we're going to have a friendly conversation, filled with reminiscence and nostalgia."

"We're on a timetable, Trevalkin. A tight timetable."

In the shuttles, the pilots—both of them carls—redplane the acceleration, ignoring the soft moans of the wounded lying in the cabins behind them, knowing they dare not slow down.

"Then we'd better proceed, Corcorigan. If you don't mind."

Holos shifted above the conference table. A translucent vertical cylinder represented a shaft leading from a Collegium Inner Court all the way up to the surface. One by one, tiny figures of arachnargoi took up their positions, tendrils fastened to the sheer walls, poised for their race upwards, to freedom.

"What are the cargos?" asked Tom.

"Manipulators, in the main. Spinpoint field manipulators." Trevalkin spoke with authority, though it was doubtful whether he had known anything of spinfields until recently. "Along with key research staff."

Tom looked at Strostiv. "Who chose them?"

"I did, along with the other surviving Altus Magisters."

"If the Anomaly guesses what we're doing," said Trevalkin, "its forces will close in immediately. Our defences can't hold back a concerted assault."

"So why is the Enemy holding back?" Tom thought he knew the answer, but wanted Trevalkin's opinion. "Why not move in now?"

"Because they don't want a repetition of their experience invading the first Collegium. If our researchers were to set off a series of self-destruct explosions, the Anomaly would lose whatever resources it finds of interest. But . . ."

"But what?"

"You know as well as I do, that its interest is only marginal. What can humankind really offer the Anomaly, beyond extra components to add to itself?" Trevalkin stared into the display. "If it knew our best researchers and equipment were in the arachnargoi, it wouldn't hesitate to destroy them."

"Perhaps it's time," said Tom, "that we got out of here."

"Possibly." Trevalkin shut down the display. "Are you ready?"

"I was hoping to meet someone else."

"Now who could that be?"

"Trevalkin . . ."

"Relax. Your friend is here, and I hope he can pull off another amazing trick. I really hope so." Trevalkin clapped his hands, and at the rear of the chamber, a door-membrane liquefied. "Here he is."

"Tom! I mean . . . Warlord."

"Avernon."

They clasped forearms.

"Did Trevalkin tell you I've got it?" Avernon's eyes were lit with the joy of logosophical discovery. "We're on the right track. With a few more tests, and brainstorming sessions . . . Anyway, I'm glad you decided to come."

Trevalkin smiled to himself. Tom wondered whether Avernon had any idea what he and Ankestion's clone-warriors had been through to get here, but all he said was, "So you've a working shield?"

"It was your suggestion, and I think," said Avernon, "we're proceeding on the right lines. It *ought* to work."

"Can't you be more certain?"

Avernon gestured towards Trevalkin. "He won't let me test the technique."

"What? Why not?"

Trevalkin looked at Avernon. "Tell the Warlord how you propose to field-test this stuff."

"Simple." Avernon's natural enthusiasm bubbled up as he reopened the display, causing a schematic to shine. "See, we send some of our soldiers into Enemy territory as a decoy . . ."

Tom glanced at Trevalkin, who said nothing.

And who were you going to get to do that?

". . . and when the Absorbed manifest themselves, our fellows get

close to one of them and set off the device. See? There's a range of phenomena that might result, but the most obvious would be—"

"How big a device? And what would it do, precisely?"

"About the size of your hand, Tom. It will collapse space around the
Absorbed individual. Surrounding him in all ten spatial dimensions."

"How will you know that? How will you know it's worked?"

"Mostly, there'll be a blaze of light, while it pinches off the seven
hyper-dimensions. It'll disconnect the Enemy soldier's mind from the
Anomaly."

And what are the other Enemy soldiers doing while all this is happening?
Tom said, "Will the individual revert back to normal?"

"The energy released," said Avernon, "would be fatal at close range.
I can't help that."

"I'd rather be dead than Absorbed." Trevalkin stood up. "We've
used simulations, or rather, Strostiv's researchers have used them, to
test Lord Avernon's methods. They appear OK."

"Simulations," said Tom.

"That's right."

"Sweet bleeding Fate."

"You have the common touch, Warlord." Trevalkin's smile was unreadable. "That's a compliment, of course."

"Right." Tom nodded as if he believed that. "Then it's time to
begin the evacuation."

But evacuation was too generous a term for the operation. Tom stood
with Ankestion Raglok on a dusty platform, staring up at the nine big
arachnargoi—some blue-green, others brown-black—perched ready to
ascend the vertical shaft.

Five small black arachnabugs hung higher up on the shaft wall,
grasers powered up, tendrils poised to fling the one-occupant vehicles
towards the top. Their job was to blast away the protective membrane
at ground level, clearing the way to the surface.

"You've got Strostiv aboard?"

"Aye, Warlord, though he wanted to remain behind. He said his place was here, with the other senior Magisters. I had to insist."

"OK, we're about ready to—"

Tom shivered.

Shuttles screaming towards the ground. Kraiv bares his teeth in a warrior's grin.

"They're here!" Tom wrenched himself back from Seeing the shuttles. "Get aboard."

Two narrow tendrils snaked down from the nearest arachnargos. One encircled Ankestion's waist and drew him upwards. The other tendril reached for Tom, but he backed off. *Something* was moving in the shadowed tunnel beyond the platform.

But it was Trevalkin who stepped into the light.

"Jumpy, Warlord?"

"Yes, for Fate's sake. Have you reconsidered? This is your last chance."

A thin-lipped smile. "Every defence force needs a leader."

"Yes." Tom hesitated, raised his arm, and the tendril fastened around him. "They do."

"Go in freedom, Warlord."

"Fate favour you, Trevalkin."

The platform fell away beneath Tom as the tendril hauled him up. Trevalkin delivered an ironic bow, and turned away. Then Tom was inside the arachnargos cabin, and the floor was sealing up.

May Fate favour us all.

The arachnargos swung into motion.

Ten minutes later the arachnargoi were racing up the shaft. At the apex, only a few tattered remnants of the protective membrane remained: the arachnabugs had done their job. The arachnargoi sped through, and then they were in the open, in the pale apricot light of dusk.

Two big shuttles were roaring downwards from the sky, their lower hatches open.

"Enemy fighters sighted." Likardion was at the arachnargos controls. "Closing fast."

Black dots above the horizon were growing larger by the second.

"Fate. Are they orbit-capable?"

"Negative on that, Warlord."

"Then let's—"

Tom's breath was knocked out of him as the cabin tipped back and the arachnargos leaped upwards, into a hovering shuttle's cargo hold. Tendrils whipped out to steady it. Three other arachnargoi leaped inside; the other five would be aiming for the second shuttle.

"We're in," said Ankestion.

The big hold's hatch puckered shut. Inside the arachnargos, Tom grabbed hold of his seat's armrest.

Then there was nothing for Tom to see as everything lurched and the shuttle flung itself into full acceleration, arcing upwards, screaming away from the planet's surface faster than the Enemy fighters, heading to a place where they could not follow: beyond the atmosphere and into orbit.

In seconds, they had left the besieged Collegium far behind and below: left them to fight as best they could against overwhelming forces that even now were moving in to crush them.

Give them Chaos, Trevalkin.

54

TERRA AD 2166–2301

<<Ro's Children>>

[16]

Further highlights from the life and times of Kian McNamara:

Kian worked hard at his ordinary career—inasmuch as any Pilot could be called ordinary—as well as setting policy, and negotiating with UNSA on his people's behalf. Senior management recognized the position he held among the natural-born Pilots (and many of the older ones) without ever giving him an official title.

No-one in the halls of power used the word *Admiral*. Not where they could be overheard.

Kian's ship was a near-twin—*ha!*—to the one Dirk had stolen. Polished bronze and banded with lustrous purple (not blue-green), it looked magnificent, and when Kian flew it he felt a deep singing joy he could never express to anyone.

No matter how political his career became, he would always find time to fly missions for his UNSA bosses. Kian never arrived late; his cargo was never damaged in transit; his passengers awoke with clear heads, not splitting migraines, at their destinations.

And if his disfigurement caused him to hate normal human beings, nothing in his actions ever indicated that.

Once, over supper in a restaurant overlooking Puget Sound, Paula—having polished off her third beer—remarked to Kian that he was the

new Mahatma Gandhi . . . at least as far as his two thousand-plus pro-
tégés were concerned. Deirdre shook her head and put down her fork,
waiting for Kian's reply.

"Gandhi was a great human being," said Kian, "but he could be a
sarcastic bastard. How does the old story go? A reporter asked him
what he thought of Western civilization; Gandhi considered a
moment, then said: *'That sounds like a good idea.'*"

Deirdre smiled, but Paula was not to be put off.

"But you are a pacifist," she said. "Just like him. And leader of your
people."

"Some people say I am."

"Y'know"—Deirdre poked at her food: some kind of spinach-and-
cheese pasta thing—"forget Gandhi. You sound more like the Dalai
fuckin' Lama every day."

"Why, does *he* think Gandhi was a sarcastic bastard?"

Paula threw her head back and laughed hard enough to fart, which
escalated the hilarity, while the other diners pretended not to pay
attention. (It was a very high-priced restaurant.) But their waiter
remained pleasant throughout, without a hint of snootiness; the tip
they left him was probably the largest he received that year.

And they tumbled, still laughing, back to Paula's and Deirdre's
house in Queen Anne Gate, where they talked until the early hours of
the morning. Then Kian went into the guest room while Paula and
Deirdre went to theirs, and all three of them were asleep within minutes, paying no attention to the surveillance drones which hovered
above the building, keeping an eye on UNSA's single most precious
asset while he moved among the ordinary folk.

During the couple's first year in Seattle, Paula worked what she called
"joe jobs": stocking shelves and working an espresso machine and
selling goods with a smile—things that an untrained ordinary joe
could do.

There was an obvious pun there, but every time Paula mentioned joe jobs in Kian's presence he just smiled, not taking the bait. He did the same on one occasion, when they were sleepy and drunk after a Thanksgiving curry, and Paula said: "So what do you do for sex?" (Deirdre made her suffer for that, practically until Christmas.)

In their third year together, Paula opened a tourist-trap boutique, selling goods from across the world. Although she was officially "*persona non* bloody *grata*" as Zoë said, being a former UN Intelligence worker gave Paula interesting contacts (some with an eye to their own retirement plans) in two dozen countries.

Deirdre's research interests shifted away from the popular focus of her contemporaries. She did a small amount of teaching at Washington State, earning enough money to finance the occasional exotic vacation for the two of them, while Paula's income paid the mortgage.

Once, they made it to Scotland, and spent an idyllic week in a stone cottage near the shore of Loch Lomond. Then they strolled through Glasgow—Paula had never even heard of Rennie Mackintosh, but she loved the architecture on first sight—and took a skimmer to Edinburgh. She made contacts in two tartan-ware shops interested in increasing their exports.

At night they climbed the cobbled slope to Edinburgh Castle, which was as forbidding as it ought to be with its black wrought-iron portcullises and ancient stones. Later, in a party of twelve, they toured the haunted tunnels and cellars below the streets. Something cold and insubstantial drifted through the group and Paula shrieked while Deirdre laughed, determined not to play the gullible tourist.

But their guide, when they climbed from the cellar, looked ashen-faced.

Then they made the trip north to Aberdeen and met up with Orla, niece of Dr. Claude Chalou who had been a tutor at Oxford when Dirk was there, and had disappeared around the same time.

An old grey-flecked retriever called Sam bumped his way over to them, tail wagging as soon as they entered the sitting-room. They sat around drinking tea for the whole afternoon, comparing notes, picking over painful memories. Deirdre could see an odd, discomfiting jealousy rise in Orla's eyes when they talked about Kian, the brother who still lived, whom Orla had never met.

On the journey home, Deirdre and Paula decided not to mention this part of their holiday to Kian.

They brought him back a set of self-playing bagpipes—one would have to look very closely to see that the "player" was not doing it for real—and he would use it, grinning broadly, on every New Year's Eve for decades to play "Amazing Grace" and "Auld Lang Syne."

During the first five years of Kian's admiralship, thirty-eight new Pilots made the grade. They took their shining ships into mu-space, plied the trade routes which UNSA devised, and produced great profits despite the cost of commissioning their vessels.

During that period, five other fledgling Pilots each managed to fly a ship into mu-space once, but refused to try a second time. Mu-space called to them—sang in their veins so much they could not withdraw sufficiently to concentrate on their vessels' systems.

Twelve others washed out in the early stages of training, because they were unsuited to long solitary voyages or simply had other over-whelming interests, despite all their background and opportunities.

An hmail joke that pervaded UNSA ran like this:

Q: When is a Pilot not a Pilot?

A: When they're scared shipless.

Kian found it amusing. (There was a weaker joke, about mu-space being the speed a cow walked at, that never quite caught on.) Still, he could see that the question of vocation was long-term and difficult. In the meantime, UNSA was happy to subsidize a dozen young Pilots in other careers: for those of scientific bent, the agency's labs made research posts available. Ilse Schwenger created a renewed funding pro-gramme for the Pilots' schools: the last decisive act in her long career.

Everyone, save the occasional anti-xeno agitator in the outside world, was happy.

Kian was careful not to abuse his privileges. When McGill University organized an academic conference entitled "Cultural Emergenics and Xenological Zen" to take place over Labor Day weekend, he used his position to ensure membership, but travelled by public suborbital. Though he did not ask for bodyguards, two fit-looking men were seated behind him all the way.

In Montréal Shuttleport the Arrivals concourse was crowded. Kian looked around for his baggage drone, ducked into the crowd, and for half a second he was out of his bodyguards' sight. That was when a narrow glass blade came arcing towards his neck from behind.

"No." Kian twisted at the last moment, faced his attacker. "There *is* no anger."

A lean-faced, unshaven man stopped, confused, his knife half-raised, blade pointing down. Then he twitched forward.

And a square fist looped out of the crowd and dropped the attacker. His blade clattered on the tiles.

"Bastard." The big woman who had thrown the punch stood ready for more.

Then the two bodyguards leaped onto the prone man and wrenched his arms back.

"We've got him, thank you, ma'am."

"You're welcome." She ran a hand through her short greying hair. "A conference in freezin' fuckin' Montreal. I thought this weekend was going to be *boring*."

"It's not that cold yet," said Kian. "And thank you very much."

"You're welcome, pal. My name's Kat."

She held out her hand, unperturbed by the ruined claw Kian offered in return.

"I'm Kian."

"Mmm. Interesting eyes you've got."

$$\Large \diamondsuit \; \diamondsuit \; \diamondsuit$$

They married the following spring.

She was Katerina Hinton, Dr. Kat to her large and boisterous clan of Iowa wrestlers and cow farmers. When Kian stayed with one of the cousins or aunts or uncles, they made no allowance for his privileged status or physical condition; he did chores with the rest of them. No-one cared about the age difference between him and Kat; and they took it for granted that Kat would teach him to milk cows.

During the long walks around the fields, she would also show him the beetles that rolled away the dung—"Or we'd be buried in cow-flap. Not just here, I mean the entire state"—and other glimpses of ecology's complexities, such as mites that saved human houses from being inundated with shed skin cells.

"Deirdre can write the coupling equations," Kian said once. "But you bring it to life, dear."

"Yeah? I'll show you coupling."

In bed, they laughed a lot.

At social events, they were K'n'K, or Two K. And they had a social life (not just with Kat's faculty colleagues at Iowa State) as Kian dropped his mu-space missions back to the minimum. UNSA, careful to show how they looked after this generation of Pilots as they matured, were more helpful than expected.

"Probably knew they'd have to answer to me," said Kat.

For reasons they never discussed with anyone else, Kian and Kat bore no biological children of their own. But they adopted a Eurasian girl called Maria, and furnished her with all the love they were capable of, which was a great deal.

One night, when Maria was fifteen, she came home from college very late, scratched and bruised. She was shaking, but neither too embarrassed nor too angry to explain how the boys she was with had drunk too much (she was not entirely innocent in that) and tried to go way too far.

Kian went to visit them in hospital.

He never repeated what he had told them, but they and their families became very quiet in the community during the final months before they packed their belongings and moved out of state.

When Maria was twenty-five, she consulted with UNSA as part of a team designing terraformer bacteria. The first full-scale trials were scheduled for a new world, nameless as yet, where the surface was uninhabitable but the geology encouraged the use of nanobores to drill out subterranean homes for the first batch of colonists.

With an eye to the future, the colonial team included half a dozen memetic engineers. The ship's cargo manifest, on the same mission that carried the first test samples from Maria's project, included a hardcopy of *Sequencing the Memome*. Deirdre, when Maria told her, was both pleased and mad. "Pissed off and proud," she said. "The first time I've understood quantum superposition in my gut. Those *bastards*."

By the time Maria was thirty-two, she was Dean of Iowa State. Despite her administrative duties, she used her authority to bully her way back into eco-research—"Because politics bores the *piss* out of me"—while acting as assistant wrestling coach.

During the final semester that year, she organized Kat's retirement party.

One cool evening at the end of May 2207, Kat told Kian she was dying.

They were sitting on the deck behind their cottage, looking out across the body of water that Kian called a lake and Kat referred to as The Pond. Tiny flies danced upon the surface. Kat put down her glass of iced tea, then pointed at a flat stone stained with pale grey-green patches.

"What do you see, Kian?"

"Life, of course, my love."

She had taught him how to look. How to see the miracle of life where others would notice only discoloration.

"Anything more complex than a bacterium," Kat said, "eventually breaks down."

After a long moment Kian took her hand.

"It's the bacterium's loss. Never knowing love."

Kat smiled. She kept hold of his hand as they watched the sun go down.

Six weeks later she was dead.

After the burial, family and friends accompanied Kian back to the cottage. From a rear window he looked out at The Pond, and silently sipped a white wine that Kat had bought when they were in Paris the year before.

"I love you, Dad," said Maria.

"You're the best daughter we could have had. And Kat . . ."

"Was the best Mom in all possible worlds."

Behind them, Paula and Deirdre looked at each other and blinked.

"She showed me how wonderful this world is."

"I know."

"But she didn't realize . . . *She* was the best part of it. The magic that was everywhere."

Deirdre shivered. Paula bit her lip.

They had known Kian long enough to sense when his words held multiple layers of meaning.

Surrounded by forest, some twenty miles from Portland, Oregon, stood an UNSA flight base with an enviable reputation within the organization. Although engineering protocols and training programmes were standardized across the globe, it was inevitable that local variations would creep in, and that some facilities would become better than others.

Enclosed in Hangar 7, in the middle of the base, a bronze, purple-banded ship, fresh from its latest service, waited.

There were armed guards at the perimeter and drones hovering overhead, scanning visible and infra-red wavelengths. That remained standard procedure at UNSA bases, though anti-xeno protest was a thing of the past.

On the fourth of July, two nights after the pallbearers lowered Kat McNamara (née Hinton) into the ground, celebratory fireworks exploded in the sky over Portland, joined by the more modest efforts of outlying communities.

And on the morning of the fifth, an engineer called Eddie Eisberg was the first person to enter Hangar 7, despite the hangover which thickened his head. It took him a full two minutes to work out the situation and press the big red alarm button.

The sound echoed through the empty hangar.

The Life and Times of Kian McNamara was one of thirteen extensive biographics, and the only one to which Maria gave approval. She even had hardcopies on a shelf in her office, mounted between two antique long-barrelled Colt .45s she somehow hung on to after firearm ownership became punishable by hypnotrauma.

No-one has seen Kian McNamara, the second Admiral, read the final paragraph, *since that fateful July night in 2207. No-one on Terra. But who can tell what mysteries await in the fractal universe that is mu-space?*

"The whole thing is fifty per cent cowshit," she told the young author. "But that's forty per cent better than the rest of the field. Those bastard newsNet articles rate ninety-eight per cent crap on my turdometer."

Her only answer was a sickly smile.

She got that a lot.

"Your genes have died out, Dad," she told Kian's portrait once, when she was pregnant with her second child, "but so fuckin' what?"

Every natural-born Pilot inherited fractolons from Ro McNamara, or rather the femto-engineered self-replicating molecule called FZA that coded for those organelles, just as they inherited mitochondrial DNA from their genetic mothers. So perhaps some paragenetic echo of her father remained.

The father of both David and Deirdre (named after her nominal aunt) was Rorion Delgasso. Rorion's father Carlos had been a pain to the McNamaras, back when Kian and Dirk were young—at school, Carlos had hero-worshipped the twins. But after Kian's disappearance it was Carlos Delgasso who became the third Admiral.

Like every other Pilot's mother, Maria gave birth aboard ship in mu-space, her mind in delta-coma to save her sanity, while machines induced labour and stood ready to perform a caesarian should it be necessary. For Maria, the need did not arise on either occasion.

"Just popped out," she would tell her friends. "Go to sleep with a bump in your belly, wake up with a mewling jet-eyed kid. Nothing to it."

Rorion was a good father when he was on Terra. Living with Maria was never part of the arrangement.

Once the kids had graduated, Maria made several mu-space voyages of her own, including some that were deliberately planned to take advantage of relativistic effects, so that she would return from a six-month (subjective) research trip a full decade after leaving.

It suited her, or so she told herself.

It meant that Maria observed geopolitics through a series of unfocused snapshots. She realized that UNSA was feeling the strain, that the third United Nations was finally pulling apart under its own momentum. That, and the growth of sociopolitical clades that crossed geographical boundaries while maintaining all of the bad features that had plagued nation states since they were invented in the nineteenth (or maybe eighteenth) century.

On returning from her final voyage, Maria learned that UNSA

existed only as the skeletal remains of that once-powerful organization. The Pilots, self-sufficient and with new vessels that came from who-knew-where, were dealing directly with trade consortia.

Maria sat on the grey wooden dock behind the old family cottage. *She* was not old—did not feel old—but on Terra ninety-four years had elapsed since Kat died and Kian abandoned realspace. (It was also one hundred and thirty-five years since Kian's brother Dirk spectacularly stole a ship and disappeared, but she did not remember that.) Maria's two children were somewhere among the stars.

"Cowshit," she told the bottle of Laphroaig in her left hand. "One hundred per cent cowshit."

With her right hand, Maria placed the muzzle of a very old and valuable Colt .45 against her temple. Because of the weight and the long barrel, she found it easier to hold the weapon in reverse, with all four fingers curled around the butt, her thumb inside the trigger.

"Hundred per cent . . ."

And squeezed.

The next day, 12 July 2301, the item that galvanized certain closed newsNets had nothing to do with an obscure academic's suicide, however interesting her antecedents might be. It was more immediate, and yet more historical: many of the item's recipients found themselves re-reading histories of the twenty-second century in order to make sense of it.

Dirk McNamara has been found.

The message came from mu-space. No newsNet in realspace made mention of Labyrinth: Pilots were masters at keeping secrets.

And he still lives!

<<MODULE ENDS>>

55

NULAPEIRON AD 3426

Tom was flying. He had come loose from his seat, and now he was spinning through the air inside the arachnargos cabin. Three clone-warriors were flailing in zero-g.

"Sorry," said Ankestion, secure in his pilot's seat. "No choice."

As the view-window whirled past him, Tom caught a glimpse of the other three arachnargoi outside, their tendrils splayed, holding them against the big cargo hold's deck. The shuttle in which all four arachnargoi crouched, including this one, was arcing high above the world. A small holodisplay showed the cloud cover below, before Tom rotated away and bumped gently into the cabin's ceiling.

"Transmission from one of the other arachnargoi," said Likardion. "For you, Warlord. From Lord Avernon."

"Open it up." Tom pushed off with his feet, steering down towards the deck. As he neared an empty chair, he reached out and grabbed hold. Hanging in place upside down, he added: "Are you all right, Avernon?"

"Um, sure . . . There's something wrong with the comms, Tom. Your image is the wrong way up."

"That's because I . . . Never mind. Why are you breaking comms blackout?"

"We're inside the shuttle's cargo hold. Can it matter?"

"I don't know. Hang on." Tom pulled himself down, turned the right way up, and hooked his legs under the chair. "What did you want to talk about?"

"Oh, I see . . . Microgravity is fun, isn't it? I was wondering if you could ask the shuttle pilot to rotate the vessel along its major axis."

Tom looked at Ankestion, then back at the display.

"Probably," he said. "How would that help?"

"Are you kidding? I only know the coriolis effect as theory. If you throw an object across a rotating cabin in zero-g, it should—"

"Destiny, Avernon. I know what it should do. Calm down, and we'll talk when we reach Axolon Array, all right? End trans—"

"No! I mean . . . Look, Tom. I've got some shield generators ready to test. We can deploy some now, while we're in orbit."

"What?"

"That's what you want to do, isn't it? Deploy a shield around the entire globe, so the Anomaly can't reach through the Calabi-Yau dimensions?"

"Um, right . . ."

"So if I could deploy just a few, it might be possible to—"

"Stay where you are," said Tom. "I'm coming over to see you."

With a tendril fastened round his waist, Tom was reminded of his schoolmate Kreevil, convicted and imprisoned inside sapphire fluid with a tentacle growing from his body, joining it to some shadowed mass whose true nature Tom had never identified. But this tendril, thin and elongated, snaked out across the echoing cargo hold, carrying Tom, and then held him in place, two metres above the deck.

Avernon was working on a big macrodrone which was mag-fastened to the deck plates. A tendril held Avernon in position, and led back to the arachnargos in which he had travelled.

The drone's hollow interior was revealed by the opened carapace. Inside, a row of fist-sized copper devices shone. They were making a high humming sound, just at the edge of audible range.

"I'm finishing up, Tom. There." Avernon waved to the pilot in the arachnargos cabin, and the tendril drew him back a few metres. "Ready to deploy."

The drone closed up, then rose from the deck, and headed towards an airlock.

"How the Fate," said Tom, "do we get to see what's happening?"

"Um . . ." Avernon frowned, then shouted to the arachnargos: "Can you get us forward, to the shuttle cabin?"

There was no reply, but two seconds later Tom and Avernon were being carried towards the front of the hold, as the tendrils elongated to impossible cord-like thinness. Then they were at a softening membrane door. The tendrils unwound from Tom's and Avernon's waists and gently pushed them through the liquefied membrane.

They tumbled into the main control cabin of the orbital shuttle. All around the huge forward view-window was the black immensity of space. Off to their right was the white, beautiful sphere of Nulapeiron, their home.

Then the shuttle was rising through the ethereal cloud that was the spinpoint layer, where tiny dots of white light shone as proudly as if they were stars in their own right.

Beside Tom, a rumbling voice said: "It's magical, by Rikleth." Kraiv was looking out into space, along with half a dozen other carls. "It's magnificent."

"Inside each point of light"—Tom pointed at the spinpoint layer—"time flows backwards. It's magic, all right, but not a kind that I approve of."

From the forward controls, a pilot called out: "No sign of Enemy vessels. We are clear to proceed with the test."

Avernon pointed.

"There goes the drone. Look."

Tom saw it: a small shape, growing smaller in the distance.

"It's slowing, relative to us," he said.

"Getting ready to launch the—There. They're out."

Copper sparkles caught the sunlight, as the tiny devices tumbled through space and the drone curved away, heading back towards the shuttle.

Such tiny things to pin our hopes on.

There was a pain in Tom's lip, and the cupric taste of blood. Biting his own lip—

Outside, space wavered.

Oh, my Destiny.

Wobbled.

"Avernon? They're in the spinpoint layer, right? Your devices."

"Shut up." Avernon had no thought of Tom's rank. "It's happening. I need to analyse . . ."

A portion of the spinpoint field grew dimmer.

"Fate, Avernon. You've done it."

Then something small and dark moved against the spinpoint field, and the shuttle pilot gestured for a magnified display. He opened subsidiary holovolumes, capturing other blackened shapes tumbling against the darkness of space.

"What—?"

Blackened, melted lumps, that had been polished copper manipulators just a few seconds before, were following Chaotic trajectories in the images.

"I . . ." Avernon looked unsure. "The collapse should have been . . . bigger. The volume . . ."

Tom held himself in place against a stanchion. The carls, too, were staring at Avernon, alerted by something in his voice.

"How much bigger?"

Avernon did not answer.

"How much bigger?"

"A lot, Tom. I . . . Two orders of magnitude."

A hundred times.

"Can we still make it work, Avernon? Can we make a shield?"

The shuttle's cabin felt like ice now.

"I don't know . . . Warlord. I'm afraid . . ."

Chaos.

". . . I just don't know."

Half an hour later, the big shuttle hung in the sky, close to Axolon Array, waiting for the terraformer sphere to extrude a morphglass corridor from one of its bays. Inside, near the airlock, Tom waited with Avernon.

"Are you all right?"

"Um, yes, Warlord. I'll be . . ."

Behind them, Kraiv and his carls loomed silently. They were warriors, not logosophers, but they had picked up enough to realize that the problem was serious. Avernon had expected the collapse volume to be a hundred times greater than it was, but it was not simply a question of building a hundred times more devices than predicted. It was obvious that Avernon was no longer sure a shield was even possible.

And they knew that Tom had no backup strategy to employ against the Anomaly. Military action could only postpone the end, and not by long: maybe days, maybe only hours.

Before them, the airlock dissolved, revealing the semi-transparent tunnel which led into the largest docking bay of Axolon Array. Elva was waiting there.

"Can you manage, Avernon?"

Walking through the tunnel, with hazy yellowish sky above and to either side, and wisps of cloud below, between them and the dark landscape . . . it was not easy, but something inside Avernon seemed to have broken. He walked alongside Tom as if he thought he was going to die, and could summon no energy to fight.

The collapse should have been . . . bigger.

Kraiv and his carls followed, their expressions grim.

Elva kept tight hold of Tom's hand as they climbed to the command centre. Scores of holos hung over the conference table, tracked by analysts, but there was one simple image that told Tom everything he needed to know: a hologlobe of Nulapeiron, almost enveloped in darkness. Only a few clear patches remained, all of them surrounded.

"We're almost lost, Tom."

Around the chamber, the carls deployed themselves and stood, impassive. It was obvious they were not going to leave Tom's presence now.

"I see. But *almost* may give me just enough to work with." Tom did not smile as he kissed Elva's hand and then released her. "Could you go back down to the lab and check on Avernon? We need him to calculate how many shield devices are required, and we *really* need him to calculate a new deployment pattern. Get him anything he wants: he's the absolute top priority."

Elva turned to a holo. "I can do that from here."

"Please, Elva. In person."

She looked at him, then: "All right."

"And drag Dr. Xyenquil away from the med-wards; put him in charge of the replication teams. I don't know the number of devices we have to create, but it's going to be huge."

"Xyenquil's a medic. He's with the most critical patients."

"And he's a damn good organizer. If this doesn't work, he won't *have* any patients to treat. Impress that fact on him."

"That I can do."

When Elva had left, Tom turned to the carls and said: "Can you wait outside, please? Just for a minute."

"Aye, Warlord."

Tom had to smile at the way they interpreted his request. The group split up: some stationed themselves by the doors on this level; two more descending the golden helical stairs that led to the deck below; the remainder stepped through the big membrane window and onto the ring-shaped balcony outside. There, they stood in the cold wind with their blue cloaks flapping.

Tom gestured a privacy field into existence, antisound cutting him off from the analysts at the table, diffraction causing the chamber to appear a blur, just as he would appear to others. At the field's centre, he opened up a comms holo.

Immediately, a leather-clad woman turned to him inside the image, and smiled.

"Well, my handsome Warlord. How goes it?"

"Hello, Thylara."

She was sweating, and her leather suit was smeared with grime. The holo rendered some background; Tom could see riders saddled on speeding arachnasprites, racing across uneven ground.

"How have you been?" Tom added.

"Are you asking whether I've bedded any man since you?"

Tom shook his head, swallowing.

"This is official, Thylara."

"And who else have you got there with you?"

"No-one right now."

"Ha. Well, lover. What is it you want of me?"

"I'm going to need transportation."

"Then buy yourself an arachnargos. You can afford it now."

"I need fast mobile warriors who can take shuttle pilots and some small, light hardware at high speed through dangerous territory. I'm not just talking about the Clades Tau. I have challenges enough for as many clans as the TauRiders deal with."

In the image, Thylara looked over her shoulder at the other riders, then turned back to Tom. "Tell me the truth. What's the situation, overall?"

"Nulapeiron is almost lost."

"Fate." Thylara leaned over to her left and spat.

"This is our last effort."

"When a member of the Clades Tau is too old to ride, they simply remain behind when the clan migrates. Without food. Facing the inevitable."

"Defeat is *not* inevitable."

"Hmm." Thylara leaned forward, and for a moment it seemed she could step through the holo. "Have you ever thought, we might be on the wrong side?"

"What?"

"The entity you call the Anomaly, from our little bedtime conversations, is a leap forward in evolution. Should we deny progress?"

"That doesn't mean—"

"The only reason there's a war is because people are fighting it. Haven't you wondered what it's like inside a fully Absorbed world, where everyone works together? I'm talking about a whole network of planets where everyone cooperates and there is only peace."

Tom's heart thudded. He felt sick.

"On the other hand"—in the holo, Thylara grinned—"I'm only thinking about soft effete bloody aristocrats like yourself. Because a rider of the Clades Tau never gives in to anyone!"

"Sweet bleeding Fate, Thylara."

"I love you too, Warlord. Send me the details when you have them."

"Soon, I—"

"Thylara out."

The holo was gone.

Tom opened another image. In it, a Zhongguo Ren man with the braided hair of a pitfighter stared out and did not speak.

"*Zài năr?*" said Tom. "I need to talk to Zhao-ji."

In the holo, the man bowed.

"Yes, Warlord."

His image was replaced by that of a drawn-faced Zhongguo Ren with a brush of black hair. Zhao-ji was clean-shaven, his narrow moustache gone.

"Tom! Good to see you."

"Yes. Listen, Zhao-ji. How much influence do you have with other, ah, societies? There's something you could help with, but not the Strontium Dragons alone."

"More than you might think"—Zhao-ji gave a soft enigmatic smile—"since I became Dragon Master."

"What?" It took Tom a moment to process that: such a fast elevation to head of a society was unheard of. "I didn't expect . . . Congratulations. Really."

"It's what your General Ygran would call a brevet rank. Promotion in the field. We've had casualties."

"I'm sorry."

"Since the years of the Manchu emperors, there have been times when we had to fight openly. Times of bloody attrition."

In the holo, Zhao-ji adjusted his sleeve, and Tom caught a glimpse of sapphire blue fluid at his wrist.

Was that an accidental gesture, old friend?

"I need to get hold of shuttles," Tom said. "Particularly orbital shuttles. Very fast."

"So you finally took notice of what I told you."

"It *was* you who told me of the spinpoint fields. Because Strostiv arranged it."

"Not because of Strostiv." Zhao-ji shrugged. "I had to. Don't ask me why, because I don't know."

Tom felt himself grow cold.

Because of the sapphire fluid?

"We're beginning tomorrow," Tom said. "Can you have a communications team standing by?"

"Absolutely, Warlord. Remember old Kolgash, talking about Ragnarok? The Twilight of the Gods?"

And final battle.

Captain Kolgash had taught them history, among other things . . . But old lessons were irrelevant. "My tac planners will hook up with your team in half an hour. We need shuttles from any sector of the globe."

"You've got it, Tom." A familiar brash grin spread across Zhao-ji's features. "Who'd have believed we'd get from the Ragged School to this?"

"Yeah, who would've?"

"Zhao-ji out, Warlord."

The image was gone.

Around Tom, shadows cloaked the control chamber. Outside, the sky had grown dark.

Ragnarok. Perhaps it is.

The outline of the carls, standing on the balcony outside, would have been familiar to those who wrote the old sagas.

Tom remembered the day he met Corduven. Sent as a servitor to Corduven's chambers, he had been there when Sylvana called via holo. She had made a reference to the way in which Old Norse sagas rhymed, which seemed to throw Corduven. Out of Sylvana's sight, Tom had silently mouthed the word *alliteration*, which was not technically correct but close enough: it jogged Corduven's memory so he could deliver a witty reply.

"*Wounded, he hung on a windswept willow . . .*" That was the part Tom remembered from a saga called The Elder Edda, when one-eyed Odin crucified himself on the Tree of Life for nine long days and nights in his search for wisdom.

And suffered.

Everyone, sooner or later, faces their own private End of Days.

But this time the whole world dies.

Tom called his carls back in, and commanded glowglobes to brighten.

You will not have Nulapeiron, Anomaly.

It occurred to him then, as the carls filed back inside the command centre, that Zhao-ji had acted more naturally just now than on any occasion since they became adults. Because Zhao-ji had attained the rank of Dragon Master? Or because of a strange affinity between two men afflicted with a sapphire curse of unknown capabilities?

Is this Ragnarok?

Perhaps it was not an idle question, coming from a man like Zhao-ji. Perhaps the new Dragon Master of the Strontium Dragons was touched with Sight, or prescience.

Twilight of the Gods.

The end of humankind in Nulapeiron.

"We need supper," Tom told the carls, "and then rest. Tomorrow we fight."

56
MU-SPACE AD 2301-UNKNOWN

<<Ro's Children>>
[17]

This is not the place to tell of the First Chaos Conflict, which endured for so long that when Pilots finally drove the Zajinets from two universes—or the Zajinets simply chose to leave—only the infinite memory banks of Labyrinth's Logos Library could contain the story. Nor may we dwell on the Stochastic Schism that so split Pilot society, though few realspace humans picked up even a hint of that tragedy.

Dirk's place among Labyrinthine society was a strange and ambiguous one. Already, by the time he and Ro arrived there, Pilot-kind's culture was diverging from its Terran roots. A young Pilot called Thierry Didier (who was an old man when Dirk met him) first laid down the upgradeable syntax and multilayered semantics of the language known as Aeternum. As more and more Pilots took wild voyages along time-dilating geodesics—by accident or intent—Aeternum became established as the first tongue of every Pilot.

When Dirk made a brief return to Terra, incognito, he found that Anglic (though the language retained the name) was incomprehensible to his ears, delivered in a sing-song rhythm he could never master. Back in Labyrinth, he lent all his support to Didier's cause, and helped to remove the final objections of those Pilots who felt that they were already too different from ordinary humankind.

(Both factions agreed on the likely effect of change, on the extent to which language influenced thought. What they disagreed on was whether new thinking was *desirable*.)

Among the Admiralty Council—for by this time a single Admiral was no longer sufficient to rule all Pilots, inasmuch as leadership was required at all—Dirk had both supporters and enemies. Admiral Schenck was foremost among those who considered Dirk a dangerous anachronism.

In a long and bloody duel that began on Poincaré Promenade among a startled crowd, ranged through Hilbert Hall and ended on Borges Boulevard, Dirk finally gained victory. They fought on many levels, through revolving layers of reality, and when Dirk struck the telling blow Admiral Schenck screamed as the air fractured into shimmering blood-red shards of geometry. Those shards swirled into a vortex, pulling Admiral Schenck inside.

Schenck died—dies still, and will forever die—crushed inside a fractal maelstrom whirling to eternity.

It was after this event that Ro, saddened and mournful, retired to the endlessly branching Aleph Annexe, where it was said that even her ship—whose whereabouts no-one knew—might be tucked away in some fractal pocket of Labyrinthine reality.

Sightings of Ro became increasingly rare, until such apparitions became the stuff of archaic legend and no-one remembered that she had once been an ordinary, feeling person who had loved in vain—Luís Starhome was long dead—and raised sons who had not turned out the way she expected.

But Aleph Annexe held wonders to beguile an enquiring mind, and miracles to soothe any hurt, in mazes that could never end.

Myths and rumours.

There were tales of a disfigured man with a scarred face and claw hand who appeared on the worlds of humankind, quietly recruiting people to his cause. He was never seen in Labyrinth; but those among the Pilots who might have been his followers became a powerful voice for moderation.

Perhaps such a body of opinion was one of the root causes of the Stochastic Schism. But it was also, centuries later, an inherent part of the Tri-Fold Way which healed the rift and unified Pilots once more.

Sigurd's World was an isolated human colony with its own way of doing things. The Admiralty Council, through its network of observers and agents-in-place, became concerned at hints of offworld trade, of goods arriving from mu-space . . . goods which had not been brought by Pilots.

Zajinets had been off the scene for some time, and the Admiralty's suspicions turned in a different direction: that those worlds were creating pseudo-Pilots of their own. The processes which had resulted in Ro's abilities were part design, part chance; anyone who thought about it expected that humankind somewhere, somewhen, would try to create Pilots again.

Pilots they could control.

The Admiralty sent a Pilot called Jared deVries to investigate undercover, in the realm of King Rasmus. But Rasmus's Palace Guard had had a great deal of practice in counterespionage, and they laid ambush to deVries, imprisoned him and put out his eyes.

Dirk led the rescue raid.

Five ships burst into the sky above the Fastness Magnusson. The raiders descended in drop-bubbles against which graser fire spattered harmlessly; and then they were inside. When the rescuers departed with Pilot deVries, they left behind King Rasmus and his Palace Guard reduced to a collection of strewn corpses from whose eye sockets steam still rose.

It turned out that King Rasmus's subjects had been trading with Zajinets, after all.

Dirk also commanded the much larger fleet which routed the Zajinets—one fleet of Zajinets at least—at the Battle of Mandelbrot Nebula. That was a long and deadly engagement inside mu-space featuring thousands of vessels on either side. Besides the violence, the battle was remembered for one other notable occurrence.

When the Zajinet position became untenable, they sent a message to the Pilots' fleet. It was the only time they had ever delivered a syntactically straightforward statement, yet its meaning remained obscure.

<<. . . we leave you to your darkness . . .>>

And then the entire surviving Zajinet fleet moved together to execute a manoeuvre whose audacity left the Pilots wondering about their own limitations. Golden mu-space rippled as the fleet turned and exited the fractal universe en masse.

But they did not return to realspace.

Instead, as the returning Pilots would analyse over and over, the Zajinets had treated mu-space like the ur-continuum it was, and used it as a launching point into an entirely different universe. Their destination might have been a parallel reality to the realspace they knew; or it might have been an unimaginable place where different physical laws applied.

The victory celebrations in Labyrinth were . . . thoughtful.

Throughout the First Chaos Conflict and after its uncertain resolution, the worlds of humankind multiplied and diverged from each other. On the paradise of Fulgor, a new entity arose through the mediation of mu-space processors that were everyday devices to the Pilots who used them.

Pilots did not move openly during the Skein Wars (though their agents made a difference to many beleaguered humans), but they arranged the evacuation which saved some of that world's inhabitants before the Anomaly engulfed it.

Different factions of the Stochastic Schism had divergent ideas about how closely to observe or even control the settled human worlds. Those who followed the Reconciled Path (which might or might not have been founded by Kian McNamara) watched closely yet did little to influence affairs.

The one thing no Pilot of any faction revealed to humanity was

<<MODULE INCOMPLETE>>
<<SEQUENCE ENDS>>
<<CRYSTAL REINITIALIZING>>

57
NULAPEIRON AD 3426

Tom hurled the lifeless crystal against the wall.

Bastard thing.

It bounced to the floor, lay still. The crystal had wiped its own contents, was empty now.

Then Tom looked around the small half-lit chamber and laughed. There was no-one to hear it besides himself. Phase space displays billowed around him.

It's too late for stories.

A chime sounded.

Too late for any distraction.

The door shimmered open.

"Planning teams are ready, Warlord." The soldier was young: far too young.

"Good. Thank you."

Eemur?

I'm ready, sweetheart.

Thanks.

Finally, Tom took a different crystal in his hand, one of a strange violet hue, and concentrated. Nothing. If there was ever a time he needed help, it was now.

He tried harder.

No . . . Yes.

Blue flames licked along his hand. Somewhere in the distance or in the past, he heard a soft singing voice. The Crystal Lady seemed very close for a moment.

—*Time, as we agreed.*

And she was gone.

Tom's heart ached for the broken contact. It seemed a dream already; but she *had* spoken to him: he was sure of it. Tom laid the violet crystal gently on the floor.

Then he looked up at the thin young soldier in his too-big uniform who was still standing by the door. The soldier swallowed.

"Don't worry," said Tom. "We're going to win."

As the action commenced, Tom sat alone in a chamber below the command centre and Saw what happened.

On a vast blue desert the sand erupts as arachnargoi leap from their hiding places, to take down the first wave of Absorbed infantry as they crawl from shafts which lead to the realm below.

Shift.

In the demesne known as Bilyarck Gébeet, a merchanalyst reaches out with a packing knife and slits an overseer's throat. Others leap into action around the dusty godown, taking down their oppressors with bare hands and everyday implements, while in the corridor outside, graser fire cracks and cold waves wash through the air as Absorbed beings manifest themselves.

Shift.

Children scream as molten lava bursts through the floor. But it is the black-bronze creatures with angled wings who fall into magma as the humans flee.

Shift.

People are queuing in an Aqua Hall, buckets in hand: just going about their everyday business as . . . nothing happens. Some failed communication, some courier screaming in an interrogation cell or lying face-down in a dank tunnel: no action kicks off here.

Shift.

A heavy battalion moves forward. Three thousand men and women, eyes wide with fear beneath their helmets, advance together along the winding series of caverns while arachnabugs, upside down, dance at speed along the broken ceilings, heading for the conflagration where Enemy forces await.

Shift.

Choking smoke. A golden dining-hall where glass songbirds wheel away in panic. A foppish-looking logosopher stops his recitation, reaches inside his sleeve, then leaps forward to thrust his bodkin through the ruling Lord's throat.

"For freedom!" he cries as scarlet-clad men step out of black flames, surrounding him.

Shift.

Fencers in a salle d'armes, a loft overlooking a narrow tunnel, stop at the sound of graser fire below. Soldiers with scarlet cravats are directly underneath the window, firing into the unarmed crowd who are rising up against them.

Several of the fencers look at each other in silence.

Then they pull the safety tips from their weapons, haul themselves out onto the sill, crouch, and jump.

Shift.

Blood-ribbons in a swimming-pool as the action rages—

Tom?

Yes.

There's too much, Tom. You can't track everything.

I know. But I can try.

Tom was muttering directions and gesturing into holo images. Upstairs—he Saw briefly—the planners were swarming around the tac displays and two hundred comm sessions were open at once as they coordinated efforts around the globe. The planners were translating Tom's mutterings into battle commands, and transmitting them to the free forces in their all-out strike against the Anomaly.

Eemur, working with Elva, was sending as many messages to the control centre as Tom himself. Eemur and Tom were each observing one hemisphere of Nulapeiron: between them, they had to cover every main strike against the Anomaly.

Had to.

Shift.

Limbs straining as the free humans fight those whose Absorbed masters have already corrupted them. Grappling, slick with sweat, no weapons or technology but basic primate struggle, and it is a free human who is first to use his teeth against his opponent's carotid artery, heedless of the screaming.

Shift.

Tom, I'm OK now. I can See your hemisphere too, for a while.

There's no—

You have to check on Avernon.

Shift.

Daggers glinting in darkness.

No. He had to let Eemur help. She was right about Avernon.

OK, Eemur.

Shift.

Broke contact.

Tom was sitting cross-legged in his chamber, drenched with sweat, while the holos around him swirled with primary colours. The soldier in charge of relaying messages looked concerned.

"Warlord?"

"Fate. It *is* too much."

"Sir? What do you want me to—?"

"Never mind." Avernon's teams would be commencing action, and Tom *had* to know.

Shift.

Shuttles against the endless night.

There are squadrons of them, hundreds of kilometres apart in orbit above Nulapeiron. To every side they spray their load of shining copper specks: each the size of a human hand.

They drift above the spinpoint field, the gossamer shell that surrounds the world.

Tom waved open a subsidiary holo.

"General Ygran? How goes it?"

"Holding our own, Warlord. No better or worse than that."

"Good. Good."

He closed the image.

From a thousand sites across the world, dart-shaped fighters rise with Absorbed pilots at the controls. They are not capable of spending extended time in orbit, but they can reach the atmosphere's edge and launch weapons against the shuttles.

"Now," says Zhao-ji, and from one commandeered facility at least a counteroffensive begins. Silver fighters with back-swept wings roar upwards to intercept the Enemy.

Shift.

Flames sweep across the clouds as smart dirigibles, released by the terraformer spheres, explode across the Enemy fighters' trajectories. A squadron is blown apart at first contact with the airborne minefield; the others break off.

And start scanning for a safe way through, a route to reach Avernon's shuttles.

Again, Tom checked the status displays, the simplified overview of the Chaos that the planners were working with in the control centre. He continued to gesture, directing the planners' efforts at the highest level, while they modulated his instructions according to their own interpretation.

"Are we *still* holding our own?" Tom asked, then answered his own question: "It looks like it . . . but only just."

The attacks were coordinated enough—perhaps—to require all the Anomaly's attention to combat them. That was all they could hope for.

Tom used urgent control gestures to attempt communication with Avernon, who was on board one of the orbital shuttles himself.

"Come on. Come on . . ."

Nothing. But even if Avernon would not talk, Tom could still See.

Shift.

Avernon stares at the feedback images.

"Sir?" The shuttle pilot calls back to him. "Down to our last thousand modules."

The copper spray continues to port and starboard.

"Stand by," Avernon says to a waiting tech, "to resonate."

There was nothing more Tom could do: not to help those in orbit. Either the modules would shift into optional alignment, or they would fail.

But the battles down below were another matter. There, his ability to See the Enemy and coordinate action might be of use.

Blue flames licked across Tom's body, were gone.

Shift.

Kraiv leads a company of carls sweeping down from a ridge. At the heart of a deep cavern, they meet the Enemy with morphospears unslung and moaning for blood.

"Blood and Axe!"

Berserkers roar, and the battle is joined.

Shift.

A thousand lev-bikes hover, quivering in the air.

"Are your people ready, Captain?"

"Yes, Viscount."

Trevalkin gives a slow, ironic smile. "Then go."

They fly forward like arrows, and fall like hail upon the Enemy.

Shift.

Thylara of the Clades Tau throws her scarlet arachnasprite to one side as a graser beam rips through the air. Up ahead, her fellow TauRiders swoop in from either side, into the mass of black-bronze beasts and their dreadful talons, avoiding the Dark Fire that flickers at the great hall's rear.

Then Thylara spins her arachnasprite in place, whipping half of its tendrils outward as weapons, beheading three Enemy soldiers before they can blink. She raises her hands overhead, brings them down to either side, firing grasers into the Enemy's midst.

A questing beam blows her torso into liquid spray.

Shift. Before Tom could react, his vision had changed.

Anomaly-controlled fighters leave the ground, heading over a mountain range to intercept the free forces just as a long-dormant caldera explodes hundreds of metres into the air, a spume of yellow-hot magma that splashes and melts and burns and takes the aircraft down.

The Crystal Lady is wielding her influence.

Shift.

A quake from nowhere. Deep in occupied territory, ceilings crack. Tonnes of broken stone descend upon the inhabitants: broken dark metallic wings protrude from the rubble when the dust begins to settle.

Shift.

Lava sprays horizontally from a sudden split in an ornate marble wall and an Absorbed human, once Lord of this demesne, falls screaming.

Shift.

Absorbed humans, by a decorative lava pool, swing up their weapons, ready to kill the rag-tag army of old people and children who have crawled up from the lower strata with nothing more than knives and bludgeons and bare hands to fight with.

The Absorbed take aim.

Then something huge moves in the pool, a hexagonal fluke bigger than a man rises from the lava, and molten Chaos falls upon the Enemy.

Tom gasped, breaking Seer-trance.

Thank you, my Lady.

But there could be no communication with the Crystal Lady now. The force of Nulapeiron's native lifeforms was on the loose, overwhelming and magnificent, and nothing Tom might say or do could control them.

Shift.

A bronze talon reaches for Zhao-ji and he yells, brings up his graser pistol already firing, and then a team of 49s, Strontium Dragons warriors, bursts in through the side door and lays down heavy fire upon the single Anomalous creature that dares invade their territory.

Shift.

It is hand-to-hand fighting now, and Trevalkin whirls and stabs his long blade with devilish accuracy into an Enemy soldier's eye.

Shift.

In the depths of Sable Ocean, armoured mantargoi crewed by Grey Shadows fighters fire grasers through the dark waters. Metallic beings face them, return terrible fire of their own.

Then an ocean vent opens, spewing superheated steam, and the Anomalous creatures writhe.

Shift. And twist.

At submicroscopic dimensions, long-outlawed smartmists and femtoviruses battle each other for control in a blaze of microwaves and subatomic predation.

Panting, Tom wrenched his attention back to his surroundings. The young soldier was looking upwards, weapon ready.

"What's wrong?"

"Nothing, sir. Warlord. The proximity detector, I thought— Nothing."

Tom opened a holo.

"Everything all right, General?"

General Lord Ygran gave a grim smile. "As well as can be expected."

"Have you had word from Avernon?" It was critical that the modules laid down in orbit align themselves correctly. Geometry was everything. "Can we detonate yet?"

"No, Warlord. We're still waiting."

"Maybe I can do better than that."

Shift.

Avernon is clawing at his own face and screaming.

"Stop it, sir. Stop it." A soldier grabs hold, hard. "This is no good."

"I know, I—"

Avernon sobs. Stops.

"It's not going to work," he says. "Do you understand? It won't work!"

Tom flipped back into the chamber.

"Warlord?"

Tom shook his head. "Avernon's not happy."

"Aren't the modules dispersed?"

"Yes . . ." He could visualize the shuttle's displays without slipping back into Seer-trance. "And their alignment looks OK to me, but not to—"

"I'd say we have to go for it now, Tom." General Ygran was looking off to one side, his expression grim. It was the first time he had addressed Tom by name, not rank. "And may Fate be with us all."

Holos swirled.

So be it.

Transmitters were poised to deliver timed signals across the globe.

"Thank you, General."

Tom raised his hand. "Ready to activate."

Damn you, Anomaly.

Gestured.

A white glow spreads through the spinpoint field.

The shield modules are doing their work, collapsing spacetime in their vicinity, linking with each other to form a barrier around Nulapeiron. Shining—

*And then the glow begins to fade. The spinpoint layer remains intact.
Nothing has changed.*

Tom flips.

> *Eemur? Is Elva OK? Are you?*
> **Which of us are you worried about?**
> *For Fate's sake.*
> **We're all right. Do whatever it is you have to, Tom.**
> Switch.

*In the shuttle cabin, Avernon is still, regarding the status displays like a
statue, while the other occupants stare out the windows at dark space, and the
dying glow of their effort.*

> *Tears track down Avernon's cheeks.*
> *"I'm sorry," he whispers. "I thought . . . I thought I could—"*
> *"Oh, Fate," murmurs the pilot.*
> *Outside, small white points that are not distant stars are glowing as always.*
> *Everyone in that cabin is aware of what it means. The collapse of space-
> time is supposed to bring the spinpoints into existence as a side effect . . . but a
> side effect in negative time. From any ordinary viewpoint, the spinpoints should
> have disappeared several seconds ago, as if they had ceased to exist.*
> *But still they shine.*
> *"We've failed."*

Flip.

> It meant failure, of their only defence against the Anomaly.
> *Failure.*
> Switch.

Nothing has changed, save that Avernon has turned away from the status displays.

> *Outside the shuttle, the spinpoints still shine.*
> *A symbol of humanity's defeat.*

And flip.

Tom stared into the holo, but General Ygran seemed to know already.

"What happened, Warlord? Enemy attacks are redoubling everywhere. If it's sensed Avernon's shield—"

"Then it should have been too late for the Anomaly to do anything."

"If the shield had worked." General Ygran rubbed his face. "Does that mean . . . ?"

"It failed," said Tom. "That's not guesswork. I Saw it fail."

For a moment, there was only silence. When General Ygran finally spoke, his voice was hollow.

"Then I guess . . . we fight. Until the end."

"I'm sorry."

"Aye, Warlord."

Tom tried.

The carls mass into a defensive circle, but Enemy forces are everywhere and in seconds they fall upon the outnumbered warriors. Every roaring berserker takes at least one Enemy soldier down with him.

But still the carls fall.

Shift.

Half the arachnasprites are riderless now, scuttling mindlessly away from the battle.

Shift.

Dark Fire rolls in black sheets across the magma, forcing the lava-dwellers back into their own domain.

Shift.

The armoured battalions fall back through the caverns as steel-blue metallic beings bigger than arachnargoi manifest themselves at the vanguard of the Anomalous forces.

Shift.

Enemy fighters converge upon the free forces' suborbitals and blow them from the sky.

Back in the chamber:

Eemur? Are things as bad in your half of the world?

You know they are.

Tom stared at the displays, seeing only defeat. Against the bulkhead, the young soldier looked frozen, his grasp tightening around the weapon he probably would not get a chance to use.

Hey, Tom? You know I'm no Oracle . . .

Right.

. . . but I always knew this would not end well.

Tom knew that was no joke.

Switch.

Armed arachnargoi spit fire while the smaller arachnabugs dart in and out, striking the advancing forces in vulnerable spots: hitting soldiers on foot behind the ponderous shielded lev-cars and aiming for the smaller non-human creatures, rather than the steel behemoths whose numbers keep increasing.

Metre by metre, the free forces fall back before the Anomaly.

Shift.

In the shuttle, Avernon sits on the deck, knees up against his chin and arms clasped around his shins: rocking, rocking, like an autistic child.

The pilot has left the controls, allowing the craft to drift through the spin-point field whose continued existence is stark evidence of humanity's failure.

Shift.

Torn corpses strewn across the Benbow Caverns.

Shift.

Dead piled high in Palace Darinia.
Shift.
In the Grand'aume Core, nothing moves.
Shift.
A *dead child's outstretched hand.*

Tom leaned back against the chamber's hard wall.
"It stinks of defeat."
"My Lord?"
"The whole world reeks of it. Defeat."
"Um . . . Yes, sir." The young soldier bobs his head.
There's nothing I can do.
There was a distant thud.
Just let things take their course.
A louder bang, and the whole chamber shook.
"What the Fate—?"
<All hands beware.> It was Axolon's voice booming throughout the sphere.
"They're here, Warlord."
Tom shook his head. He was stunned by his ongoing effort, by the inevitability of failure.
"*Who's* here?"
"The Enemy." The young soldier looked up as the terraformer shook once more, and yells echoed from the command centre overhead. "They're inside."
<We are being boarded. We are being boarded.>
"Oh, Fate. Not now."
Anomaly. You've come for me.
It was the end.

58

NULAPEIRON AD 3426

The young soldier looked scared. As the chamber rocked once more, Tom grabbed hold of the doorway.

"What's your name, soldier?"

"Er, Vize, sir. Pentor Vize."

"You know how to operate external comms, Pentor?"

"Yes, Warlord."

Someone screamed as they died outside.

"Get me in contact with Lord Avernon. Talk to the shuttle pilot. Tell him to do whatever's necessary. He can kick a member of the nobility in the balls if that's what it takes. Just get Avernon online, Pentor."

"I'll do it, sir." Pentor Vize struggled across to the holos. "I'm not—"

Tom's thumb ring sparked.

"You're authorized now." The doorshimmer opened, and Tom swung through to the corridor. "Fate be with you . . . And throw me that crystal, would you?"

It arced through the air and Tom caught it.

Muscular carls were kneeling on the other side, facing both ways down the corridor, each with a heavy graser in one fist, a short wide morphblade in the other.

"Axolon? Where is the Enemy?"

<Above you in the command centre. Lady Elva's in trouble.>

"No."

I will not let this happen.

"Come on."

Tom vaulted straight over the carls, headed for the golden helical stairs and hit them running, and sprinted up. Behind him, the carls moved very fast, shifting their muscular bulk to follow Tom as wild berserker rage lit up their eyes.

"*Blood and Death!*"

Just for a moment, Tom Saw:

Three black angular craft hover outside Axolon Array. They are similar to the vessel Tom boarded on Siganth: the Enemy. Even though the Anomaly has its own forces already on board the terraformer, the lead craft turns to bring its major weapons to bear.

<I should not have allowed you this close.>

The terraformer itself revolves on its vertical axis, until the face of Axolon regards the vessels with his own microfaceted eyes. Axolon's voice is like rumbling thunder.

<I made a mistake.>

It seems that time slows down as a soft bronze glimmer in the Enemy craft accompanies the resonance cavities' excitation and the graser beams about to—

<I will not make another.>

Subnuclear forces tear the air apart as Axolon unleashes his defences. The Enemy craft explodes.

Tom flung himself into the command centre and was in the thick of it.

Scarlet uniforms of the Anomalous forces were everywhere, roiling through the chamber in hand-to-hand fighting. Old General Ygran knocked an Enemy soldier onto the table where he sprawled amid tactical holos then brought his graser to bear on Ygran.

A carl's morphblade severed the Enemy soldier's hand above the wrist and arterial blood spurted as bright and scarlet as the invaders' uniforms.

"Elva!"

Fighting men and women stumbled close and Tom whipped out a raking blow that destroyed an Enemy fighter's eyes. The maelstrom of struggling bodies was everywhere.

"Tom!"

He saw Elva then, fists flashing polished brass—*knuckledusters?*—
as she pummelled the man in front of her. Fighting figures obscured
the view, then rolled past. Behind Elva, Jissie stood with a short
dagger held point-up, ready for an upward thrust.

Fate. She's a child.

A boiling mass of Enemy fighters surrounded Elva, a pandemonium of limbs and torsos, and Jissie was blotted from Tom's sight once
more.

With a roar Tom struck out, elbowed a face, spun around another
man's back, clawed his way through a third man's guard, rotated
another's shoulder to push two men into each other's way, and made a
direct line towards Elva and Jissie.

A fist from nowhere snapped against the side of Tom's jaw.

Tom spun and lashed back with a hammer-fist of his own and then
leaped high, knee into the larynx, and the man was down and choking
his final breath.

Elva!

Too late.

The Enemy were upon her and Jissie screamed and Tom threw off
someone who tried to grab but he could *not* get there in time. A black-
bronze creature was rising, its wings spreading as its rows of pitted
eyes focused on Elva. It paused, poised to fall upon her.

That was its mistake.

Tom stopped in the midst of battle, statue-still as Chaos rolled past
on every side, a screaming mêlée and the stench of fear and blood. Blue
flames flickered as Tom lowered his head and Saw into the alien creature—*inside its skull*—and when Tom stretched his hand out to squeeze
the hand was enveloped in a blaze of sapphire blue and the creature
threw back its head and howled.

Good.

Tom squeezed harder.

The great bulk stumbled as Elva threw four men aside in a massive adrenaline rage and turned both fists towards the creature. Parallel graser beams ripped out of the brass devices that were more than knuckledusters, and cut the thing's head away from its torso.

Then Elva turned the beams upon the men who had cut Jissie but failed to kill her and butchered their bodies into smoking offal.

Tom's bodyguard, the enraged carls, howled their berserker roar and the Enemy fell back. Between Tom and the carls stood the bulk of the Enemy. Whatever Tom's fighting skills had been it was time to transcend them now.

He spun and his right heel hooked into the first man's temple; then he used the momentum transfer to reverse his spin, twist his torso the other way and thrust out his left leg, to target another's lower ribs. He heard the crunch. Something arced towards Tom's head and he dropped, palm on the floor as he spun and scissored someone's leg, snapping their kneecap onto the deck and clawing at their eyes as he rose, still twisting, and was on his feet once more.

A scarlet-uniformed woman was swinging a graser pistol towards Tom and his foot was closest so he used a crescent kick then the edge of his hand to snap her collarbone—*speed up*—and hit her three times, fast, and she was down.

Two men came at Tom together—*faster*—and he went for the nerve-points and they died without a sound as he used a fallen body as a stepping-stone to leap high, into the heart of the Enemy force, a thrusting kick with the blade edge of his foot snapping a neck before he landed and pivoted and accelerated again.

The warrior who grabbed him from behind was as big as a carl but Tom's head snapped back and he twisted, and butted twice from side to side. Tom slid down the big man's torso, hooked his arm under the groin and launched himself upwards.

The big man's bulk flew against his comrades and Tom snapped out a low kick to split someone's knee, then a whipping kick, shin against thigh to paralyse the nerve, and two more were down. Another was close and Tom whipped his elbow in hard and followed with the knee and that was another to his tally but he should *not* congratulate himself because danger was everywhere.

Tom struck again and a soldier screamed but suddenly strong hands had hold of Tom and the chamber spun as the man threw Tom over his outstretched leg—*faster*—but Tom twisted in the air, landing crouched on his feet instead of on his head and then he sprang up with his hips to execute a counter-throw.

Had he held the man's tunic it would not have done serious damage but Tom's grip was around the man's neck and as he fell Tom ripped back—*crack*—and the body that hit the floor was dead.

Something touched Tom from behind and he spun with hand upraised—*faster*—but it was a carl whose blood-lust was as great as Tom's own and then he realized.

"It's done, Warlord."

Blood rushed in Tom's ears and yellow fluorescence edged his vision and he wanted only to fight but—*no*—he had to stop now—*calm down*—and he was panting and glistening beneath a sheet of sweat—*calm*—and slowly he brought himself back to a point where he could begin to process rational thought.

There were bodies strewn everywhere, great sucking chest wounds and severed torsos and those who whimpered and those who howled in the face of death.

Bodies of friends. Bodies of the Enemy: scarlet uniforms soaked with scarlet blood that splashed across the chamber.

But the only sign of movement among those who wore scarlet was the twitch of the mortally wounded and the sudden shudder as Jissie delivered a *coup de grâce* and despatched a dying man.

"We've won. For now, we've beaten them off."

"Aye, Warlord."

But now the Anomaly knows where we are.

In the corner, Elva placed her hand on Jissie's shoulder, looked up at Tom, wiped blood from her face. And gave a tiny smile.

Tom closed his eyes, collecting his thoughts.

Avernon.

He opened his eyes, dug out the crystal from his waistband: the crystal that the young soldier, Pentor Vize, had thrown to him.

Chaos . . .

It was the wrong one. Tom had wanted the violet crystal that might allow him to contact the Grey Shadows and the Crystal Lady once more. But he had no rational reason to suppose that they would answer the call again, or that they could redouble their efforts inside Nulapeiron in any way.

What Tom was holding was a blank crystal, its internal lattice neatly reset to the original configuration, all record of its tales of Pilots and Zajinets and mu-space wiped clean.

Useless.

"Pilots . . ."

The crystal was useless. But perhaps it was the idea, not the medium, that was important.

"What, Tom?" It was Elva. "Are you hurt?"

"No."

His black tunic was wet with blood, but none of it was his.

"I've looked at the tac displays," said Elva. "Ninety-seven of our terraformers have been destroyed."

"Fate."

"Things are going badly down inside the remaining free sectors. There's no point in even trying to coordinate things. It's too messy, and everything's a rout."

Tom looked at General Ygran, who was leaning against the conference table, his face ashen, his left arm tucked inside his belt: broken, for sure.

"Do the best you can."

Then he turned to the remaining carls.

"You're with me."

Young Pentor Vize was still in the chamber, and he jerked his rifle up when Tom came in.

"Relax. We're safe for now."

"Sir."

Inside one holo, a bulkhead was visible, and the edge of a man's arm.

"Do you have contact with the shuttle, Pentor?"

"Yes, Warlord."

"Good man. Let me sit there."

Tom took his place, and called into the holo: "Avernon. Are you there?"

"*Oh, Tom. Yes.*"

"What happened? What went wrong?"

"*Those orders of magnitude . . . I misjudged a single factor in the equation, approximated it as a constant when I should have known . . . Should have.*"

"How do we fix it?"

"*We can't. We just . . . can't.*"

Tom kept his breathing shallow and calm. "*Theoretically*, what could we do to make it work? The devices perform their basic function, don't they?"

"*I don't know . . .*"

"Do we just need more of them? To disperse them in a different configuration?"

"*I . . .*"

"Are the ones in orbit right now still operational, or do we need to start again?"

Tom paused. He was pushing too hard.

But we don't have time.

In the image, another man's hand appeared, offering a cup to Avernon with the murmured words: *"Here. Drink this, my Lord."*

Tom waited.

Finally:

"Most of them still work. We need more, but not many more. A new con-figuration . . . Yes, kind of."

"What does that mean?"

"Tom, I . . . There's no way to work with the precision I need. The geom-etry . . . It's so sensitive to the initial placement that a tiny perturbation from the exact point throws the field wildly off kilter. It's Chaotic!"

"Send me the equations."

"There's no point. No-one can work in orbit to that exact a—"

"Send it now."

"I . . . Yes, Warlord."

Tom held up the blank crystal, hesitated.

It seems appropriate.

So that was the crystal Tom used, downloading Avernon's equations into the core which once held tales of ancient Pilots.

"Is that everything, Avernon?"

"Yes."

"Then I hope to see you later. Out."

The more Tom considered, the more he could think of only one person who might help: Brino of Kilware Associates. But even if he lived, Brino could be anywhere in Nulapeiron.

Elva will try to stop me.

Tom looked at young Pentor Vize.

"Here." Tom began to pull off his black, bloodstained tunic. "I need you to—Mmph."

He dragged the heavy garment over his head.

"I need you to wear this," he told Pentor. "I'm sorry about the blood."

Tom's white undershirt was crimson where it had soaked through.

"Um . . . Yes, Warlord."

Pentor Vize tugged the tunic on.

"Keep the doorshimmer half-manifest," Tom said. "I want it translucent, so if anyone looks inside, they'll think that you are me. Got it?"

"Yes, Warlord. Um . . . No, not really."

"Good."

Tom plucked his blood-damp undershirt away from his skin, then shrugged and pulled it right off. He wiped blood from his bare torso, and tossed the garment aside.

The stallion talisman hung against his sternum. The air was cool against his bare torso, and welcome.

Moving quickly now, Tom inserted the crystal inside the talisman, sealing it up once more as he strode towards the doorshimmer.

"Fate be with you, Warlord."

In the corridor outside, if the carls were startled to see their one-armed Warlord bare above the waist, they revealed no sign of it.

"I want three of you to come with me," Tom said, "and the rest to remain stationed here."

"But, Warlord. We took an oath to protect—"

"I guessed that. And if anyone sees you here, they'll think I'm inside the chamber. Right?"

"Aye, sir."

"Then that's how you'll be protecting me. Because I won't be here."

"Er . . ." Then a knowing expression spread across the carl's face, and his voice grew hollow with disappointment: "Yes, sir."

You think I'm fleeing.

But, "Good," was all Tom said. "Let's get on with it."

With three carls tagging along, Tom crossed to the corridor's end, checked there was no-one to see, then took descending stairs to the next level down. They were near the highest level of drop-bug bays, designed for emergency escape.

"Can you three clear that corridor? I don't want anyone to see me."

"Aye, Warlord."

The carls moved ahead.

After a moment, one of them waved Tom forward. "All clear," the carl said. "The drop-bug in that bay is ready to go."

"I'm using the other bay. Once I've gone, try to look . . . unobtrusive."

"But sir . . ."

"What, warrior?"

"*That* bay is empty. There's no drop-bug inside it."

"I know." Tom grinned at him. "You don't expect me to miss the fun, do you?"

Inside the bay, cold draughts moaned. There was no membrane sealing off the bay from the outside, nothing to obstruct Tom's view of the cloudy lemon sky.

There'll be Anomaly vessels to darken it soon enough.

Tom did not know how much time he had.

But it can't be much.

So why was he delaying?

Tom grasped the stallion talisman in his fist. He remembered Father's big blunt hands moving the graser cutter, sculpting the raised hooves and flying mane from a featureless metal block. He remembered the Pilot, Petra deVries: her fine triangular olive features, and the tension in her voice when she secreted that first crystal inside the stallion, entrusting it to Tom before she fled.

Before she died.

It's all led up to this.

Tom trembled from more than the chill.

Everything. Since I was fourteen SY old.

Trembled from more than fear.

Every single step since then.

Tom walked to the bay's outer doorway and stopped. Wind caressed his bare chest. He moved so his toes were at the edge.

Standing at the threshold of the void.

59

NULAPEIRON AD 3426

Lashed to the terraformer, crucified before the elements, back arched against hard freezing piercing stone, Tom wept and whimpered and Saw.

It hurts.

Tom Saw everything.

The climb down had been fast. He picked his way down the convex surface, slowing as he neared the equatorial rim and the slope became almost vertical. Here, a mistake could not be corrected, would spring him out over the drop.

Tom halted his descent at the rim, hooked his hand around a cable and crouched near Axolon's pale weathered face.

"Did I do right by you, old friend? Bringing you this instead of death?"

<Death will come soon enough.>

"I know. What I mean is—"

<You have provided me with more than you realize, Warlord.>

Tom shook his head, blinked away tears caused by the wind.

"Then will you help me now?"

<I will help.>

After a moment, Tom nodded, and swung himself to one side. Then he began to descend further, on the underside: a convex overhang, and he a tiny insect on the vast stone globe, using counterpressure against the tug of gravity.

Some five metres below Axolon's head, he stopped.

"Here, I think."

Then he turned to face outwards as cables that had once formed a cyborg's sinews wrapped themselves around his torso, his three limbs, and splayed him against the terraformer sphere.

Crucified him.

<Now?>

"Yes."

Pain caught his breath. Cold slipstream rushed past.

Now.

Tom opened himself up to the visions.

And Saw.

The Lady cries as the bronze talon slides closer and above the lake the edelaces wait to drop while the great hall stands empty and glassbirds sing where none is left to hear and flames lick across the abandoned warehouse as hemp catches fire and smoke blackens and in the church they are praying without seeing the doubt that lurks behind the priestess's eyes or the empty tunnel empty hall empty boulevard empty lake and all the empty empty empty realms and that is just the start.

Tom howled into the wind.

Face like paper as the old woman prays over her husband stroking the fore-head but the eyes unmoving and the resonance catches and they overlap in their thousands all those mourning widows with their new-fallen men but they could have been Absorbed moving in their mindless armies in steady enthralled marching rhythm through corridors that once formed their homes where the ruined babies lie unmourned and none to taste the stench that hangs in the silent boulevard or the quiet family home where the stocky man holds his children to his chest and stares at the faded hanging and waits.

It was not enough.

How can you See an entire world and every person in it?

Even components of the greater whole must eat but their nutritional intake is balanced only chemically as in the mess a thousand Absorbed individuals in scarlet uniform eat fresh slop with synchronized raising and lowering of a thou-

*sand spoons while in the destroyed tunnel a family crawls through the gap left
by the rubble in their search for food and a ciliate feasts upon a fallen Lord and
a Lady gasps as the noose—*

Tom. I'm with you.

*—tightens around her neck and the spatter of urine on tiles below as her
body jerks but her spirit is free and her chief of security finds her just in time to
turn his graser upon himself before black flames push the air apart while in the
Aqua Hall the old councilman with the bandaged eye doles out careful rations
of—*

I can help the search.

*—water to the queuing broken men and women except that at the door a
big man with a livid scar holds a curved knife at the ready—*

Focus there.

*—and wipes a stain from the blade and straight blade in its sheath and
another and a needle-like stiletto lies in her lap ready for anything like a
whistling glassbird the scimitar whistles as the cycle-eunuch swings and the
Dragoon's sabre and his comrade's lance—*

Weapons. Resonate on weapons.

*—and the endless shining array of weapon upon weapon upon weapon and
the steady grip and the shaven head saying to the wounded man that everything
will be fine as he washes the wound and applies the healing gel* and Tom
knows Brino's voice and the olive features of the man who helps him
and that is something.

You've found him!

Both.

The agony was unbearable.

I want both of them.

Struggling to maintain the vision.

Hang on, Tom.

Blue fire exploding all around.

Come on.

Blue nova.

It's happening.
Try . . .
Something snapped in the air.
Got them.

A link tunnelled through realspace.

Tom's crucified form was on Axolon Array but it also hung in the weapons shop deep below ground where Brino and the Pilot, Janis deVries, were treating the wounded. Janis wore contacts, as he had when he visited Tom on the day of his wedding.

"*I need your help.*" Tom's words split the air like sapphire flames.

"What?" Janis deVries rose quickly.

"*To contact Labyrinth. Someone in the Admiralty Council.*"

Perhaps the term was outmoded, but Janis would know what he meant.

I'm still with you, Tom.

"I can't—" Janis looked at Brino.

"You ought to help, Pilot," said Brino. "That's my opinion."

Those wounded who were conscious were moaning in fear, but Brino gestured and black hangings slid into place, deadening sound: forming a space where only he and the Pilot and the floating apparition that was Tom Corcorigan appeared to exist.

"*I was looking for Brino,*" said Tom. "*But truly, I need a Pilot.*"

"I'm supposed to observe. Not fight."

"*Can you open a comms channel inside mu-space? To Labyrinth?*"

"I won't ask how you know of that place. I can, but . . . Not from here."

"*Take me with you.*"

"You mean . . .?"

"*Go to your ship, and I will follow as I am.*"

Janis smiled grimly.

"Follow, then. If you can."

The floor rotated and a shaft opened beneath his feet.

"With me."

Janis dropped.

Tom followed.

The ship was submerged in molten magma that boiled red and yellow below the habitable strata. Janis slid through an impermeable shaft while Tom followed.

The Grey Shadows. Of course.

It was Pilots who had formed that centuries-old organization, though few of its members would be aware of it.

Then Janis was inside the control cabin of his vessel and the hatch was sealing shut. He stared at the crucified apparition floating beside him.

It hurts.

Tom felt the stone terraformer breaking his back and the cold wind tearing at his skin even as he felt the heat inside this cabin. He was in both places; he was in neither.

It is agony.

He was in a Pilot's ship, a thing that he had dreamed of.

Hurts—

I know. I'm here, Tom.

Janis was opening something like—yet unlike—a holodisplay, swirling with perspectives no human mind could grasp.

"Your ship can exit into mu-space from here," said Tom.

"Yes." Janis looked at him. "How did you know that?"

Tom remembered the old tale, and the empty hangar in a spaceport the morning after Kian McNamara disappeared.

"Lucky guess. Can you hang there, without movement?"

"Relative to insertion? Does that mean you'll be able to tunnel through the event barrier, if I hold steady? To enter mu-space with me, from . . . wherever you are now?"

"*I think so.*"

"Then here goes."

If the torture that preceded it was agony, then no single word matched the fire that raged along Tom's nerves and split his mind apart as the ship moved in a way that corresponded to no angle in realspace and the universe exploded and died and was reborn and then he was in the ship's cabin in a place beyond reality.

<<Do you still hear me, Lord Corcorigan?>> Janis's voice was no longer sound, exactly.

In a way.

Energies washed all around. Amber fluid seemed to permeate everything, and the cabin's image threatened to slip away from Tom.

***I'm* still here.**

But even Eemur's silent words in his mind were a distant, attenuated thing.

<<Who do you want to talk to, and why?>>

Someone in a position of power. We need ships to help, at no cost to you. No risk to Pilots' lives.

<<Against the darkness? There is always risk.>>

Help to fix the shield we almost *have in place.*

Janis said nothing.

Tom strained with the effort of merely remaining inside the cabin.

I know . . .

It was the only thing he had to offer.

. . . where Kian McNamara is!

That caused Janis to react.

<<Are you sure?>>

Oh, yes. I've Seen him.

Then Janis's hands blurred into motion. That strange holo-that-was-not-a-holo opened and twisted—

Labyrinth!

++Who is this?++

Tom rode the carrier wave.

++Who—?++

Tom rode the wave to Labyrinth.

60

MU-SPACE AD 3426

Strange shimmerings and twisting perspectives and light/not-light bombarded Tom's eyes.

++Why are you here?++

Where is this?

++We call it the Aleph Annexe. I repeat: Why are you here? ++

Kian McNamara . . . I saw him on Siganth.

Tidal shifting. Tom can see nothing beyond kaleidoscopic Chaos. Mu-space is not for the likes of him.

++Siganth?++

A moving shape, closer now.

Can it be a woman?

He's a prisoner.

++Tell me where.++

Tom shudders, lost for a moment in the splendour.

Then he concentrates.

Yes, my love. Focus.

And performs a feat of logosophical calculation perhaps only Avernon could appreciate, as Tom takes the remembered feeling of Eemur's Seeing into the hellworld—**that's right**—and transforms it into a displacement vector and shouts out the numbers: the location of the captive, trapped upon Siganth.

It is as if a person, walking along, suddenly reeled off the second-order differential equations that mapped the motion of their muscles. That is what Tom achieves, with Eemur's help.

Is that enough information?

++Yes.++

To mount a rescue?

++Twenty ships just left.++

Time cannot pass in the ordinary way in this place.

Tom floats.

Who are you? He needs to know.

Floats for a timeless duration.

++Perhaps I'm the one you think I am.++

An aeon.

++Perhaps I'm not.++

An eternity.

Magic all around.

Will you help us?

Twisting.

Waiting.

++They're back. My . . . Kian is safe.++

Shifting.

Glimpses of wonder.

Rotations in ways he could never—

++We will help.++

Slams out of existence.

61

NULAPEIRON AD 3426

Wounded he hung on a windswept willow . . .

Braced against the stone sphere, crucified, Tom could barely see with ordinary eyes the surrounding sky.

<Warlord. Are you all right?>

"I'll . . . live . . . Axolon." Pain defined every nerve and muscle in his body.

<I hope so.>

Black dots against the clouds. Tom could just make them out.

"What—?"

<The Anomaly is back.>

An entire fleet of fighters and suborbitals was heading straight for them.

"No . . ."

They're almost ready.

Tom's head bowed. Far below, Nulapeiron's landscape was a blur. He was freezing, but at some point his body had ceased to shiver. Not just the crucifixion: the excruciating stress on cramped, screaming muscles and the exposure, too, were killing him.

Tom?

Yes. We have to See.

Ignoring the pain, ignoring the approaching Enemy, he forced it to happen once more.

A great ship formed of silver and gold spreads its wings above the orbital shuttle. It is Janis deVries's mu-space vessel.

Inside the shuttle, Avernon is wide-eyed, but still able to perform work as

his fingers dance control gestures, transmitting the shield modules' command
codes to the Pilot.
　　"When . . . When will your fleet arrive, Pilot?"
　　"Soon."
　　"I hope you're—"
　　Then one of the shuttle pilots, Feltima, turns from her display.
　　"Enemy missiles are rising."

Tom lost concentration, slipped back to his physical surroundings and
the feel of hard stone pressed against his back, the constricting cables
that supported him but cut off blood flow.

　　Enemy fighters were drawing close.

　　A wave of blackness washed over Tom—*Anomaly*—but then he
raised his head and squinted at the sky, and knew it was only his own
weakness, the incipient coma trying to take hold of him.

　　Then a squadron of dart-shaped flyers swooped in from the left,
and each one carried the sigil of the Strontium Dragons—*Zhao-ji, my*
old friend—and the air rippled as Axolon brought his own defences to
bear and graser fire streamed in all directions and an explosion blew
out a hole from the terraformer, below Tom, and the vibration was a
giant fist punching through his back.

　　Black flames, somewhere overhead.

　　Tom's head lolled—*fight it*—and he pushed it back up, forced his
eyes to open.

　　Dark Fire.

　　It was manifesting itself on the stone sphere's surface above Tom,
the air darkening and wavering and clearing once more, and the beings
who crouched there now were different: black and bronze but human-
sized and wingless, their metallic talons digging into stone while they
hung and swivelled their horned, wedge-shaped heads and focused on
Tom.

　　"So . . . kill me." Saliva gathered, dry and sticky, at the edge of

Tom's mouth. He tried to spit. "You're too . . . late."

Tom closed his eyes.

And Saw:

What he had never hoped to see: a Pilot's ship in action. For as the Enemy missiles rise through the atmosphere, Janis deVries's great silver-gold ship shimmers from existence.

Then reappears far below the spinpoint field, light stabbing out in all directions and the missiles vaporizing with no true explosion, transformed into dust.

And then, high in orbit above the world, a new apparition.

Ten thousand Pilots' ships spring into existence: a myriad polished bronze and silver vessels spreading their delta wings above Nulapeiron.

An entire fleet of Pilots.

Something sliced through the skin of Tom's shoulder. His mouth opened but he could not breathe as the deadly being reversed the swing, aiming for his eye—

NO.

—and arched its back, screaming as a white beam pierced its torso, and then it was toppling from the sphere over the long drop to ground.

Adam Gervicort's commandos were rappelling down from the terraformer's apex, firing heavy grasers as they came.

Tom? Are you—?

Still here.

But the dark beings were returning fire of their own, spewing graser beams from encrusted growths on their bodies, and all was crackling fire and confusion above Tom.

They know who you are. You're a target now.

Good. That's what we want.

While farther out, Enemy fighters were trying to reach Axolon Array, but Zhao-ji's flyers were laying down heavy fire and Axolon's own defences were deflecting the main attack: a holding action he could not sustain.

We don't need to win.

It was a question of distracting the Enemy while the real solution materialized far above the world, in space.

Just survive for a few minutes longer.

And Tom Saw:

The Pilot ships spread out now, tossing out sparkling motes to reinforce the number of shield devices, replicas of Avernon's design. They hover above the spinpoint field where millions of tiny spots of light shine: the ongoing sign of something strange and powerful surrounding the world.

Then those ten thousand ships use their fine-honed control systems, designed to navigate in a fractal universe where a microscopic divergence from an intended position can result in a near-infinite difference in result, to manipulate the orbiting devices into the configuration they were designed for.

"Now . . ."

A soft white glow suffuses the spinpoint field.

Surrounds Nulapeiron with light.

Pain jerked Tom back into place as two more beings crawled down the convex stone towards him. One had spat graser fire close to Tom's face, searing skin, but now their mouths opened in what could only be blood lust as they came for him with talons extended.

Then one of the commandos was in their midst—

Adam!

—and it was Tom's former servitor who now fought like a berserker, hanging from a smartrope and firing his graser at close range so that one dark being's guts exploded through its lower back and it was done for. But a talon raked as it fell away into the void, and Adam's graser went spinning with it.

The other being turned its attention to Tom.

Eemur? Tell Elva that I—

Then a shape came hurtling downwards as a freed rope whipped back.

Fate, no!

And Adam's hands hooked under the Enemy creature's mandible and momentum dragged its talons free from the stone surface and then they were hanging in the air. For a moment Adam's gaze met Tom's.

Then he and the struggling being were falling.

Down into the void.

No, Adam.

Dwindling specks.

No . . .

Gone.

Tom hung his head.

<Tom?>

It's only Axolon.

<Tom, wake up.>

Ignore him.

<Warlord!>

The voice boomed, vibrated, shook him into momentary wakefulness.

<Look up.>

The sky was shining.

A glow . . .

Shining a pure, beautiful white.

It gave Tom the strength to See.

Above the world, the encompassing field blazes, surrounding Nulapeiron with light, while ten thousand mu-space vessels move farther into space and hang there, regarding the marvel they have wrought.

May have wrought. Things are not certain yet.

So they wait.

I never hoped to See such a . . .

Wait.

Glorious light, fading.

Dying down.

Nothing.

Where the spinpoints used to shine, nothing at all. The collapse has taken place.

Tom. You don't know how much I . . .

Eemur?

The shield is in place.

One word is broadcast around the fleet: "Success."

Nulapeiron is safe.

The tiniest hint of blue washed across Tom's skin as he tried to See for the last time.

Inside the shadowed chamber, a silver lev-tray floats. And on it . . .

No. Please, no.

. . . sideways, lies a flensed head, looking dry and purple now.

A black moirée cap lies like a veil half across the skinless face, over one spherical eye already growing opaque.

No. Not because of me.

The air shimmers as Tom bends it to his will.

Inside the nearest med-ward containers of parablood spin in place and medics step back in horror as the blood squirts into nowhere—

You can not *die.*

—through unseen dimensions into the disembodied head—

Come on.

—forcing the nutrients inside—

Come on.

—forcing life—

Don't.

—forcing—

Die.

—trying.

No.

But he forces until blood springs out around the eyes like tears, nothing inside her is responding, and he forces more but there is no point and then he stops.

Eemur, you know I—

No.

Blackness comes.

62

NULAPEIRON AD 3427

They waited until Tom could walk without a cane. The beginning of a new year.

And, as he waited in the wings and peeked into the vast auditorium, he thought they must have used the delay to scour Nulapeiron for the biggest Convocation Hall they could find.

So many people.

They were taking their seats, excited murmurs filling the air as they made themselves comfortable, leaning back to take in the setting. Circular lev-steps formed two arcs in the air, rising from ground-level wings to the circular crystal platform that hung above the expectant crowd.

"Tom?" Elva squeezed his arm.

"I'm all right, my love."

From higher up, a bright illumination shone. Hidden backstage, Tom could not make out the holo, but he had read it earlier when the auditorium was empty.

*** PEACE REGAINED ***

And, beneath:

PRAISE TO
LORD CORCORIGAN
WARLORD PRIMUS
RULER OF NULAPEIRON

No-one could deny him that position now.

There were nobles in the audience, in their finest capes and stoles and coronets and torcs, dripping with precious stones. There were freemen and freewomen who had fought in the war. And there were the pale, ashen figures who walked slowly as though measuring their surroundings, unable to forget the dark flood that once claimed their minds.

"They'll recover," said Elva, knowing what Tom was looking at. "Just like this realm."

But for all the opulent magnificence of the new-looking Convocation Hall, they had seen tunnels strewn with rubble still, and the broken boulevards where vendors set up stalls amid charred devastation: the merest beginning of regrowth.

"Maybe not," Tom answered. "But their children will."

Others waited in the wings to take places beside their Warlord. Volksurd wore the ornate helm of a clan ruler; beside him, so did Kraiv: chieftain of the new Clan Guelfsson.

Viscount Trevalkin, dressed in black, was wrapped in filigree silver wire: an exoskeleton with style. His physical recovery would take longer than Tom's. Trevalkin stood next to General Lord Ygran, though the two men had little to say to each other.

Tom thought about those who should have been here: Corduven, and Adam Gervicort. And Eemur.

I'll not betray anyone today.

But that was the moment that Viscount Trevalkin chose to walk over to Tom, in the strange fluid-yet-jerky gait provided by his exoskeleton.

"Well, Warlord. Are you ready for your big moment?"

"I could do without more big moments in my life."

"Ha." Trevalkin's smile was full of triumph. "Nevertheless, you have my congratulations, sir."

"We survived. We all survived. Nothing more."

"But you know they'll offer you the position today, don't you? They'll ratify you as ruler. Ask old Ygran. He knows his history."

Tom shook his head, knowing Trevalkin was right. Every tyrant, every caesar, every shogun had been through this: having taken control during war, they maintained their position when they won the peace.

"This is a ceremony of thanksgiving, Trevalkin. Nothing more."

"Certainly. My congratulations again, Warlord."

Trevalkin bowed and withdrew two paces.

Of course he's correct.

Tom did not like agreeing with Trevalkin, that was all.

They waited until the hall was full. Then a majordomo came to Tom, went down on one knee and bowed his head.

"Warlord, we are ready to commence."

"Stand up. Thank you."

Tom looked around. Elva was ready. So were the others. But before Tom could begin his stately walk to the floating stage, Trevalkin sank his final barb: "Can I convey Lord A'Dekal's congratulations also, sir? They are well meant."

Tom stopped.

"He stands for everything I despise, Trevalkin. I thought you knew that."

"But you've saved the system he and I fought for, Warlord." To someone who did not know Trevalkin, the tone in his voice might have seemed innocent puzzlement. "Fate, sir. In a real sense, it was Tom Corcorigan who founded the entire aristocracy which has existed for over a millennium. You enabled it to work."

"No."

"Don't tell me you haven't thought about it, Warlord."

"I *have* thought about it, and you're wrong."

"But the spinpoints existed backwards in time. When they apparently ceased to exist—when the shield fell into place—that was really the moment of their creation, not their death."

"Go heisenberg yourself, Trevalkin."

"Ah. But there's no avoiding it, Warlord. You created the spin-points as a side effect of the shield."

"No."

"Yes. *You* made the Oracles, Tom Corcorigan. Only you."

Trevalkin's words burned. Tom turned and walked out onto the first step but the words remained like trickling acid in his mind.

An Oracle killed my father.

Applause rushed through the auditorium, a tidal wave of sound.

One of the Oracles . . .

Every person stood.

. . . that I created.

Tom stood on the floating crystal stage and received the massive adulation of those below, while Dukes and Lords from every sector ascended a pathway formed of lev-steps. Their presence would grant the proceedings full legality, would ratify any decisions taken here.

They'll offer you the position today.

Would they call him Warlord still? Or grant him some other title as peacetime ruler of Nulapeiron?

Father. I wish you could see this.

A sea of faces below. In every pair of eyes, the light of adoration glowed.

It was a bulky white-bearded man called Count Schilko who made the official speech. Tom had not met the Count, but knew of his formidable record in fighting against the Anomaly. The powers-that-be had chosen their representative well. His words were straightforward, his manner blunt yet dignified, as he delineated the steps by which Thomas Corcorigan, Warlord Primus, had achieved victory against the Enemy.

Finally, the speech wound towards its real conclusion, to say the thing which everyone in their hearts had thought about, had discussed among their friends.

"—unanimous verdict of every Council in every sector of the world, we do hereby offer you, Warlord Primus Thomas Corcorigan, the continuing command of all Nulapeiron which you alone did save—"

Applause began to rise once more.

"—and invest in you sole authority as—"

Louder, the rushing sound, the audience standing to shout their approval.

"—Lord Primus of the world."

A huge climax of yelling and cheering and clapping.

This is the moment.

Then Tom walked forward to the floating platform's edge.

This is my time.

Looked down upon his people.

My time.

A hush settled upon the hall.

Tom waited, allowed the tension to rise . . . And waited.

Not a whisper. Not a movement.

No sound, as the gathered thousands dared not breathe.

And then he spoke.

"I accept the position."

Jubilation burst through the air. A roar of approval, of celebration, echoed and redoubled through the hall. Tom waited for it to die down, before raising his hand.

Silence settled.

"As I understand it, a formal command issued by the Lord Primus carries the full weight of statute law." Tom looked towards the high aristocracy assembled on the platform with him. "Is that right, my honoured Lords and Ladies?"

There were nods, from those who were not too spellbound to move.

"Then I give you this command from the Lord Primus. *All noble titles, all Lordships and Ladyships, are abolished.* Including the rank of Lord Primus."

Tom let the silence hang there.

"Feel free to resolve that legal paradox, my logosophical friends."

A murmur rippled among the thousands seated below.

They'll turn on you eventually. That was what Eemur had told him.

Not if I don't give them the chance, Eemur, my love.

Tom took a deep breath. Then he spoke in commanding tones that the system carried throughout the hall, sounded deep in the audience's bones.

"Nulapeiron is free. Let's keep it that way."

He turned away.

And descended the lev-steps amid tumultuous, gigantic roars and cheers of admiration dwarfing everything that went before.

63

NULAPEIRON AD 3429

The embassy—for now, one shared facility for ambassadors of all other free worlds—stood on a ridge upon the surface. On three sides, heathland covered with long silver grasses stretched into the distance. The fourth side overlooked a slope at whose foot lay the Lake of Glass, in which two hundred and fifty thousand corpses were frozen for ever.

The location was deliberate: a reminder of things no-one should forget.

Banners fluttered, and in the open courtyard the majestic opening of *Ode to Victory* sounded. The waiting crowd, dressed in their finest, automatically straightened their stances. Tom and Elva stood together near the rear. Neither of them was giving a speech today; they were honoured to be attendees, no more.

The crowd remained standing.

Ode to Victory reached its swelling climax.

And seven mu-space ships burst into being overhead.

Next to Elva, Citizen Avernon looked up at the polished undersides of the great craft, and smiled like an awestruck child. Everyone watched the vessels descend.

It was a steady, bracing breeze which caused the banners to flutter, and Tom had an odd thought unaccompanied by fear.

I will die on a day like this.

Elva had not been in that vision. But two youngsters had called him Grandfather, and one of them had obsidian eyes, and that was enough.

When the first ambassadors descended from the ships, they were accompanied by Pilots, Janis deVries among them.

"He *is* coming to dinner afterwards, isn't he?"

"Don't worry." Tom squeezed Elva's hand. "He'll make it."

"Jissie will play havoc if he doesn't."

Then something clenched Tom's heart.

At the rear of the entourage stood a man dressed in a long cape, hood drawn forward to hide his face. But just for a moment, Tom thought he glimpsed a ruined hand, curled into the shape of a claw; then the man moved out of sight.

They did not have long to wait before Speaker Trevalkin (for the old nobles still held on to influence, whatever their positions were called) cleared his throat, and his words drifted across the gathered crowd.

"As elected representative to the Assembly of Free Worlds, I hereby declare this embassy open. We welcome links to all the worlds of humankind—"

With cheers growing all around, Tom hugged Elva close, and kissed her. For a while, they watched the official proceedings unfold amid pageantry appropriate to the occasion: the clasped forearms and handshakes and formal speeches with genuine smiles, as Nulapeiron became part of the greater fraternity of free peoples, its isolation broken and forgotten after twelve hundred Standard Years of following a bitter path alone.

Then Tom and Elva slipped away unnoticed, and headed towards home.

ACKNOWLEDGMENTS

For their books on networks and connectivity, thanks to Steven Strogatz and Mark Buchanan; likewise to Brian Greene for his works on superstring theory. *Resolution* builds on the weird ideas of the previous Nulapeiron novels, so thanks again to Huw Price, John Gribbin, Ian Stewart, and the inimitable Jack Cohen. You guys enrich the universe.

The "ancient proto-logosopher" referred to in the text is Richard Dawkins, of course. His clarity of thought leaves me in awe. (So I admire two biologists with differing views on emergent properties. So sue me.)

The Combat Conditioning methods used by both Dirk McNamara and Tom are real. A thousand thanks to fitness guru Matt Furey (see www.mattfurey.com) for revitalizing my health and martial arts practice.

After several years as a wandering ronin, I have a new home in martial arts. Thanks to Sensei Mick Foster for welcoming me into his dojo. *Osu!* And let me pay my respects here to the indomitable spirit of the late great Enoeda Sensei, the true shotokan tiger. He was the greatest and the best.

For camaraderie and rambling conversations on Zen, physics, philosophy, and fighting, muchas gracias to Bob Bridges, Paul Storer-Martin, and Zenon Wozniakowski. Cheers, guys.

And the writing . . . In the UK, thanks to Simon Taylor, John Jarrold, and Elizabeth Dobson. Stateside, respect and eternal, boundless thanks to Lou Anders and everyone at Pyr. Globally, my agent, John Richard Parker, is simply a superstar!

Finally, *diolch yn fawr* (for putting up with me) and loads of love to Yvonne.

JOHN MEANEY has a degree in physics and computer science, and is a black belt in Shotokan karate. He has been hooked on science fiction since the age of eight, and his short fiction has appeared in *Interzone* and in a number of anthologies. His début novel, *To Hold Infinity*, was published to great acclaim in 1998, shortlisted for the BSFA Award, and subsequently selected as one of the *Daily Telegraph*'s "Books of the Year." *Resolution* is the third (and final) novel in the Nulapeiron Sequence.